MW00416839

THE PEARL
OF
GREAT PRICE

APRIL ESTES

Blessings!
April Estes
2019

The Pearl of Great Price

© 2019 by April Estes

All rights reserved. No part of this book may be reproduced, stored in a retrieval system, or transmitted in any form or by any means – electronic, mechanical, photocopy, recording, or otherwise – without written permission of the author, except for brief quotations and reviews. Author may be contacted for permissions at sweetmimosadevos@gmail.com

Distribution of digital editions of this book in any format via the internet or any other means without the author's written permission or by license agreement is a violation of copyright law and is subject to substantial fines and penalties. Thank you for supporting the author by purchasing only authorized editions.

The persons and events portrayed in this work are the creations of the author, and any resemblance to persons, living or dead, is purely coincidental.

Scriptural quotations are from various versions of the Bible.

ISBN-13c 978-1-6870-1705-5

"It is my honor to have had the opportunity to edit such a well told story. April Estes' *The Pearl of Great Price* is a highly relatable story of redemption with likeable, flawed characters. Only a BIG God can delight in redeeming our past mistakes. I laughed and cried while reading this book, and I heartedly give this entertaining book two thumbs up!"
--Diana L. Flegal, Literary Agent/Coach and Freelance Editor

"*The Pearl of Great Price* is a captivating novel about love, life, and faith set in a small, Southern town. The author weaves a story that keeps the reader engaged while avoiding predictable plot lines. I enjoyed the story arc as I cheered for these imperfect characters page after page. Life rarely turns out the way we expect, and this poignant novel points readers to God's truths while providing a memorable reading experience!"
-- Allison K. Flexer, author of *Truth, Lies, and the Single Woman*

"April Estes has penned a unique story with characters that are real and relatable. *The Pearl of Great Price* takes us through a journey of questions and brings us out on the other side with new understanding. I look forward to more."
--Cindy K. Sproles, best-selling and award-winning author of *Mercy's Rain* and *Liar's Winter*

Dedicated to Savannah, Alyssa, Jace & Lacey
who encouraged me to pursue the dream,
To Jay, who provided a way,
And to Panera Bread
for providing the place.

Special thanks to Diana Flegal, Cindy Sproles,
Mark Harper, Mary Anne Allen, Allison Flexer McGaha,
Kerri Bell and April Wireman who provided
invaluable feedback and assistance.

And to Dad, who always asks,
"So, have you done any writing today?"

Let me tell you what I know about the devil.

He's patient.

He's dirty.

He's a sneaky conman who doesn't play by the rules.

And he's slick. Oh, how he is slick.

He plants seeds…tiny seeds you don't even notice.

And then he waits.

Waits 'til you're down. And depressed. And worn out. And hardly have the strength to tell what's even right or wrong.

Then he attacks.

He offers you your greatest desire on a silver platter, with all the promises of it fulfilling that big, empty place in your heart that seems to grow larger with each passing day.

For those who take the bait, it seems to fill that gap - until you realize that instead of filling the hole, you were just feeding it.

And by then?

It's too late. The trap has already been laid: the cycle of needing and feeding and feeding and needing becomes endless. You become a slave to the craving, the puppet of the Puppeteer. For most, this is where the struggle ends and the surrender to sin begins.

No, the devil doesn't approach you when you're feeling fine and had a full eight hours of sleep.

No.

He waits.

ONE

Dickson, Tennessee
Present Day

"Lacey, are you OK?! What happened?" Mya shook her friend after finding her passed out cold by her mailbox.

"Is it news about Kit? Did someone attack you?!"

"No, I haven't been attacked. Just help me inside," Lacey muttered, too disoriented to stand alone but still clutching the letter from Vanderbilt hospital tightly in her hand.

Mya helped Lacey into the house and onto the couch, and grabbed a wet cloth and some water from the kitchen. Lacey's family was dealing with a lot related to her daughter Kit's kidney failure, but Mya had no clue what had caused Lacey to pass out.

Mya put the water on the coffee table and placed the washcloth on Lacey's forehead. A goose egg was popping up around her left eye.

Mya and Lacey were close. They had the same number of kids, attended the same church, and knew one another as well as any two friends could. Mya wanted to be supportive, and not pry, though her eyes begged an explanation.

When Lacey's daughter Kit was diagnosed with Polycystic Kidney Disease (PKD) five years earlier, the doctors had been optimistic. Before Kit's diagnosis, it had been a light-hearted time for their family. But as Kit's condition worsened, there were some days Lacey wanted to run away. Ironically, it *was* running - and her faith - that kept her sane.

This week she'd been especially nervous. The doctors at Vanderbilt said they were out of options, and the next step in the course of treatment for Kit was a kidney transplant. Since it can take years to find a matching kidney donor, it was suggested they search for a kidney within their families. Lacey and her husband, Grant, had been tested and they were eagerly awaiting the results.

Lacey hadn't known when she went for her routine jog that brisk morning her world as she knew it would crumble. She'd gotten the kids and her husband up and out the door like she normally did. While she ran, she prayed. Kit's health was at the top of her list, followed by prayers for the rest of her family, her friends, and the members of her church listed in the bulletin that week. It helped Lacey to pray for others…one can get lost in their own problems if they focus too much on themselves.

Mya usually joined her on her cool-down lap. Today, Lacey had stopped by the mailbox and said a quick prayer before opening it. The next thing she knew, Mya was bending over her.

Once inside, Mya's concern was magnified as Lacey alternated between pacing the floor and sitting with her head in her hands.

"Really, God?!" Lacey yelled to the air. "As if we don't have enough to deal with, You bring me *this*?!"

"Lacey, you're starting to scare me…what is this all about?" Mya asked.

"Mya, there's a whole part of my life I've never shared with you," Lacey sat in shocking disbelief as the past enveloped her.

"Long story short? My sins have found me out." She timidly sipped her water before waving the letter that had arrived that morning.

"Grant is not Kit's father."

TWO

Dawsonville, Tennessee

May, 1991

"Laaaaaacey Grace! Get in the car! We *cannot* be late today!" Momma Kim's voice cut across the wide front yard, stirring up the chickens. "And don't forget to grab those pies off the counter!"

It was the fourth Sunday of the month, and the ladies of the church had been baking all weekend. Unlike regular Sundays, every fourth Sunday brought Pastor Gill - the "circuit riding preacher" – to town and the energy in the air and quality of the food always seemed to be better. And it attracted more visitors which all young, eligible teenagers were well aware of. The girls especially, since they outnumbered the boys two to one. The Pastor's new foster son, Brett, didn't interest Lacey the *least bit*. She'd already pegged him as a "city-fied," pompous, private-schooled boy. Not her type in the least bit.

Lacey grabbed a fork and poked the chess pie to "test" if it was done. Relieved, she packed up the pies and placed them on the wooden carrier her guitar teacher had made for her, put her Bible under her arm, and ran out the front door.

Lacey was an excellent baker. Cookies, fudge, cobbler, meringue…she could bake anything! On potluck Sunday the members who had their priorities straight would head to the dessert table first, knowing Lacey's desserts were always the first to go.

"Make room in the back, sweetie. We gotta pick up Grandma and Grandpa," Lacey's mother instructed.

Grandpa Charlie and Grandma Kate, Lacey's paternal grandparents, lived "over the river" and "through the woods" – a fact Grandpa Charlie always jokingly pointed out every time they were given a ride home, even though the river was little more than a creek.

Momma Kim chose the "river" route. It was May, and she was able to drive across with little more than a splash.

Grandpa Charlie ran ahead of Grandma Kate and yelled, "Shotgun!" as he opened the car door for her. The cute couple inspired everyone with their loving, playful, banter. They had made it through the Great Depression and "the Last Great War" and were still holding steady forty years later.

Grandma Kate wedged herself into the back with Lacey between all the food, straddling chicken spaghetti, green bean and pineapple casseroles, fried chicken, and zucchini bread - along with their famous pies.

"We'd better pray we don't have a wreck, honey, cause if we do they're not gonna be able to identify us for all the mess!"

They both giggled as Grandma Kate squeezed Lacey's hand. Grandma Kate had a tight grip from all the milking she used to do on her family's farm. Lacey looked down at her Grandma's strong, beautifully manicured hands, and was once again struck by the dichotomy.

"Strength and beauty, tender and tough," Lacey had noted to her mom once. "Her hands are just like her."

"And just like *you*!" Momma Kate had said. "That's how you got your name…'cause lace is both beautiful *and* strong." Lacey agreed, the women who graced their hills had both delicate beauty and immense strength – like the dogwood trees that rose from the limestone cliffs high around them.

Lacey's thoughts were brought back by laughter.

"Lacey, do you have any singing gigs coming up?" Grandpa Charlie asked. Lacey shared her plans with her family as they made their way toward church.

When their '82 Citation pulled into the church lot, Lacey couldn't help but smile. She knew it was Spring in Dixie when the willow flies were hatching and every pickup truck towed a fishing boat in some form or fashion - from little dinghies with Evinrude trolling motors to Ranger bass boats.

"A sign of a church whose priorities are in order - Lovers of God and Fishers of Men," Grandpa Charlie said with a smile.

Grandpa Charlie had pastored some small churches scattered about in the mountains after the war, churches struggling to survive. But most of his ministry happened on the river, fishing with different folks he invited. Many a soul would accept the invitation to salvation after hearing the Good News and, like the Eunuch in the Bible, ask to be baptized. So, they would anchor off bank, go into the water and perform an impromptu baptism. Unlike Phillip, who disappeared immediately, Grandpa Charlie and his guest would then get back into the boat and continue fishing if it was a warm day.

"Priorities," Grandpa Charlie would always say with a smile.

At the church, Lacey jumped out of the car and grabbed the pies. She wanted time to do her makeup in case some "potential prospects" showed up.

"Lacey!" Mom yelled, holding up Lacey's Bible. Lacey turned and retrieved it from her mom's waving hand before turning to jog away.

"Lacey! Apron!" Mom yelled again, pointing to her chest, signaling she had forgotten to leave the pink, ruffled coverlet at home. Lacey sighed and rolled her eyes as she wiggled out of the apron and tossed it to her mom.

Grandpa Charlie chuckled and shook his head, "That girl'd forget her head if it weren't attached to her body."

"Good thing she's pretty," Momma Kim teased to Grandma Kate as she carried the dishes toward the church building.

****

Jennifer sang as she sashayed through the girl's bathroom at the church in the new dress they had admired the week before. A shimmery blue-green, purple, it perfectly matched Lacey's eyes – but not her budget. Lacey put on her makeup and swallowed her slight jealousy. While the dress might've perfectly matched her eyes, it accentuated Jenn's figure.

"You got the dress! I'm sure Pastor Gill's son will *love* it!" Lacey shot over her shoulder as she gave her friend a knowing smile.

Jennifer grabbed Lacey's lipstick & tried to smother her agitation. Jennifer didn't know how Lacey always knew what people were thinking and feeling. It was as if she could read minds. And it wasn't just with her! Jennifer had seen Lacey on more than one occasion say someone was sick, cheating, or pregnant – and later, low and behold, they were! People in these parts called it "The Gift." So, it was no use for Jenn to feign innocence. She would downplay it, though, until her crush reciprocated her feelings.

"Maybe," Jennifer mumbled. "But I got this dress for the band banquet. Have you gotten yours?"

"I swear, Jenn, I don't see how we can have so much in common and have such total opposite tastes in boys! I know you have highbrow tastes, but a PRIVATE SCHOOL boy?! *Really*?! And did you *see* that bowtie?? I bet he pees sittin' down!"

"LACEY GRACE! Don't talk like that in church! And I think he looks downright distinguished! That's the latest style, I'll have you know...everyone in Nashville is wearing them right now! You are such a snob, Lacey. Just because you are ninety-nine percent right about most people, you aren't right *all* the time! You need to stop judging a book by its cover and give people a chance to prove themselves!" Jennifer retorted.

Lacey held her lipstick midair.

"And just when have I *ever* been wrong about people, Jenn?" Lacey asked as she held her gaze.

Jennifer shrugged and blinked, annoyed at not being able to think of a single time.

"Well, still, Lacey, it's just not healthy the way you sum people up so fast!" Jennifer spit out.

"It might not be "healthy," Lacey said between mascara strokes, "but it sure saves a lot of time and trouble! Anyway, you've seen one, you've seen 'em all, sweetie. But go ahead. Shoot for the stars," Lacey mumbled as she adjusted her dress. She'd met the likes of Mr. Brett many times in Nashville when she went for her guitar lessons, and was none too impressed. A bunch of boys who'd never been hunting, much less field dressed a deer, and most with hands smoother than hers. No, Lacey preferred her boyfriends a little rougher around the edges, with *real* life skills. Ones who didn't wear bows – even if they *were* around their necks.

"Girls! The singing has started. You'd better grab a seat!" Mrs. Story's voice rang out.

They shoved the last bit of makeup into their bags and whizzed out the door, but not before Mrs. Story tugged on Jenn's skirt and did a silent tisk, tisk with her eyes. It was a big church, but a small town, and the older women took their Titus 2 directive of "teaching the younger women how to behave" seriously – especially in areas of modesty. And *especially* Mrs. Story, since she had six sons.

The singing echoed up the corridor. They would have to be slick so as not to be noticed for their tardiness. As Jenn started to enter, Lacey grabbed her arm.

"Wait until the prayer, when Dad's eyes are closed," Lacey mouthed.

They waited for Brother Sid's "Shall we pray…" before sliding into the second, middle pew.

As the preacher was speaking, Lacey wasn't sure exactly WHAT he was speaking on, but she was sure Pastor Gill was not in tune with the vernacular of the day. His voice rose in volume as he exposed the ridiculousness of a philosophy,

"…Now that would be like cutting cheese with a string!"

Lacey giggled, knowing the Pastor hadn't a clue "cutting the cheese" was modern day slang for something not the least *bit* holy. She looked to Jenn for a shared laugh, but Jenn was being reverent.

"Or like cutting cheese with a hay straw…"

The visual was too much and Lacey accidentally snorted! She nudged Jenn, but Jenn pinched her to hush her up.

Lacey wasn't the only one who noticed the Pastor's choice of words. The pastor's son could barely contain himself. He glanced over at his friend, but Will was out cold, sleeping off his ROTC weekend. At the second reference to cheese, Brett looked to see if anyone else appreciated his guardian's mishap.

He spied the telltale, shaky shoulders of a giggler in front of him. Brett had to meet this girl with the same sense of humor.

He grabbed a pencil and an attendance card, scribbled a note in his engineering block letters, and tossed it forward. As planned, it landed right beside her. Lacey opened the folded card and read the following:

CHURCH CITATION
You are hereby sentenced to church jail for failing
To remain quiet and pious.

Lacey was caught off guard. Who had seen her? She bowed her head as if taking notes and snuck a glance over her shoulder. To her chagrin, Brett was shaking his pointer finger at her in a "tisk, tisk" fashion. Their eyes connected before Lacey turned her head back to the front and went into reverent mode.

Of all people to catch her! Bowtie himself! Lacey vowed to remain stoic so as not to attract any more attention from anyone… particularly *him*.

The service was cut short when the air conditioner went out and the fans couldn't keep up with the heat. The scents from the foods wafted up to the auditorium. By the time they said the last "Amen" every mouth was watering. The teen boys rushed to set up the tables and chairs while the girls went to lay out the food.

If Brett had an interest in Jennifer, he played it off well, focusing his full attention on the chore before him, but Will gave her best friend the eye. Lacey knew he had a thing for Jenn, but up to now he'd lacked the confidence to approach her. Lacey overheard him flirting with Jenn as she walked by, and, boy, was he laying it on thick! Jennifer's high-pitched laughter echoed off the plaster walls.

"Guess she's adjusted her sails and given up on the Preacher's Kid," Lacey thought as she grabbed the crystal tea pitchers. When Pastor Gill was in town, they hauled out the crystal and silver usually reserved for weddings. Lacey found that comical, since they still served the tea in plastic, disposable cups and ate off paper plates.

"Half formal, half relaxed," Lacey mused, just like their congregation. With only one main church in town, there were old money, wealthy families who drove to Nashville once a month to buy their Sunday best from the Belk stores – and the town's proud, dirt-poor who bathed in the creeks, with the majority of the congregation in the middle. It was always a culture shock just entering the door. However, the poor brought their humorous stories, and the wealthy were generous with their money, so they all got along pretty well.

It was the teens' job to serve at these Potlucks. Lacey always refilled the cups. She had trouble sitting still, and this allowed her time to socialize.

"Lacebug, you got tables six to ten today," Lacey's grandmother directed as she handed her the tea pitcher and an apron. "Get to steppin."

It was only after tying her apron strings Lacey noticed she would be serving "private school" himself.

"Great – I bet he's used to people waiting on him hand and foot," Lacey internally rolled her eyes as she grabbed the pitchers. She would be civil, but nothing more. She wasn't required to fellowship with him. She started at table ten and worked her way down, hoping to avoid a run-in with Mr. Bowtie and the boys at table seven.

Maybe the boys would eat quickly and head out to the court, but no such luck. Despite her lack of self-confidence, Lacey was used to being noticed on stage and by boys, but she *was* selective in *whom* she welcomed the attention from.

She stalled as long as she could, even listening to old Mrs. White talk in great detail about the corn on the side of her foot. As she neared table seven, she heard the boys talking about Bulldog's mare that had just delivered a colt the Saturday before. They were discussing the intricacies of horse behavior. For being a newbie, Brett didn't have a problem making conversation or friends. Lacey was a bit jealous. It had taken her years to find her core "niche" of friends, but here he was surrounded, the guys hanging on every word.

"What could a city boy like him have to say that *they* need to hear?" she wondered. She tried to eavesdrop without appearing to do so.

Lacey knew how all the boys took their tea except Brett and wondered by his mannerisms if he was a Yankee and took it plain.

"...I just can't figure how to get her to cross the creek. She's scared to death!" Bulldog said.

"Sweet tea?" Lacey quickly interjected, hoping she'd asked loudly enough so she wouldn't have to repeat it.

"Yes, Ma'am," Brett drawled, absent mindedly holding his cup in the air, before turning to tell Bulldog, "Don't try to ride her across. Take the reins, make and keep eye contact, hold her head high and lead her slowly as you wade through the creek. Get her used to the water a bit at a time," he advised.

Lacey was taken off guard on two counts. "Ma'am" was what you call an older woman. Was he insulting her? And what did this city slicker know about horses? Lacey could smell an imposter a mile away, and he reeked of it. He was definitely hiding something. There was no way she was gonna let him get away pulling one over on her friends.

"Ma'am?!" Lacey mimicked, with her hand on her hip. "And just what do YOU know about horses?"

The whole table stopped and stared. Everyone knew Lacey could be sassy, but Brett was seeing it for the first time. He'd been watching this beautiful girl since he'd caught her giggling during the sermon. Her blue-green eyes were angrily demanding an answer.

Brett hadn't expected to be put on the spot, but he loved a challenge - and he had to admit he was intrigued. Her eyes had darkened two shades darker like Percy Priest Lake before a storm.

The boys, especially Robert (the only boy who had been able to score a date with her), enjoyed seeing her fire directed at someone else for a change. Her beauty and quick-fire temper were intimidating, and few boys were brave enough to try to take her - or her Daddy - on. But Brett saw her unpredictability for what it really was: passion - a trait in women that attracted him. He knew to tread lightly if he had any hopes of getting to know this beautiful, sassy girl better.

"Well, I don't know a *lot* about horses, but I know if you push too hard, she'll push back. And if you have to, you should let her lead. And if you want her to do your bidding you have to prove you care about her. And if she's still hesitant, you'd better lead her with a soft and gentle touch," Brett kept strong eye contact and was surprised and impressed when she didn't flinch, though a hint of blush darkened under her jaw.

What nerve! His double meaning hadn't escaped her.

"Nice play on words there, Private School. Do all the ladies get embarrassed by your double entendres?" Lacey held his stare despite the blush she was trying to hold back. Let's see if he knows how to dance…

Brett was caught off guard by her quick response, but his pride won out as the boys waited for his response.

"Only the dirty minded ones," he shot back.

The table erupted with hoots and "You told HER's!" Brett knew he had won the match but he wasn't prepared for the bad feeling in the pit of his stomach – or the half pitcher of sweet tea that was poured over his head!

****

Lacey's mind spun wildly. How dare that snobby, rich kid tarnish her reputation just to win an argument.

"What a jerk!" she fumed as she ran out the back door.

Lacey's Dad hadn't heard Brett's comment, but he did see his quick-tempered daughter dump a pitcher of tea on the Pastor's boy and heard his fellow deacons mumble he needed to "get control of his household." Try as he might to keep her in line, Lacey liked to color outside the lines. And worse, it was Elder selection season and she'd doused the Preacher's son! Private matters were one thing, but this was an entirely new level of embarrassment. He followed her into the back graveyard.

Lacey rarely cried in public, but all kinds of emotion ran through her. Brett didn't know about the rumors she had faced last year – when she had refused a boy's advances and he'd attempted to change her mind the old-fashioned way. Though she was small, she was fierce, and was able to thwart his attempts. He had retaliated by spreading lies about her the rest of the quarter. The kids who knew Lacey knew full well the boy was lying, but that didn't keep her from getting phone calls from guys seeking wares she wasn't selling. Not knowing how to weed the good from the bad, she hadn't dated for a year. She finally put that behind her, and now this incident could stir it all back up. She had acted without thinking. It was a trait that was both her salvation and her demise.

She heard footsteps behind her and turned to give Mr. Bowtie another piece of her mind, only it wasn't Brett, but her father. He gave her a grave look.

Their differing personalities had shaken the foundation of their family more than once. Not that Lacey didn't *try*. She took the commandment of "children obey your parents" very seriously. Trouble was, she never knew what her dad was expecting. But today she knew it hadn't included a pitcher of tea.

"Do you mind explaining to me what merited such behavior, young lady?" Her dad always asked questions he didn't expect answers to when he was really upset. Once he made up his mind on something, she never got through to him. But this time it wasn't about losing her temper. This time her actions were vindicated, so she felt it was worth a shot at an explanation – especially with the Band Banquet looming on the horizon.

"He insulted me, Dad," she mumbled, trying to remain calm.

"I don't care if he insulted your MOMMA, Lacey! We do NOT bring harm to others. No matter what they say. You are grounded for four weeks, young lady. Now get yourself back up there and apologize to that boy right now! And do it quickly, because we are leaving in ten minutes." Mr. Wilson turned around and headed back toward the church.

Lacey knew better than to argue. He'd only add another week of punishment. But APOLOGIZE? She most certainly was *not* sorry. He was the one who owed *her* an apology!

THREE

Halfway back to the church, Jenn came whizzing out the backdoor, mouth flapping as fast as her dress.

"Oh my word, Lacey, what in the world were you thinking?! I mean, I know he had it coming, don't get me wrong, but the Band Banquet is right around the corner and you're gonna go and get yourself grounded?!"

"Already did," Lacey grumbled. "And now I've gotta find that jerk and apologize. APOLOGIZE! Humph!"

Jennifer stopped in her tracks. They'd been friends since toddlers, and she knew better than to give her friend grief over something she could barely control. She'd always had a love-hate relationship with Lacey's personality. She loved her spontaneity and free spirit that led them to do fun things, things Jenn herself would never *think* to do, must less actually *try*. But it was that same spontaneity that fueled her quick-fire temper and led to major groundings that ruined lots of their *planned* events. So, she held her tongue – pleasantly surprised her bestie was actually planning on apologizing. Maybe this was a sign of maturing on her part.

"Well, if you're looking for him, you'll probably find him down at the creek. I saw him with a pole," Jenn directed.

"Thanks," Lacey said, unable to return Jenn's gaze. She knew her temper had caused more than one disappointment for her best friend, and she always felt horrible for it. And, every time, Lacey vowed it would be the last. And she meant it…until the next time.

Lacey circled around the building and made her way toward the creek, taking her heels off to avoid sinking in the wet ground. She could see Brett in a ballcap, crouching on the creek bank. As she wound her way around the mud bogs and weeping willow roots, she tried to formulate an adequate apology that would suffice while still saving face. She was NOT going to say, "I'm sorry," because she wasn't. Lacey could be hot tempered, but she was also sincere - usually to a fault. This was going to be difficult, but she never backed down from a challenge. She decided she'd start with buttering up the boy.

Brett had set his fishing pole and was now absorbed in the creek. Unlike the muddy creeks in East Texas, here they were crystal clear. Smooth, rounded rocks of every color – brown, cream, red, bright blue - arrayed the creek floor like a sunset.

"Beautiful and unpredictable. Kinda like that Lacey girl," he mused. Despite his promise to himself not to date this baseball season, he couldn't get her off his mind. And besides, she lived two hours away and he didn't have a car yet – but if he did…

"Just as well," he thought, as his fishing rod jerked beside him. He unwedged the pole from the rocks, reeled in the line, and pulled out a bluegill.

"That's a big one!" he heard someone yell. He turned around to see Lacey tiptoeing toward him, shoes in one hand, and her purple, flowered skirt in the other. Her outfit was what his city friends would call "shabby chic". The lace trim and pearls made her outfit seem more elegant and the sash ribbon that tied in back showed she had a nice figure – a fact Brett was trying hard not to focus on.

"You coming to baptize me again?" Brett shouted as he adjusted his baseball cap, hoping she had a sense of humor along with her sense of fashion. Brett was all about getting a laugh, but he'd been raised right enough to know he'd overstepped his bounds. Even *he* knew an apology was in order.

"Very funny," Lacey retorted gently.

His Southern drawl rolled off his tongue, thick and heavy. She wasn't sure just *where* he was from. Alabama? Georgia? She couldn't say, but she knew it wasn't Nashville.

"I was about to come find you to apologize," he said.

Brett could see he'd surprised her by the way she paused and shifted her gaze. He knew she wasn't expecting an apology after he so brazenly shamed her publicly.

"Well, I should think so," Lacey answered coldly, recovering quickly and then holding his gaze. Once again, this girl was throwing him. He was starting to doubt his "never fail" intuition until he saw the corners of her glossy lips curl up in a teasing grin.

"But, I guess I'll let it slide. Just this *one* time," Lacey winked, secretly grateful she did not have to apologize herself. Now when her father asked, she could honestly say they had made amends and an apology was given – she'd just withhold that it was *he*, not *she*, who extended the *actual* apology. Despite taking God's commands seriously, she wasn't above saving face whenever possible.

Brett laughed, half relieved and half impressed. *Impressed* because he had met a female who could effortlessly turn things in her favor. And *relieved*, because he had strict orders from his guardian to return only after delivering a sincere apology. God had smiled on him with this foster family, and he knew better than to mess it up. Sometimes, though, it was a full-time job keeping himself in line.

Lacey noticed how handsome he was. Not the deep, quiet type she was usually attracted to. No, this boy was cut from a whole different cloth. Athletic, confident, loud. Perhaps it was his unexpected laugh, or his crooked smile but she'd glimpsed something besides his "jock" façade. She saw genuine joy mixed with a humble sincerity ...traits sometimes rare in confident athletes.

"Well, I appreciate that," he said, as he picked up a smooth stone and tossed it across the still water. It skipped an impressive seven times before landing on the opposite bank.

"Now where did you learn to throw like that?" Lacey asked, hoping his answer would explain where he'd got his deep accent – and strong biceps.

14

"I was pitcher for my school in Houston," Brett replied, grabbing another stone.

"Texas. So that explains the accent. And the boots," Lacey thought.

"So, what brought you up this way?" she asked, curiosity getting the better of her.

Her question caught Brett off guard. Usually when strangers asked, he would say his Dad got transferred. But this girl knew his foster Dad wasn't his real father. He couldn't give her the white-lie answer, nor did he want to. Even though they'd just met, and she'd insulted him more than once, there was something about her that let him think he could trust her. Though her eyes were kind, he went with a half-truth.

"My Dad's health ain't the best so he sent me to stay with Pastor Gill for a while." He withheld it was his Dad's *mental* health along with the abuse he suffered that put him in Foster Care. To avoid questions, he quickly changed the subject.

"C'mere," he waved her over with his left hand. "Lemme show you how to land a crappie."

All of a sudden, Lacey's easy going demeanor changed. "And just what do *you* think YOU are going to teach ME about catching fish, Private School?" Lacey asked, insulted.

"Whoa, girl! Easy!" Brett interrupted, hands up in the air. She'd gone from 0-60 so quickly that her eyes had changed again, this time from blue-green to a deep purple...the exact colors he'd seen in the freshwater pearl he'd just found minutes before.

"It's just a tip Will shared with me!" Brett said. "Man! Don't have a heart attack! How's your pulse?" he joked.

Lacey would normally be offended at someone teasing her, but Brett seemed genuinely amused, and laughing *with* – not *at* – her. And when he asked about her pulse – and felt her wrist for it – she felt the unmistakable flutter of butterflies in her stomach. Despite herself, she felt herself softening.

"I guess I could stand to improve my game," Lacey grinned.

"A'iiight," Brett drawled. He was glad to see her smile, and it only made her more beautiful.

"Now, the secret is to aim at the shadowy parts, that blue-grey area where the tree shadows meet the sun on the water, like this," Brett pulled back the line and threw it dead center. "You try."

"Oh, I don't know…" Lacey stalled, feigning apprehension.

"Oh, c'mere, you scaredy cat," Brett waved her over.

Lacey decided to play "ig-nert" as Bulldog would say, and see what this city slicker knew. He at least knew where to aim his cast.

She took aim at the tree branches, closed her eyes and tossed. To her pleasure, her line stuck in the overhanging elm branches. Grandpa Charlie said you could tell a lot about a person by how he dealt with disappointments, so she watched for his reaction.

"Good try," Brett encouraged. "Now, try throwing it from the side like this." Brett gave the line another fling, and it landed with a plop.

Lacey found trying to cast badly was like trying to sing off key - more difficult than it seemed. So, she grabbed the pole and cast the line with her *left* hand. Luckily, the line fell short.

"Almost!" Brett said, retrieving the line.

"Here, lemme show you," he motioned her to fall into his arms. Lacey obliged, molding her back into his chest, ignoring the way the nape of her neck fit on his right shoulder like it was made to…the same fact Brett was *etching* into his memory. A few curls that had escaped her bun were tickling his neck, but he dared not move, for fear she would pull away.

"You gotta push in the button, pull back, then release as you throw," Brett instructed as he showed her. Lacey noticed he lingered on the "pull back," when his arms were fully wrapped around her.

She was enjoying the smell of his cologne as she noticed the tea stained circles on his cuffed Izod. It was then she saw the blisters on the inside of his palms.

"Oh my word, Brett! What's a preppy boy like you doing with hands like that?" she pointedly asked, as she whirled around to face him.

"Preppy?! Humph! I'm a foster boy who works to earn his keep!" Brett laughed as he tossed the line again, disappointed that something from his past was once again ruining his present.

Brett made a mental note, "She's definitely observant."

Despite her resolve, this stranger was slowly chipping away her walls, causing Lacey to question her previous assumptions. Lacey relied on her sixth sense the way most people relied on their sense of sight or hearing. It was always "on" and never wrong, until, perhaps, today.

"Well, your dwellings must be mighty fine, then, if you're workin' that hard," Lacey said.

"Oh, they are, kiddo. Better than I deserve," Brett looked down for a moment, as if trying to forget something.

In an effort to lighten the mood, Lacey took the pole and flung the line...with her *right* hand this time. The bobber gave a deep, solid "plop," indicating it had hit its mark. Brett cheered, impressed.

"Wow! Awesome! You're a quick learner!" he teased, trying to rile her up again. But this time she was too happy to go for it. Instead, she accepted the high-five he gave her.

"You'll have to tell your Dad you..."

Lacey's mouth dropped and she pulled her hand out of his.

"Oh my word! My Dad!" She'd totally forgotten her Dad's ten-minute warning.

"I'm sorry Brett, but I have GOT to go!" Lacey yelled over her shoulder as she whirled around and ran.

"Wait! What's wrong?" Brett yelled after her, but she was already halfway to the church parking lot by the time the words left his lips.

Lacey arrived back at the church just in time to see her dad's car pulling out of the parking lot. Without a second thought, she ran. She was more concerned about the consequential punishments that would come if she didn't catch the leaving car than any embarrassment. Her dress billowed behind her as her spirits sank. She knew her dad could see her in his rearview mirror – how could he not, with her trailing behind on the double yellow line? Yet, he didn't stop, or pull over to let her in. She was tired of failing. And tired of trying.

Huffing and puffing, she stopped to catch her breath. She wasn't prepared for the feeling of defeat and despair that suddenly darkened her heart. She also wasn't prepared to turn around and find Brett and the entire youth group standing at the edge of the churchyard, taking in the whole scene.

Her friends all quickly diverted their eyes, embarrassed for her, except for Brett. He looked straight at her, unflinching. He was not embarrassed or intimidated by her pain, and he didn't back down – with his gaze or his attention. She didn't know why, but it bothered her like nothing ever had. She felt naked, stripped bare. Even though his eyes were kind, she felt tears welling up. It wasn't her friends' looks of pity, but the *lack* of pity in Brett's eyes that sent her over the top. There was only sadness, understanding and sorrow. She did not know how to react to such an intimate connection, so she ran.

She ran across the highway to the neighboring Nature Reserve's walking trail, breezed past the daffodil meadow and continued up to the old covered bridge. As she ran, hot tears spilled out pent up confusion and frustration, emotions that had plagued her for years. It had recently occurred to her that her Dad was different. She now knew the Vietnam War had changed him, but the knowledge offered little comfort, now. No matter how hard she tried to be the dutiful daughter, she always fell short of his military expectations.

It was exhausting.

She twisted her ankle as she slowed down at the covered bridge.

"Aaaaaahhhhhhh!" her cry echoed up the holler. She limped over to the side of the gravel road and rested on the wooden post. She knew better than to run in heels. What was she thinking? She was in the middle of reprimanding herself when she heard footsteps jogging her way. Brett rounded the bend, huffing and puffing.

"Man! For a short girl, you sure run fast! WOW! Do you run track, too?" Brett wheezed. Lacey looked up to see him bent over, trying to catch his breath.

"Great," she fumed. "The *one time* I fall apart in public, I get an audience…" She cocked her ankle up a bit, turned her head past the wooden post and quickly dried her tears.

Brett figured she needed time to pull herself together so he took extra time by tying his shoe. She could use a good cheering up and maybe a ride home. He had seen it all: her chasing after the car, and finally stopping, defeated. Her dad had to have seen her running after him. Why hadn't he stopped?

Brett wondered if they had more in common than he'd originally thought, namely abuse. He made a mental note to investigate further, later. He'd planned on ignoring the fact she was crying, but when she turned around her eyes were splotchy, and she couldn't stop the hiccups, a tell-tale sign of a hard cry.

"I twisted it," Lacey mumbled, pointing to her ankle.

Her ankle had already started to swell and was turning a nice shade of blue.

"Yep. You sure did," Brett nodded. "Let's get it cooled off."

Without asking, he picked her up like a groom carrying a bride over a threshold and walked toward the creek. Lacey would have objected, or at least feigned insult at someone insinuating she was not strong or able bodied, but today she was neither. He had swooped her up so fast, it was too late to say anything anyway.

Too tired to fight, she relaxed and rested her head on his shoulder. Listening to his steady breathing, she felt no pressure to talk. The silence of nature wrapped around them. Large rocks lined the path, but his gait was steady and his footing, sure. He was intent on getting her to the water safely. Lacey had to admit she liked him carrying her. For the first time in a very long time, she felt safe and protected.

Brett placed her on a small boulder near the edge of the creek and elevated her injured foot on a rock in front of her. He scooped the cold water onto her ankle and washed the dirt off her foot, careful not to harm her.

He thought about making light of the situation, but the air was thick with her sadness. Instead, they sat in comfortable silence as Brett skipped an occasional rock. They watched the water ebb and flow before he finally spoke.

"Things difficult at home, huh?" he asked, looking straight ahead, squinting out over the water. Lacey nodded a silent "yes" between sporadic sniffs. Her heart was taking its own sweet time pulling itself back together. At this point, she honestly didn't care. She'd been too strong for too long and needed a rest. For some reason, God chose to let Brett be here with her at this appointed time, and she didn't have the strength to question it.

"I sure know what that's like," Brett mumbled, skipping another rock across the face of the water to the opposite bank.

Lacey chanced a look at him, wondering if he was patronizing her, but the far-away look in his eyes told a different story.

"Sucks," he knowingly whispered as he turned toward her. His eyes told her he understood her pain.

He continued, "It's hard when the people we love don't know how to love us back."

"My Dad's got issues," Lacey explained. "He loves the Lord, and has a good heart, but he's a little off-kilter. A little hard to predict, since he returned from 'Nam," her voice softened. Brett was surprised she was being so transparent. He saw deep pain beneath the surface, signs of someone who had wrestled with a problem that had no solution for far too long. He knew it firsthand.

"Your Dad is lucky to have a daughter so wise and kind hearted," Brett observed. "I know all about unpredictable dads, but mine wouldn't be what you'd call *good* hearted," Brett revealed.

"It's like walking on eggshells, never knowing what's going to irritate him," Lacey said. She was keenly aware it might be the same for him. She wanted to know more, but it was too early to ask such a question, so she swallowed her curiosity. It was comfort enough to finally meet someone who had fought a similar battle.

"Is that why you're living with Pastor Gill now?" she squinted at him under the bright, sun.

"Yep," Brett curtly murmured. He was not used to baring his soul, but he had to admit it was easy and natural to do with her. Despite their rough beginning, he was comfortable in this relationship – and that made him *un*comfortable. But in a good way.

Lacey let her hair down and twirled it around her finger - grateful, but sad.

"I'm sorry," was all she could think to say.

Brett shrugged, "It is what it is." He stood and brushed off his khakis.

"Anyway, I'm starting to like Tennessee… as of today, anyway." He winked as he extended a hand to help her stand.

Lacey accepted his help, and felt him hesitate before letting her hands go. She would remember this moment a very long time.

"Now, how are we gonna get you all the way back to church, Missy?" Brett asked, his right dimple growing deeper as his smile widened. Before she could answer, he said, "Tater sack!" and pulled her forward as he dipped down so that she fell across his shoulder...like a sack of taters.

"You're gonna throw your back out, Tex," Lacey teased, half serious.

"Hush, I'm trying to focus, here," he scolded her with a chuckle, balancing atop the rocks on the creek bank toward the daffodil field.

"So, do you have a name? Maybe an Indian name?" Brett quizzed as he walked her back toward the church, cutting through the fields of yellow daffodils.

"Something like "Drowns MenInTea"? Or "Feisty SassyGirl?""

The names did, indeed, sound Indian the way they flew off his tongue. Lacey was impressed by his quick humor.

"Lacey. Lacey Grace," she said between chuckles. It felt good to smile again.

"Lacey...Lacey..." Brett said her name slowly, analytically, before shaking his head. "Nope. I'm gonna call you Pearl."

"Pearl?! You can't just change someone's name!" Lacey objected with a laugh.

"Ok...Sassy, then," Brett said playfully.

Lacey could tell it was a losing battle. She'd better accept her new nickname before she got stuck with one she absolutely detested. She had to admit, though; this strange character was growing on her.

"Let's see if we can get you a ride home," Brett put her back on her feet and handed her a daffodil that sprouted near the gravel road. Her eyes were dry now, but still retained the blue-green, purply hue, just like the pearl he had put in his pocket.

FOUR

Pastor Gill offered to give his damsel in distress a ride home, but if Brett had known his guardian was going to use it as a chance to teach him how to court a girl, he might have just walked her the seven miles home. In Pastor Gill's defense, when someone sees a boy carrying a girl in his arms, who *wouldn't* assume their intentions were romantic? Despite his calm exterior, Brett was mortified.

When they pulled up to her porch, Brett remembered his "dating etiquette" and ran around to open Lacey's car door, but she hardly noticed. She knew her having to walk home was a "punishment that fit the crime" in her Dad's eyes, but how would her dad react to her accepting a ride home? Her worries were temporarily interrupted when Brett extended his hand to help her out of the car and tater sacked her again and effortlessly climbed her front porch steps. Lacey laughed when she heard Pastor Gill give a big sigh and his wife mutter with a chuckle, "That move works, too, dear."

Even though the day had started stressfully, Lacey couldn't remember the last time she had laughed so much. This Brett character was turning out to be a good egg, after all.

"Well, I'd say that was a successful church day," Brett said as he placed her in front of her door. "…what with the baptism and foot washing," he joked – pointing to her ankle and his tea-stained shirt. Lacey's laughter bubbled out, natural and easy. Before she could respond, their lab, Riley, jumped up onto the porch and whizzed through the two-inch gap Lacey had made when she started to open the door.

Lacey hadn't planned on asking Brett in, but when she hobbled after the dog, Brett followed her inside – the dog offering Brett and excuse to enter.

Brett was fiercely protective, especially of women – a souvenir from his abusive home. He knew her Dad was a bit gruff, but he wanted to verify there was nothing more sinister …with his own eyes.

He entered the home to find everything tidy – a place for everything, and everything in its place – except for a messy desk in the corner of the living room. After shooing the overactive pup out the back, Lacey saw Brett eyeing the disorganized corner and confirmed, "Yes, that is MY area," she sheepishly informed him. "I'm the black sheep of this tidy family," she explained.

"Baaaaa," her younger brother said as he whizzed past. Lacey good-naturedly swatted at him as he cocked his shoulder just out of her reach. He had to admit he liked the way Lacey was comfortable with herself – even her unappealing, messy qualities.

"So, you like Bible verses?" Brett pointed to the gray, weathered signs that lined the walls, then singled out the one with Philippians 1:24 written in black calligraphy:

"Whatever happens, act worthy of the Gospel of Christ"

Lacey nodded, "And calligraphy! I'm going to sell these at the Dogwood Festival next month. And of course I like Bible verses! They keep you on the right track!"

"Takes a little more than verses to keep me in line," Brett mumbled.

"There's a verse for everything in life. You should know that, Private school!"

"Everything?" Brett teased.

"Everything," Lacey stated confidently.

"What about children?"

"Children obey your parents in the Lord," Lacey cited.

"Work?"

"Work as unto the Lord and not men" Lacey stated.

"What about… passionate love?" Brett asked, moving closer, keeping a steady eye on hers.

"That would be Song of Solomon," Lacey whispered, trying to camouflage the lump forming in her throat. She had always prided herself on being in control of her emotions, but this boy had a grip on her.

She had put her hair up when fetching the dog and Brett could see her pulse quickening in her neck. He also noted the daffodil he had given her was now in her loose bun. Shiny, amethyst earrings competed with her freshly glossed lips. For the second time that day Brett found himself wondering what her lips might taste like. Before he could try, Lacey's Dad yelled from the back of the house.

"Lacey. We need to talk," her Dad's stern voice wafted down the hallway, indicating a "talk" was eminent. Lacey sighed and slouched her shoulders.

"You're gonna have to go," Lacey whined.

As he headed for the front door, he turned to find a mass of fish mounts covering the living room wall. There were bass, crappie, and even some catfish – bigger than he had ever seen! Brett was impressed, thinking this might be a chance to get in good with Lacey's old man.

"Your Dad's quite the angler," Brett said to Lacey's brother as he came tearing through the front door, the screen door slamming behind him.

"Yeah, he is," Jax said, flopping down on the couch. "But most of those are Lacey's."

Brett laughed. He knew when his leg was being pulled. "Good one, sport." He chuckled.

"What?" Jax asked, as he stood up from picking up his soccer ball, giving Brett a quizzical look.

"Lacey catchin' those. Ha-ha. Good one, buddy," Brett said dryly.

"No, I'm serious. She took first place in most of the casting competitions in Junior High and Mom's been mounting her best the past few years. That bass on the end is her most recent," Jax pointed to a shiny, green bass that had to be at least ten pounds. Sure enough, there in the corner, was a picture of Lacey holding the bass by the mouth – sun kissed grin shining from ear to ear.

"Well whaddaya know...swindled by a swindler!" Brett mused as he remembered how earlier at the creek, she'd awkwardly tossed the line and got it caught in the overhanging branches.

"Looks like fish wasn't all she was trying to reel in," Brett thought.

Brett smiled, half out of relief and half out of admiration for a hand well played.

FIVE

June, 1991

Lacey watched the dust fairies dance in the June sunlight through the high school windows. Lately she found herself drifting off. Maybe it was teenage hormones...or *maybe* it was a certain Texan. It had been a month since Pastor Gill had visited, and Lacey was itchin' to see Brett – though how a long-distance relationship would work, she had no idea. The odds were against them, but she had to admit though, the thought of not taking a risk on this possible chance saddened her. Could she *really* be falling for a city boy? Her initial impression of Brett had been wrong. There was a depth to him few guys his age had. And what about his blisters? Blisters don't lie – they testify to grit and hard work.

Lacey's thoughts were interrupted by an announcement.

"Delivery for Lacey!" someone's voice rang out. It wasn't everyday a girl got flowers in Dawsonville, and even rarer for no reason. Behind the flowers trailed a line of nosey Freshmen girls, eager to hear who the flowers were from, and trying to vicariously live through Lacey's moment.

"Ohhhhhhhhhhh!" Will sang up and down the scale as the office staffer brought in the flowers.

"From Rooooooooobeeeeerrrrttttt," he sang the scale again.

"It would be just like Robert to send flowers," Lacey mused. Despite the way she kept him at arms' length, he really was a nice guy. Steady. Stable. Dependable. Predictable.

All eyes were on the long, white box tied with a pretty, yellow bow. The Senior staffer placed a yellow feather duster alongside the box of flowers on her desk.

"Hey! You forgot your duster!" Lacey yelled, but the office volunteer had already whizzed out the door.

Lacey slipped the ribbon off the box and was surprised by a bouquet of deep yellow roses. Over a dozen! They were so beautiful! As soon as she saw the vibrant, butter colored blooms, her mind went back to the last time she saw yellow flowers. It was Memorial Day weekend, the first day she was with -

"Brett!" Her heart leaped as she realized *who* the flowers were from. Her classmates had turned back to their activities, but the Freshmen girls were waiting to hear what the card said.

"Not today," Lacey chided the girls, shooing them away.

As shocked as she was, she nearly fell out of her seat when she read the words:

Sorry for insulting your honor Sunday, but I've been reading my Bible like you told me (Song of Solomon 1:2)
- Brett

She quickly grabbed the Gideon Bible off the shelf and found the referenced verse and blushed:

"Kiss me and kiss me again, for your love is sweeter than wine."

"What did Robert say?" Jenn asked. Lacey silently handed her the card, awaiting her response.

"Oh my word!!" Jenn squealed. "Brett?!" she reached for the Bible, read the verse, then squealed again.

"So that's what the duster is for!" she said.

Lacey gave her a quizzical look.

"Read the PS!" Jenn nudged, handing her the card.

In her hurry to look up the bible verse, Lacey hadn't noticed a PS. She grabbed the card and was shocked into stunned silence when she read what was at the bottom of the card:

PS. Your bass mounts need dusting...

Lacey dug her face into the flowers, sniffed their fragrance, and smiled - knowing that Brett knew she had purposefully played innocent to get into his arms.

Checkmate.

SIX

Lacey woke up before her alarm, and tore around the kitchen. Today was the one- hundred-year celebration of their church, and the ladies were going all-out, dressing in period clothes. Lacey had found a dress at the thrift store a couple weeks before that resembled a patchwork quilt with light blue, purple and pink patch patterns. But instead of the long, billowy, hot skirts her ancestors wore, hers was tea length with an in-style, sweetheart waistline. At the bodice, a pink ribbon weaved back and forth like a corset, and tied into a pretty, feminine bow at the top, in front. It was a bit "racy" for church, but she was hoping it looked enough like the time period clothing to get a pass wearing it. Since Brett was going to be there, Lacey took extra time getting ready. She rolled her long hair on the sides and pulled it back into a clip at the base of her neck. She was a picture of country elegance, a mixture of Anne of Green Gables and Scarlett O'Hara rolled into one. Some daisies from the churchyard in her hair would add the final touch.

The Wilson ladies were in charge of set-up, which meant they wouldn't have to wait around all night and help with the cleanup. But they had to get there on time, lest someone "cover" for them, forcing them to switch volunteer duties.

When they topped the hill, Lacey caught her breath. Helium balloons in all colors and a one hundred-year celebration banner decorated a huge tent and various booths were set up around the lawn.

Lacey felt a buzz in the air as everyone worked their assigned tasks. She scanned the crowd looking for Brett. It had been eight weeks since she had received the surprise bouquet, and she was eager to speak with him, but Jenn found her before she spied him.

"You're looking very pioneerish today. Dressing for Brett, I see," Jenn teased, speaking loudly to embarrass her friend.

"Hush it, Jenn. I haven't heard a word from him since the flowers. I'm not even sure he'll come today," Lacey tossed her low ponytail over her shoulder.

Jenn looked at her friend with a dead-eyed stare. "Lacey. His Dad is the FEATURED SPEAKER."

"Well, that don't mean nothing," Lacey said defensively. "There's plenty of times Brother Gill comes and Brett doesn't..."

"Well, hey, Brett! Speak of the devil!" Jenn waved past Lacey, yelling greetings to an imaginary Brett.

Lacey whirled around, all smiles, expecting to see Brett. Instead she saw nothing but air as Jenn passed along side, mumbling "Uh-huh..." over her shoulder. Lacey threw a kitchen towel at her bestie. She knew she'd been discovered.

The choir began the service with an upbeat "Give me that Old Time Religion" to get things going. In honor of the celebration, they were doing songs relevant to that era. About mid-song, Will nudged Brett.

"D'you bid on Lacey's desert yet?" Will asked Brett.

"What are you talkin 'bout?" Brett asked, confused.

"All the girls made desserts for the building fund. Highest bidder gets the dessert...AND a date with the cook," Will winked and nodded to his buddy. He knew Brett and Lacey had been simmerin, and this was just the chance his buddy needed to swoop in under her Daddy's nose.

Brett pulled out his wallet. Nothing.

"I gotta get some cash quick," he thought.

"Will, can you spot me a twenty?" he begged.

"Sorry, dude, but I laid down my bet right before service," Will whispered. Brett was desperate. This was his one shot at getting a date with Lacey. He had to get some money, and fast.

He leaned over and asked Bulldog, adding he needed it to get back in Lacey's good graces.

Bulldog was no help either. "Sorry, bro. All mine's reserved for Kendal's brownies."

Just as Brett was contemplating what to do, the offering basket full of money passed by. Tempted as he was, he couldn't do it.

Brett looked for and finally found Lacey – front and center, beside Robert. Robert slyly put his arm around Lacey, meeting eyes with Brett to make sure he saw what he was missing. The gantlet had been thrown. Brett had to find a way to get that money now!

At the last Amen, Brett shot out the back door and made a beeline for the big tent to see if he could locate Lacey's dessert. He needed to know how much money he was going to have to hustle.

Brett was sweating bullets scanning the dessert table. The desserts were not labeled – no one was supposed to know WHO made WHAT. Grandma Kate spied him browsing, and made her way over to him, still steadily mashing potatoes in a bowl.

"Well! How you been, Mr. Wright?" she smiled, the Appalachian accent so thick her "well" sounded like "wail." Brett loved it.

"Fair to midlin', I reckon, Ms. Wilson. And you?" Brett asked, visibly distracted.

"'Bout the same, 'bout the same. The heat's about to kill me's, all." Brett was beginning to wonder why Grandma Kate was engaging him in small talk. In all the times he'd seen her she was never NOT doing something productive.

"…'Course I'm all tuckered out, too, from baking and helping Lacebug mix chess pies all week," she said as she nodded her head down the table.

"Chess pies, huh?" Brett asked.

"Yepppp," Grandma Kate drawled as she winked his way, her "yep" sounding like a "yayyyyy-up".

Brett finally had a clue! "Yes, ma'am!" he gave her his biggest smile as he walked down the table. Grandma Kate walked alongside him.

"You know, I also hear tell Robert sold his Holstein calf for $85 last Friday."

"Eighty-five bucks, huh? You don't say…" Brett mumbled as he made his way toward the pies. There on a white doily was a yellow and brown crusted chess pie, number fourteen. *Eighty-five bucks though?!* "Why couldn't his competition have been a poor man?" he wondered, as he wrote down his entry bid. He picked up box fourteen and, sure enough, there were at least a dozen bids.

"Lace wasn't lyin' about being the best baker in Houston County," Brett thought. She knew it and apparently so did everyone else. He wrote down his token bid then headed back up to the church building. Someday he'd have to thank Grandma Kate.

He was so engrossed in thought; he almost ran into Lacey as he rounded the corner.

"Well, hey, Sassy! Where've you been hiding?" Brett chuckled as he grabbed Lacey's hand and twirled her around. He was not prepared for the way his heart skipped. She was full of light and her very presence made him light headed.

Lacey's stomach flip-flopped, but she knew to play it cool. Part of the attraction for Brett was the pursuit, so she was careful not to appear too excited or eager, though her convictions were being challenged as his fingers laced through hers and he pulled her toward him. If she didn't act quick, he'd have his arm around her waist in no time.

"I'll have you know, Private, while you were goofing off, others of us were working ourselves to the bone preparing for this little shin-dig," Lacey teased, as she turned his twirl into a full dosey-doe and released herself from his grasp, but not before squeezing his hand first. Her words were cold, but her eyes were dancing, tempting him.

"Goofing off?" Brett decided to bite, "I'll have you know I've been stacking hay bales all day with your farming buddies," He joked as he flexed his biceps.

"Stacking bales, huh? Well, you certainly don't LOOK stacked," she teased, as she poked his bicep.

"Well, *you* certainly do," he quickly retorted, glancing at her cleavage and laughing. He was rewarded with her shocked gape. Lacey couldn't help but laugh. Before she could reprimand him, he changed the subject.

"Say, d'you ever get those mounts polished?" Brett asked, giving her a "knowing" smile.

"Uh-huh," Lacey cooed, shooting him a sideways glance and coy grin.

"Well, maybe *you* can show *me* a thing or two next time, huh?" Brett asked, moving in closer.

She was relieved to hear the flirtiness in his voice, so she responded in likewise fashion.

"Oh, I could teach you *many* things, Bowtie!" she said.

"I think I'd like that..." Brett said, moving in closer.

"And it's good to hear you've been reading your Bible," Lacey interjected with a sheepish grin. Was that a blush she saw creeping up his neck?

"Oh, yes," Brett nodded. "I'm particular to that Song of Solomon book...*so* glad you recommended it," he teased.

"*I* recommended? Oh, no! I think you have me mistaken for someone *else*," Lacey refuted.

"No, no, I distinctly remember a sassy, pretty girl referring me to Song of Solomon a few months ago. Haven't been able to put the book down since...although I *was* a little shocked," Brett teased, lowering his voice to a whisper. "Did you know it talks about *nakedness* and such?? *Scandalous!*" he leaned in, easing his mouth closer to her ear, keeping eye contact. He knew he was pushing her limits, but he couldn't resist. He was bound and determined to see her squirm.

Even though Lacey was playing it cool, she was secretly excited. She stood her ground, meeting his steely gaze coolly, even though it took everything she had.

"Things shocking to a city boy like yourself, I presume," Lacey was ready to go toe to toe with him, but allowed a gentle smile to creep out of the sides of her mouth. Before she could revel in her comeback, Brett had his own ready.

"So, I hear some women who can actually bake made some desserts for today," Brett said. Lacey saw how he was trying to get her goat, but decided not to retaliate.

"*We* certainly have!" Lacey said as they walked toward the building, letting him know his insinuation was not lost on her.

"*You* wouldn't happen to have a dessert in there, would you Lacey?" he asked, giving her a sideways grin.

"As a matter of fact, I do, Private. You bidding?" she asked.

"Nah..." Brett drew out his words slowly, reminiscently. "Only one pie's worth it's price and that pie is in Texas. Nobody here ever even heard of it. So, I'll be saving my money, I guess…" Brett looked off in the distance, chewing on a piece of hay straw, trying to look nonchalant.

"Oh, really? And just WHAT pie would that be?" Lacey asked, her eyes starting to dilate as the red started creeping onto her neck. Man, she was beautiful when she was angry!

"Eh…You wouldn't know it," Brett said, dismissively.

"Try me." Lacey stood her ground, crossing her arms across her chest.

"Well…It's called chess pie. Not "chest," as in all that *you're* showing today, missy, but Chess. C-h-e-s…"

"I *know* how to spell it, Cowboy, and yes, I am well aware of that pie. As a matter of fact, *that* is the pie I baked for today, Mr. Wright!" By now Lacey was almost nose-to-nose with him.

"Really? You don't say? Well, I guess I'm gonna have to bid after all," he said, tossing the straw and looking at her.

"Well, you better plan on bidding high, Mister, 'cause I'm the best baker in Houston County! And winner gets a DATE with the cook!" She was not going to let his insinuations dampen her confidence.

"So, I can kiss the cook?" Brett asked, moving in closer.

Lacey looked at him slyly, "No…but the winning bidder just might…" she teased with a playful grin.

"You don't say?" Brett drawled, his Texas tongue sitting hard on that final "a." Lacey thought she would melt.

"Uh-huh," Lacey quickly pulled away, "So, may the best man win!" she sang, as she twirled her hands over her head and her skirt panned out in a circle. She glanced over her shoulder, issuing the challenge with her eyes.

"Oh, I will!" Brett yelled after her. "Trust me."

****

If Brett was going to get a winning bet on Lacey's dessert, he was going to have to get a lot of cash fast. He had been around the Dawsonville guys long enough to know he wasn't the surest shooter or strongest hitter. He decided his best bet was to play off the other guys' prides.

He rounded the church building to find ten of the teen guys on the court.

"Hey, Texas! What's your vote?" Bulldog yelled, holding up the football and basketball.

"Neither. My knee's out," Brett lied. "Let's do something different. Arm wrestle. Five dollar ante, winner takes all."

All the "I'm in's" were music to his ears. Even if he won, it wouldn't be enough to beat Robert, but he was only looking to reel them in on the first round. As predicted, all the guys gave it their all. It was easy for Brett to lose. He honestly didn't stand a chance against the bush hoggin' farmers. Bulldog took away the pile of money, bragging and laughing.

Will whispered to him, "Boy, you ain't ever gonna get that pie!"

"Not by arm wrestling, but I got a plan," Brett shot back.

"Just what're you gonna do?" Will asked, genuinely wondering.

"Turn the odds in my favor..." Brett gave him a confident wink as he walked toward center court. He picked out the shortest guy there. Brett knew they were always willing to prove how tough they were.

"Hey, Josh! You think your pretty tough, huh?" Brett yelled down-court.

"Yeah, private school, I think it's pretty clear I can handle myself," Josh retorted, bowing up

"If you're as tough as all that, then let's up the ante. Double or nothing," Brett wasn't a praying man, but he was pleading with the heavenly hosts to make Josh accept his challenge, especially before Bulldog counted the money and noticed his missing five. If he didn't, he had no plan B.

"What'chew got in mind, Bow Tie?" Josh sneered.

"Burn out," Brett shouted. The guys erupted in a gale of laughter.

"Burn out?! Is 'at the best you got, private school? Some elementary school game?" Josh jeered, still laughing.

"No...Burn out...*Texas* style. It's really not hard, you just gotta be tough," Brett continued. He knew how to play off their machismo egos. As hoped, he'd now attracted almost all the males from the youth group. "Ten dollar entry," he finished.

A throng of "I'm in's" echoed as the guys rolled up their sleeves. It would be hard, but Brett believed he could beat them. He'd had lots of practice at his Dad's house…

"Gimme a lighter, Jason" Brett ordered, hand out. "And I know you got some cigarettes, Bulldog…" The guys handed over the materials and formed a circle barrier to limit visibility. The little old ladies probably wouldn't take too kindly to them smoking on the church grounds. They barely tolerated it from the Veterans in the Smoking Area at the back of the church property!

The game was underway – each guy taking the heat from the cigarette on his bare arm as long as he could before giving up. The current time was 6 seconds.

"A'ight. Let's see what you got," Will said, looking at Brett and rubbing his wound. He had to admit his friend had determination. And gumption.

Bulldog held the watch as Jason readied the cigarette over Brett's arm. "Six seconds," Will whispered to him. "You just gotta beat 6 seconds."

"Nah…" Brett shot back. "I'm going for 10," he said, through clenched teeth. Will never fully understood Brett. He always had to push it a little too far. He was tenacious with a dash of dangerous.

Bulldog counted down. "Ready…go!"

To the observers, Brett had his eyes closed tight to shut out the pain. But it was another pain he was trying to block. As soon as the ashes hit his arm, he was eight years old again, riddled with fear. Fear of what was coming, but more fear of what would happen if he ran. If he took the beatings and burns it would deflect attention off his younger brother. Tyson! God, was he still living in that hell? The flashbacks were vivid. He could smell the alcohol and see the busted up room. He needed to get back to Ty…the guilt was too much. The guys that saw the tear escape his eye thought it was from the pain on his arm. They had no idea it was something else entirely. Part of going for ten was to sock it to his Dad. To show him how tough he really was now and that he could take whatever was thrown at him. Anything, that is, except the guilt of having to leave his brother behind.

The guys' chants brought him back to the present. "Eight! Nine! Ten!!" As planned and hoped, Brett held out longer than every male there, and walked away with a hundred dollars.

"Pleasure doing business with you, boys," Brett said as he tipped his cowboy hat and jogged to the big tent where the auction was about to take place.

****

By the time the guys reached the main tent, the auction had begun. The girls were standing at the front, eager to see which of their wares would reap the biggest bid. Sherri's brownies were the first to go at thirty dollars, followed by old Ms. Davis' raspberry blondies at forty. The bids were averaging thirty-five dollars with some netting fifty dollars! Lacey was popping her fingers with anxiety. Not being a vain girl, she wasn't stuck on appearances. You could call her ugly and she wouldn't care. You could say she couldn't sing, and she wouldn't bat an eye. But to insult her baking? That's something she'd never get over. And now her best work was about to be bid on in *public* - in front of God and everybody! What if NO ONE bid? What if she only netted ten dollars?! The thought was too much. She buried her face in her hands.

"It's gonna be ok, Lace," Jenn whispered. "I'll be lucky if I get a twenty-five dollar bid. At least you've got some real competition to boost your bids."

"Oh, no…" Lacey's voice was quivering now. "Jenn, what if he *emptied my bid box*?!" Lacey frantically whispered; her eyes as wide as a hypnotized doe. Jenn admired her friend's creative imagination, but sometimes it got the better of her. Seemed she spent half her time in amazed amusement and the other half talking her off a cliff.

"LACEY. CHILL." Jenn commanded. To most girls, such a statement would be upsetting, even offensive. But for Lacey it was comforting. She needed a strong voice of reason to keep her nerves calm.

Even though she was peeved at Brett for not writing like he promised, she still wanted him to be the winning bidder.

"And now, number fourteen!" Brother Pollard's booming voice echoed down the holler. "Mmm-mmmm! Oh, my, fellas! It looks like we are in for a TREAT! Looks like a pie my Momma used to make! What is this, Martha? Buttermilk? Custard?"

"I think it's chess," Martha whispered from the side. Brother Pollard lowered the microphone like he was shocked into a state of wonderful nostalgia. "Lord have MERCY, men! It's CHESS. A little piece of heaven on a platter!" Brother Pollard was getting theatrical now, and Lacey was grateful. "All of you who now wished you'd bought in, please step aside and let the bidders step up." The men shifted around, flanked by the ladies on the sidelines, but no one was leaving. This was going to be a humdinger of a bidding war.

"Alright, men, it feels like a lot of you looooove chess pie!" Brother Pollard swooned as he shook the bid box. Judging by the size of the group moving forward, he was correct. It wasn't only the pie they were shooting for, however, but the coveted date with Lacey. As intimidating as Lacey was, boys loved her energetic spirit and fun personality...and her svelte figure didn't hurt, either.

"We shoulda let Lacey enter FIVE pies! We could've added another wing to the new building!" Brother Pollard chuckled to himself. Even though he knew he could start the bidding high, Brother Pollard decided to stretch out the excitement.

"I'm going to start the bidding at five dollars...Do I have five?" Brother Pollard purposefully slowed his voice to build the tension. To his pleasure, every head nodded.

The bidding got into full swing, a couple of men falling out incrementally as the bids went higher.

"Sixty dollars! Do we have sixty-five?" Brother Pollard asked. The bids remained steady and strong, unlike Lacey's heartbeat. But Lacey wasn't prepared for what was to come.

The men's voices grew louder as the totals rose. It was clear to everyone who the real competitors were – Robert on the left, and Brett on the right. Brett had just bid ninety dollars and was awaiting his win. To his shock, Robert nodded a bid of ninety-five.

Will leaned over and whispered "Looks like they've pooled their money to beat you."

Brett's heart sank. He could only lay one more bid. He prayed like he'd never prayed before, and said dramatically, "ONE HUNDRED DOLLARS!" as he eyed Lacey to make sure she saw his efforts. His drama did not go unrewarded, as the ooh's and ahh's of the crowd commenced. Lacey sent a small wink his way.

Brother Pollard, exuberant with the tension and competition, shouted, "ONE HUNDRED DOLLARS, ladies and gentleman! Highest bid of the day!"

To Brett's pleasure, Robert looked shocked and dismayed, murmuring amongst his friends.

"ONE HUNDRED DOLLARS!" Brother Pollard sang out again, using his handkerchief to fan himself and dab sweat from his brow. "Praise the Lord! Praise the Lord! Praise the Lord!" Brother Pollard started pumping his hands up toward heaven and did a little jig. The crowd erupted in cheers and laughter before Brother Pollard stopped abruptly. "Oh, but can I get a hundred ten? One hundred ten?" He asked, his voice climbing on the last syllable. But his request was met with silence as quiet necks looked this way and that for a possible bidder. The silence was golden to Brett, and deafening to the crowd. Three seconds felt like thirty.

Robert bet he could wrangle five dollars out of SOMEBODY before collection time came. There was no way he'd let himself be beaten by Brett.

"ONE HUNDRED AND FIVE," Robert stated, his voice breaking the silence, sending a bullet straight through Brett...and ricocheting off his buddies, who knew he didn't have one cent over a hundred.

Brett's head fell, and Lacey gasped, her pleasure of winning the highest bid over overshadowed by her dismay at Brett's loss. To be honest, she had seen the positives of both boys, but now, in this moment, she knew who her heart yearned for – and he had just lost the bid. She teased him for being a rich, private school boy, but she knew the reality of his situation, and was shocked he'd bid anything. No telling what he had to do to get all that cash – or what he had to give up. Lacey smiled. At least now she knew where she stood with him. Ever the lady, she kept her true feelings hidden, not wanting to offend Robert – or put a damper on the auction.

The high fives on the left side of the auditorium commenced as Lacey and Robert headed to the front of the tent, assured of his win. Brett was crushed. Scheming and hustling, turning zero dollars into one hundred dollars in under an hour, giving himself up to literally be *burned* and for *what*? To be beaten by five measly dollars!

Brother Pollard's voice rang out happily. "ONE HUNDRED AND FIVE DOLLARS, brothers and sisters! ONE HUNDRED AND FIVE! Going once…"

Brett couldn't bear to watch. As he turned to leave, Grandpa Charlie bumped into him.

"Oh, sorry, Mr. Wilson," Brett mumbled, grabbing his arm, worried he'd knocked the elderly man off balance.

"Going twice…

"Oh, that's fine, that's fine," Grandpa Charlie said, shaking his hand – and leaving behind a new, crisp twenty-dollar bill. Brett looked up at him in disbelief, and, without missing a beat, threw the twenty up in the air, and yelled, "ONE TWENTY!" just as Brother Pollard was about to slam the gavel and pronounce Robert the winner! Lacey squealed and breathed a sigh of relief.

Pleased as punch with the outcome – and wanting to help the underdog – Brother Pollard yelled, "Once, twice, SOLD! SOLD to Brett Wright for ONE HUNDRED AND TWWWEEENNNNTTTYYYY DOOOLLLLARRRSSS!" Brother Pollard theatrically flopped himself down in a chair, exhausted, as Brett jumped onto the stage and lifted the pie in one hand and Lacey's hand in the other. They both bowed, hand in hand, as the congregation erupted in happy cheers. Ignoring her daddy's scowls, Brett tapped his hat at Grandpa Charlie, who met his stare with a quick wink.

"Well, it's about time!" Lacey teased, above the roar, her face flushed red from all the excitement. "I was beginning to think I wasn't worth it to you," Lacey smiled big, squeezing his hand and capturing his gaze.

"You're worth everything to me, Lace," Brett smiled back, kissing her hand before pulling it back up in the air and cheering with the crowd. He quickly hopped off stage, whisking Lacey off by her waist and twirling her, before running with her, hand in hand, through the tent toward the horse and buggy waiting for them.

Lacey's Mom had seen the whole scene. "Just why ya'll like that boy so much?" she asked her in laws, good-naturedly.

"Cause he reminds me of Charlie at that age!" Grandma Kate said, hugging Charlie's arm.

"And Lacey's gonna need a boy with spunk like that to keep her in line!" Grandpa Charlie joked with a twinkle in his eye.

****

"This wasn't exactly the date I had envisioned when I was hustling money for your dessert," Brett grumbled, as he sat behind Lacey on the second row of hay bales in the cart, the coveted chess pie beside him. The thought made Lacey laugh.

"Well, this is a hundred-year celebration, and it's what a date was back then," she answered diplomatically, tossing her voice over her shoulder and hiding a tickled smile.

"Oh, no! Uh-uh! No, ma'am! I didn't give them hundred-year-old money, so I don't expect a hundred-year-old date!" Brett complained, stating his case to the deaf driver. Lacey couldn't stop laughing. Bless his heart, he had scrounged up one hundred, twenty dollars – only to be rewarded with a chaperoned buggy ride.

"Oh, did the boys leave off the details?" Lacey was starting to feel for him.

"Heck, yeah, they left out the details!" Brett exclaimed. Lacey instantly shushed him.

"Brett Wright! Don't talk like that!" she reprimanded him, pointing to the driver.

"What? Him?! Heck, he can't hear a *blasted* thing!" Brett retorted.

"BRETT!" Lacey tisk'ed.

"Watch this...HEY OLD MAN!" Brett yelled, to which Lacey turned around and put her hand over his mouth. Brett took advantage of the situation to grab her wrist and pull her in toward him, wrapping his arms around her waist.

"Do you mean to tell me you regret winning?" Lacey asked, wrapping her arms around his neck and picking the stray hay out of his hair.

"Now, I didn't say *that*! There you go again putting words in my mouth...and ideas in my head," He was pleasantly surprised she'd let him hold her for so long.

"You know, a hundred years ago you woulda been married by now. You're technically an old spinster," Brett mumbled, letting his eyes ride up to meet hers as his sideways grin deepened.

Lacey stopped the happy gasp from reaching her throat. As happy as she was to hear him hint at marriage, she still wasn't exactly sure where his teasing ended and his sincerity began, always making a play on words, speaking in riddles and rhymes. She decided to return the serve, but with a serious face.

"And a hundred years ago a suitor would have made his intentions clear," Lacey said, toying with his hair. She liked the way it felt to be in his arms and didn't want this moment to end.

"Well, you keep baking like that, and I just might let you marry me," Brett said with a serious face.

Lacey let his words sink in. They gave her a dizzy high when she thought about the picture they evoked.

Brett was going for a kiss when the carriage came to a halt. "HERE'S YER STOP!" the driver yelled.

"But we haven't had a chance to eat the pie!" Brett objected.

"Your pleas are falling on deaf ears," Lacey quipped as she waited for Brett to help her off the carriage.

"A hundred-and-twenty-dollar chess pie and NO SUGAR!" Brett wailed. "I want a refund!"

Lacey laughed at his predicament – and desperation. "The day is still young, Mister Wright…Who knows what it might bring?"

It wasn't a promise, but it was how he'd gotten through life…on a hope and a prayer.

SEVEN

Back at the church, they were whisked in separate directions –
Lacey was serving food and Brett had duty at the dunking booth.

The serving was easy, under the tent instead of in the hot
kitchen. Lacey was wedged in between Jenn and Sheryl, a girl
from high school who liked to poke her nose where it didn't
belong. She had the special "gift" of making people feel badly
about themselves while seeming to be nice.

"She is *nice*, but not *kind*," Grandma Kate once observed.

"Congrats on the big win, Lacey," Sheryl drawled. "That
was *some show*!"

Lacey mumbled a quick, "Uh-huh," and acted busy with
her serving, hoping that would be the end of the conversation, but
Sheryl hadn't drawn enough blood. She never did know when to
leave well enough alone.

"I just don't understand, Lacey… what's a country girl like
you see in a preppy guy like him anyway?" She pried, looking at
Brett.

As luck would have it, Brett had just taken off his Sunday
shirt to get into the dunking booth, revealing the rewards of endless
football and baseball practices.

"I think you just found your answer right there, Sheryl,"
Jenn laughed at her gaping stare.

Lacey tried to keep the conversation light, knowing Sheryl
was like a pit bull intent on getting the answers and reaction she
wanted.

"Oh, I don't know," Lacey said nonchalantly, hoping her
deeper feelings didn't show.

Brett hadn't been in the booth two seconds when Pastor Gill approached with four tickets.

"Brett Wright, I told you I was gonna get you baptized by the year's end..." he teased, taking off his suit coat and rolling up his sleeves.

Brett gave a loud laugh. "It's still not gonna happen, old geezer! You couldn't hit the side of a barn! I think you need to buy a dozen more tickets," he good-naturedly ribbed him.

Pastor Gill spoke slowly as he handed his jacket to his wife and started rolling up his sleeves. By now half the congregation had gathered round. "Brett, did you hear my sermon last month where I said we all have a past?"

"Yes, sir," Brett answered cautiously.

Pastor Gill pushed his sleeves, "Well, my past is centered around the pitching mound at the University of Tennessee!"

The church crowd erupted into laughter, oohs and ahhs and applause as Pastor Gill's fast pitch landed squarely on the dunking booth target!

Without time to react, Brett was dumped into the tub of water. He came up sputtering.

"I told you I'd get you dunked!" Pastor Gill yelled to Brett.

The girls turned back to their serving line. Lacey counted down the minutes to her shift's end, hoping to steal some time away with Brett before he left, but Sheryl wasn't done with her yet.

"Well, Lacey, I guess you feel mighty special the way Brett got the money for that pie and all," Sheryl cooed.

"What do you mean?" Lacey asked, eager to hear what she had heard.

"Oh! Didn't you *know*?" Sheryl's voice was drenched in fake innocence. "Brett was GAMBLING! On church property! Wiped poor Josh clean outta all his seed money!" Sheryl tisk'ed. "And Ms. Andrews said they were SMOKING! Like SMOKE STACKS! All the while..."

Jenn saw the look on Lacey's face and tried to change the subject with the only thing that would divert Sheryl's attention. "Hey, Sheryl, you heard from Brandon lately?" Her question worked.

"Why, yes! He called LONG DISTANCE just yesterday...in the MIDDLE OF THE DAY..." Sheryl said, cutting her eyes toward the cluster of girls, making sure they caught just how important her boyfriend must think her to be by calling at peak phone hours, paying premium costs.

Lacey saw her knight in shining armor tarnish before her, fading as a husband option. "Excuse me, girls," she took off her apron and strutted over to the dunking booth. Jenn's voice trailing behind her, "Lacey! WAIT! *DON'T!*" But it was too late. She was on a mission.

****

By the time Lacey got to Brett he was out of the dunking booth and toweling off, getting ready for their real date. He heard her footsteps before he saw her.

"You must've sensed I was half naked," he grinned wide, but Lacey was having none of it.

"Just WHAT IN THE WORLD do you think you were doing today?" she asked, hands on her hips, wild eyed and angry, and oh, so beautiful.

"There go her eyes again, getting that pearly violet," Brett thought, but instead said, "Pipe down, Sassy! I don't think this is any way to start our real date now, do you?"

"Were you gambling on church property? And smoking?" Her eyes narrowed and her jaw was tight. He knew he was in deep, now.

"Well, *were* you?" she demanded. Brett knew he'd better fess up.

"I was," Brett said seriously.

"You beat ALL, Brett Wright!" Lacey spat her words out before spinning around and stomping off.

Brett continued to towel off, yelling after her, "So I'll see you at the bridge at eight?"

"Humph!" Lacey kept on walking.

Will threw Brett his Oxford shirt and shook his head, "All of that for nothing, Brett..." he said under his breath, sadly.

EIGHT

Grandma Kate overheard their conversation and followed her granddaughter to the cemetery. She knew what high morals Lacey ascribed to and expected from others, but she also knew how her good intentions got in the way of relationships.

"People over things," was a family motto. Grandma Kate knew her granddaughter might need some guidance maneuvering this one.

Lacey was in full-on cry mode when her grandmother found her. "Best to tread lightly," Kate thought.

"Lacey..." Grandma Kate whispered. Lacey jerked around then wailed, "Do you know what he *DID*?"

"Yes, I heard," Grandma Kate replied. "But do we know all the facts, shoog?"

Lacey grimaced through clenched teeth, then relenting. "He INFURIATES me! I know you've said to give people the benefit of the doubt, but he is *beyond*! He was SMOKING ANDDDD gambling on church grounds – to win MY PIE, no less! How is that OK?"

Grandma Kate stroked Lacey's hair. She knew Lacey relied on logic and rules to help her feel in control of her world, but there was a time for grace and mercy. "Baby, not everybody in this world has been raised like you in this sheltered town with caring family," Grandma Kate explained.

"Grandma! Everybody with a lick of sense *knows* you don't SMOKE AND GAMBLE on the church grounds!" Lacey said, bewildered.

Grandma Kate chuckled. "Oh, really? And what is the difference, might I ask, between the boys betting each other versus placing bets in an auction raffle as a church fundraiser? Didn't all the money go to the fundraiser in the long run?" Grandma Kate was hoping to help her granddaughter see things from a different perspective. "And I would dare say MORE was earned than normally would have been because they DID bet! Anyway, men's logic goes out the window when their egos get involved," Grandma Kate whispered the last line.

Lacey wiped her tears away. "You are just defending him because you like him Grandma!"

"...*And* because YOU like him, sweetie!" Grandma Kate said. Lacey started to argue, then saw Grandma give her a knowing smile. "Lacey, there's some things you need to know. You've made some assumptions about Brett that just aren't correct. Brett is not an entitled rich kid staying with his "Uncle." Brett is staying with Brother Gill cause…

"…cause his dad is sick. I know," Lacey interrupted.

Grandma Kate gave her a quizzical stare. "I'm not sure where you heard that (probably Sheryl - her mom never can get nothin' straight) but that's not right. Brett got taken away from his parents. His Dad used to beat him. Real bad. When they finally got him out of there, he hadn't eaten for God knows how long cause he gave all the food he ever got to his younger brother. He had bruises and burn marks all over his scrawny body."

Lacey looked up, surprised and concerned. Grandma quietly nodded "yes" to confirm.

"He then bounced from foster home to foster home until he was able to rest with Brother Gill and Sister Nancy. He hasn't had good raisin' like you, honey. We've got to give people grace, as well as the benefit of the doubt," Grandma Kate coaxed.

"And he is FAR from "rich," sweetie…He gets free tuition to that expensive private school cause his foster dad is a preacher. He probably learned about that auction today and had no way of getting money before hand, so he did whatever he could. And I can see, if one hasn't been raised in the church, how one would not see a difference between betting ON a pie and betting FOR one…I actually *admire* the boy for being resourceful!" Grandma Kate said, impressed.

"Grandma! What would the Ladies Prayer Committee say if they heard you say that?!" Lacey asked with a giggle.

"Honey, you gotta cut that boy some slack! He's in culture shock and doing the best he can...and you, my dear, are missing the big picture for the details! The point, sweetie, is you've got a boy back there who wanted a date with you so badly that he FOUND a way to get that money!"

"Love makes boys do strange things, sometimes..." Grandma Kate mumbled. Lacey was shocked she used the word "love," but Grandma Kate always called a spade a spade.

"Once, your Granddad pawned his Granddaddy's pocket watch for money to take me on a date - He did!" she shared, nodding affirmatively. "But that's when I knew how much he cared for me. Sounds like Brett cares an awful lot for you, too, sweetie...

"Now, get yourself back up there!" Grandma Kate said, swatting her fanny. "You owe that boy a date!"

****

Lacey had a little time to think after talking to Grandma Kate as she helped Jax churn the peach ice cream for the social. The new information about Brett was swirling in her mind. Despite her conscience, she felt honored that he had gone to such pains to make sure he won the bid on her pie. She hadn't seen Brett to tell him their date was still on, but at eight o'clock, she grabbed a couple of forks off the table and a quilt and headed toward the whippoorwill. She wasn't sure he was going to show. Brett might not have much, but he had pride...

She spread the quilt out so they'd have a place to sit and eat. There had been a wedding the night before, and all the candled mason jars were still in place, flanking the pathway and hanging from the branches. As Brett approached, carrying the pie, she nervously picked make-believe fuzz off the blanket.

"You're late, Cowboy!" She sounded stern, but softened the blow with a smile.

Brett looked up, relieved and pleasantly surprised. "On Texas time, I'm an hour *early*," he teased. "I see you rolled out the red carpet for me," he said, pointing to the mason jars.

Lacey smiled, happy to see him relaxing. "Well, I'd *like* to take credit for all this, but it's actually leftover décor from the Spann wedding yesterday," Lacey explained as Brett retrieved Bulldog's lighter from his pocket and lit a few of the candles.

"I'm glad you're here; I was worried you wouldn't show. You were pretty hot at me earlier," Brett said, with a questioning tone.

"Well, I had time to think things through – and I can admit when I'm wrong…"

Brett fell back in feigned amazement. "Is that the first time you've done that?"

"What?!" she asked, confused.

"Admitted you're wrong?" Brett laughed.

"Maybe," Lacey said, coyly, as she cut into the chess pie.

"Ok, open up, Private. You've earned this!" she fed him a bite of chess pie.

"Now. *TALE* me that ain't the best pie you've ever had, Brett Wright!" Lacey's southern twang was thick and confident.

Brett chewed thoughtfully. "Hmmm…I'm gonna need another bite to decide," he grinned mischievously.

Lacey obliged, putting another forkful up to his lips. "Better'n Texas?"

Brett chewed, swallowed, nodded "yes", then "no." "Umm… I'm not sure. I'd say it's a close *second*…" He joked, still chewing. Riled up, Lacey's pearl eyes danced.

"Second! Second, my *fanny*, Brett! I'll have you know I won *first prize* in the 4-H contest with that *very recipe* two years ago!"

Brett chuckled. "4-H, huh? Wow! Well, then I guess I *am* wrong. Yes, ma'am! I'll have to defer to the wisdom of 4-H!" They both started laughing, Brett steady eating the pie.

"Listen, Lacey, I really am sorry. I've never been what you'd call "churched." I'm not sure about all the rules, but I'm trying," his voice trailed off.

"It's OK, Brett. I overreacted. I can be a little tightly wound sometimes. I still can't believe you bid a hundred and twenty dollars! I mean, come on! That's too much!"

Brett blushed. "Naw…" he said as they shared a look "Some things are worth what they cost," his deepening voice reflected his strong feelings. Silence emphasized his sentiments as he finished the piece of pie.

"And...I gotta say...that is the *best dang pie* I have *ever had*!" He said as he wiped his mouth. Lacey decided to accept the compliment.

"So...am I forgiven?" Brett asked, leaning in, keeping her gaze.

Lacey gazed back. "Just this one time," she said with a smile. Brett adjusted his cowboy hat, and Lacey saw the fresh burns peeping out of his rolled up sleeves.

"Oh my word, Brett! How did you get those?! Is that from today?" She asked, pulling his arm down for her to inspect. He knew better than to try to deflect.

"Yeah," he mumbled, trying to pull his arm from Lacey's tight grip. Old, white scars, roughly the same shape, lay beside his fresh wounds. She pulled his sleeve up to see even more. Grandma Kate's words echoed in her head, "...by the time they found him, he had bruises and BURNS all over his scrawny, little body..."

Brett didn't pull away, grateful to be near her. She realized he purposefully endured the same type of abuse today he had suffered for years at the hand of his dad - just to win some time with her.

"Is that what ya'll were bettin' on today? Is that how you got your pie money?" she asked.

Brett nodded.

"And these?" she asked, pointing to the old, white scars.

Brett paused, "I guess that's what you'd call my "training," he said sadly. They shared a knowing look, bonded by their mutual understanding of being hurt by things you cannot change. Lacey leaned in close, softly rubbing the old wounds, hoping somehow her present sympathies could make up for all his past injuries. She felt immense sadness and love for him, all at the same time. She smiled as she chose to focus on the positive, and let her heart feel just how much he must be feeling for her.

"Well, then, I'd say you must *love* chess pie," she whispered, face to face.

Brett, moved in, "Somethin' like that," he whispered back, confirming her unspoken question before moving in for a kiss. The fireflies had started their nightly dance, and the crickets offered an impromptu serenade. He wrapped his arms around her and pulled her in close, kissing her slowly. She fell into him, her lips responding naturally to his. She'd hoped this moment would happen tonight, but wasn't prepared for the fireworks igniting her senses, a match for the ones the church was setting off. She'd felt attraction before, but not passion. It was enough to make her forget logic, rules and reason. That moment she knew her heart was his.

"You sure are something, Lacey Wilson," Brett said as he pulled away, holding her close, his lips on her forehead.

"Is that good or bad?" Lacey asked.

Brett laughed: "Oh, that's good. *Very* good!" he kissed her again, as the sky lit up and the sounds matched the beat of her heart.

****

Mya sat open mouthed, as Lacey took a sip of her coffee.

"My word, Lacey!" Mya said finally, bewildered and concerned. "So does Grant know about Brett? How are you ever going to tell him about this?! Did you and Brett get *married*?!"

Lacey laughed, then her face filled with sorrow. "Well, no, the distance didn't do much to help our relationship. I'd go weeks without hearing a word. He was busy with sports and I was busy with band and by the time we could talk, it would be late at night. Things were not easy for us... "

NINE
AUGUST, 1992

It had been two long months since Pastor Gill had visited Dawsonville due to his conference speaking circuit, and Lacey couldn't wait to see Brett. It was the fourth Sunday and Pastor Gill was due to speak.

"Leaving in five!" Lacey's Dad's booming voice jolted her as she did a final primping in the mirror by the door before grabbing her Bible and heading for the car. She made sure to hide a towel in her purse. This was also the first Sunday after the start of school, which meant the high schoolers were going to sneak to the river for their annual School Kickoff celebration.

The church was abuzz with the double excitement. If the adults knew about the party, they *acted* like they didn't, knowing it was good to let the kids think they were "getting away with" some innocent fun. Lacey's Dad wouldn't approve of his daughter participating in an unstructured, unsupervised activity – and everyone was determined Mr. Wilson would not find out.

Teens stood whispering in the corners and the guys stood a little taller, anticipating the afternoon's events. Robert had won the biggest catch two years running, and all the boys were eager to beat his record.

Lacey scanned the auditorium. She hadn't seen Brett yet, but was confident he was there – she had seen his baseball glove in the rear window of his Dad's car.

"I bet you're strung tighter than a new banjo," Jenn whispered.

"What're you talkin' 'bout?" Lacey asked absent mindedly, scanning the crowd.

"Aren't you nervous 'bout Robert seeing Brett?" Jenn asked. "Word is he's not happy about Brett stealing your attention."

Jenn tried to warn her friend, but Lacey wasn't listening.

"What? Nah," Lacey schluffed off the idea. "Robert knows we're not steady," Lacey said.

Jenn didn't know if she should envy or pity her friend. Lacey had always lived outside the box, but she seemed oblivious to the rules everyone else chose to follow, not realizing how it might make them feel when she did differently. It was Lacey's greatest asset, as well as her Achilles heel. Jenn felt it was her job to be the "social norm whisperer," and warn Lacey so other's reactions didn't catch her off guard. Lacey had a good heart, she was just a nonconforming, different kinda girl, bless her heart. It'd been a full year since she and Brett had tried to make a go of things – dating sporadically and, occasionally, others. It wasn't ideal, but neither was the long distance between them.

"There he is," Lacey had only eight minutes to make her way across the crowded room and talk to him.

She hadn't heard from Brett. No letter, no call, nothing for weeks. Did he have the same feelings she did? She decided to play it cool until she could figure him out, but Brett beat her to the punch.

She was happy to see him smile when he saw her and stand up straight, but before she could say anything Sheryl ran up to them, breathless.

"Lacey, Brother Miller has been lookin' all over for you! You're on the music roster today," Sheryl interrupted.

"Shoot!" Lacey thought. "That means I can't sit with Brett."

"Music, too?!" Brett whistled, surprised and genuinely impressed.

Lacey laughed nervously, "Well, you haven't heard me yet, so I'd hold off those compliments, Private..." Lacey said as she backed away.

Brett chuckled, "Ah, naw! You're not foolin' anybody, sweetheart..." Lacey heard him yell to her as she excused herself and went up the church steps.

She took a seat up front, angry she had forgotten today was her solo. She was going to have to remember to ask Brother Miller to schedule her solos for any time other than the fourth Sunday.

Brett's disappointment with the seating arrangements turned to dismay when he saw Lacey sitting between Brother Miller and Robert. Robert caught his eye and made a pouty face at him, then smirked as he leaned back and draped his arm on the pew behind Lacey.

"Challenge accepted," Brett thought.

He might not have been the luckiest, but Brett Wright was resourceful and strategic. He'd find a way to get what he wanted. He scanned the bulletin and noticed Will was scheduled to lead opening prayer.

"Dude, let me have your prayer spot," Brett commanded, nudging Will.

"Have at it, bro," Will shrugged, eager to be off the hook.

Services began, and Brett's thoughts were interrupted when Lacey and Robert got up and walked to the piano.

"I didn't know Lacey played piano," Brett whispered to Will.

"She don't. She sings," Will whispered.

"She any good?" Brett asked.

Will shot him a look, "You'll see."

Lacey closed her eyes as Robert finished the entry on the piano, awaiting her cue. The whole church grew still. Dawsonville was a small, some would say "hick" town, but they knew talent when they heard it. And Lacey had it.

Brett was astonished as Lacey began singing *This One's for You, God.** He didn't know what he expected, but he definitely wasn't expecting such jazzy, raspy sounds to come from such a petite girl. He didn't know exactly what he was expecting, but he definitely wasn't expecting this!

The sanctuary filled with Lacey's emotive voice. Like a roller coaster, her voice rang high and low, circling their ears and making their toes tap. Brett almost forgot his turn to pray.

As Lacey ended on a long note, Brett walked to the podium. Now it was her turn to be shocked. Lacey held her breath but began to relax as she heard his sincere voice. She breathed a sigh of relief. His prayer was believable and none too shabby, even garnering a few "yeses" from the amen section.

"There's more to this cowboy than meets the eye," Lacey thought.

Brett went down the stairs first, and as Lacey was descending, gave her his hand to help steady her. As she sat down, he slid in beside her, to Robert's chagrin, and returned the pouty face Robert had made earlier. Robert knew better than to play a player, so he took a seat at the back of the auditorium - a move that escaped most of the members' attentions, except Grandpa Charlie's. He couldn't help chuckle. That preacher's boy was green, but he was sly!

If Lacey was wise to Brett's plot she didn't let on. She was glad to be beside him. Their times together at church every other week or so didn't leave much time to see each other, so every second was cherished. She was also happy to note that Brett could sing and he had a nice voice. Lacey went through her mental checklist on her "ideal husband" checklist – Prayer, check. Singing, check. Things were definitely slanting in Brett's favor.

He grabbed the Bible in front of them, and opened it between them. She took the hint and held the other side of the bible from underneath. His right hand slowly searched for hers beneath the Holy Word. Not one to be overconfident, he put his hand lightly over hers and waited. Just when he thought he might have overstepped, she laced her fingers through his. He had trouble playing it cool and hiding his smile. For the first time Brett Wright felt accepted and loved. He liked what he was feeling. It was like something someone had described to him once...HOME.

TEN

The services ended and preparations for the potluck began. Will and Brett were getting tables set up in the fellowship hall while the girls were busy laying out the food in the kitchen.

"You got more gumption than I thought you did, Tex – moving in on Robert's girl like you did and then pullin' that sly move this mornin'," Will said.

"*Robert's* girl? What're you talkin' 'bout?" Brett asked, feigning innocence.

"Robert's had a thing for Lacey for a couple years now, and…he is NOT HAPPY."

"You don't say…" Brett said as he set up the tables, "Good thing I don't rightly much care," he said, but made a mental note to be on his best game.

Today was Potluck Sunday, as the old timers called it, but the young folk knew this particular Sunday in August as "Eat-as-fast-as-you-can-so-you-can-have-more-time-on-the-riverside" Day. This year they would have more time to enjoy the water, since this was the "men's meeting/church planning" day. All the adults would be busy and distracted until well into suppertime.

As soon as the teens finished their plates, they started meandering separately out the door toward the creek, so as not to arouse attention. Some Potluck Sundays it was too rainy to creek walk, but not today. The end of August was going out with a scorching bang! But it would only make their time in the water all the more enjoyable.

55

On the way out the door, Lacey noticed some guys gathered around Bulldog's new truck.

"What'chew boys doin' over here?" Lacey inquired. She was met with prompt shushing by the boys.

"Shh, Lacey! Keep your voice down!" Jason warned. "We're prankin' Bulldog!"

Will and Brett came around the building, Will still gnawing on a chicken leg.

"What're they up to, Will?" Jenn asked as she tossed her apron onto the church stair's iron railing.

"They're pulling a fast one on Bulldog. When he got that truck a couple weeks ago, they added a little gas into the tank every day. He's been bragging all about the great gas mileage! Today, they've started siphoning out a bit. Bulldog's gonna be stumped!" Will laughed.

They all waded up the creek as a group until the creek widened. When the trees cleared, Brett stood in wide-eyed wonder. A rope swing hung from a tree over the water, fishing poles and coolers were on the bank, and a trampoline sat in the shallow parts of the water. There was even a PVC pipe slide that would shoot the brave riders into the air before they fell into the cool water.

"*That's* how we do it in the country!" Will laughed as he patted Brett on the back.

By the time they caught up with the girls, Lacey had flung off her shoes and was trying to wiggle up out of her dress! Brett froze in wide-eyed wonder. As much as he liked where this was going, this wasn't like her at all! Quickly, he tried to pull her dress back down before she showed too much.

"Good night, Lacey! What are you thinking? Have you been drinking?!" Brett grabbed her hands and tried to immobilize her. He had once tried to wrestle a calf in Dallas, but this was proving harder. Try as he might, she wiggled out of his clutches like a greased pig, laughing.

"Yep. She's done got lit somehow," he thought. By this time, Lacey was in a full-on laughing fit.

"Didn't you listen to the sermon, Private? The wise virgins show up *prepared*!" Lacey teased as she took off her dress to reveal a bathing suit underneath, and wiped the laughing tears from her eyes. She was flattered that underneath his cool, aloof manner lurked a gentlemanly side. As she dove into the water, she vowed to remember his shocked, gaping stare – to savor later.

It was only after Lacey dove in that Brett noticed the others laughing and stripping down, too.

"I thought you were gonna hog tie that girl," Will said between chuckles as he took off his button-up Oxford and threw Brett some trunks.

"I swear I thought she was tipsy! I was startin' to wonder if they'd swapped out the grape juice for the real stuff in the Communion!"

"Hey! If they did, we might have more converts!" Will agreed.

"I gotta tell ya, I was in a quandary: protect her virtue or step back and enjoy the show. That must be what Pastor Gill was talking about this morning when he spoke about wrestling with temptation. I never did much wrestling before," Brett laughed.

"Well, you definitely earned brownie points with the ladies for that chivalrous act. True fact," Will nodded affirmatively as he pulled on his ball cap, complete with a huge fishing hook on the rim.

"That's what I'm counting on," Brett murmured under his breath as he grabbed the poles and bait pail. Truth be told, he'd much rather be alone with Lacey, but fishing would have to do. They made their way up the waterway to where the still, clear water acted as a mirror, reflecting the blue August sky and full, luscious green hills. Mimosa trees and Queen Ann's Lace dotted the creek bank between the water and the sky, creating a quilt of pink, white, green and blue, reminding Brett of the dress Lacey had worn last year at the Centennial Celebration.

"They got anything like *this* in the big city?" Will asked. Brett could only nod "no."

They spent the half-hour fishing and talking. Brett learned Will was serving in the Jr. ROTC, with plans to join the National Guard as soon as he could. He'd most likely get to be in the same unit as his Dad and brothers if they stayed in Dawsonville.

"That's nice for when you go overseas, I bet, being with your family like that," Brett mused.

"Yeah...unless a grenade takes out your unit," Will's voice became somber. "That's what happened with Bulldog's family. One grenade, three generations...all gone in two seconds."

Brett looked at him in silence. He'd never known about Bulldog. Who've ever thought such a fun guy could have experienced such tragedy?

They fished in silence for another half-hour, the quiet as still as the crystal-clear water beneath them, with only the plopping bobbers and an occasional finch making any sound. "Restores the spirit as well as the soul," Brett thought.

The sounds of *Rolling in My Sweet Baby's Arms* wafted down from the watering hole.

"That's our cue," Will said, as he reeled in his line and collected his gear. Brett followed suit. As they were packing up, Will put his wildlife knowledge to work for him. He knew that Tennessee crawdads turned from their typical normal red undertones into a light blue hue in the Fall, so he decided now was as good a time as any to lay the groundwork for a prank he'd pull later.

"Oh, hey, I almost forgot: see that right there?" Will asked, pointing to a crawdad.

"That crawdad?" Brett asked.

"Don't touch it! Looks like a crawdad, but see that blue on its back? That's a *water scorpion*. It'll kill you in three minutes flat!" Will said sternly. "They stick to themselves, so you don't have to worry unless they feel threatened," he said.

Brett nodded, making a mental picture of the fierce little critter with the little pinchers and poisonous tail.

They walked up on an impromptu concert. Jason was strumming a Martin guitar and Lacey was in full swing, singing the lyrics, "She's a real good girl who wants to be bad."*

"Fitting," Brett thought.

Lacey had changed out of her suit & back into her dress, but she had tied the sleeves around her neck. The sun bounced off her bare shoulders, and Brett was fighting the urge to go kiss one of them. Her hair was pulled back into a messy bun and she was still barefoot.

"A Southern angel," Brett thought. He stayed in the shadows, leaning against an Oak, watching her. It wasn't her good looks, but her confidence, that made her shine. He'd never seen a girl so radiant and happy. Man, he loved her.

Lacey finished her song and walked back to join Brett by the creek bank. She hiked up her dress to wade in the water one last time. She was always sorry to send summer off, knowing the drab winter was on the way. Dawsonville was situated between two valleys, so skies were especially grey in the winter.

She'd seen Brett go off fishing and hoped she'd get to see him before he left, but she didn't want to appear desperate.

"There's nothing worse a woman can wear than desperation," Grandma Kate used to say. "Men can smell it a mile away, and run."

"Wow! You got some pipes on you, kiddo. How long you been singing like that?" Brett shot her an admiring look as they waded knee deep into the water.

"Well…" she trailed off as she saw Brett's face turn stone cold.

"Lacey. Oh, man…DON'T MOVE," Brett said, as he got gravely still. Most might not have noticed, but Brett's color blindness allowed him to see through things easily – like camouflage and water clouds. He was hoping what he saw was just a shadow, but there was no mistake – there was the telltale blue on the back of a water scorpion…right beside Lacey's left foot! Brett knew time was of the essence. Quick as lightning, he leaped from the knee-deep water, flew through the air, grabbed her around the waist like a linebacker as fast as he could and pulled her into the water – clothes and all – away from the danger.

"What in the world?" Lacey wondered as Brett swam them out further, his right arm wrapped tightly around her waist, his left arm steadily taking them out into deeper water. Lacey was scared, but she couldn't help noticing how strong his arms were. Pitching was definitely working in his favor!

"Was it a water moccasin?!" Lacey screamed as he swam them both toward the middle of the creek.

"No!" Brett exclaimed, speaking through quick breaths, "It was a water scorpion! It almost *had* you, Lacey!"

By now they were off-shore and treading water about chest deep. "That must be a Texas term, lost in translation," Lacey had no clue what he was talking about, but noticed the fear that had crept into his voice.

"If you want to know what people love, watch what they fear. People love what they fear to lose," Grandpa Charlie's words rang in her ears.

"Water scorpion?! What in the world are you TALKING ABOUT?!" Lacey yelled, confused. He looked genuinely afraid for her, but why, she couldn't decipher. They swam back toward the shore into waist deep water, Brett still scanning the shallow water with a protective hand around her waist.

"A water scorpion! There was one by your foot, ready to pounce!" By this time, their commotion had drawn everyone's attention. "Get back guys! Don't get in right there!" Brett yelled, pointing. "There's a water scorpion 'round that big rock!" Everyone stood, in wide-eyed wonder, not knowing what he was talking about, but not wanting to chance any dangers.

"Uhhhh...Just what *is* a water scorpion?" Bulldog asked from the grill on shore.

"It's that little critter with a poisonous tail and pinchers," Brett was literally doing "pincher hands" with his own hands, demonstrating. "The one with the blue on it's back!" Brett yelled, still scanning the area for other small enemies. "Will told me about 'em..."

"Will, huh? Will told you that critter was a poisonous water scorpion?!" Bulldog asked, starting to grin. The whole bank erupted in a gaggle of laughs, with Will leading the pack.

"Water scorpion!!" Bulldog yelled, tapping his BBQ tongs together like crawdad pinchers and hee-hawing so hard he had to stop so he could breathe. All the others naturally followed suit.

"Oh, Brett, sweetie! That is no water scorpion! That is nothin' but a common, everyday CRAWDAD! Harmless as can be unless you get pinched, but even then, it's not bad. I mean, we EAT those things!" By now Lacey's ribs hurt from laughing. She tread water as she floated in a circle, teasing him. Some of the guys caught some "water scorpions" and were throwing them at him in good natured fun.

"But these are *blue*!" Brett yelled, still a bit confused.

Brett, not usually one to take a joke well, realized the guys were laughing *with* him, not *at* him. He floated on his back and joined them. It felt good to laugh. It'd been too long.

"Oh, gracious! Will got you good! I am going to be laughing at that *all week*!" Lacey said, as she swam teasingly toward Brett with a crawdad in her hand. Brett caught her from behind around the waist, and pulled her out into the deep again.

"Oh, that's funny, huh? You deserve a spankin' for that one, missy," Brett threatened as he continued to pull her away from the shore.

"Well, I highly doubt you're fast enough to catch me, Tex," Lacey wiggled from his grasp and darted from left to right.

With one swift move, he caught her and dunked her full under the water. But he was not prepared for the reaction that followed. Lacey came up sputtering, and angry.

"Dang it, Private, not my HAIR!!"

Brett couldn't stop laughing. "I never took *you* for a Miss Priss!" he teased.

"I'm not! But Daddy's gonna tan me alive now! Or worse, ground me. Thanks a lot," Lacey started to swim away, but Brett grabbed her by the wrist just before she got away.

"Hey, Lacey, I'm sorry – I was just tryin' to rile you up a bit. You really gonna get in trouble?" Lacey was taken aback by the sincerity in his voice.

"Probably," she muttered, frustrated that her Dad would make her life hard for the next week or so.

"Well, let's see if we can find a way so he don't find out. Bulldog, you got any fans up in that shed?"

"Don't think so," he yelled back.

"Don't worry, baby! We can fix this," Brett had already started swimming to shore. By the time Lacey got there Brett had asked Jason to fetch his truck. When the truck arrived, Brett was waiting ...and shirtless.

"OK, Sassy, now strip to your skivvies," Brett directed. Lacey laughed. Brett stared at her soberly.

"Oh! You're serious?" she asked, in wide-eyed wonder.

"Here, wear this," Brett said, throwing her his Izod shirt.

"Listen, Buddy, I don't know how the women act where YOU come from, but around here women don't just drop-trou when told!" Lacey remarked stubbornly.

"Would it help if I kissed you first?" Brett teased, as he moved in closer. For a second Lacey thought he was serious. Should she be insulted or excited? She'd never had a boy be so daring toward her. She felt desired – but not in the lustful way she got from the guys in school. No, this was deeper. But even so, she couldn't let him get away with half-way insulting her virtue.

"Brett Wright! There you go again making false insinuations of the kind of girl I am NOT..."

"Ok! Ok! Pipe down, Martha! Just kiddin'...I *know* what a good girl you are," he said, sensing her anger. "But it's not gonna do us any good if we get your hair *dry* but you show up all soppin' wet, now, is it?" Brett blinked back at her in feigned wide-eyed wonder.

He did have a point. Lacey reluctantly snatched the shirt.

"Fine!" she sighed as she turned to hop into the cab of the truck. "But no peeking!"

"I wouldn't *dream* of it," Brett promised, putting his hands up innocently, and turning his back to the cab. "I prefer girls who've been blessed on top, anyway," he joked, knowing she couldn't slap him from the cab. With that statement he was promptly rewarded with an empty coke can to the head.

"...now I KNOW you're a liar," Lacey called from the cab of the truck.

"Tisk, tisk, Miss Lacey. I do believe that is the *second* false accusation you have made today. I am shocked and insulted!" Brett said over his shoulder.

"Well, you just keep looking straight ahead, Mister, or that shock and appalled feeling's bound to continue if you catch a glimpse," Lacey yelled back, laughing at her own self-deprecating humor. Brett laughed with her, partly out of relief that she wasn't still mad at him, and partly because, from what he could make out of the back reflection of his sunglasses, her silhouette revealed she was lying, too.

"Need any help back there? Maybe with those buttons? They can be tricky..." Brett chuckled at his own joke.

"I believe I mastered "buttons" back in kindergarten, but thank you for being so concerned," Lacey said dryly.

"Always willing to help," Brett reminded her as he waited.

"Looks like my days of changing on the band bus are coming in handy," she shouted, as she wiggled out of her wet dress. She had to admit she liked the way his shirt smelled. She made a mental note to stop by the Dillard's cologne counter next week to find out which cologne it was. She didn't have the guts to come out and ask him – it'd go straight to his head.

"And just what exactly do you DO on that bus?! I *knew* I shoulda done band!" he said. His question was met with a thump on the head. This time it was her drenched dress.

"Oh, hush, and get to wringing!" Lacey ordered.

Jenn jumped in the cab with Lacey as Brett wrung out her cotton frock before throwing it to Jason, who promptly hung it from his passenger window and sped down the highway, air drying it as best he could. Jason turned the heat in his F-150 on full blast and instructed her to put her hair against the vent, and then proceeded to tell her not to worry about the gas because his new truck was "getting almost fifty miles to the gallon!" Jenn and Lacey shared a knowing smile and stifled their giggles before cranking up the heat.

Jenn helped by fluffing Lacey's hair in the wind. It wasn't the best plan, but it was better than nothing.

Surprisingly, Brett's plan worked. Not surprisingly, her hair acted predictably and was frizzed out like a Caucasian afro. Brett couldn't resist.

"Whoa, Momma! You need a whip to tame all that?" Brett laughed. Lacey couldn't help but laugh. She *knew* what blow drying did to her hair, and it wasn't pretty in the least.

"Good litmus test," she thought. "If he sticks around after seeing me like this, his intentions are more than skin deep," she reasoned.

Jenn pulled her fingers through Lacey's hair and did a half decent up-do.

"I really am sorry, Lace," Brett apologized. "Your dad must be somethin' fierce."

"He's somethin, alright," Jenn confirmed.

How could Lacey explain to outsiders what she barely understood herself? Like, how her dad could have the best heart but be so tough sometimes? Or how her dad's outbursts were a response to anxiety, not anger? Or how his military style parenting was out of a sense of love – to prepare them for anything the world would throw at them?

Brett leaned on the passenger side door. "So, you forgive me then?" Brett tried to keep the desperation out of his voice, but his eyes revealed a longing that seemed too deep for the amount of time they'd known each other. Lacey felt it, too.

"Just this *one* time, I guess," Lacey teased, emphasizing the "one." She leaned over the open truck window and twirled her finger around a few wayward strands of hair at the base of her neck. "But only under *one* condition," she gazed up at him, doe eyed.

"What's that?"

"You gotta promise to write me while you're away," Her request was two-fold. First, to test his dedication and, second, to keep his mind on her – just in case he DID have a girl in "every town" like her dad espoused.

"They never taught us how to read and write in Texas, babe," Brett winked as he readjusted his cap and tweaked her pug nose. Her wrinkled brow told him this was a bigger deal than he'd thought, though.

"I'll do my best," he said.

Lacey sincerely hoped his best could meet her needs. She could only hope he was up to the challenge. And pray.

And pray she did, right then and there, sealed with a kiss for good luck.

ELEVEN
FALL, 1992

Lacey's high school football team was playing Brett's tonight, and the band was going. Lacey was going to be on duty as drum major, but still hoped she might be able to see him as she snuck to the bathroom. She'd called and left a few messages with his foster mom that she would be there, but hadn't heard back from him. Mrs. Gill had said he was busy until ten thirty every night. Lacey always got mixed signals with Brett. When they were together, the chemistry couldn't be beat. But when they were separated, she never knew how he felt. He wasn't consistent with how he contacted her when they were parted – but every once in a while, out of the blue, he would drop her a letter or call. Being separated really threw a kink in their relationship.

Brett was hoping Lacey would get to come to the game, but by the time of kickoff he still hadn't heard a band in the stands. He knew her dad would never allow her to go anywhere on a school night, much less travel two hours to watch a football game unless the band was playing. He was sure wishing she would show up, though...he wanted to show out for her.

"Wilson! What's wrong with you tonight? Get your head in the game!" his coach yelled as he hit him upside his helmet. "Sorry, coach," Brett mumbled.

He was distracted and making stupid mistakes. So far, the prospect of seeing her wasn't looking good, and neither was Brett's team. Brett was quarterback for the Spartans, and though they were fast, Dawsonville had a strong defensive line. He was starting to be glad Lacey *wasn't* here to see this.

"Hey, Bowtie! You got butter on your hands?" Brett heard Bulldog's voice yelling and laughing. Despite the jeering, Brett had to smile. It was good to see the guys again, even if it was as rivals for the night.

"Nah, that'd be lotion on his soft, girly hands," Jason's voice came from the centerline, half muffled by a chaw of tobacco.

Brett wasn't prepared to be singled out like that in front of his teammates. Their quizzical looks let him know they could tell the other team knew him intimately, but they had no clue as to how or why. He decided the best course of action was to ignore it all. But he just couldn't focus. At halftime, he barely heard the pep talk.

Second quarter started slow, with the Dawsonville Panthers leading seven to zero. Then Jason broke through the line and body slammed Brett full force. An immediate "Oh!" erupted from the crowd, almost drowning out the sounds on the field, except Jason's breath on the back of his neck, "That's for the pie you stole from Robert at the tent meetin…"

The coach scowled and benched Brett. He sat out almost the entire third quarter and decided Lacey must not be coming. Brett had just grabbed his Gatorade when he heard the faint but clear echo of drum taps coming from the visitor's side. Lacey was on her way.

He watched as the band filed in, looking for the silver sequins and white mesh. There she was. "Like an angel," Brett thought. He waited until the band had settled in the stands before he approached the coach.

"Coach, you gotta put me in," Brett begged.

"Oh, no! Your head ain't right tonight," Coach Raines replied without even looking up.

Right then, Jason broke their line and laid out the second-string running back. Brett had his helmet on and buckled when the coach looked at him, sighed and said, "It's your lucky day, son," and nodded him in.

"Welcome back, Tex! Back for another beat down?" Bulldog jeered.

"If you can catch me first," Brett retorted.

"Oh! That's a challenge, Bubba!" Jason yelled right before the handoff.

Before the guys could advance, the Spartans had gotten the ball to Brett and he was off! Faster than a greased pig running through a forest fire, he zigged and zagged like a skier on a mountainside, running the ball in for a seventy-yard touchdown before the third quarter buzzer.

"Holy smokes, Wright!! What in th' world HAPPENED to you?!" Coach Raines screamed.

Brett gave him a big, dimpled grin, "I found my motivation."

"Well, for Pete's sake, do whatever you gotta do to keep it!" his coach said, half threatening, half begging.

"Yes, sir!" Brett yelled back, focusing on the white, sparkly silhouette behind his coach's left shoulder. "I intend to..." he promised himself, newly resolved to get back in Lacey's good graces.

The game picked up once Brett got back in, with a great show of defense and offense. With only minutes to go in the fourth quarter, the Spartans had upped their score from zero to seven, tying the game. Not wanting to lose in front of his girl, Brett prayed for a miracle and got it. The ball slid out of Bulldog's hands on the pass and Brett intercepted it, running it in for a last second touchdown! The Spartans won, thirteen to seven! The field flooded into a sea of red and yellow!

Brett had planned on heading to the visitor's side as soon as the game was over, but didn't know he'd run the winning touchdown and be stuck on the shoulders of his teammates, trapped. For all his scanning, he couldn't find Lacey in the stands.

Right as the newspaper reporter took his photo, Ashley, the cheerleader captain, leaned in and laid one on him. She'd been waiting for *months* to get with him, and choose her moment well.

"Chad, I gotta get over there," Brett said to the guy below him.

"I got you, boss," Chad nodded, and started walking Brett, still on his shoulders, toward the Panther side. The team followed, but the crowd wouldn't budge. They piled into a huddle right on the field and had their final wrap up. As soon as the team huddle broke, Brett was off – running faster than he had all game! Coach looked perplexed.

"Girl," Chad told him, his one word saying it all.

Coach Raines chuckled, "We gotta find a way to get her to *all* his games!"

By the time Brett got to the parking lot, Lacey's bus had pulled away. He was left standing with his helmet – and his heart – in his hand. But it wasn't for nothing. Brett learned two valuable things that night: he could trust his gut when calling an audible, and he was one hundred percent in love with Lacey Wilson.

Despite knowing better, Lacey had joined the "enemy" team on the field, her sequined, royal blue and silver outfit standing out in a sea of red and yellow. Lacey was too short to see much, but followed the crowd, hoping it would reach him.

Sure enough, the crowd circled around the players, Brett in the center, on the shoulders of the linemen. She'd never seen him so happy! She watched as his teammates took turns high-fiving him and each other, helmets in the air. The cheerleaders joined them, pompoms waving and flashing. Lacey was about to move forward to hug him when the lead cheerleader, on the shoulders of another girl, moved in and kissed him! Smack dab on the mouth! The cheering continued, at a deafening level. Lacey stepped back, turned, and ran as fast as she could back to the visitor's side and onto the bus, tears flowing without restraint. Jenn was the first to hear the story.

"I told you Lacey, he's not marriage material. He's hot, then cold and totally unpredictable...you can't plan a future with someone so fickle!" Jenn tried to console her, but felt it was her first job to protect her friend. "Why are you doing this to yourself?" Jenn asked, genuinely curious.

Lacey paused, wondering if she should say what she needed to say. "Cause he's 'The One'," she said, her voice barely above a whisper.

Jenn stopped stroking her friend's hair and stared. Over the years she'd always wondered how Lacey "knew" things about people. Then, one night, she'd heard a sermon about the gifts of the Spirit, including the gift of discernment and prophesy. As soon as she'd heard it, she knew Lacey had The Gift. She'd told Lacey about it, and, though skeptical, it set right with her and provided an explanation to the unexplainable.

"Do *you* just feel that way, or –"

"No. I *sense* it…verging on *Know It*," Lacey interrupted. Ever since Jenn had told her about the gift of discernment, she started paying more attention to her "inklings." She noticed what seemed to be three distinct "feelings." One was when she "sensed" something about people. That could usually be chalked up to a keen understanding of human behavior and non-verbals. The second was a "knowing." She would see someone across the room and a thought would enter her mind, like, "She's pregnant," and, low and behold, a few days later the woman herself would find out. The third was what might be defined as prophecy. She'd be going about her daily routine and, usually at a quiet moment, "imagine" a story. Once, she'd been taking a bath and imagined a young husband having a brain aneurysm and the wife having to raise three children virtually alone. The next week the very thing happened to a family in their church. These moments did not happen every day, but they happened often enough not to be ignored or denied. In every case, they all came to fruition.

"Oh, wow," Jenn whispered, knowing the meaning and burden those words held. Lacey could no longer be willy-nilly in regards to Brett. There was more on the table now than was before.

Just then Robert was heading to the back of the bus and noticed Lacey had been crying. "What's wrong with Lacey?" he asked Jennifer, who silently mouthed, "Brett" to him. It hurt Robert to see the girl he cared for go through such heartache. He spoke the words that were on both of their hearts as he put his uniform away,

"You deserve better'n that, Lacey," he said softly.

She agreed with him, but couldn't deny what she'd sensed, and knew better than to ignore what the Spirit was whispering. Prophecy and discernment were given to warn and prepare people for what was to come.

What was to come.

The thought both excited and scared Lacey. She knew she genuinely loved Brett, but they had their share of obstacles. It was going to be a bumpy ride.

Good thing she was built tough.

TWELVE
October, 1992

By the time band practice was over Lacey had just enough time to finish her chores before saying her prayers and heading to bed. She prayed for those fighting overseas, for the struggling and sick listed in the bulletin that week and, lastly, Brett. Always Brett. It'd been a week since she'd seen him kiss the cheerleader at his game.

Her prayers usually asked God to give them more time to be together, or for him to nudge Brett to communicate more. But this time she prayed for *clarity*. Seeing that kiss put things in a whole new perspective. *Could* her dad be right? *Could* he have a girl in every city his Dad preached in? Was she just one of a *handful* to him?

Those questions danced in her head as she drifted off to sleep. A few hours later she was startled awake. At first, she thought branches were hitting her window. But the sound was louder than the branches should've been.

Lacey reached under her mattress for her 9mm pistol.

"There's nothing scarier than a woman with a loaded gun," her Dad said with a chuckle. And anyone who crossed Lacey's path would have just cause to be scared. Lacey shot as accurately as she tossed a line.

Before she could take three steps, she turned to see a silhouette STANDING right outside her window. But how could anyone be outside her second story window? She pushed the questions out of her mind as she steadied her pistol.

Before she could yell, "Who is it?" the figure threw up his hands.

"Holy Smokes!" he yelled.

As soon as she heard the deep drawl, she knew who it was.

"Brett!" she screamed in a whisper. "What in the *world*?!" She ran to the partially opened window to see Brett, in his repelling gear, standing on her house wall beside her window, the ropes taut and steady.

"You almost got yourself SHOT!" Lacey yelled, as she fully opened her window, again in a whisper, so as not to awaken her family.

"Oh! Don't shoot!" Brett said, unafraid, mimicking her. "You can't stop a bad guy with a BB pistol, babe," he said, mockingly.

Without losing eye contact or cracking a smile, Lacey raised the pistol and pushed the button for the clip with her right hand, letting it fall into her left, revealing the gun was, indeed, a 9mm.

"They don't stop cats either. That's why I carry this," she said, returning his mocking smile as she reassembled her gun and put it on her bookcase beside the window.

"Dang, babe!" he said, the color partially drained out of his face.

"I was aiming at your *shoulder*!" Lacey cried defensively.

"Oh, well *that's* better!" Brett said sarcastically.

"What are you *doing*, anyway?!" Lacey asked, pulling her big sweatshirt tighter around herself. She was more curious than mad, so she waited for his answer.

"Will told me 'bout you seeing Ashley plant one on me after the game. I had to let you know I didn't know that was coming," Brett's voice and gaze were steady.

"That Ashley's had a thing for me since last year. I've been able to dodge all her advances but she saw her opportunity that night and took it," Brett told her.

He was relieved when a smile spread across her face.

"You coulda just called, you know…" Lacey said, leaning closer, relief washing over her.

"Some things you just gotta say in person," Brett said as he readjusted his harness.

"What kinds of things?" Lacey asked, demurely.

"Oh, things like apologies," Brett said loftily as he looked up at his equipment, playing coy but adjusting it to get closer.

"Any *other* things?" Lacey asked, her voice coy.

"Telling someone their dog has died. Or their mom got arrested for streaking," Brett waited for her laugh. He wasn't disappointed.

"Anything else?" Lacey asked, through chuckles.

"Nope, that's about it," Brett said, looking at her and shrugging his shoulders.

Lacey sighed. "Are you *sure* there's nothing else that needs to be said in person for the first time?" She asked sweetly.

Brett continued the dance, "Not that I can think of…what are *you* thinking?" He asked, egging her on, inches from her now.

"Hurry up! Don't leave me hanging!" he said, tugging on his ropes with a grin.

"Oh, no!" Lacey shook her first finger in the air in a "no-no" wave, "I'm not gonna be the first one to say it!"

"Say what?" Brett asked, not-so-innocently. He was rewarded when he saw her feisty side rearing its head.

"Brett Wright! YOU are the man! And MEN are supposed to make the first mo-

Before she could finish, Brett leaned into her window, grabbed her behind her neck, and brought her lips to meet his. It wasn't a first time, nervous kiss this time, but a *sure* one, full of passion. Lacey felt swoony and light headed.

"There's some things you just know…but me too," Brett said with a wink as he leaned back a bit

"I did not say it first!" Lacey insisted.

"Oh, you said it, girl! You didn't use words, but you sure 'nuff said it!" His deep dimples were shining bright now. It was enough to make Lacey relent.

"Well…I do, you know…" Lacey confessed.

Brett beamed. "Me, too…but could you tell me again?" he whispered, leaning in for another kiss.

"What time do you have to leave?" Lacey asked, plotting their night.

"I got a couple of hours," Brett said.

"Dad gets up in three. I'll meet you outside."

Brett quietly bounced down the house while Lacey threw on her jeans and boots. She maneuvered her way down the stairs like a thief avoiding laser beams and silently headed out. She threw open the screen door and held her breath. It opened with only a whisper.

Brett was taking off his gear under the corner oak tree when Lacey got to him.

"I coasted and parked the truck down a ways," Brett said, pointing.

"Leave your stuff behind this tree," Lacey pointed. "I wanna show you something."

She took his hand as they walked down a well-traveled path across the grazing fields. They were blessed by a full moon, and could see their way pretty easily. A coyote howled in the background.

"Got your gun?" Brett asked, half joking, half hoping.

"Always," Lacey said, patting her hip.

"Only in Tennessee," he said with a chuckle.

They headed up a hill in a zig zag fashion, getting steadily higher with each stride.

"I was hoping you were gonna take my breath away, but I wasn't picturing it like this," Brett joked, huffing and puffing.

"Just wait. You'll see," Lacey said mysteriously.

The trail leveled off a bit and Lacey pointed to a thin, yellow rope. "Last climb," she sighed.

The hill wasn't as steep as the repelling Brett had just done, but it was a good angle. Lacey led the way, and Brett followed her every step, with a tight grip on the rope. After a few feet they topped the hill and came to a clearing. "Beautiful!" Brett breathed.

"Wait 'til we cross over," Lacey said.

"I wasn't talking about the landscape," Brett said as he pulled her in for another kiss. She melted into his arms. For the first time, she felt free. No prying eyes, no hiding from her Dad, just free.

"You can't do *that* over the phone, either," Brett said.

She took his hand and walked to the top of the grassy hill, then had him cover his eyes as she led him to the other side of the clearing.

"This would be a great place for a newlywed couple's house," Brett hinted, his eyes still closed.

"Lay down and close your eyes," she instructed.

"Yes, ma'am!" Brett flopped down on his back as quick as a wink.

Brett dodged the swat he knew she'd send his way. Lacey laid down beside him and held his hand.

"Ok. Open," she said.

Brett opened his eyes to a starry wonderland. Even with the moon shining so bright, the night sky was a glittery display of diamonds on a velvet sea. Brett was taken aback by it all.

"Ain't God something?" she asked, looking at the wonders above them.

"He sure can paint a pretty sky," Brett agreed.

They lay in silence, taking it all in.

Eventually, Lacey sat up, pointing to the valley, below. The river was narrow this time of year, but the full moon reflected on the water, making it look twice the size it really was.

"If you come out here around nine o'clock in early June the fireflies do their mating dance and the whole valley sparkles," Lacey said. "Between the stars and the lightning bugs, you feel like you're in outer space."

Suddenly, Lacey sat up straighter. "Oh my word, Brett. Do you see that?!" She pointed down the valley at the small forest of trees to the right.

"That glow! Do you see that glow??" She was excited now. Brett looked to where her finger was pointing, but couldn't see anything.

"That yellowish glow! Near the bottom of the trees!" Lacey said. Lacey sighed, forgetting he didn't have hunting or military training, "Don't look directly at that area, look a hair to the left or right and focus your eyes," she'd learned as a child from her grandfather how to "see" things better in the woods.

Yes! There it was! A mysterious, almost spooky, moving orb.

"What the - -" Brett was bewildered.

"That's foxfire," Lacey said, the excitement rising in her voice. "An unexplainable glow in the deep forest. Its legend is how the yellow butterfly came to symbolize the never-ending love between lovers," Lacey said, thinking of the yellow daffodil field they walked through the first time they really got to know each other.

"You know, I used to think love like that never existed," Brett whispered.

"*Used* to?" Lacey questioned, looking at him.

"*Used* to," Brett stated. They shared a quiet moment, happy to be together, and thinking of the possible future ahead of them. It was one of the things she loved most about them. Even their silences were not awkward. Instead, it wrapped itself around them like a blanket of contentment and waited patiently. Even time, it seemed, sensed their connection and respected them.

"We're gonna have to head back," Lacey said sadly. "Dad will be waking up soon."

"Five more minutes," Brett said, pulling her close, trying to memorize the feel of her neck on the curve of his arm and the smell of her hair.

"Hey, tell me you love me again," Lacey cooed, referring to the kisses at her window. Brett obliged, taking the credit for saying "I love you" first in exchange for the kisses that followed.

THIRTEEN
Present Day

"Have you ever heard of foxfire?" Lacey asked Mya.

"Foxfire? No, I haven't." Mya shook her head.

"The proper term is "P. luminescence." It's a rare glow that happens in forests sometimes. At Shiloh, some of the soldiers waiting for medical treatment noticed their wounds were glowing. They freaked out, but later noticed their comrads with the glowing wounds healed faster and had a higher survival rate than those without the glow. They say if anyone gets near it the orb will follow them for a while. But I think they made that up to keep people away," Lacey explained.

"What is it really?" she asked.

"I don't know, but there's an old Indian tale that says a young Indian, Abornazine, fell in love with a beautiful squaw who happened to be the Chief's daughter. The boy was in no position to marry her, but the Chief could not deny the love he saw between them. So, he devised a plan to facilitate their marriage. Knowing Abornazine was an excellent tracker, he said a husband for his daughter must be strong and brave and a good hunter. In a contest to find the appropriate suitor, they would place his daughter somewhere in the forest, and whoever was the first to find her would become the Squaw's husband. They placed the Chief's daughter under the tall trees where she would be safe and well hidden. The young suitors began the search as the Chief started preparing the wedding feast, confident she would quickly be found. However, Abornazine searched everywhere but could not find his bride-to-be. The Chief and the men of the tribe formed a search party and scoured the forest. When they returned to the place she had been placed, she was gone! Not a trace of her. But, curiously, there were hundreds of bright, yellow butterflies in the place where she had sat. Abornazine was heartbroken and spent the remainder of his life looking for his love. They say the yellow glow is the spirit of the boy still searching for his soul mate."

"That's beautiful and tragic all at the same time," Mya said. Lacey nodded.

"So did you and Brett fizzle out then?"

"Not exactly," Lacey said, stirring her tea.

FOURTEEN
April, 1993

"So, you and Lacey "on" or "off" right now?" Will asked Brett as they baited their hooks. Brett's guardian was preaching in Dawsonville that Sunday, and Brett chose to go down the Friday before to relax…and hopefully see Lacey.

Will had cut school to show Brett his secret fishing spot on Hurricane Creek. The willow flies were as thick as moths on a porch light, which meant the fish were biting heavy. Brett's fishing had improved a lot since he and Will first fished together, and a lot had happened in that time. Will and Jenn were already engaged, and he was trying to graduate early so he could enlist and they could begin their life together. Brett and Lacey were still going strong, too…when they were "on."

"Off, but I'm 'bout to change that," Brett shot back over his shoulder. It wasn't normal for he and Lacey to go so long without seeing each other, but Brett's father had added an extra church to his preaching circuit last month, making it double the time away from her.

"You two beat all I ever saw, man. Total opposites. Fire and ice. Oil and water…"

"…more like gasoline and fire," Brett interrupted, winking.

Will laughed, "Tru dat, tru dat…but how you gonna get back in her good graces? I heard she was full-on, mad-as-a-bat this time – and you know she's seen Robert a couple times since, right? Word is she might be seeing him right now."

"Robert? Pfffft! *He's* no competition," Brett mumbled. "She might be seeing him, but she'll always be my girl."

"No competition? Are you kiddin' me? His Dad owns First Federal bank and half the town. And he's got a *boat*..."

Brett adjusted his Cowboys ballcap. "He might have money, but I've got game. Money's great, but it ain't Lacey's thing."

Will was always in half-awe around Brett. There seemed to be things he was just born knowing and good at, like how to pitch no-hitters, find and reel in the biggest catfish – and how to reach Lacey. He had a quiet confidence that was strong and assured, yet humble. Will often wondered if he just *knew* how things were gonna go, or if his assured confidence *made* them go his way. Either way, one thing was sure: he could tame the most stubborn, feisty girl in Houston County. Many had dreamed of dating Lacey Wilson, but few got a second look. Brett had not only dated her, but seemingly won her heart. No matter how many times they fought and separated, they always found their way back to each other. God only knows why! They had about as much in common as a nun and a side street conman, but together they just worked. Nobody could beat the chemistry between the two of them – which is why Lacey so seldom went on any dates on their "off" times. Guys knew they couldn't compete with a love like that, so very few even asked her out. Once you've seen true love in real life, everything else pales in comparison. Will would give his whole bait collection & his Daddy's old Nova without batting an eye to have that cocky confidence – and relationship. Will and Jenn were engaged and as happy as could be – but they didn't have what Brett and Lacey had. Nobody did.

"How can you be so sure, man?" Will squinted at Brett under the late morning sun. Brett's response fit his typically assured manner.

"Cause I know her," Brett stated knowingly, more to assure himself than Will.

What Will didn't know was that underneath Brett's calm grip and cool grin he was really nervous, and growing a bit concerned. It wasn't like Lacey to not call him after getting a letter, but he'd heard nothing this time. Nada. Zero. Not one single call or letter. He'd always felt they were gonna end up together, and he thought she felt it too. Perhaps he had put too much confidence in his assumptions and not enough effort in their relationship? He wasn't sure just what Lacey was thinking, but he knew it was time to be clear...they were almost adults, now, after all.

Brett always seemed to have a cool calmness about him. He had been through so much in life, nothing much riled him. Nothing, that is, except the thought of losing Lacey. Abused and neglected by his father, he'd learned early in life how to be self-reliant. "The only person you can really rely on is yourself," he reasoned. So, early-on he convinced himself he didn't need anyone else. And he didn't, until he met Lacey. From their first day, when he followed her through the field of daffodils and saw her crying, his guard dropped. It was in her eyes he found understanding – an unspoken, shared "knowing." And it was in her heart he found unconditional love and comfort. Going so long without seeing her wasn't good for him – or anyone in his path, for that matter. By week three he'd almost gotten into two fights. Being with Lacey just about drove Brett crazy, but being without her was a guaranteed one-way ticket to Insanity. But he preferred a roller coaster to a desert of loneliness.

Try as he might to be independent, Lacey had gotten through. She had soaked through to the marrow of his soul, knowing him in ways no one else did. It was her approval that propelled him on the field, and it was her quiet wince that made him give up almost all his vices. Only she could push him to such greatness and only she could keep him in line. He *needed* her even more than he *wanted* her.

He reprimanded himself for not reaching out more. Being so far away *did* make things difficult, but he could have tried harder, done more. He had been coy with her in the past, but they had a lot of miles behind them now, and were getting older – college would be coming in another year. He now knew, despite how they teased, she was The One – and he needed to find a way to make "them" work, despite the distance. He vowed to start taking the needed steps to convince her of that.

"Well, you've got just the chance to make your move. I heard she was gonna be singing at the bonfire tonight," Will said.

"You don't say," Brett mumbled, already plotting his moves.

FIFTEEN

By the time Lacey got to the bonfire it was in full blaze. When the boys of Houston County did a bonfire, they did it right! No small backyard pit – no siree! The guys had stacked crates and pallets nine feet high and doused it all with gasoline before lighting the match. They all used to joke that the blaze could be seen clear to Davidson County. With flames dancing up to twelve feet high, there might be truth in their claim!

Jenn saw Lacey walking in with her band – alone. Jenn knew Brett was coming since he and Will left early for fishing that morning, so she wondered why Brett wasn't with her. "Will said Brett came down and is at his place. Planning on coming to the Bonfire," she mentioned, feeling Lacey out. But Lacey remained silent.

"Say," Jenn said louder, commanding her attention.

"I know, Jenn, but I don't rightly care," Lacey shrugged, busying herself unwrapping the amp chords and helping Robert get the microphones set up. She and Robert had formed a band with a couple of the other kids from school, and they were performing regularly. Robert and Lacey had good harmony and chemistry – but it was limited to the stage. Even though Robert's heart pined for Lacey, she did not have the same feelings for him.

Jenn wasn't surprised Lacey knew Brett was in town, and she knew what Lacey meant when she said she "knew." Early on, Lacey had developed an almost psychic-like connection with Brett. It was what made being away from him so hard. And it was also the thing that assured Lacey they were going to be together a very long time - which made waiting and being apart so very difficult.

Jenn noticed Lacey was being coy, so she decided to play along. "Good girl!" she said with a pat on the back.

Jenn never knew how to deal with Lacey and Brett. She could see their chemistry like everyone else, but *she* was the one left to comfort her friend every time he didn't follow through with staying in touch. She honestly didn't know if they were better off together or apart. The distance always managed to put a kink in things. She hated to see her friend ride the emotional roller coaster. But she was a dutiful bestie, so when they were together, she celebrated with Lacey, and when they were apart, she soothed her. There was no in between with the two of them.

"Yeah, but you know how I get around him," Lacey mused. "You gotta *promise* to stop me if I start going his way!"

"I will hogtie you, if need be!" Jenn assured her, grinning.

The evening rolled into night, and the band was in full swing. Lacey had already sung a full set by the time Will and Brett rolled in. They walked up just as she was finishing her new song, *Southern Chic.**

"Lacey must've written that one about herself," Brett said when she got to the chorus:

She's got that Southern Chic, Relaxed and refined,
Classy, kinda sassy 'Bout to blow my mind
*Unpredictable but that's a part of the mystique...**

"Sounds like it," Will chuckled as he took a sip. Brett never tired of seeing Lacey perform. She always looked natural and radiant, totally at home on the stage.

Lacey finished her song and went to the back where the boys were to get a drink. She knew full well where Brett was, but she was going to play hard to get.

Brett saw her striding his way and grinned, but then she walked past him.

"I shoulda seen that one coming," Brett muttered to Will. She made sure to stand right behind Brett, though, at the makeshift, haybale "bar" as she asked Jeff to hand her a Dr. Pepper.

"A'ight, guys. Let's say grace 'fore we eat," Robert announced from the center. Brett knew this was a perfect time to talk to her. She couldn't walk away now.

"So...you gonna ignore me all night?" he asked, turning her way.

Lacey just picked at her bottle wrapper, acting distracted. Brett knew it was time to up the ante.

"I SAID, *YOU GONNA IGNORE ME ALL NIGHT*?!" he yelled, upsetting the prayer. Teens four feet away turned around with disapproving looks.

"*Shh*! Hush, Brett!" Lacey whispered, taking him by the elbow and leading him behind the wall of dually trucks. She knew he was willing to do whatever it took to get her attention. "You're one to talk about ignoring! Not one letter or phone call for *weeks...*"

Brett interrupted in a loud voice, "I REPELLED DOWN YOUR HOUSE, LACEY! Don't that count for nothing?! And anyway, finals were last week and I haven't had a second to do anything!" he tried to explain.

Lacey was watching him closely. He seemed truly frustrated and stressed, but she was still hurt.

"People make time for the things they love, Brett," Lacey said. Brett could see she was still guarded, and was getting nervous. They had always done this same dance, but he hadn't seen her hurt like this, and he hated that he might've caused it. He needed to lighten the mood.

Brett stepped in closer. "Oh, I can *make* time," he said grinning mischievously. Lacey looked up. Was that a grin starting at the corners of her lips? Just as he was gonna go in for a kiss, the band started playing a quick intro.

"Hold up. I gotta sing," Lacey said, as she handed Brett her Dr. Pepper and ran off. Brett sighed. Her sweet confidence and magnetic smile made the audience like putty in her hands. This time it was as if she had selected the song to send a message to him.

Everything is always up in the air,
Here you come, there you go, without a single care.
I'm sick and tired of all your come and go rules,
That kinda game is the kind of love that's better played by fools!
Boomerang...you boomerang...
Spinning round up in the air,
Here we go again,
Boomerang!*

Brett rejoined Will on the hay bale. "Lacey looks like an ice queen tonight," Will said.

"Yeah, I've never seen her this bad," Brett grimaced as he watched Robert and Lacey smiling and having a good time performing.

"I gotta up my game – Hey, you think you could back me on that duet we heard coming over?" he asked Will. Will had the uncanny ability of playing anything by ear.

"Yeah I can. But Brett: YOU DON'T SING." Will said, wide eyed.

"I do tonight," Brett said, determined, eyeing Robert and Lacey.

"Oh, no," Will mumbled as he took one last swig for luck.

"She can't say no to a good duet," Brett thought to himself. He decided to start the song in front of everyone, while Lacey's band was still in the aisle. He was hoping this move would encourage the drummer and guitarist to stick around and accompany them, as well as encourage Lacey to sing without Brett having to ask her. "Best to ask forgiveness than permission," Brett reasoned - an anthem that could sum up his life.

The song ended, and the crowd's applause and whistles gave Brett and Will time to hop on stage. Without a second to spare, Brett started in on verse one:

*How were we to know, it'd all start with a little hello, ***
Spark the best love story this town has ever known

Lacey and the band turned around, surprised, as Will came in on the guitar.

And how were we to know, we would share our first kiss
Giving us sweet memories we'd always love and always miss

How were we to know? How could we have known?
All those years ago

After that line, Brett raised his eyebrows and held out the other mic, sending her a nonverbal invitation to sing. He prayed she wouldn't leave him hanging, because he had no plan B – and there was no way he could hit the high notes of the song.

How were we to know, war'd come knocking at our door
Taking us away to different shores…

Will hit the key change and Brett held his breath. He thought he might pass out before Lacey put the mic to her lips and started to sing:

And how were we to know, you'd come to mean so much to
me
To challenge and encourage me through every joy and
tragedy... *

Much to everyone's surprise they sounded *great* together! No one was more surprised than Brett himself! "All those church services are finally paying off!" he laughed to himself. Of course, anyone would sound good if Lacey were singing with him.

Lacey couldn't believe what she was seeing – and hearing. "Brett must be *desperate* to pull something like this!" she chuckled to herself. She had to admit she felt honored. As their voices blended on the duet, she was once again reminded of how well they fit together: from their voices, to their hands, to their lips...

Jenn was videoing the whole scene in unsurprised wonder and leaned over to Bulldog. "You got any rope in your truck, Bulldog?" she whispered.

"Yeah, why?" he asked.

"Because it looks like I'm gonna have to hogtie someone before the night's through," Jenn answered with a smirk.

By the time they hit the second chorus, they were holding hands again, all the past weeks forgiven.

How were we to know? How could we have known?
All those years ago... *

By the time they hit the last note, they were in each other's arms. In the back of his mind, Brett was wondered if Lacey was just performing – but when she turned fully toward him and let him kiss her forehead, he knew he was forgiven.

The crowd erupted into a gale of cheers, shouting "Encore" – but before they could consider another song Brett saw something. A girl was moving away from a guy, but the guy wasn't letting up, talking in her face. When the guy gripped her elbow and grabbed her face with his other hand, making her look at him, Brett jumped off the stage and ran to them. He pushed the girl out of the way and hit the guy. By the time the other guys got to him, Brett was straddling the guy.

All the girls screamed but Lacey. She knew what was going

on in Brett's head, but she'd never seen him act like this. It scared her speechless. Jenn caught Lacey's eye as she put the video camera down and gave her an "I told you so" look before Lacey ran to him.

"Good Lord, Brett! What in the world is wrong with you?" Lacey asked.

"He was roughing her up!" Brett was still wild-eyed, in another time and place. This was not just about the guy and girl. This was a flashback to his childhood.

"I know, baby, but you almost *killed* him!" Lacey said, gently cleaning off his bleeding knuckles with a wet napkin someone had given her.

"He deserved it," Brett muttered, unapologetically.

Lacey started to wipe the blood off his shirt, and that's when she saw it: a tattoo on the right side of his chest, over his heart.

No! It couldn't be!

She ripped his shirt wide open to reveal an eagle tattoo. A cold chill shot through her. To a typical girl, it would be just an eagle – but the Houston County girls were not typical. They knew a 101st Army eagle when they saw one.

"What is that?!" she half yelled, looking up, scared, at Brett.

Brett looked down, then back at Lacey. "I was gonna tell you tonight, Lace," he whispered.

Lacey froze. Operation Desert Storm had ended, but the 101st were still there. Brett would now be over there soon, too.

"Hey – at least my temper will be put to good use, right? Special Forces need tough guys…" Brett's voice droned on but Lacey couldn't hear anything he was saying. What was Brett *thinking*? He had *no* military training! Had he ever even *fired* a gun?!

"No!" she heard herself yell before running toward the river. Brett was quick on her heals. Across the field, through the woods, and out the other side to another clearing she ran. The light of the full moon caused sparkling ripples on the river. When Brett overtook her, he tackled her like a lineman. They took a tumble, but he wrapped her tight in his arms and rolled with her. By the time they stopped rolling they'd been kissing – passionately this time - no pretenses, no masks. Skin to skin and soul to soul. There was no going back now on hiding their feelings. They were both all in, whether they'd planned to be by now or not. War has a way of pushing deadlines and timetables. They literally and symbolically were now learning how to roll with it.

Tears streamed down Lacey's face, illuminated by the full moon above. Lacey felt every emotion all at once – anguish, joy, anxiety, love…

Brett took a minute just to look at her. Even with her hair a tussle and her face a wet mess she was gorgeous. He wanted to remember her just like this – natural and emotionally naked and clinging to him.

"Baby, it's gonna be ok…when I saw the recent bombing, I couldn't NOT join," he pleaded as he buried his face in her neck.

Of course she understood. She, of *all* people, understood. Living in the county bordering Fort Campbell, how could she not? Every male within fifty miles had served or had plans of joining the military one day. She knew all about freedom and pride and doing one's duty…it was not the *lack* of knowledge that had her in tears, it was the *full knowing* that plagued her.

"When do you leave for BASIC?" she asked, trying to be brave through her tears.

"Not sure yet. I just joined up," Brett answered.

"Fort Benning?" Lacey asked, already knowledgeable about the timelines and places.

"Most likely," Brett nodded, tenderly tracing her face with his finger, still atop her.

Lacey knew she needed to lighten the mood and not scare the poor boy. She tried to push out of her mind all the things she knew and he didn't.

"Hey…that means I can keep callin' you Private!" she said with a sly smile and a nudge.

Brett laughed before closing in for another kiss.

THE PEARL OF GREAT PRICE

SIXTEEN

The boiling teapot brought Lacey and Mya back to reality. Mya ran to the pot, quickly poured the tea, and hurried back to her perch on the couch, like an old lady running around during the commercials of her favorite soap opera, trying to get back before the show started again.

"Lacey! I can't believe all this happened! It's like a romance novel! I need some popcorn!" Mya laughed.

Lacey couldn't help but laugh at her friend's reaction. She was hoping to paint the full picture of what things were like between her and Brett, so Mya wouldn't judge her too harshly.

"Well, things always look better, looking back," Lacey said, cooling her coffee. "When we were together it was the fairytale kind of stuff they write books about, but occasionally, there was *something* I could never put my finger on, like an undertow warning that a storm might be on the horizon," Lacey stirred her coffee absentmindedly, trying to find the right words for something unexplainable. She shrugged, "But what I *do* know is it wasn't all in my mind - Jenn sensed it, too. She was supportive, but also played devil's advocate, especially when that silent undertow started whispering…"

"But you stayed with him?" Mya asked.

"From that moment on, yeah – as much as we *could* living two counties away. Once word got out we sang well together, we were asked to sing together every Sunday pastor Gill was there. We even got to sing at The Boardwalk when he was in town on Saturday nights. We got to be quite the hit! Life was carefree and easy, and we were counting the days until graduation so we could elope."

"What happened?!" Mya asked, bewildered.

Lacey paused, then said thoughtfully, "Graduation came and all our boyfriends, with their Daddies and Granddaddies, went to fight in the sand. Overnight our boys became men. Boys who couldn't buy a pistol were given a gun and expected to stand and defend. And they did. Bravely. We swallowed our fears and supported our guys. I remember vividly the office dismissing class and announcing the first convoy was on the way out. We all lined the streets with our little American flags to wave to the local National Guard – our friends and families. Men, who just the year before were considered boys, jumped off the trucks to kiss their high school girls, one last time, before jumping back in the wagons. We all knew from past experience when the Guard went it wouldn't be long before the troops would be called out," Lacey shuddered as she remembered the emotions of the past.

"Brett didn't ship out with them. He had to go through BASIC first. I was sad he wouldn't be with Will and all the guys, but relieved his training would give us more time before he would head overseas."

"Did y'all elope then?" Mya asked.

"No, I still had a year of high school left," Lacey sighed.

"Well, what happened?!" Mya asked, trying to sound more caring than curious.

"War happened," Lacey said with a sigh.

SEVENTEEN
August, 1993

Lacey didn't have to *try* to stay busy to keep her mind off things, she truly was. Even though she wanted to spend every moment with Brett, she had Graduation parties and her girlfriends' wedding showers to help with. Deployments were always met with wedding bells.

This particular Sunday the church was having a graduation/military sendoff party, complete with the Panther Singers performing their state championship show. Lacey had just finished cutting and serving cake, and was standing at the back watching the show when, without knowing, Brett arrived. He shushed his buddies, and slid up behind Lacey and gave her a quick hug and peck on the cheek.

Lacey was startled, then let out a happy squeal when she realized it was Brett. The old folk let them have their welcome before hushing them. Brett started to tell her something, but Lacey said, "Shh! This is the best part…watch!"

The chorus had added some hand motions to their routine, much to Robert's delight, and he had memorized the gestures *and* the song. The chorus got new outfits that year, swapping their bright, blue sequined vests for traditional white tops and black pants. As soon as the director gave the downbeat, the crowd saw a flash of blue! Suddenly, Robert popped up on the top tier – a blue peacock amidst a sea of white, starched shirts – and performed the whole routine with them! Hand gestures and *all*!

"Oh my!" Brett wheezed, wiping away tears. Everyone was in stitches. And then, as soon as the song was over, Robert hopped down, and ran out the side entrance. The director was all red faced, which made it all the more hilarious.

"He's been watching them for weeks!" Lacey explained between belly laughs.

Brett watched her laughing, making a mental picture of the way her pug nose crinkled and eyes got bright from tears just before busting into laughter.

He didn't know how he was going to tell her his news, so he just blurted out, "They're shipping me out tomorrow, Lace."

Lacey stopped laughing.

"I'll be in Fort Benning for thirteen weeks, then back to Fort Campbell."

"Tomorrow?" Lacey formed the words slowly, her mind fighting to comprehend his words and what they meant for her. For the first time in her life, she was speechless.

Brett led her outside the tent to the weeping willow tree.

"Let's elope tonight," Brett said, hoping she'd say yes.

"Tonight?" Lacey was still shocked but the question jolted her out of her trance. "I can't, Brett! Do you know what that shock would do to my Dad??"

"Always thinking of others," Brett thought. It was sweet and frustrating all at the same time. Brett knew she, too, always needed extra time for new ideas to "soak in," so he quickly changed the subject.

"Here, I got you something." He pulled out a decorative, pink box with pictures of flowers and lace all over it.

"That's for you to put all my letters in. I'm gonna write you, babe! Every day!" he crossed his heart with his fingers then kissed them to seal the promise.

"Holding you to it, Private," Lacey said as she wrapped her arms around his waist and looked longingly at him. They shared a long gaze, content knowing what the other was feeling and thinking, but both *still* too stubborn to be the first to say "I love you." It was Brett who broke the silence with three words, but not the three that hung, waiting, between them.

"Me too, kiddo…" Brett went in for a goodbye kiss, getting his message across without saying a single word.

****

"It was our silly way of saying, "I love you," without actually saying the words...just saying, "Me too" and implying that the other had said it first," Lacey explained as she sipped her coffee, a far-away look on her face. She quickly shrugged, though, and came back to the present.

"And we always tried to beat each other to it," Lacey chuckled. "I guess our stubbornness affected everything."

"I thought that was the last time I would see him for at least three months, but after crying all night, Jenn had a great idea..."

****

"Let's sneak up to Nashville and see Brett off!" Jenn shouted, wondering why they hadn't thought of it before. "I can pick you up tomorrow morning, and we'll have enough time to get there and come back before school is over!"

Lacey was ecstatic. She was so blessed to have such a caring friend. She knew she had put her friend's emotions through the ringer. Across four years, she was with her through every breakup and makeup – yet was still supportive of whatever stage they happened to be in at the time.

They made plans to leave at the usual time, so as not to raise their parents' suspicions, but Lacey wondered how she was going to sleep that night. Little did she know; Jenn had called Brett to give him a heads up so he'd arrive early enough to get a proper sendoff.

Jenn arrived at Lacey's house right at seven thirty. Send off time was high noon, so that left two hours to say goodbye. They listened to Nashville radio, gabbing all the way about their upcoming weddings and futures. Jenn and Will had gotten engaged the year before, and Lacey knew she and Brett would be married relatively soon.

They had been talking about wedding colors when Lacey saw a truck swerve, and barely had time to scream "Look out!!" before the eighteen-wheeler jackknifed, his back wheels pushing their car ahead like at ball on a pinball machine. Luckily, instead of pushing them under the rig, the car began to roll. Metal and parts flew all over the road with every flip. By the time their car stopped, there was barely a metal frame – or a pulse – left.

EIGHTEEN

Brett had gotten the call from Jenn the night before telling him that Lacey was coming to see him off. He had arrived a full hour early to spend as much time as he could with her. He had stamps – and a ring – in his pocket, the purple-blue pearl he'd found in the creek the first day they really got to know each other set in white gold and flanked by two small diamonds. He was hoping *she* would be the one truly surprised! But he was sweating bullets. Lacey liked to make plans – and stick to them. Marriage probably wasn't even on her radar, with graduation and college looming. Heck, they hadn't even been a steady couple throughout the years– but he knew how they both felt, and was hoping her love for him would surpass her need to stick to her preplanned life schedule.

He'd wanted to do something romantic, maybe take her to a nice restaurant or ask her onstage at a concert, but time didn't allow it. He did what he could with the time and resources he had, grabbing three dozen yellow roses on the way to the reception station.

He'd hoped for daffodils, but they were out of season, so he settled. At least they were yellow.

"Roses, check…ring, check…Now I just need my girl," Brett thought. "*My* girl…" he liked the way those words sounded. He couldn't wipe the grin off his face when he thought of Lacey Wilson becoming his wife.

Ten o'clock turned to eleven and then eleven thirty. By the time eleven forty-five rolled around, Brett was devastated, his head hanging lower than the wilting roses. What happened? He thought their moment last night was genuine, but she had always been fickle on things… Did she get cold feet and change her mind? Or did her Dad foil her plans? Brett didn't know what to think, as he got on the bus – the roses going home with his comrades' girls instead of his.

He slumped low into his seat, feeling the ring in his pocket but no answers to his questions.

NINETEEN

While both girls had been injured, Lacey suffered the worst. Lacey was unconscious when the paramedics arrived, but Vanderbilt was just a couple of blocks away, and they got her right in.

Lacey woke up to a beeping machine. Thinking it was her alarm, she was surprised when she couldn't move her arm. She opened her eyes to find herself in a hospital room, an IV bag attached to her restrained arm. Even though she couldn't see the five-inch gash on her forehead and the shards of glass that still clung to her hair, she knew she was in a precarious situation when she saw the heart monitor and her right foot elevated in a sling. Her mom and dad were at the foot of her bed, talking to some nurses. Momma Kim went over to Lacey when she saw her moving.

"Oh, sweetie, how are you feeling? You've been in a wreck, but you are okay," Momma Kim was good at putting a positive spin on every situation – even a near death wreck.

"What happened?" Lacey asked, genuinely wondering.

"Well, you and Jenn were in Nashville and a semi ran you off the road," Momma Kim explained, a little concerned her daughter didn't know how she got there.

"She must've taken a harder hit on her head than we thought," Momma Kim thought as she brushed the hair away from Lacey's forehead laceration.

"Oh, no! Where's Jenn?!" Lacey shouted, fearing the worst.

"She's okay, honey, she's just getting some x-rays done," her Mom said.

"What were we doing in Nashville?" Lacey asked – not remembering she wasn't supposed to be there, but in school.

"That's what I was hoping you could tell us," her Dad's voice boomed across the room.

"Jim, I think I saw the doctors in the hall. Go talk to them while I help Lacey get cleaned up," Momma Kim said as she sent her husband down the hall. She didn't want him upsetting Lacey before she'd fully "come to."

Her Dad had contacted their family lawyer, an elder at their sister church in Nashville, so he hurried over to give them advice *and* prayer. By the time her dad escorted him in, Lacey's cut– and tears - had dried.

When Attorney Andrews walked through the room, he brought a young, male assistant with him. This was the assistant's first time in the field and he was eager to be out from behind his desk. When he heard the term "totaled car" he prepared himself for a gruesome scene. What he had not prepared himself for was the sight of a beautiful young lady with wavy hair that reflected the light like diamonds flashing in an African mine. She looked like a fairy princess! He could barely take his eyes off her.

"Grant. Grant!" Attorney Andrews bellowed, knocking Grant out of his daydream.

"Oh, yes sir," Grant fumbled through the papers in his manila folder, praying he'd packed everything needed for this visit.

"Come on, boy!" Attorney Andrews said. "I swear, you're as slow and unorganized as your father!" he said with a wink to Lacey's father.

"Here it is, Dad…uh…sir," Grant mumbled. His father had told him it would be best to call him sir while working, so people wouldn't assume he had ridden his father's coattails into his position. Grant almost laughed aloud every time. In his family the idea of getting any charity of that sort was comical. If anything, his parents went out of their way to make it harder, not easier, for their children to earn their way in life.

"Builds character," his father would always say with an assured nod.

As the men talked of procedures and plans of action, Grant took the opportunity to observe the pretty subject before him. She had a radiant beauty despite the injuries, but there was a sadness in her eyes. "From the accident, no doubt," Grant reasoned.

The meeting lasted only a few minutes, but Grant determined he would be calling to check up on Ms. Lacey very soon.

****

"So that's how you and Grant met up…" Mya said.

Lacey shook her head, smiling. "He tried so hard to get me to go out with him! I had a long recovery ahead of me. I woke up thinking it was 1991, but Grant would not give up! First, he came by with some papers for me to sign, and then he needed to interview me about the accident. Then, he had *more* papers for me to sign! He later told me he had copied the first set of papers and brought those same papers over to the house three separate times, just to be able to see me! He wound up taking classes at my college, so we saw each other every other day…" Lacey's face broke into a big smile, remembering.

"He would push me around in my wheelchair, popping wheelies all over campus, and he gave me these crazy looking socks to fit over my leg cast to keep my toes warm," Lacey laughed.

"And what about Brett?" Mya asked,

Lacey paused and shrugged. "I never heard from him," she said soberly, her smile fading. "I had no memories of us after 1991, when things had gotten serious. I had no memory of our recent past or future plans, which was *good* since I had enough on my plate trying to heal physically. Grant and I hit it off so well that my family decided not to "remind" me of Brett. Jenn, of course, agreed – albeit a little reluctantly. However, his lack of contacting me led her to be more convinced than ever about her sixth sense feeling about him. Everyone agreed moving on and focusing on healing and new prospects was the best thing for me. Every once in a while, I would hear rumor of where he might be, but he never wrote to me like he promised. Actually, he wrote one letter – but that was it. It hurt a little, but I had no memories of our serious times so I moved on. The real heartache didn't come until much later…" Lacey's voice – and mind – trailed off.

"But it was OK," Lacey piped up matter of factly. "Grant and I were happy, and it was all great. It was nice dating someone whose feelings about me I knew were sure and steady - with the only hiccup being his family, of course. You know how things have always been awkward there..."

TWENTY
July 4, 1994

Lacey held onto her chess pie as she and Grant drove around the windy, wooded roads toward Dickson. It was July of 1994 and they had been dating a full year now. Grant's brother's high school graduation was the perfect time for Grant to introduce Lacey to the entire family, and show them how serious he was about her. Family celebrations were usually strictly reserved for family *only*, but Grant had called to let his parents know another seat would be needed at the table. He was hoping this action would prevent him from having to have an uncomfortable talk with his parents. He was aware of the timetable his parents had in mind for their sons, and that it did not include marriage until *after* college. He was also well aware of the potential fallout argument that was sure to ensue if that timetable should be altered. He cringed at the thought. Truth be told, marriage hadn't been in his plans either, but he knew a good thing when he saw it. And Lacey Wilson was definitely a good thing. He wasn't willing to risk letting her get away – or risk "the hell fire," as his preacher used to say, referencing I Corinthians 7:9 and bellowing out, "It is better to marry than BUUUURRRNNNN, men!" Perhaps the delivery of the message was a bit silly, but the message itself held true, and Grant took it seriously. He would keep the vow of purity he had made to the Lord and his future wife in high school, but Lacey didn't make that an easy task. If they had to date for three more years while he finished his degree, it wasn't likely he'd make it. He was trying to be both an attorney *and* a godly man, a task that had never been a problem until now. But that meant an adjustment to his plans was going to be necessary.

Lacey was visibly nervous. She knew meeting his family was a big deal, and wanted to be liked. Normally she had no qualms about meeting people, but as they drove further the homes grew bigger and pricier. Lacey knew Grant's family had more money than hers, but she didn't own or even know the names of the clothing designers people in these parts admired. She knew one thing, though: she didn't have a one of them in her closet...or her duffle bag. She began to regret not asking Grant more questions about his family.

Grant took her nervous hand in his and kissed the back of it, "They're gonna love you," and gave her an assured wink.

As they pulled into the drive, Lacey's suspicions were confirmed: Grant came from money. Old money. The paved driveway was as long as the single lane highway that her friends cruised on through her small hometown. The craftsman style mansion was unassuming, yet much attention had been given to quality.

"People that notice details," Lacey thought nervously, already counting the number of labels missing from her luggage, watch, and purse.

As they pulled in front of the house, Grant turned up the radio and said, "I *love* this song!" Much to her surprise "All Those Years Ago*"* filled the car, enveloping her in memories of Brett and the bonfire. Lacey was not prepared for the feelings that came swirling back, uninvited, at the sound of a few notes. The music took her back to the bonfire in Dawsonville and the scent of burning pine mixed with Brett's cologne as she sang with him, falling deeply in love. She froze, stuck between one reality and another. Luckily, Grant's brother swung open Grant's jeep door, ending his serenade. Lacey put on a happy face, but knew the nostalgic feeling was going to be with her for a while. As hard as she tried, she couldn't get over Brett.

"Some things in life you can't get over, you just have to move on." Grandma Kate said, the day she found Lacey at the river wailing in sorrow, the day her amnesia broke.

"Some things just go too deep, sweetie," Grandma Kate said with tears in her eyes as she rubbed her granddaughter's hair, her own heartbreaking memories from the War flooding her mind and stealing her voice. So that's what Lacey decided to do – move on. She packed away her memories, literally and figuratively, and focused on the future. Yet, there was always a ghost memory lurking in the shadows – waiting to creep up and steal her joy, dragging her back to yesterday. She'd learned to keep herself busy until the memory passed. Her strategy wasn't ideal, but it beat trying to *forget*. *That* was a *proven* losing battle.

Grant's family were welcoming and friendly, with the exception of his mother, who was distant, and his elitist aunts. But Grant had forewarned her of their ways, so Lacey tried not to take anything too personally. His brothers and sister were very warm, joking with Grant and taking turns telling her embarrassing stories from his youth. Graduation lunch had gone smoothly, a fact she relayed to Jenn when she had called to check up on her. But there were definitely hints here and there Lacey wasn't at home anymore.

While the guys played football outside, Lacey went inside to bond with the women. As she wound her way through the living room, she heard snippets of the uncles' conversations.

"… thing is, you give those poor people some money, six months later they'll be poor again…"

As she slid past the "elitist aunts with the poufy hair" she couldn't help overhearing them discuss a recent luncheon.

"…I mean, the girl used PAPER TOWELS for her napkins, for Pete's sake!" they whispered, as they chuckled knowingly. Lacey couldn't help but question if she really fit in at all. Grant jogged into the kitchen just as his Great Aunt started to quiz Lacey.

"So, Ms. Lacey, what are your plans for this coming year? Grant says you are headed to Nashville. Will you still be attending Lipscomb or Belmont?"

Lacey responded quickly, happy to finally be acknowledged, "Well, I think I'm gonna hold off on college for a bit…"

She knew it was the wrong thing to say as soon as the ladies stopped their conversations cold turkey and looked at her.

His Aunt nodded, knowingly, "So you're taking a sabbatical? To Europe? Perhaps a hiking tour?"

Lacey hurried to explain, so they wouldn't think she was lazy. "No, I'm heading up to Music Row. I've got a friend in East Nashville I'm gonna room with and I've got a few gigs lined up…"

His aunt looked shocked and confused, as if she had just heard someone respond in Mandarin Chinese.

"Mistake number two," Lacey thought, as, this time, the ladies stopped prepping food and turned to look at Grant's mother.

Grant's mother interjected with a nervous laugh. "Well, I hope none of those gigs is in a BAR, because people in OUR family just don't sing in *BARS*..." she ended her sentence with a laugh of utter ridiculousness to the other ladies, drumming up supportive chuckles from them and eyeing Lacey through slit eyes.

Lacey recalled the times she had sung at The Boardwalk back home, and all the fun they'd all had...good natured, family fun. She'd never thought to be embarrassed about it, until today. Her face turned a shade of crimson. Lacey wasn't prepared for such cattiness and wasn't sure how to respond, since the subtle insults were coming from Grant's mom. Lacey was at a loss for words.

But Grant wasn't.

"So, singing in bars is off limits, but selling to bars is ok?" he interjected with a sly smile, as he grabbed a roll and hopped onto the counter. Grant's immediate family was in law, but their family's wealth had been acquired during the Prohibition Era– and was still earning dividends off the invested stock shares...a fact the family liked to keep quiet.

Grant's mom gave a quick laugh, "Oh, you silly!" she said with a wave of her hand, shooing him out of the kitchen. Grant went, but not before he grabbed Lacey's hand and took her along. He had hoped his mom would behave, but was glad he had been there to intervene when she wasn't. Lacey's sad face was not lost on him.

"C'mere, I wanna show you something," he said as he walked her deeper into the woods. It wasn't long before they came to a big, Sugar Maple tree. It stood at least ninety feet tall with long, thick branches. It had to be well over two hundred years old!

"Oh, Grant! It is BEAUTIFUL!" Lacey sighed. She had always had an affinity for trees, capturing many of them in photos that lined her walls. But this one was better than she'd ever seen: round and full and majestic.

"I thought you'd like it. I know what a thing you have for trees," Grant said, watching her face light up as she took it all in.

"It's pretty during every season, too. In winter it looks like a crystal palace when the ice clings to its bare branches. In the Spring, it's full of red, chandelier shaped blooms before it breaks into this full, round greenery. But the best, by far, is fall! Bright yellows and oranges fade into deep reds and burgundies toward the top. And when the sun is setting it slants at the perfect angle to make it look ablaze! Dad calls it the Burning Bush."

They stood there, taking in all its glory.

"Walk this way," Grant whispered as he took her hand and walked her toward the tree. Grant pointed out a few spots with various lover's initials and hearts. "This is my sisters' favorite family tradition. When someone gets married, they get to carve their initials in the trunk, becoming an official part of the family tree," Grant laughed, emphasizing the word "tree." Lacey rubbed her hand along the carved letters. "The initials go all the way back to my great, great grandfather." As she got closer to the tree, she could see a small, wooden circle hanging from a branch with a carved heart and the initials in the middle:

LW + GS

Lacey was so touched. "Is that what you were doing last night?" she asked, smiling.

Grant nodded, stepping closer. "Yes. I thought a Christmas ornament might be nice, since maybe next time you're here I can carve our initials *on* that tree with a *new* last initial…" It was the first time either one of them had actually voiced plans for the future aloud, even though they both knew where their relationship was heading. Lacey felt her mouth break into a wide smile as Grant's lips met hers. For the first time in a year, she felt truly happy – the ghost in the shadows barely a whisper, now. Life seemed blissful.

As they went back to the house, though, reality set back in. As Lacey headed to the bathroom, she heard hints that seemed to scream, "You don't belong here…" The final blow came when she overheard one of the aunts talking about her son.

"…I mean, if he doesn't get his tail in gear, he's gonna have to go work for the *government*…or…the MILITARY!" As she said "military," she lowered her voice and whispered it like it was something to be ashamed of. Lacey felt her head spin. She knew how she felt about Grant, and now knew how he felt about her, but how in the world would she ever fit into this world of his? And…did she even *want* to?

She checked her phone in the bathroom and had a voicemail from Jenn:

"Come out to the Barn! Everybody's here and askin' about you!"

Lacey smiled. The thought of being back home, relaxed around all her old buddies, gave her a warm, fuzzy feeling. She longed to let her hair down – literally and figuratively – surrounded by her friends who "spoke her language."

She left the bathroom, thanked Grant's parents for their hospitality, and convinced Grant to drive her back to her car, promising to find him as soon as they got back to school the next week.

****

"I didn't know Grant had such a romantic side!" Mya said, impressed.

Lacey laughed "Oh, he did! Definitely! Although, our initials still aren't on that tree…" Lacey frowned. It was such a seemingly small thing, yet the fact that Grant's Mother *still* had not seen to it that their initials were on the tree spoke volumes to Lacey.

"*Spoke* volumes," Lacey chuckled at the term. In Grant's family, they never *spoke* disparagingly words, they just spoke volumes…with their silences. And the silence on this simple act said Grant's parents still did not accept her as part of the family.

"So did y'all have a long engagement while he finished school?" Mya asked, trying to count back the years in her head.

Lacey paused. "Well, not exactly…"

TWENTY-ONE
JULY 4, 1994

The closer Lacey got to home, the more relaxed she felt. The way she shimmied out of her clothes while driving home – from her hat to her shrug, to her shoes – was symbolic of all the masks and appearances she felt falling away. College had been good that year, but that environment required a more refined way of talking and acting that was not natural for her. "Like at Grant's house," Lacey thought. She immediately rebuked herself and tried to push the thought out of her mind. After all, Grant did not judge her on the basis of her family's issues, so it wasn't fair for her to do it to him. She instead focused her thoughts on all her high school buddies she'd get to see soon. Jason and Robert would not be there. Robert was on a mission trip to Ghana and Jason was serving overseas with Desert Storm. "Serving with Brett and everyone else, no doubt," her breath caught in her throat at the thought of him.

"A perfect example of how my heart keeps holding on, even though I've tried to move on," Lacey sighed. "And how his ghost always casts a shadow on my new life."

Grandma Kate always used to say the devil was in the details, and in a strange twist of fate it had been a tiny detail that brought Lacey's memory back.

It was Christmas break, and Lacey had been doing charity work with Operation Homefront. This particular year she was lucky enough to deliver some gifts to the families in the Clarksville area. As the door opened at the third apartment, Lacey was greeted by a shirtless soldier. It wasn't his bare chest, but the 101st eagle tattoo on the right side of his chest that gave her pause. The soldier was grateful for the gifts, but none of his kind words got through to her. Forgotten moments filled Lacey's mind. Moments with Brett; the Bonfire where she'd seen his tattoo and his chase when she'd run from him, knowing all the eagle represented. Their roll down the hill, their shared passionate kiss and his promise to stay in touch...

It'd taken seven months for the forgotten memories to come back, and they came at her - swift, strong, unexpected and powerful...just like their love. The soldier she had been talking to caught her before her knees gave way. This brought back the memory of Brett carrying her back to church when she had twisted her ankle the first day they'd talked. In a state of memory overload, she'd had just enough strength to get herself to her jeep before falling apart. It was all too much to bear. Jenn came immediately and rocked her in her arms. Lacey didn't have to explain; Jenn knew this day might come. What do you say to your best friend when she realizes all she's lost?

Lacey had so many unanswered questions, but she'd been dating Grant steadily for a few months. Mourning a lost love in secret was *unbearable*, her heart breaking like the tiny glass shards she had seen when she first opened her eyes after the fateful wreck that had changed her destiny. How could she mend her heart while still dating Grant? There is nothing worse than grieving alone.

Gratefully, the revelation hit during her four-week Christmas Break when Grant and Lacey spent time with their respective families. Lacey spent the break in bed at the Lakehouse, only waking to relieve herself and eat. Grandma Kate dropped off her favorite foods in the hope of getting Lacey to eat: fried pies, cornbread and sweet tea, but hadn't pushed Lacey to talk. She knew Lacey needed time to sort things through – and mourn. One night, Lacey called her, "Have you gotten any letters, Grandma?" To which Grandma Kate had to give a reluctant "No, sweetie." Kate knew, more than anyone, how much Lacey needed this down time. She had always rooted for Brett, but, like Lacey, felt the faint, nagging feeling of "something amiss." But even with that feeling, Grandma Kate wasn't prepared for how Brett fell off the map without a word. She didn't know quite *what* to make of it, or what to advise. Everyone knew what the two of them shared was precious and rare, a true love only found once in a lifetime. But Grandma Kate also knew you can't plan a future with a man you can't depend on, a piece of advice she had written Lacey on a card in her third food delivery basket.

Her heart broke for her granddaughter. She remembered the way she would light up when Brett was around, in stark contrast to her days of recovery after her wreck. In addition to her physical injuries, Lacey had also suffered a personality change. She was still creative and smart, but she became more reserved and introverted. She swapped her singing for writing, and guitar for oil pastels. Her family would never admit that they were saddened by this. They were thankful she was alive. No one knew if the somber changes were from the head injury or her heartbreak. Grandma Kate attributed it to a little of both.

Lacey's saving grace was Grant. It was he who had brought joy back into Lacey's life, and probably the reason she didn't lose her sanity. Lacey spent two weeks grieving and mourning before Grandpa Charlie decided it was time to have a talk with Miss Lacey.

Grandpa Charlie always had a joke to share, but few knew what a difficult life he had lived. Orphaned at eight, he was forced to make his own way and ended up in the Army. He was one of the first Rangers in the Philippines, and only the tough survived. He had the respect of all the Army guys – young and old - once they knew.

"I hear you can't get out of your foxhole," Grandpa Charlie yelled up to Lacey from the front yard. She had run out onto the balcony, frizzy haired and wild-eyed, after being awakened by three rounds to the air from her granddad's pistol. He sure knew how to command attention when he needed to!

"Land sakes alive, Lacey! You look like a POW all pale and skinny like that! Get yourself down here in ten. We're going fishing," he ordered.

Even in Lacey's down and depressed state, she knew better than to try to argue with Grandpa Charlie when he was ordering commands, so she slid a rubber band around her wild mane and creek shoes on her feet and was in the jeep within eight minutes. They wound their way along the gravel roads toward the river, Grandpa Charlie teasing and trying to cheer her all the way. By the time they got to the boat ramp, Lacey had smiled a few times and was starting to feel better.

Lacey remembered Grandpa Charlie's words of encouragement and advice.

"Lacey, I was planning on making a career of the Army. Nobody knows this, but I held the highest sharpshooter record – for years - and was working my way up the ranks."

"What happened?" Lacey had asked.

"God had other plans, namely a five-foot, five-inch beauty with light auburn hair that looked like ripe harvest wheat dancing in the bright sun just before sunset. She could cook and kiss better'n any I'd ever met," Grandpa Charlie smiled. "Thing is, we don't always live the life we think we will. Proverbs says, "The mind of a man plans his way, but the Lord directs his steps." That means, "Plan your life but watch out! God might have other plans and His will wins, so you'd better hold onto your plans with a loose grip…that's the GCV," he said as he chuckled, knowing Lacey knew he meant the "Grandpa Charlie Version" of the Bible.

"But I can tell you, sweetie, God's direction is *always* better than our best laid plans. What if I had chosen the Army over your Grandma?" Grandpa Charlie shuddered. "I'd still be as skinny as a rail and never have matching socks!" He laughed at his own joke, his gaffs rocking the boat.

"Lacebug, I know you're heartbroken. And we are sorry. Truly. We were going to fill you in on your missing memories eventually, but decided to wait and see what Brett would or wouldn't do. You know how negligent he could be sometimes," Grandpa Charlie said with a slight frown.

"But we always pray for *God's* will to be done, first and foremost. So, when things don't go the way *we* want or the way *we've* planned, we've gotta believe God is up to something *different*. And TRUST Him in that," Grandpa Charlie's voice was firm and sure.

Once again, Lacey found comfort and redemption in her family's words. She knew the Godly wisdom behind them, so she followed their advice, pulled herself together, and pressed forward. By the time she returned to school, she felt God had mended her broken heart. Almost.

TWENTY-TWO
July 4, 1994

The sight of the gigantic bonfire brought her back to reality, and by the time she got to the Barn, the place was in full swing: hay bales scattered in a circle around the bonfire pit, lights strung from the old barn down to the tables, country music floating out from the loft and what looked like nearly all the past two graduating classes wandering around. Lacey breathed it all in deeply. It was good to be home.

Jenn wrapped Lacey up in a big bear hug before Lacey could even turn around.

"Oh my word, Lacey! I was praying you'd come! Everybody's here!" She squealed, as she put a Coke in her hand.

"How'd it go at Grant's?" Jenn asked, as she scanned the food table.

"Fine..." Lacey mumbled, grabbing a plate. She felt her friend's concerned stare.

"Oh, Grant was great! Just great! It's just...they live a little higher on the hog than I'm used to, I guess," Lacey shrugged. "They dine on filet mignon and I'm more used to Vienna sausages!"

Jenn laughed. "It's gonna take some getting used to, I guess," Jenn encouraged her. "Of course, it's a whole lot easier to go from franks to steak than vice versa!" Jenn joked.

"Yeah, that's for sure!" Lacey laughed. "It's just hard to think of marrying someone whose family doesn't feel like home to you. And Dad always says, "You marry the man, you marry the family...""

"Well, your Dad says a LOT of things, Lacey," Jenn looked at her friend sympathetically. "Home isn't always where we think it will be..."

Lacey nodded, "I know..."

The late afternoon wore on into dusk, the setting sun of the bright July sky reflecting over the river. The band played a mix of Charlie Daniels, McGraw and Chesney. Lacey and Jenn were finishing their desserts when there was a big commotion. Before Lacey even heard his name, she knew - the same way she had always known. She looked up at Jenn's shocked face for confirmation, then heard it.

"Brett! Jason!" cheers and loud welcomes filled the night air. Jenn grabbed Lacey by the shoulders, whirled her around and looked deep into her eyes.

"Lacey! Look at me! You have to promise me you will not be hoodwinked by his sugarcoated tongue this time; do you hear me? You have a good thing going right now, and Grant is a GOOD MAN..." Jennifer hoped her pleas would somehow protect Lacey's heart from the slippery slope it always rode toward Brett.

Lacey shrugged her friend off nonchalantly, "Please, Jenn! I'm OVER Brett! Anyway, I love Grant..." she said, a little more confidently than she felt.

"I know you love Grant, but your chemistry is programmed for *Brett*! You know how you two are!" Jenn begged, worried she would once again, tonight, find herself consoling her crying friend. "I'm *serious*, Lacey! *Promise* me!"

Lacey put her hands on Jenn's shoulders, "I promise!" she said before giving her a pinky swear.

Lacey knew her two biggest weaknesses: Brett Wright and men in uniform.

"Steady my heart, Lord," she prayed as she took a deep breath and turned around.

The crowd around the soldiers dwindled as the band began to tune up. Soon there was no one left between Brett and Lacey. Brett was in his desert fatigues. "At least he's not in his dress greens," Lacey breathed a small sigh of relief.

Brett had been longing for and dreading this moment, hoping to get an answer as to why she hadn't kept in touch with him. It was her face and the hope of rekindling the fire between them that had kept him going these past months. He was hoping he'd see by the look in her eyes if there was a chance they could still connect. He was wanting a definitive signal but he'd settle for a whisper of a hint. After all, he liked a challenge and wasn't scared to fight.

Before he walked over, he took her in. She was even more beautiful than in his dreams. Flowing sundress, hair long and pulled back with a few stray curls around her ears that and refused to stay in place, and that *smile*...he'd been on the mainland for a couple of hours but just now he felt like he'd come home. Will told him she was dating some college boy pretty steady. He didn't know how to approach her, but knew he had to. Over one hundred letters and not one response...could he really have misread Lacey like that? After the third month and no responses, he'd finally given up. It seemed clear she didn't want him in her life after all. But he still had many unanswered questions, like why hadn't she come to see him off like she'd said? That night by the river - they were both so genuine and raw...it just didn't make sense. He was hoping to get some answers, but now, seeing her there, he knew he wanted more. He was willing to swallow his pride if it meant getting her back. He had learned a lot overseas – the most important was learning to identify what is most important, make that your objective and stop at nothing to attain it. That "most important thing" was now standing before him, barefoot and bare shouldered, scaring the mess outta him – same as an unsecured bomb he once had to detonate. But, unlike knowing how to detonate a bomb, there was no manual on how to win back the love of your life. He was just gonna have to do what he did best: wing it.

She had been tidying the card tables, staying busy. He *knew* she knew he was there by the way she *hadn't* responded to the commotion. Lacey, always in the thick of the action, was purposefully keeping her distance. He was gonna have to play it carefully.

Almost as if reading his mind, Will nodded over at Lacey. Brett nodded back and began walking toward her, praying for courage the whole way. He'd just spent eight months in enemy territory, marching through mine pits and dodging bullets, but this walk was far scarier and more unpredictable. And much more was at stake. Both his love *and* his future were on the line. One wrong move and it could all blow up in his face.

By the time Brett made it to her, Lacey stood watching the band.

"Hey, Lace," Brett said in a friendly way.

Lacey gave him a slight, friendly smile. "Brett...when'd you get in?" she tried to keep her voice steady and nonchalant, but the dimples and uniform were making that a difficult task. She had told herself there was no sense in being rude.

"I touched down in Nashville two hours ago. Will told me everyone was out here, and I was hoping to see you. I've still got sand in my boots!"

Despite her promise to herself, his sand comment made her chuckle, but she quickly reeled herself back in. "Well, here I am..." she said coolly.

In her desperation to ease the awkward tension, Lacey pointed to one of his badges.

"What're those for?" she asked innocently.

"Unit awards and campaigns I participated in," Brett said.

"What's that one for?" Lacey asked, pointing to one.

"That one there?" Brett asked, looking down at his chest. "Oh, that's for waterboarding."

Lacey pulled back, surprised. She was truly shocked. She was familiar with most all the ribbons for the National Guard, but not the Army. Had they seriously added *waterboarding* to their training since Desert Shield? She could not hide her fearful admiration.

"Oh my word, Brett! Are you SERIOUS?! They WATERBOARD ya'll now?!" She asked, seriously scared for him. She could not keep the concern out of her voice.

Brett's chuckle turned into a hearty laugh, "NO, silly! *No!* That one's for combat infantry."

"You're still gullible, I see," he liked the way her face turned a soft shade of pink. Their laughter drew attention from their friends who were keeping an ear out for them, despite acting as if they were oblivious to the soap opera playing out in their midst. She turned her face to the sky, laughing, and that's when he saw it.

"And just what've *you* been doin, Sassy?" he asked jovially, pushing her bangs out of her eyes. "Rollin 'round in barbed wire?" he chuckled, as he brushed his thumb over the scar on her forehead from the wreck. Their eavesdropping friends stopped and stared, horrified, waiting for Lacey to lash out.

Lacey stopped smiling and looked down. His question cut through her as deep as the glass had on her forehead, reminding her anew of what they were and what they had lost.

"That's from the wreck, Brett," she whispered softly. *So softly Brett almost didn't hear her.*

Brett stopped grinning, "What wreck?" he asked, confused and concerned.

Lacey looked up, amazed. She couldn't believe he would deny knowing.

"The wreck I had on the way to see you off last year," she said coldly.

Brett was dumbstruck. "What are you *talking* about, Lace? Is that why you never showed up?!" His voice was starting to get frantic, half out of concern and half out of relief. If she had been delayed instead of deciding not to come, there might still be hope.

Lacey turned away, but Brett was not giving up. "Lace!" he said louder.

Lacey shook her head, "Don't do it Brett," she commanded, turning and walking away. Her voice warning him to stop, because the road he was about to go down was a bumpy one. They had the crowd's full attention by now so Lacey decided to move their conversation elsewhere and started toward the lake.

"Do what?" Brett asked, following.

"Try to make yourself look better by denying you *knew* anything. You were never really as "all in" as I was...I've always known that, and I get it. It's OK..." Lacey was trying to be nonchalant but her quivering voice was deceiving her.

Brett was flabbergasted. He didn't know which topic to tackle first: this "wreck" he'd just learned of, or her accusation he never had deep feelings for her.

"Never "all in"?! Is *that* what you think? Wow. Wow!"

As his voice started rising, so did Lacey's pulse. Her personality had changed drastically since the wreck, but some things go deeper (like the fight or flight response) and she had to run. And, as always, Brett ran after her, away from the barn, past the bonfire and toward the river, his words following her the whole way.

"Does somebody who's not all in write a girl every day for a HUNDRED DAYS even though she never wrote back?? Does somebody who's not all in come crawling back, tail t'wixt his legs like a neutered dog to see if there's any hope left? Does he get a tattoo of her name on his arm, Lacey?" he asked, swiping at his bicep. Lacey had planned on ignoring any of his attempts to connect, but she stopped running and twirled around in frustration, hands already flailing.

"Stop it Brett, just stop it!" she yelled, pushing him back by his chest, trying not to notice the new muscles that had developed. "You *always* DO this! Proclaim your undying devotion to me, promise me the moon and stars, and then NEVER FOLLOW THROUGH. It's interesting you say you wrote everyday 'cause know how many letters I got? ONE. ONE, Brett."

Brett was confused, but distracted by her scar. When she had twirled around, she had absent-mindedly tossed her hair to the other side. The bright moonlight revealed it had been a deep cut.

"What about this wreck you're talkin 'bout? Were you hurt bad?" he asked, looking at her scar, his eyes searching the rest of her for more.

Lacey relaxed a bit. Could he be telling the truth? She knew they weren't allowed any contact for nine weeks during BASIC…

"Not too bad," Lacey lied. "I got this pretty souvenir, of course," she said, pointing to her forehead, "…and I only had to be in a wheelchair for a couple months."

"*Wheelchair*?! Are you *kidding me*??" There was no hiding it now. His voice was raised an octave.

"The physical injuries weren't that serious, it was just --" before she could say "memory lapses that were so bad" Brett swooped in and kissed her like he had a right to, the way he used to. She didn't know if she wanted to, or if she was conditioned to, but she found herself relaxing in his arms.

"Man, Lacey, I'd die if I ever lost you…" he said in her ear, hugging her tight.

Before Lacey had a chance to think of how she would respond, the whole gang came running down to the river. Brett and

Lacey quickly pulled apart as the guys scooped Brett up onto their shoulders and announced, "We're going to Nash Vegas, baby!" they yelled as they handed him over, rave style, toward the trucks.

Jenn took the opportunity to sidle up to her friend. "So much for pinky promises," she scolded.

Lacey sighed. "I didn't kiss him back, Jenn," she said, still feeling his lips on hers and trying to ignore the butterflies that had taken flight within her a few seconds before.

TWENTY-THREE

By the time the crew had made it to Nashville, Music Row was in full swing. It was July fourth weekend, and military personnel were being celebrated, which meant free cover charges and drinks - if a soldier was in his fatigues.

"If you serve *us*, we serve *you*!" the bartenders said with a wink. "If you're old enough to fight, you're old enough to drink!" they'd say as they ignored their "underage" stamp.

Lacey, Will, Jenn and Brett had ridden up together, and Lacey had to admit it was fun and felt natural. She'd had two hours to think about all Brett had said. It just didn't make sense: Brett was aggressive and he was a fighter, but he didn't lie. Maybe he didn't know about the wreck...but where were all the letters he claimed to have written? She decided to put her judgments on hold for the time being.

As half the group hit the dance floor at Tequila Cowboy, the other half stayed behind in the booths as Brett told some of his Army stories. It wasn't long before all the guys were in stitches. Brett was an excellent storyteller. He nonchalantly put his arm around Lacey, as if nothing had changed between them, and she was conflicted about her feelings. She never believed someone could love two people at the same time, yet she did.

She absentmindedly toyed with the bracelet Grant had given her shortly after she had met his mother for the first time, and discovered her distain for artistic debutants.

It said, "Artists must be a little strange to make such beautiful and magical things." She remembered his sheepish grin when he told her, "Don't let my Mom get to you. Stay just like you are, Lacey."

And that was Grant: encouraging, genuine, true, and totally in love with her.

The thought made her feel a twinge of guilt. He had just made his intentions and plans of a future with her known. Even though there hadn't been an *official* engagement, they both knew where things were headed ...at least until five hours ago. Either way, Lacey needed to settle the question whether she had any feelings for Brett Wright once and for all before accepting a proposal from Grant. And there was only one way to figure that out. She needed time with Brett before she settled on an answer.

Lacey was at a crossroads with Brett on one hand, and Grant on the other. Her choice would determine her future. She hoped she would make the right decision. She knew how she FELT about Brett, but she didn't want to make a decision based purely on their physical attraction...there were other issues to consider as well. She and Brett had chemistry to rival any romance novel, but she and Grant had everything *else* important in common, from their ideology on life to their strong faith. And they were a good team: he was strong where she was weak and vice versa.

As she was weighing her options, Brett pulled her close. "Man, it's good to be home," and kissed her on the forehead.

Home.

A word drenched in meaning, almost sacred, for the two of them. A word whose meaning had eluded them until they met each other. A word that held promise and forever. *Together.*

Lacey could feel herself getting drunk on nostalgia.

Just then the band started playing *First Love Rights.** As everyone got up to dance, Brett put out his hand to lead Lacey onto the floor.

Lacey stayed in the booth, "I'm not as light on my feet as I used to be, Cowboy." Brett saw her hesitancy and knew there was something deeper in her statement.

"Brett, I can't do a lot of the things I used to do easily, and I'm not even sure I'm the same girl." She looked up at him with questioning eyes. He didn't know the full extent of her injuries, and she worried perhaps they would make him feel differently about her.

"Nothing could ever make me love you any less, babe. We'll just do things different. Now, get up quick 'fore someone from church sees you!" Brett joked.

Lacey laughed as she took his hand. "I think today, even old Widow Clemmons would allow dancing!" Lacey said, referring to the American victory they'd just seen reported on the news. She felt his hand on the small of her back, and noticed how he slowed to adapt to her weakness. It touched Lacey's heart.

The group took to the dance floor, dancing in rhythm to the cadenced steps. Brett did not falter in his gentle treatment of her, repeating the same steps over and over. At one point, he had her step on his boots and whisked her around the floor! Everyone was having fun. It was just like old times.

Brett felt the hesitancy in Lacey. Her spunk was a bit dimmer and her gait, a bit slower. But she was still Lacey, and that's all that mattered to him. He'd help her find her old spark if she'd let him...

When the song was over, Lacey went back to the table to get a drink of water. While there, she saw she had missed multiple calls from Grant. She quickly turned her phone off, surprising herself. She wasn't ready to confront her feelings just yet. She still wanted to give Brett a fair shot.

Brett came up from behind her, wrapping his arms around her middle and kissed her cheek. *Before We Let Love Go** began playing, and Brett led her onto the floor to join the other couples. As the music played on, they drew closer, their bodies moving in perfect rhythm.

"Lacey, I feel really bad for not being here for you when you needed me. I can't imagine my life without you. This year has been murder..." Brett's voice faded away, more sincere than she had ever heard him. She knew there was something more in his words – only God knew what he'd seen overseas.

As they fell into step, she put her head on his chest. It was as if nothing – and everything – had changed. They saw the differences in each other. The service had definitely changed Brett. There was a more disciplined calm in his mannerisms. Brett noticed the same in her - she seemed quieter, more serious. It's funny how different traumas produce the same results in people.

Yet they both felt a familiar peace just being together. When Lacey was with him, it was as if all the strange things about her made sense. Despite their opposing energies, they balanced each other out.

Lacey lifted her head for the kiss she knew was coming, but when she looked up, his eyes weren't on her. He'd noticed a commotion behind her, some guy getting in Will's face and poking his finger in his chest. The guy then reared back. Without hesitation, Brett pushed Lacey aside with his right arm as he went in for the punch with his left. Brett caught the brunt of the hit that was designed for Will, but one hit from Brett was all it took to end things. The guy was out cold.

"Go! Go! Get outta here!" the guys yelled; worried Brett would get court-martialed.

Brett grabbed Lacey's hand and they hurried out – but not before she shared a wary glance with Jenn. She knew Jenn was worried about her getting her heart broken again, and she shared her concerns.

They ran up Music Row, away from Tequila Cowboy and caught a taxi in front of Tootsie's to divert bouncers that might be tailing them.

"Brett! What were you thinking? That guy was twice your size!" Lacey said, huffing and puffing as they slid into the cab.

Brett brushed it off. "That's what I do for a living, protect and defend," he said coolly. He saw her look of concern, then got somber.

"You never leave a man behind, babe," he said seriously. Lacey knew better than to argue and instead tended to his left eye. It wasn't a big cut, but it was bleeding a little. Brett used the time to get closer to her, enjoying being doted over, just taking her in. She still smelled of mangos and flowers, the same perfume that used to linger on his Sunday shirt when he would get home after church services with her.

Brett cradled her in his arms as she lay in his lap, looking up at him, just like he used to when they would sit in his car waiting for his guardian after evening services, talking about their future plans or just sitting in silence listening to the radio.

The taxi stopped in front of Brett's hotel. Brett tipped and thanked the driver and said, "Come up, Lace. I got something to show you."

"Oh, I bet you do..." she said with a laugh.

Brett feigned exasperation and rolled his eyes with a grin. "Turn off that public school brain and get in there!" he said, swatting her on the fanny as she walked through the front lobby door.

Pastor and Sister Gill had moved to Kentucky, so Brett couldn't stay with them that night. He was going to drive out there in a couple of days, but he was hoping he might bring a bride with him.

Ever the hopeful optimistic, Brett had booked a room with a balcony and a great view, hoping beyond hope he might carry Lacey over the threshold that weekend. When the hotel learned that Brett had just returned from overseas, they upgraded him to a penthouse suite, free of charge. Tennessee always looked after their Volunteers.

Lacey wandered out onto the balcony as Brett was rummaged around in his duffle. The view was beautiful, and the lights of Nashville sprawled out below them, twinkling like stars in the country.

"Like the view from the other side of heaven," Lacey mused.

Brett came up behind Lacey and wrapped his arms around her. "Reminds me of the moon bouncing off your river at home," Brett nodded to the sparkling lights, echoing the thought in Lacey's mind. Lacey asked Brett questions about his time in BASIC, and his tour. She knew better than to ask locations or details, but he shared with her what he could. Their conversation was now slow and easy, having lost its awkwardness long before, as if no time had passed and they had never been apart.

"Since they might be switching me to Green berets, you'll probably be able to join me at Fort Hood," Brett said, pulling away.

Lacey's confusion changed to shock as she turned to see him on one knee. Her hands flew to her mouth in surprise, feeling a mixture of surprise, confusion, and joy.

"Lacey Grace, will you marry me?" Brett asked her with a big grin, void of any doubt as to what her answer would be.

Lacey had hoped to have more time to think things through, but time and circumstances were demanding an answer...now. Reject the past and move ahead with a man she'd known only a year? Or claim the destiny she'd always assumed she'd have? And always wanted? She'd prayed and, truth be told, hadn't gotten a clear answer. She'd always been able to rely on God when she was seeking an answer, sometimes through sermons on the radio, or godly counsel or even through fleece prayers. Maybe God was saying, "Either is fine – it's your decision." Grandpa Charlie used to remind her God doesn't always have an opinion on a matter, and He was big enough to fix it if we made the wrong choice.

But a doubt is not a good thing to base your future upon. The bracelet from Grant dug into her wrist, reminding her of her assumed promise. But what good is making a home with someone who doesn't feel like home?

A different future possibility knelt before her now, waiting for an answer.

The ring he held wasn't a typical diamond, but a freshwater pearl like the ones found back home. She gasped in delight and searched his face for an answer.

"It's a pearl from your river, Lace. I found it the day we met," he explained.

"I heard you might be seeing someone, and I know we've joked around in the past, but you're the only woman I've ever loved, Lacey. You're home to me..." There was nothing between them now - no pretense, no pride, no misunderstandings. All of the doubts lurking in the shadows faded away as Lacey melted into his arms. She didn't know what the future would look like for them, but she was sure of one thing: she wanted to be with Brett, forever.

"It's you, Lacey. It's always been you," Brett said, slipping the ring on her finger. "You're the only woman I've ever loved."

Lacey finally surrendered, tired of the battle between her heart and mind, questioning herself and over analyzing. She knew she hadn't heard a clear answer from God, but how do you leave a man waiting on one knee?! She had loved Brett from the day he had comforted her on the bridge all those years ago. She didn't know all the answers, or if he had even written as he had claimed, but she didn't care. She was ready to be his – heart, soul and name.

His lips found hers, muffling her happy, tearful reply. Lacey melted into his arms. Every kiss, every touch reminded her of just how homesick she had been since he had left. Now home had returned to her. She slipped into the ring and out of her dress, her moral convictions falling with it to the floor. Her pang of guilt that they weren't married faded away as they got closer and their kisses grew longer. With nothing but dog tags between them, she reminded herself they'd be married first thing the next morning, and all would be okay.

****

Lacey looked up to see Mya wide eyed, mouth agape, stunned.

"I told you I wasn't the same person then as I am now," Lacey whispered, ashamed, before continuing.

TWENTY-FOUR

Lacey woke up in Brett's arms the next morning with a tinge of guilt yet couldn't help but smile, when she saw her name on his arm and started to picture their future together. Brett went into the bathroom and, out of habit, Lacey grabbed the Gideon Bible in the nightstand drawer. As she reached for the it, the cross pendant from Grant slid off the nightstand and snagged on the drawer, swinging midair.

"Double guilt," Lacey thought and winced. How in the world would she tell Grant? *WHAT* would she tell him? She had never told him anything about Brett! There was really no need to until today. Just because her heart had chosen Brett didn't mean she didn't love Grant. After all, love doesn't die in a day.

When Brett came out of the bathroom and saw her in his shirt with the Bible on her lap, he felt love and conviction all at the same time. He knew how strong Lacey's devotion to the Lord and his commands were. Lord knows she was about as close to an angel as one could get on earth - and he felt a twinge of remorse for being partial cause for the guilt she was probably feeling.

"You are something else, babygirl," Brett whispered as he scooped her up and put her on his lap. He could tell his suspicions about her guilt were on target by the way she kept her head on his shoulder, not looking up.

"Hey," Brett cajoled, lifting her chin to look into her eyes. "It's ok…In about two hours, we'll be licensed and certified! I'll make a good woman outta you, yet!" he said, playfully pinching her nose.

Lacey felt herself grin. Brett was right. She was being too hard on herself, as usual. Her guilt faded as she rubbed the new ring on her left hand and smiled– the promise of a future together as husband and wife filling her mind.

Brett went to shower and left Lacey to finish getting ready, vowing to himself to get more serious about church once they were married since it was so important to her.

Married.

That word felt good next to Lacey's name. He couldn't believe he was about to have a wife.

And a home.

All his own.

Finally.

Lacey's devo was interrupted by Brett's phone. She flipped it open and was greeted with the picture of a cute little baby with the message: Baby boy, 6 lbs. 1 oz.

"Aww! Whose baby?" she typed, wondering if this was one of the first rounds of deployment babies that would be arriving. "Maybe we can start our *own* family in a year or two," Lacey thought. The thought made her smile.

It took a minute before the phone buzzed again. Lacey opened the phone and gasped.

"Yours"

Lacey laughed. "I think you have the wrong number," she typed.

She wasn't expecting the text that followed. "You are a JERK, Brett Wright! I know it was a one-night stand, but I thought you were a better man than that."

Lacey's knees gave way and she sank onto the bed. Her heart fell to the floor and she couldn't breathe. *What was happening?!*

She threw on her clothes, her hands trembling so she could barely pull on her shoes. "No time to think, just leave," Lacey told herself. How could she have been so *stupid*? She had always tried to ignore that "something" as it whispered and nagged at her gut. The "something" she had tried to explain away as her fears or cold feet. The "something" that was now before her, ironically and symbolically, demanding to be dealt with – refusing to stay in the shadows any longer…the "something" that had now produced a BABY! A *one-night stand*, no less!

She had hoped to be gone before Brett came out of the bathroom, and she had almost made it. Just as she had opened the door, Brett opened the bathroom door beside her. As he went to hug her, she pushed him away.

"So, I'm the only woman you've ever loved, huh?" Lacey's eyes were wild and the deepest violet he had even seen. "My Daddy was *so right*! You're a LIAR!!" she yelled, as she threw the ring and the phone at him and ran out of the room.

Brett opened the phone and stared at the screen, bewildered, as he read the messages.

"Oh no!" Without a second thought, he ran down the hall after her, holding onto his towel with one hand and his phone with the other.

"Lacey! Stop! Let me explain!" but he was too late. Without a glance back, Lacey jumped into a waiting taxi and sped away – leaving her foiled destiny behind her.

Brett looked down at the fuzzy picture on his flip phone in disbelief. The night they had gotten their first leave was one week to the day he had sent Lacey his one hundredth letter. He'd never heard back from her. He was heartbroken, and he did what most heartbroken, young men do when on leave. He drowned his sorrows so much so he woke up the next morning beside a red-headed stranger not knowing how he got there. A message came a month later saying this stranger was pregnant, but, thinking it was too early to tell, he didn't believe it. He had assumed he was right, until this text. Bad assumption.

Somehow Lacey made it to the lake house without attracting any attention except for Grandma Kate's. Always the early riser, Kate had seen the cloud of dust from the road as she watered her petunias that morning. Anyone traveling on that road that early was either a couple of lovebirds looking to kiss a bit by the lake before school or Lacey Grace. Judging by the speed of the dust that was billowing up, she was willing to put money down that it is was her granddaughter.

Grandma Kate waited until nine o'clock, then went over to make Lacey her famous hot cakes. Whatever was eating at her granddaughter had to be a biggie for her to fly down to the lake house without so much as a howdy to anyone. Grandma Kate had heard Brett Wright was back in town and most likely the source of her pain. She had really liked the way that boy made Lacey relax and light up, and he reminded her of her own sweetheart when he was young, but no matter how she felt about the boy one thing was a fact: he always brought her baby to tears.

Having exhausted herself between her tears and the wheel, Lacey fell sound asleep when her head hit the feather pillow.

Lacey awoke to the smell of Grandma Kate's flapjacks and the sound of her hum-singing *O Beautiful Star of Bethlehem*. Grandma Kate had honored her privacy and set the pancakes and juice outside her door. Lacey was thankful for the gesture. She wasn't sure how she could look her family in the eye after what she'd done *and* what was done *to* her. She felt like her sin was written all over her for all to see, and "Brett cheated on me" was scrawled across her forehead in red ink. So much had happened in one short day! Every emotion imaginable, from the highest of highs to the lowest of lows. Love and betrayal. Welcome home reunions and angry goodbyes, mixed with romantic elation and sin and guilt. It was all just too much.

Lacey took her breakfast out onto the bedroom balcony and let the quiet flood her soul. This is where she always came for restoration, and it never failed. She always left this natural spot with either an answer or peace – both of which she was seeking today.

She ended her breakfast in a long prayer, asking for forgiveness from the night before, of course, and for plowing ahead without waiting for a firm answer from God. How could God ever forgive me? Lacey thought. She knew better than to do what she'd done! She had always thought she was better than that. Now she didn't know who she was, exactly.

Later, Lacey made her way down to the swing overlooking the lake. Grandma Kate joined her and they sat in silence for a long time, Grandma Kate rubbing her arm and Lacey resting her head on her shoulder. "No matter how big they get, they will always be our little ones," Grandma Kate thought.

"You wanna talk about it, baby?" Grandma Kate broke the silence with her question.

Lacey shook her head "no."

"It's not like you to be this quiet, Shoog..." Grandma Kate's statement was more of an observation than a plea to talk.

Lacey thought she deserved an explanation.

"Dad was right after all," Lacey said, forlornly.

"Brett?" Grandma Kate asked softly. Lacey nodded affirmatively, her eyes filling with tears.

Grandma Kate leaned back, and sighed thoughtfully – assuming her granddaughter was trying to decide between her first love and possibly her last. Finally, she spoke with kindness, as always.

"I'm so sorry, sweetie! Choosing between two loves is a big decision and I'm not gonna lie - I don't envy you. I know what you had with Brett, but I also see what you have with Grant. You are blessed to be loved so deeply by such good men – but that makes the decision all the harder. My grandmother used to tell me, 'Katherine, if you want to know what kind of husband a man will make, watch how he treats his mother and his relationship with God. One will tell you how caring he will be. The other, how dedicated,' And I've noticed that's about right." Grandma Kate continued to swing with Lacey as she thought.

"Brett IS a hard kind of man to love. The thing with men like that is you either never let 'em in, or you never let 'em go..."

"He's not the man I thought he was, Grandma! Not at all!" Lacey buried her face in her hands and cried deep, heavy tears. Grandma Kate nodded.

"War changes them, hon. Lots of men come back from battle different at first. They have to find their footing, but they eventually do. It just takes time. You have both been through a battle of sorts, and sometimes it changes people. Sometimes our hardest battle in life is knowing when to hold on and when to let go," Grandma Kate explained, not really knowing what she was dealing with.

"Did you pray about it?" Grandma Kate asked. Lacey nodded. Kate continued, "Well, if you prayed God into it, He is there! He always shows up when we call to Him, sweetie. We doubt it sometimes because there is not an earthquake or lightning or trumpet to announce "God is here, working." But jus' like with Moses on the mountain, he was not in the earthquake, or in the rushing wind, but in the gentle whisper. You will hear a soft voice saying, "This is the way, walk in it." Don't just ask what Lacey wants or feels. Instead, ask for God's guidance. Man looks with the eyes, but God sees the heart and knows things we don't. He is all knowing and timeless. Lay it out before Him and wait for His answer. Ask yourself, "What is that small voice telling me to do? What path is it directing me to take?" and do *that*."

"But I didn't wait," Lacey wailed. "I didn't get a clear answer and I plowed ahead."

"Ahhh," Grandma Kate nodded. "Well, now you know the hardest part: waiting. Faith in God also includes faith in His timing," she kept the swing moving with her foot, but remained looking ahead.

"We do the best we can where we are with the information we have at the time. Yesterday you made decisions based on yesterday's information. Today, you will make decisions based on today's information. Hindsight is 20/20, shoog. We all could've made better decisions with future knowledge, but life doesn't work that way. You just gotta do the best where you are with what you've got and pray God into every decision."

"Well, I *didn't* wait, but it doesn't matter anyway," Lacey whispered. "Brett made the decision for me – and it's definitely not what I would have wanted." Lacey said, sinking lower into the swing and depression.

Grandma Kate was angry. First the wreck, then a heartbreak, followed by another heartbreak. No matter what chemistry existed between the two, their fruit was not good, a factor the Appalachian people were taught to watch for in spiritual discernment. Grandma Kate was starting to worry now. The only time she'd seen her granddaughter this low was back in December when all her memories of Brett had come flooding back. It had taken her the whole break – four weeks! – to mourn and recover. Grandma Kate wasn't sure Lacebug's heart could take another episode like that. She needed to lighten the mood.

"Well, in that case, consider it a blessing! I know you are hurting, sweetie, but life doesn't always go the way we think it's gonna go...or even the way we want it to go. Things change and people change. It's nobody's fault, and nobody plans it, it just happens." Grandma Kate smiled sympathetically at her. "And I know you've always had the gift of discernment, but sometimes how we think people are isn't necessarily the way they really are…or the way they are now." Grandma Kate squeezed her shoulder comfortingly. "And if anyone can make it through anything, it is *you*, Sweet Pea."

Lacey nodded, her young heart breaking all over again. She didn't have the heart to tell Grandma Kate what had happened, but, as usual, Grandma Kate's words spoke exactly what her heart needed to hear.

Later that night Brett called. Grandpa Charlie made Lacey take the call, but before she could even say hello Brett was talking a mile a minute.

"Oh my word, Lace, you gotta listen to me. I'm shipping out tonight and I'm not sure when I'm gonna be back. I've only got one minute to explain but it's not what you think, I promise," Lacey listened in numbed silence. Grandpa Charlie could make her listen, but he couldn't make her talk.

"Lace, are you there? I've only got thirty more seconds! Are you there?!" Brett's voice was filled with frantic desperation.

"Yes, I'm here," Lacey said, her voice null of any emotion.

Brett was relieved. "Lace, I don't have time to explain now, but promise me you'll wait for me??" Then she heard the line that had become their reunion motto.

"You gotta forgive me, Lace…" he begged in a whisper, resting his head against the pay phone and praying to hear her usual reply.

This time, however, she tossed him a new one.

"Not *this* time," she said, just before the line went dead. Despite the silence and one reaching out and the other fleeing, they had one thing in common this night: both their hearts were breaking.

TWENTY-FIVE

Present day

Lacey teared up. When she finally had the courage to look up, there was no judgment in her friend's face, only sadness. "Sweet Mya," Lacey thought for the hundredth time in her life. Never before had she been so grateful to have such a merciful, loving friend.

"Oh, Lacey! I'm so sorry!" Mya said.

"So what'd you do next?" Mya asked, mesmerized.

"Well, after a week of praying, fasting and crying, I ran to Grant. After I'd had time to think things through, I was sure, more than ever, Grant was the one God was leading me to. I returned to school the next week and we eloped, and I never looked back. It was intoxicating, being sure of Grant's feelings and character, and knowing how he felt about me, like having solid ground under my feet after being at sea for weeks. It was nice to have someone I could count on, never having to decode mixed messages. He passed Grandma Kate's litmus test of treating his Mom well, and His faith was as strong, if not stronger, than mine. We would be equally yoked, and that automatically solved a lot of potential problems. Our whirlwind elopement to the Bahamas did not go over well with his mother, though."

Mya laughed, thinking about it. "What happened to Brett?"

Lacey paused her stirring. His name still took her to another time and place.

"I don't know," Lacey said, furrowing her brow. "Last I'd heard, he was stationed in Clarksville playing some minor league baseball on the side, but I'm not sure…" her voice faded off. "I've tried to leave the past in the past…until today. And now, my past has caught up with me," Lacey sighed. Mya could see her anxiety.

Lacey was clearly pained, as if carrying a very heavy burden. Mya knew her friend was a strong woman and nothing easily rattled her, but today Lacey's hands were shaking.

"Honey, if you're feeling guilt over your past, God forgives! Jesus' blood cleanses not only the *stain* of sin, but the *guilt* as well! If it comforts you to know, Kevin and I didn't wait until we were married, and while I am not proud of that, it's not a life sentence!" Mya tried to comfort her friend.

Lacey nodded, "Oh, I know! It's not that…." Lacey stopped, unsure if she could continue.

"Lacey, what is going *on*??" Mya finally asked, worried.

Lacey took a big, jagged breath and prayed for strength. Her pride almost prevented her from telling Mya the full story, but she needed her friend's feedback – especially since she might be alone in this for a while, and potentially shunned by others later. She needed her best prayer warrior to cover her in prayer.

"Well, you know how the doctor told us a couple weeks ago they had exhausted every treatment possible and the medicines were not helping Kit any longer?"

"Yes, and you said Kit's only option was a Kidney transplant. Does that letter have something to do with that?" Mya asked.

Lacey continued, "Well, the first step was to see if her closest kin were a match. We did that test a couple of weeks ago, and have been waiting for the results, and they came today." Lacey explained, resting her head in her hands and closing her eyes.

"And no one is a match?" Mya asked, fearfully.

"Not yet," Lacey said. Mya's heart sank. She knew what a battle the family had gone through and how draining it had been – physically, emotionally - all around, really.

"But that's not why I fainted," Lacey continued, nervously.

"What is it?" Mya was almost too scared to ask. Her normally forthcoming friend was holding back and looked scared. Definitely scared. She let her friend have a moment to get her composure, but nothing could have prepared Mya for what Lacey said next.

"Grant is not Kit's father."

The words hung in the quiet. Mya had heard Lacey the first time, but had assumed she was talking nonsense from her fall. Grant was not Kit's father. Sweet Grant. The man who'd raised her and loved her. The perfect family man. How devastating!

The moment weighed heavy on Lacey's heart, not knowing how her friend would respond. She felt as if she had just stripped bare, waiting for rightfully deserved judgment and scorn. When Lacey found the courage, she looked up at her friend. Mya was still in shock, the reality of those words - and all they meant and all they *would* mean- still sinking in. But there was no hint of judgement, only shock.

"I can't believe it…I just can't believe it…" Lacey stood and started to pace.

"Wait…are you saying *you* didn't know either?!" Mya's eyes widened.

"*NO*, I didn't *KNOW*!" Lacey wailed, frustrated. "That night with Brett was just a week before Grant and I eloped!" Lacey was frantic. "How can this *be*?!" she asked, chewing on her thumb nail.

Mya was dumb founded but forced herself to remain calm for Lacey's sake. She had never seen her somber friend like this before.

"Mya, oh my word! Grant's gonna kill me. He is gonna STRAIGHT UP *DIVORCE* me!" Lacey was nearing a full-on fit. "And his family?! Oh my word! His *MOM*! Good thing they never put our initials on their family tree, 'cause she'd sho 'nuff be chainsawin' that mug down! She will stone me in the front yard and mount my head on the wall!" Lacey yelled, her Tennessee twang and colloquialisms sneaking in, pronouncing "head" as "HAY-ED".

"Calm down, Lacey! Breathe!" Mya commanded. "We gotta keep our wits about us. Just breathe." Lacey dropped to her knees and put her head down on the couch, and covered her head with her arms.

"What am I gonna DO, Mya?" Lacey asked through short, choppy breaths.

"I don't rightly know, but, girl, we gon' be prayin' like crazy! Pentecostal style!" Mya's deep, Southern Georgia accent rang out loud and clear. Suddenly, Lacey jerked her head up and whirled around to Mya.

"Wait! Mya! Brett could be a match! For Kit!" Lacey jumped up and grabbed the local newspaper, "Oh my word! Oh my word! I think there's a minor league game at the stadium Thursday!"

Mya looked confused, until Lacey pointed to the paper and said, "Yes. Minor League Tournament."

Mya was amazed at Lacey's quick emotional change, "Wait, Lacey...so you think you're just gonna show up after dissin' this man and thirteen years later say, "Oh, by the way, we have a daughter and can I have your kidney?" Mya asked.

Even Lacey, though she rarely let social norms dictate her actions, could see the absurdity in this situation.

"I *have* to...I don't rightly have any other choice."

TWENTY-SIX

Fort Campbell

Present day

Lacey was second-guessing her sundress as she pulled into the stadium. She didn't want to overdress, but what are you supposed to wear when you're seeing your first love again after fourteen years to tell him he has a daughter he didn't know existed? And you also want one of his kidneys? She didn't want to send the wrong message. She, with Mya's help, had tried on every outfit, from jeans to capris to the sundress. At the last minute she chunked the capris and slid into the sundress and floppy hat. At least her outfit would keep her cool in the stands. She was wearing the hat for two reasons: to keep the sun, and Brett's prying eyes, at bay. The goose egg that had popped up when she fainted had gone down, but some bruising remained. She was proud of the makeup job Mya had done to help hide it, but Brett wasn't a typical anyone. He had the eyes of a hawk.

She'd already spilled her coffee in the console and missed the stadium exit. Despite her best efforts, her nerves were raw and her head was spinning. What would Brett do? Would he even agree to see her? She could only pray he would. And how would she tell him about Kit?! She'd tried to write it all out and rehearse how she might tell him the news, but it all seemed stilted and disingenuous. She'd been tempted to send a certified letter, and let her lawyer handle it, but too much was riding on this to be impersonal.

She was praying double-time. Mya was right. Things had ended badly, and at the end of the day Lacey was having to ride on the good graces of a man she had rejected. She didn't know the future, but she knew one thing: At one time, Brett would never leave a man – or his daughter – behind. She was praying that hadn't changed through the years.

She parked the car and walked toward the stadium. She felt her heart speed up with every step, and it took all her willpower not to turn back to the car.

"Kit's kidney…Kit's kidney…" became her mantra as she marched through the gates and to her seat.

The game was in full swing – six to eight and bottom of the eighth. She scanned the players, trying to decipher which might be Brett.

"Number sixteen, maybe? That was his number in high school," Kit mused as she scanned the blue and grey uniforms. Her eyes paused on the batter. Something about him….

The batter connected with the ball in a loud CRACK and started running. A lefthanded hitter. Lacey didn't have to check the roster – she knew it was Brett when he pivoted to run.

"And it's a homerun by Brett Wright!" The announcer's voice echoed off the walls.

A cold flash swept over her as butterflies took flight in her stomach and her mind went back to the sounds in the stands, the beer and bratz…Lacey's phone jerked her back to reality.

"Did you find him?" Mya's voice cut through her thoughts.

"Oh, I found him. He just hit a homerun," Lacey replied as she saw him striding over home plate.

"Well, just breathe deep and call me after," Mya advised. "I'm praying for you!"

"Uh-huh," Lacey mumbled.

Lacey watched the rest of the game, praying for a win. She needed Brett to be in the best mood possible before she laid the big news on him.

Remembering how he hated surprises, she'd come up with a plan. She flagged down the ball boy, handed him the package she'd brought from home, and told him to tell Brett a lady was waiting to talk to him. She knew the pie would let him know who the lady might be and she hoped he would be willing to talk with her.

And then she waited.

And prayed.

Fervently.

****

It had been fourteen years since Brett had eaten chess pie, partly from lack of access, but mostly for the heartstrings it would pull. But now one had landed in his lap, and the batboy said a lady asked him to tell Brett she'd be waiting outside. Could it really be Lacey? Who else would've sent a chess pie?

Nothing rattled Brett. Not a bases loaded, two out hit, not enemy fire, nothing. But today? He'd already nicked himself shaving after the game, and dropped his equipment.

"Dude! What's wrong?" Stubbs asked.

"Stubbs, do me a favor. Bite into that pie and tell me what it is," Brett commanded.

"Uh...what?" Stubbs stopped and stared at him quizzically.

"Seriously. Just do it."

Stubbs didn't know what had Brett riled up tighter than a girdle on a Southern woman at an all-you-can-eat pancake breakfast, but Stubbs wasn't the kind to question or deny a pie so he dug in.

Brett had spent years trying to put Lacey behind him. Will had even told him to move on, closure wasn't gonna happen with him and Lacey. And with that piece of advice, he had. And never felt much of anything else since. Until today.

Despite not wanting to dredge up anything that had been painstakingly buried, he shut his eyes and prayed.

"Chess."

His heart leaped. This meant only one thing: Lacey Wilson was standing just outside the door. His biggest dream and greatest fear now lay before him.

"What in the world was she doing here? Now?"

****

"Someone said a pretty lady was looking for me," Brett's voice cut through the silent corridor. Lacey took a deep breath and walked out of the shadows.

"Hi, Brett," Lacey tried to steady her voice.

"Is that *you*, Lace? I never thought in a million years...."
Brett's voice trailed off as he walked closer. He'd decided to play
things cool and confident, but that was before he saw her.

A lean, curvy silhouette stepped out of the bleacher
shadows and into the bright sun. She'd always been able to steal
his breath. Her dress resembled the one she had been wearing
down at the river the night he had tackled her while running, when
they had stayed in each other's arms and both finally admitted how
deeply they felt about each other... Brett tried to push those
memories down.

"Man, Lace, you look good," he said softly, sincerely.

Lacey tried to hide a smile. Lace. No one had called her
that in years. It felt good – and guilty – to be reminded how
intimately someone once knew you.

Lacey chided herself. A lot of things had changed since
they had last seen each other. Lacey felt like an entirely different
person, and in most ways she was. From her personality to her
habits to her hobbies – everything *had* changed.

When she saw his fit physique, she was glad she had
chosen the sundress, and had joined the gym a year before. She
didn't want to lead him on, but at the end of the day he *was* her ex.
The ex, to be exact.

Momma Kim always said, 'Always put your face on when
you go out in public. You never know if you might run into your
ex or his new girlfriend.'

"You too, Brett," she returned.

For someone who was great at reading people, Brett was at
a loss. One thing was sure, though: she was still gorgeous.

"I was wondering if you'd like to grab a bite to eat. Maybe
LaParilla?"

"Sure," Brett replied. "I'll bring the truck around."

"No, I'll meet you there," Lacey quickly interjected. "I
have to leave right after, anyway," Lacey said.

Brett was puzzled, but let it lie. That wasn't a good sign,
her planning on a short visit.

Lacey arrived first and slid into a booth. She had picked a
Mexican restaurant since it was Brett's favorite, and she was
relieved they had won the game. So much was riding on this

meeting! The future of her child – *their* child, to be exact. She needed every angel on her side for this one.

She scanned the restaurant and, to her dismay, spied a couple of old ladies from her church.

"Lovely," Lacey thought sarcastically. She ducked low and tried to stay out of sight. Maybe they wouldn't recognize her.

"Wow. Mexican AND my favorite drink! You tryin' to get me liquored up and take advantage of me, little lady?" Brett's eyes teased her as he took his seat.

"You can't *take* what is freely given," she bit her lip, shocked at how quickly she had quipped at him. He brought out the best, the worst, and the "best-worst" in her. But it was that chemistry, their natural "tit for tat" comebacks that had made their relationship so special. But, really, after all these years?! It would be *amazing* if it weren't so annoying. She refused to look at him, worried he'd be encouraged.

Brett laughed. "Well, I'm glad to see you've retained your spunk, Sassy," he teased, though secretly impressed. She always did know how to dish it out as well as take it. There was no shortage of women trying to impress him, but he missed Lacey's smart mouth and how she always put him in his place when he needed it.

"Wow, Lacey, it's good to see you again. So, how've you been?" he asked as he reached across the table to take her hand, mainly to feel for a ring on a certain finger.

"Good!" Lacey said, disappointed by the way her voice cracked.

The waiter came to take their orders and Lacey used the opportunity to free her hand by grabbing the menu. Brett ordered in fluent Spanish. A skill he picked up in the military, Lacey correctly guessed. Try as she might, she couldn't ignore the attraction of it, or all the things she used to love: his good-natured disposition…his dimples…his physique. Lacey reprimanded herself as she sipped her tea.

"So, you still married?" Brett blurted as soon as the waiter left. He looked at her unashamedly, steel gazed.

"Yes," she said evenly, caught off guard, but returning his gaze.

"Happily?" His audacity was insulting yet charming. Typical Brett, always setting things up for the next move. She gave in to a chuckle as she said, "Not that it *matters*, but yes."

Brett felt sucker punched.

"Well, that's too bad... I mean, for *me*," he mumbled.

Lacey racked her brain. She needed to change the subject to a safer topic to get her attention off her pounding heart and improve his mood.

"So, you still look great out there! Have you been playing long?" she asked. But her mind was too distracted to hear his response.

Lacey's thoughts raced and her stomach did flip flops as he rambled on about his team. Her head swam as she noticed all the things that had first attracted her: his chiseled chin, those dimples, that Southern drawl...could he *BE* more handsome? *Seriously*?!

She had prepared herself for a confrontation. She had *NOT* prepared herself for *attraction*.

"Dang, baby, you ok? You don't look so good," Brett asked.

"Baby" echoed through Lacey's mind as she tried to steady herself.

"I gotta get outta here," Lacey heard herself mumble as she ran out the door. Brett laid down some cash and followed close behind. By the time he reached her, Lacey was in a full-blown panic, pacing back and forth on the sidewalk. Brett knew her well enough to wait.

Lacey finally landed on a bench, her head in her hands. Brett went to sit beside her.

"Good night, Lace! What in the world is *wrong*?"

Lacey's head shot up like a rocket. It was all just too much. She was foolish to ever think she could handle this on her own. Why didn't she just have the lawyer send a letter?!

She got up, pacing again, hands clasped in a prayer stance, visibly anxious.

"I...I had everything all planned out in my mind what to say, Brett, but..." by now she had both hands on the side of her face, shaking her head back in forth as if she was trying to forget something. Her look of terror quickly turned to anger, however, as she pointed her finger in Brett's face and yelled, "And stop callin' me Baby!"

With that, she whirled around and sat back on the bench, defeated, with her head back in her hands. Dumbfounded, Brett waited silently, now gravely concerned.

"Heyyy," Brett knelt before her, took her hands off her face, and pulled her toward him, letting her collapse on his shoulder. He rubbed her hair as she caught her breath. "Calm down, firecracker! Breathe…"

Accepting defeat, Lacey tried to exhale her fears while looking him eye to eye.

Brett tenderly stroked her face and waited. Lacey pulled his hand down and wiped a lone tear. "Brett…I need to tell you some—

"What is *that*, Lace?!" Brett interrupted her. Without waiting for an answer, he licked his thumb and wiped the makeup off her bruise.

"Dang, Lacey! Is he beating you?!" Brett was all bowed up, alert and poised for a fight.

"What? No…" Lacey sighed. Now his adrenaline would be pumping when she told him the shocking news. "No! I got this little bruise when I fainted the other day."

"Fainted? Lacey, are you sick?" Brett's angry concern had morphed into worry. She was getting all off track.

"No, Brett! Listen! I need to tell you something that might make you mad, but I didn't know either, 'til last week so I'm hoping you'll forgive me. I don't know how to say this, so I'm just gonna come out and say it.…we have a daughter."

Brett paused before laughing, "There you go with your Indian talk again! Sounded like you said We…Haveadaughter," he said, slurring the words together like she had. Lacey stared, too nervous to offer a charity chuckle. Brett interpreted her silence as her trying to play off her joke.

"Hardy har, kiddo. Wouldn't *that* be something?! No, seriously…what's got you all riled up?" Brett pressed. He still wasn't convinced she was telling the truth about her eye…

Lacey was emotionally drained, and spent. With nothing left to say, she let the tears fall, hoping her expression might convey the sincerity her words lacked.

Brett was confused. Could she be *serious*? But how in the world? There was only that one time in...

"Nashville?!" he asked.

Lacey nodded affirmatively.

"Wow....Wow!" Brett leaned back, then stood and walked to a nearby tree, looking out over the grassy square in stunned silence. She'd rarely seen Brett stunned. Was he angry? Happy? Sad? Lacey kept quiet. He deserved to have this moment.

It seemed like an eternity before he cleared his throat. "I...I... don't know what to say..." his voice trailed off.

Lacey summoned her last bit of courage she had. "Well, that's not all..."

Brett turned, hoping she was going to say she wanted to be a family.

"She's sick, Brett. She needs a kidney..."

"What's her name?" Brett asked, seemingly oblivious to the horrible news. Lacey knew he needed to take things in his own way, in his own time.

"Katherine. After Grandma..."

"...Kate," Brett broke in, his voice in unison with hers.

"We call her Kit..." Lacey explained.

Brett looked off in silent disbelief. "So... she's...13, now?"

"Yes. And she's beautiful, Brett. And smart...and spunky." Lacey pulled a picture from her purse she'd brought to give him.

"She's the spittin' image of you, Lace..." Brett whispered.

"...with your dimples..." Lacey chimed in.

They stood in silence; the air heavy with the news she'd just delivered. With so many swirling emotions, it was hard to know how to act or what to say. The elation of having a child, alongside the regret of all the missed years, was bittersweet. Brett would deal with the emotions later, like he always did.

"What do I need to do?" Brett asked. Lacey instinctively knew he was talking about the medical procedures.

"Well, we start with a blood test. That's how I found all this out last week..."

"What'd your husband say?" Brett interrupted, past the point of small talk.

Lacey paused. "Grant doesn't know yet..."

"Dang, Lacey!" Brett said, amazed.

"I know, I know! I gotta find the right time. I thought if I could tell him you were willing to donate it might soften the blow…"

"Humph! Good luck with that!" Brett scoffed.

"I know, right?! How could I not have KNOWN?!" Lacey started to wail. "She has your temper and fire, for Pete's sake!"

"Yeah, cause NONE of that could 'a come from her Momma," Brett let a grin slide and nudged her to lighten the mood. Lacey chuckled through the tears. They sat quietly, coming to grips with all that it meant and all it would change.

"You'd better be glad she's got that, Lace…" Brett interjected causing Lacey to stop and stare, confused.

"She's gonna need every bit of it to get her through this…" he said, seriously.

Lacey nodded in solemn agreement.

The heavy moment was interrupted by a ringtone alert, reminding Lacey to pick up the kids. Lacey hated to leave things like this, so stilted and all, but she had no choice.

"I'm so sorry, Brett, but I've got to pick up the kids…can I call you later?"

"Of course," they quickly exchanged numbers.

"How many children do you have, other than Kit?" Brett asked as she stood.

"One more. Jake. He's nine years old. I'm sorry, Brett, but I really have to go."

"I understand. And Lace? It's good to see you again. I hope you know I will do anything I can to help Kit."

Lacey nodded and quickly walked away, leaving Brett on the bench alone with his thoughts.

If this were a business negotiation, what had just transpired would be considered a win, so Lacey chose to be content with it. It was a start.

TWENTY-SEVEN

Dickson, Tennessee

"That was a lovely shower," Mya said, as she and Lacey walked up the drive to Lacey's house.

"Uh-huh," Lacey absent-mindedly grunted as she unlocked the front door. It had, indeed, been a beautiful wedding shower, complete with large Sunday hats, heels and pearls. However, Lacey's mind wasn't on the shower, but the guest that would soon be arriving. Brett was coming over to talk about the possible upcoming procedure and all its implications before their official meeting, and Lacey thought it best to have Mya present. It was the proper thing to do, after all.

Mya busied herself by helping their little ones get into their swimsuits. They were blessed to be neighbors and good friends. When Mya went back inside, Lacey was visibly nervous, fluffing already fluffed couch pillows and brushing off imaginary crumbs.

"You're gonna work yourself into a lather!" Mya warned. "I've never seen you like this, Lacey! Calm down! Remember what we talked about? About God holding you? Just relax! God's *got* you!"

"I don't doubt God, it's just all those old feelings that started coming back when I saw him that I'm worried about. And, Mya, he's gotten even better looking over the years..."

"Grant is handsome!" Mya defended, pointing to the smiling picture of him and Lacey on the wall.

"Oh, I know! He IS! But...well..." Lacey paused to choose her words carefully. "Brett is a *different* kind of handsome, you might say," she tried to explain.

Mya brushed off her friend's worries. "Well, don't worry. Like I said, you are not a new Christian still on the milk – you've dealt with fleshly feelings before and learned to keep your emotions in check a long time ago. This is the same thing, just a different form. You are gonna be fine!"

Lacey put on a calm face for her friend, but inwardly she wasn't so confident. Yes, she had dealt with temptations before, but saying no to cupcakes was a lot different than saying no to unfulfilled desires and dashed dreams. Brett couldn't be so easily ignored. Throughout the years, he'd crept into her thoughts and dreams uninvited, but she'd always managed to put him back in the box he belonged in. But now they were going to have to see each other and interact. Despite how she wanted to forget her past, it was demanding to be dealt with.

Lacey remembered how Grandma Kate used to say, 'All pain we shove aside or push down eventually creeps up, uninvited, and demands a reckoning.'

Well, this was her time of reckoning.

The roar of a motorcycle jolted Lacey out of her thoughts, and forced her back into the present.

"Well, here he comes," Lacey announced as they headed out to greet him. As always, his arrival came with fanfare and noise. Lacey wondered if the HOA was going to write her up for her guest's muffler. Well, she didn't mind in the least bit if he ticked off the HOA. The thought made her chuckle.

As if the motorcycle wasn't enough, Brett was dressed in his leather jacket, faded jeans, cowboy boots and sunglasses.

Mya stood wide-eyed, mouth gaping. Lacey's previous statement about Brett being a "different kind of handsome" was hammered home as Brett took off his jacket, revealing tattoos peeking out from under the rolled-up sleeves of his tight Oxford shirt. Lacey took a minute to catch her breath as he took off his helmet and started up the walkway.

"The only thing missing is horns and a pitchfork," Lacey thought, pushing Mya's bottom jaw up and recalling their preacher's sermon warning that Satan usually sends temptation beautifully wrapped as the thing we most desire.

Mya, now visibly nervous, leaned over and whispered, "Remember what I said about you being able to handle this?"

Lacey nodded in the affirmative, still speechless. "Well, scratch that! Girl, you bes' be like Joseph and RUN from temptation! He's like a real life *Top Gun*! Lord have mercy!" Mya started fanning herself, nervously. Lacey slyly smiled, secretly happy to be vindicated.

"He's definitely brought his A game," Lacey mumbled out the side of her mouth, taking note of the yellow daffodils he held in his hand.

Lacey was correct. Brett had a lot of time to think since they'd last seen each other, and one thing was certain, he definitely wanted the family he'd been denied. He and Lacey belonged together, and he was willing to do whatever it took to try to see that happen. While he might not be able to predict exactly what Lacey would *do*, he definitely knew how she *felt*. She could play coy, but there was no hiding the pink hue that crept onto her chest as they were talking about the past at the restaurant. Or the way she bit her bottom lip when he had asked her if she was happily married. Time might change a lot of things, but human behavioral response usually wasn't one of them. Brett's work in Special Ops called for noticing people's nonverbals, and he was skilled in the art more than most. It was a skill that helped him in his work as well as his personal life.

Brett stopped in front of the women at the bottom of the steps and took off his shades.

"Ladies..." he greeted them in his deep, Texan accent. Lacey swore Mya swooned.

"Brett, this is my friend Mya..." Lacey introduced them as Brett gave her a gentlemanly nod.

"Ma'am..." he said, the twang rolling off of his tongue thick as gravy. Mya had gone from swooning to full-on woozy, much to Lacey's chagrin.

"Judas," Lacey thought as she shot her a "get it together" glare before turning back to Brett.

"Lace," he greeted Lacey, handing her the daffodils. They shared a knowing glance, but Lacey quickly looked away. Neither the daffodils nor the yellow butterfly in the middle of the bouquet escaped Lacey's attention. Her words to him long ago, *"The yellow butterfly signifies the never-ending love between two lovers,"* rang in her head and gave her a slight headache. He was definitely making his desires clear, in a subtle way.

Brett gave her a quick once over. She was dressed to impress in her high heels, pearls and Sunday hat. "Good sign," Brett thought.

"Well, don't you clean up nice, Sassy?" Brett teased. Lacey bristled when he said "Sassy," feeling Mya's quick glance. Seriously, could her friend gawk any harder? Lacey was starting to regret asking her friend to be present.

Lacey turned to lead Brett inside, seemingly unrattled. "We've just come from a wedding shower. Would you like some iced tea?" she asked in business fashion.

"Tea is fine," Brett said, as Mya dismissed herself to watch the kids in the pool out back. Kit was in school, and Grant was at work, so it left an opportunity for the two to meet up.

"So, how did the appointment go?" Lacey asked, arranging the flowers in a mason jar. Brett had gone to the doctor for the bloodwork to see if he was a match – in paternity and for the kidney donation. Lacey had wanted official confirmation before telling Grant that Brett was Kit's father. No need to fight a battle she didn't have to.

"Fine. Painless. They asked when the baby was due and I said 1995," Brett said, referring to Kit's birth date thirteen years *prior*. Lacey reared her head back and laughed. That was one of the best things about Brett – he had a way of lightening the mood. It felt good to laugh again. It had been too long since she had.

The phone interrupted their conversation and Brett used her distraction as an opportunity to look around. If he was going to make it through the visit, he was going to have to clear his head.

"Business mode...business mode," he repeated as he looked around the house, trying to imagine what the last fourteen years had been like for Lacey. He found himself in a long hallway, its walls filled with photos of all sizes, floor to ceiling. Pictures of people and moments lined the walls. The photos created a virtual timeline of Lacey's life, snapshots of a life well lived...without him. Black and white stills mixed with bright colors of treasured moments. There were birth and marriage photos, toasts and joyful tears, pictures of children's feet in creek water and generational hands on bouquets. Some memories had gilded gold frames, while others had rustic wooden ones. "Elegant *and* homey," Brett thought. "Just like her."

Brett was relieved to see that, while formal, Lacey *did* look happy. He noticed a picture of Lacey when she was younger, then started. It was not Lacey, but Kit. He was amazed at how much she looked like her Mom so many years ago, the spitting image except for a pair of deep dimples. The photos allowed him to see her life in reverse as he walked down the hallway, theater and band and toddler ballet…all the way down to Kit's birth, flanked by Lacey and Grant. He couldn't stop the frown that furrowed his brow. He noticed their happy faces, exuberant with their first newborn, ignorant of the secret that lay between them.

A crocheted doily labeled "Wilson" was in the center – stitched by Grandma Kate, no doubt. He was glad to see Lacey still cherished her humble beginnings. The thought of Grandma Kate brought an unexpected lump to his throat. It is both a blessing and a curse to be loved so unconditionally, a blessing he'd assumed would continue through Lacey. Unconditional love fills the heart like nothing else can, and leaves the deepest ache when it's gone. Grandma Kate was the first woman to ever believe in and root for him, his first cheerleader.

He smiled as he spied a photo of Grandpa Charlie, his mischievous grin shining through. His eyes grew misty as he realized they had passed on. He never got a chance to thank them.

"If you want to know what people cherish, watch what they photograph," his foster mom used to say. By the looks of things, Lacey still loved people and treasured the moments with them. He was happy the years hadn't changed her heart. He wondered if she would think the same about him if she could see into the past and his years without her. He cringed at the thought. No one could make him feel more guilty, or forgiven, than Lacey.

But life's events had put him in situations where hard choices had to be made. Hard choices chipped away at even the best of hearts under the right circumstances. Life had sledgehammered him from the very beginning, but Lacey had seen something good in him and it was her unwavering faith that made him believe he was better than he thought he was. He remembered her smiling young eyes as she took his face in her hands all those years ago and said, assuredly,

"You can play tough all you want, Cowboy, but I KNOW YOU! I know you are *good hearted* to the very *core*! Don't try to deny it!"

He had always wondered if he really *was* good, or if it was just her *faith* in him that made him that way. Nothing keeps a man on the right track like the faith of a good woman, and Lacey's faith kept him steady for many years. In that moment it was clear: Lacey's faith was what he'd lost. It was like finding a treasure chest just out of reach.

As he neared the end of the wall, a photo grabbed his eye. It was a small, unassuming 5x5, everyone else might quickly glance over. A bright blue sky overlooked a country church behind a sea of yellow daffodils. And to the right? A lone, light green weeping willow. Only two people in the world knew it as the place where two young loves shared their first kiss. Brett smiled, knowing today's bouquet would not be lost on Lacey. Despite her cool composure, Brett knew: she remembered.

"Maybe there's hope after all," he mused.

"Here you go," Lacey's voice broke through his thoughts as she handed him his sweet tea, complete with lime on the rim. The thoughtful gesture caught him off guard. Brett was still a bachelor, and his life in Special Ops didn't leave room for lasting relationships. For guys like him, relationship was the intimacy he craved. Truth be told, there was only one girl he could claim as a "relationship" and she was now standing before him, unavailable - handing him his tea, made just the way he liked it - lime and all. Unbeknownst to Lacey, this simple gesture felt intimate and audacious to Brett, almost rude. It was a sweet irritation to have someone once again know him so well, and be so considerate.

Almost as if she was reading his mind, Lacey pointed to his lime and whispered, "Some things never change," with an innocent wink and smile.

"That's what I'm hoping for," Brett quickly retorted and held her glaze as her playful mood changed to quiet reflection.

She *did* remember.

But she had also *forgotten*.

In all of the memories that would occasionally sneak into her dreams, she had forgotten...*THIS*. How Brett always seemed to be thinking or feeling the same thing at the same time as her, and how quickly he would go for her emotional jugular. It was both extremely romantic and terribly imposing. It was the trait she missed the most. The way he would say what was on her heart without restraint was seducing, and made her time with him have such an easy flow. It was a trait she and Grant did not have. Despite having so much in common, and a strong love, things were just not as easy with Grant. She shrugged off the thought. Comparing would only end in discontent.

Lacey was still an angler, and she knew when someone was fishing. The bright yellow daffodils he brought that day were clue number one and she guessed they had sent red flames up to her cheeks. Other clues let her know he was hoping for reconciliation. As tempted as she was to retort with a flirting comment like she used to, she refrained. She knew these moments were laying the foundation for the new relationship they would have, and to resort to flirting – no matter how innocent – would be playing with fire.

"Kit takes her tea like that, lime instead of lemon," Lacey said, swallowing a lump that had risen in her throat. She looked out to the pool where Mya's son was showing off his latest cannonball moves, soaking Mya to the core! Lacey made a mental note to gift her with a hair appointment, since she knew she had just gotten her hair done.

"Is that right?" Brett said. Lacey nodded.

"She actually has a lot of your mannerisms," Lacey mused, almost absentmindedly. "It's amazing I never put two and two together...."

"Probably 'cause you didn't want to," Brett said. It was hard being here. He wasn't prepared for this emotional roller coaster, but he knew he shouldn't have said that.

"I mean," Brett gestured to the photos on the wall, "Grant's a great husband and father, looks like...He's definitely taken good care of you," Brett said quickly. "...better'n I ever could..." he muttered, a bit remorsefully, as he put his glass to his lips. It wasn't the best response, but he felt her soften.

"Yeah..." Lacey realized she had been responding in quick trigger fashion and did not like seeing her old self emerging. She made a mental note to keep her guard up. Emotions are not logical, and despite people's best intentions, or vows, emotions tend to go as they are inclined, and (where Brett was concerned) her inclination was not prudent for a married woman. They were going to have to carve out a new path of dealing with each other.

Brett looked around the room, eager to change the subject. Some of her Bible verse signs decorated her walls, and in the corner was Grandpa Charlie's old Martin guitar.

"So where do you sing around here?" Brett asked.

Lacey paused, "Um...well...I don't..." Lacey admitted, embarrassingly.

Brett looked up surprised, "Well that's a shame," he said as he glanced away.

Lacey, chuckled nervously, " I..I don't have time now, anyway, what with the kids and all..."

"A wise person once told me we *make* time for the things we love..." Brett whispered. There was no ignoring his gaze this time.

"Miss Lacey! We need snacks!" Jordan yelled, breaking the spell. After the kids returned outside, Brett and Lacey made small talk. Lacey explained the eagles poster board that was prominently displayed in their kitchen, where they updated and recorded the eagle's eggs progress. She learned Brett's life mainly consisted of military and baseball for the past thirteen years. Most of his missions were classified, so he mainly talked of baseball.

Suddenly, he stopped mid-sentence. "You sure you're happy, Lace?"

He caught her off guard by his question, one she'd not asked herself in the hubbub of raising a family. Her life was filled with the routines of her family. Without warning, her uncomfortable times with Grant's family flooded her mind in sharp contrast to her carefree days, laughing with Brett.

She wasn't going to go there with him, though. Not today.

She laughed, nervously, "Of course I am!" She nodded as she looked down, re-chopping the apples she'd just cut.

"Is that what you tell yourself?" Brett asked, pointedly.

This was too much. They had been skating over the thin veneer of civility, avoiding the emotional undercurrent, but there was no avoiding the elephant in the room anymore. Lacey put the knife down, irritated, shattering whatever veil of false, polite appearances was left and dove head-first into the deep waters of unresolved conflict.

"Listen, Brett, just because you are privy to certain information *about* me does not give you the right to use it *against* me..." Lacey was no longer looking down, but straight ahead, eye to eye.

"All I did was ask if you are happy, Lace," Brett lowered his voice as he moved in closer.

Lacey backed away. "Why are you trying to make me feel bad, Brett? I know I'm not the woman I once was..."

"That's for sure," Brett interrupted. It was more of a statement than an insult, but Lacey took things as she interpreted them, not as they were meant, where Brett was concerned.

"Dang it, Brett, this is hard on me!" Lacey yelled.

"Hard on you? Hard on you?! It's no picnic for me either, babe! The love of my life, the "one that got away" shows up after thirteen years and tells me I have a DAUGHTER I never even knew about? Then I have to come here and play nice – in a house that should have been ours, with a woman that shoulda been my wife, with kids that should've been ours?! Walking into a life we were supposed to have together? A life we had planned on?" All the old dormant hurts were now resurrecting. There was no hiding now.

"Brett, I...Grant was here for me," Lacey heard her voice raise, despite the promise she had made to herself to keep her composure. She was thinking of her time in the hospital, but Brett took it a different way.

Brett was speechless. "Dang, Lacey, I was at WAR! You gonna front a man for fightin' in a WAR??"

Lacey softened a bit. "I needed you, Brett, and you weren't there. Yes, you were in the dessert – but you didn't even write! I recovered from the wreck only to have my memory return later, and do you know what memories they were? JUNIOR and SENIOR YEAR, Brett! Yes. It all came flooding over me – wonderful, blissful memories and all the plans we had made and then the haunting realization that you hadn't written 'cause YOU MEANT *NONE* OF IT! There I was, stuck in a wheelchair and in the middle of a new relationship, and not knowing if you were dead or alive, much less interested. Just what was I supposed to do, Brett?!"

"Wait for me," Brett said flatly. "You were supposed to wait for me." His answer was free of emotion but poignant and dead on, filled with the hard truth.

"I wrote you *every day*, Lacey! And *"interested"*?! You were my whole LIFE, Lace! I waited *3 months* with nothing but silence from you and then made ONE mistake – one stupid, drunk mistake I can hardly remember and you took off! *GONE*! Didn't even let me *explain…*"

He absentmindedly picked up the paring knife she'd put down and threw it at the cutting board hanging on the wall, where it stuck. In any other house, with any other two people, that action would've been strange, even threatening. But not with Lacey and Brett. She'd actually taught him how to throw a knife, leading with blade in hand! With them, things were just different.

"It sounds like neither one of us waited," Lacey whispered, defending herself but softening the moment.

Silence enveloped them, each scared of what the next statement would bring. Finally, Brett spoke, but gently this time.

"Don't you remember, Lace? Can you not still feel it? Don't you have a heart?"

Lacey chuckled, shocked and amazed. "Do I have a heart? Do I have a *heart*, you ask?! Every time I *see* you my heart jumps up to my throat so fast I can't even breathe! Comin' up in here with that Southern drawl and those annoying dimples…" As if on cue, Brett smiled, flashing them.

"Could you please just put those things away?! Seriously!" Lacey was full on aggravated now, her Southern dialect thick and heavy. He knew the storm that was rolling in her eyes was going to bring a violet hue to them any second.

"Every time you say my name in that Texas drawl, I feel sixteen again and have to remind myself, "Lacey, you're married now…Lacey, you're married now!" she was practically in his face by now. "Pardon me if I think it's comical that you're askin' me if I even have a heart when I feel it's blatantly obvious to you and everyone else that I'm constantly wrestling you for it!"

With that, Brett grabbed her and pulled her in for a kiss. Without thinking, Lacey fell prey to the chemistry, like she always did.

Mya, having herded the kids out of the pool toward the house, saw the scene through the sliding glass door. Ever the good friend, she instantly whirled them back into the pool, distracting them with a loud "Watch this!" and did a running belly flop! Lacey was definitely going to owe her for this one!

Lacey was the first to pull away. Looking down, she said the only thing she could think of, "I'm married, Brett."

Undeterred, he slowly raised her chin and started to move in again. Lacey raised her hand and pushed back against his chest, "I'm still gonna be married if you kiss me again."

Brett reluctantly pulled away. They were both visibly torn and sad. Brett hadn't planned on kissing Lacey that day, but it felt so natural to have Lacey back in his arms. He decided to not let the moment slip past him.

"Does he make you feel like that?" Brett asked sincerely.

Lacey looked down and saw the cross pendant Grant had given her, the same cross that had once pained her the night she was with Brett. The sight of it now gave her strength.

"The question isn't what I feel, but who I love," Lacey whispered.

Brett paused a minute, lost in thought. "You always did love him more than me..." his voice trailed off.

Lacey looked up, confused, "But I didn't know Grant until college..."

"Not Grant...GOD," Brett said, nodding to the cross on her neck and looking back up at her again. He pulled away, collecting his wits and his pride.

"Which *is* as it *should be*..." he said, kissing her forehead before pulling away.

Lacey said nothing. Brett backed away, started to say something, thought better of it, and instead turned to go.

"I'll call you when I hear something from Vanderbilt," Brett said over his shoulder as he walked out the door. Lacey nodded, frozen and torn between the past and the present, one world and another.

The rev of Brett's motorcycle brought Lacey out of her comatose state. Without a word, she exited the kitchen, walked stone-faced past Mya to the pool, turned to stand on the edge with her back to the water, and fell back into the pool, fully clothed, heels and all.

As she surfaced, Mya stood on the side, waiting with a towel. They looked like a set of drowned rats in their wet outfits.

"Oh my word, Lacey! What in the world happened in there?" Mya asked as they moved onto the pool chairs.

"I think my thwarted destiny and God's will collided," Lacey
replied.

"Well I know one thing's for sure," Mya said.

"What's that?" Lacey asked.

"You'd better give Grant a steak dinner tonight when you tell him."

TWENTY-EIGHT

By the time Grant rolled in from work, Lacey had delivered the kids to Mya's house, got "presentable," and had almost finished preparing dinner. She was dreading having to tell him the news. She had hoped to wait a while before telling Grant, to get used to the news herself first, but Vanderbilt had said the turnaround time for the results could just take a couple of days this time. Whether *she* was ready or not, Grant was going to need time to absorb everything – even more time than her.

She had tried to plan out what she was going to say, and even made notes and practiced how she might tell him in the mirror, but nothing sounded right. She wanted to lead with a positive, but no matter how she tried to spin it, she knew the news would devastate him. How do you tell your godly husband the daughter he has called his own for thirteen years is not actually *his*? And *you*, the *mother*, didn't know? He would, of course, take her to be a double liar…first in deed and, then, in word. For most couples, this might not be as big of a deal, but Grant and Lacey had prided themselves on being pure on their wedding day – had even taken precautions so as not to tempt themselves. How in the world could she ever explain that she had been chaste with *him*, but not *another man*?! It would truly feel like infidelity to him. Unlike her hometown friends, Grant had *no knowledge* of her life before him, no knowledge of the chemistry and history she and Brett had shared, no knowledge of who she *used* to be. Grant had never even told another girl he loved her! How in the world was he going to understand *THIS*?! When she imagined the betrayal he would feel, and how he might look at her in shame…she just couldn't handle the thought.

"And his *family*!! Oh my word, his *FAMILY*!" She literally shook her head "no" at the thought. One crisis at a time was enough.

"I deserve whatever comes my way," Lacey thought. She had *known* better, and she had always *done* better, but she stepped outside of God's will and now she was reaping what she and Brett had sown.

"Your sins will always find you out," her father's words played in her head. And they were. What was done in private would now be dealt with in public, for all the world to gawk at. Lacey had never meant to be deceiving, she was just in such shock and pain when she heard Brett had lied to her, she did what she'd always done: fled, ignored the pain, and pushed forward without looking back, not thinking of the potential repercussions. She never imagined *this* would even be a *possibility*! She'd always just assumed she'd gotten pregnant on her honeymoon…

Lacey couldn't think of all of that right now. Now she had to deal with Grant, and she was fully expecting him to leave her. She'd even packed a bag for herself and stored it at Mya's, just in case. When she saw her suitcase sitting in Mya's guest room, the reality of the situation had taken ahold of her.

She wanted to die, but there were steaks to get off the grill and potatoes to poach.

Grant came in the front door, and sniffed the air pleasantly. "Steak and potatoes night?" he asked Lacey from the living room.

"Uh-huh," Lacey said from the kitchen, too nervous to even talk. She had asked Mya to cover her in prayer the whole time they would be talking – and fast while she was at it. This was not a time to be chintzy. Her whole future was riding on this.

"Where's the kids?" Grant asked.

"I sent them to Mya's so we could have dinner," Lacey explained. Grant dropped his computer bag and snuggled up behind her at the stove, kissing her neck.

"Really?" he asked, happy to finally have some alone time without the kids underfoot.

Lacey pulled away as stove timer went off. "Uh-huh," she said, as she grabbed the potatoes out of the microwave.

Dinner went well, consisting of small talk. Like Queen Esther, Lacey had decided to wait until Grant's tummy was full until she broached the subject.

"That was awesome, sweetie," Grant said.

"Yes, it was!" Lacey agreed. "Honey, we need to talk," she whispered, her voice cracking.

"Are you pregnant?" Grant asked, hopeful excitement lacing his words. It was right he should ask since every time she had sprung the news of a baby, she'd always done it over a private meal she'd prepared, a fact Lacey had forgotten until this moment.

"Another good tradition ruined because of my sin," Lacey thought sadly.

"No, we got the results back from Vanderbilt, but neither one of us is a candidate," Lacey said softly. She felt Grant's spirit sink along with his head. It was not the news they'd hoped for. She let the news sink in before continuing.

"So what's the next step?" Grant asked.

"Well, we go further up the family line and look for a viable candidate," Lacey explained.

"We'll start with my parents," Grant stated, knowing his parents were in better health than Lacey's at the moment.

Lacey nodded. "Well, there might be another option as well," Lacey hurriedly continued, before she chickened out. "The results gave some interesting information that *I* didn't even know..." she tried to emphasize that point, hoping he'd keep it in mind when he heard the real news.

"Great! What?" Grant asked.

"Well..." Lacey had no clue what to say next. "God give me strength," she silently prayed, but then hung her head. Grant was such a tenderhearted man, and she worried the news might kill him. At least emotionally.

"Grant, I've got to tell you something but before I do, I need you to know the news was a shock to me too. Promise me you will remember that, okay?" Lacey begged.

"Okay...you're starting to scare me, honey," Grant rubbed her hand consolingly. "Always thinking of the other person," Lacey thought, "Unlike me." The guilt weighed heavy and she felt as low as the candles that had burned down during dinner.

"Grant, I learned…Kit is not our daughter." Lacey let the words just spill out, then clasped her hands over her mouth like they actually had. She didn't have the heart to say *he* wasn't *her* father.

Again, for the second time that week, the words just hung in the air, their meaning waiting to be caught.

"Oh my word! The hospital switched her at birth?!" Grant's reaction was even worse! He believed in her so much he couldn't imagine another possibility. Lacey braced herself.

"No, Grant…Kit *is* MY daughter…" Lacey forced herself to say with emphasis. She couldn't bring herself to say, "but not yours." She waited as the meaning started attaching to the words he'd heard.

He didn't respond in anger. She knew he wouldn't. That would have been easier than having to answer his questions – some of which didn't have answers.

"What are you talking about, Lacey? We'd only known *each other*…You told me…"

"…and that was all TRUE, Grant – until the Summer of '94…" Lacey hung her head. She couldn't look at him, thinking of what he might be picturing in his mind.

Grant remained silent in what seemed like forever, his mind racing, trying to put all the pieces together.

" '94, huh?" he said, calculating and pondering. Lacey knew he was focusing on the fact that they had been dating steady during that time and were all *but* officially engaged.

This time Grant's eyes did all the talking. There was confusion and hurt, disappointment and anger – and it was all directed at her.

"Brett," Grant said stoically. He was all too familiar with that name. A name he'd heard whispered at Lacey's high school reunion behind questioning eyes and cupped hands as he and Lacey walked by. He'd always suspected there was *something,* but he dared not pry. "Nothing good could come from that," he always told himself. On more than one occasion he was met by a male classmate shaking his hand and proclaiming in awe, "So THIS is the guy who beat out Brett Wright!" Lacey had always shrugged and explained it away as "puppy love" – an answer that had

159

satisfied Grant, until today. He had never *met* this "Brett," but, oh, he knew him!

"What month?" Grant asked, coming out of his stunned state. Lacey looked away, not wanting to respond. She didn't know she'd have to answer detailed questions tonight. "Honey, let's think about what this could mean for Kit," she said.

"WHAT. *MONTH*?!" Grant slammed his fist on the table. Lacey had never heard him yell. Ever.

"July," Lacey said – briskly but firmly, so she wouldn't have to repeat it.

"What day?" Grant was not backing down.

Lacey hung her head in shame. "The fourth," she whispered.

"The fourth," Grant repeated. They both knew what he was thinking. She had given herself to another man just seven days before they had eloped. It was too much for Grant to take in.

Without a word, Grant threw his napkin on his plate and walked to the door.

Lacey as too scared to talk, but managed to eke out, "Are you coming back?"

Grant turned around, stunned, blinked and walked away.

Lacey slumped to ground and sobbed deeply, the likes of which she hadn't done since July 5, 1994... the day after the event that caused the pain they were all living now.

TWENTY-NINE

Grant didn't remember where all he had driven, or gone. All he knew was life as he had known it was changed forever…and built on a lie. One lie with roots that spread far and wide.

Around 2AM he grabbed his Bible from his glovebox, searching the scriptures for wisdom. Grant knew in situations like this, one had to cut off his own feelings, clear his head and find what God had to say on the subject. If Grant acted on his feelings right now…. the thought made him shudder.

As he came out of the fog, he began to have questions. A lot of questions. Who was "Brett" really? Had Lacey been two-timing him back then, or was this a one-night stand? He would have never thought Lacey was the type of girl to do that, but apparently, he didn't know his wife as well as he thought he did. His whole world felt off kilter.

By sunrise he had made his way to Pastor Holt's house. It just seemed like the right place to go. Before he even got to the porch, Pastor Holt was greeting him.

"I was hoping you'd show up," he welcomed him. "Lacey called last night," he explained, as he put a leash on his Yorkie. "Let's go for a walk."

They walked down a shady, winding trail, surrounded by hardwoods. It seemed people were more relaxed and forth coming in the outdoors, walking the trail. It was the best counseling tool he had, besides God's guidance.

They walked in silence while Pastor Holt allowed Grant to collect his thoughts and eat the blueberry muffins Melissa had made for them. Grant looked like he'd not slept at all the night before – which would be expected, considering the news he'd gotten yesterday.

Lacey had called and explained the situation to Brother Holt and Melissa. He heard deep sadness and desperation in her voice, and after hearing the whole story, he knew Lacey's emotions were not exaggerated. Having known Lacey and Grant so long - their characters and values – he was surprised by the news. Surprised, but not shocked. He'd learned a long time ago *everyone* has baggage and most have a past, especially in a military town during wartime. Now Lacey's past was catching up with her...and Grant.

They made their way to a clearing where a man-made beach preceded a small pond flanked with Adirondack chairs. Grant had finally told the preacher what Lacey had told him the night before, and Brother Holt realized he possessed information that Grant *didn't* have yet. Lacey had warned him she hadn't been able to divulge a lot to Grant since he'd left so quickly, and now it was up to Brother Holt to share some of the vital stats. In this case, he agreed Grant needed to hear some of it from a third party instead of Lacey herself. Emotions were running too high right now for them to talk face to face.

"...I've been lied to my whole life, Dan. I don't even know my own wife!" Grant sighed, his head slumping low.

"I know this is rough, and I know it *feels* like a lie, Grant, but she didn't know. You are both hurting and having to come to terms with the same reality right now. In a way, *she* was deceived as well – not only by a person, but by circumstances. I talked to her last night, Grant, and she honestly *did not know...*"

Grant cut him off. "She knew she'd slept with some other guy a week before we got married! She knew *THAT*!" Grant spat out the words, his face red. Brother Holt nodded in agreement. They sat in silence a while, letting the new reality and all its implications catch up with them.

He'd never seen Grant upset. Feelings weren't something his family of origin wrestled with much. They didn't *deal* with feelings, they swallowed them. Brother Dan knew he was going to have to help Grant maneuver through and deal with the deep emotions coming his way - his marriage and family were at stake.

"Grant, what do you NOT know that you *need* to know? Let's start with that," Brother Holt asked.

Grant swallowed and thought a second. "I don't know *who* this Brett is, and if my wife was two-timing me or why she cheated on me," a lump crept into Grant's throat.

Brother Holt took a deep breath. "I think there are some things Lacey needs to fill you in on herself, but you need to know right now that this was *not* a seedy, one night stand, nor was she two-timing you. She told me it was an ex-boyfriend that she had dated and loved deeply for years who showed up unexpectedly..." Pastor Dan left off the part about their plans to be married – he'd leave that one to Lacey.

Grant felt some relief, knowing his wife hadn't given her heart and body to just *anyone*...but it was little consolation in light of all the rest that was lost.

"It feels like I've been cheated on, Dan, but it happened *before* our vows so I can't justify a divorce!" Grant hung his head in sorrowful defeat.

"It sounds like you've been researching your options," Dan said, sad Grant was already thinking of an exit plan. Grant was embarrassed. He knew that shouldn't be his first line of thinking, but he was going off sheer anger right now.

"Are you wanting reconciliation or revenge, Grant?"

Grant looked at him, shocked. First, that Brother Holt would have to ask that question, and, worse, that he had to *think* about his answer.

"I'm supposed to say reconciliation, but I'm not sure..." Grant admitted.

"Grant, this is a bombshell. Don't make any decisions right now. Just try to digest everything. But know this: Lacey made a mistake but she did not do it *TO* you, to hurt you. She's hurting, too! Try to not spend too much time in anger, but focus on this question: What does God want you to do? Not what do you WANT to do – because your feelings will lead you astray. Not what do OTHER people do, but WHAT DOES GOD WANT YOU TO DO? Love will never steer you wrong."

Pastor Holt continued, "Lacey is going to Vanderbilt this weekend, right?"

Grant nodded.

"Use this time to absorb everything and pray, and we'll all meet up next week. In the meantime, I need you to chop us a bundle of firewood."

"Dan, it's *June*," Grant objected, confused.

"So?" Dan responded. "It'll help you blow off some steam, and sometimes we have to do things we don't want to do."

"Touché," Grant said, grabbing an ax.

****

By the time Grant got home after work the next day Lacey and the kids had already left for Nashville. It was good the house was so quiet, for two reasons: one, to give him time to let everything sink in, and also, to show him just how empty the house would be if he and Lacey didn't resolve things. So far, he did not like the thought of it.

Despite wanting to work things through, Grant wasn't sure how to. Brother Holt had advised him to think on the things that had drawn them together and focus on those.

"No better place to start than the beginning," Grant reasoned. So, he dug through old videos in the attic, grabbed a handful of VHS home tapes and plopped on the couch, ready for a long night.

He started with videos of the kids…Kit and Jake toddling around with messy birthday cake on their faces and clumsy first steps. He worked his way backward until he finally found their wedding video.

It seemed like it was yesterday, and Lacey was gorgeous. As radiant as the white gown she wore. Both so filled with joy, neither one knowing all the challenges that lay ahead. Seeing the video reminded him of all the love they felt for each other.

He grabbed another video with no label. As the video started to play, Grant couldn't place where the video was filmed. It was a country setting, complete with hay bales, white lights strung from a barn loft, and a huge bonfire.

"Houston County," Grant realized, chuckling in respectful amazement. Grant was instantly transported to another time and place. The band was playing one of Lacey's songs he'd heard on her old CD. As she was singing, the video zoomed in on a young

Lacey, no more than seventeen. Her hair fell in soft, natural waves and the cowboy boots paired with her blue jean skirt reminded him just how different their upbringing truly was.

"Country girl and city boy," they used to joke. But now, seeing it in color, he felt a twinge of jealousy. Lacey looked so relaxed as she pushed into the chorus, her confidence rose along with the notes. Grant watched in wonder, as his refined wife morphed into a young, carefree singer. He couldn't believe his eyes. Lacey had always been beautiful, but reserved. He didn't quite know what to make of this brazen girl on the screen, but he liked what he saw.

Just as she was stepping offstage two guys moved in. One grabbed a guitar and the taller one grabbed a microphone and started singing. He watched as Lacey stopped, turned and listened – just before the singer took her hand and led her back to center stage. Grant watched, mesmerized, as their voices blended, moving them closer and closer as the song went on. By the end, they were holding hands, their bodies as tight as the harmony between them. The crowd erupted into thunderous applause and southern yells as the male singer pulled Lacey in close and kissed her forehead – the same way Grant, himself, did regularly. Grant could feel his face getting hot. He watched in jealousy as Lacey looked at the guy like he hung the moon – with an expression of pure, blissful happiness…and love.

Brett.

Even though it was sixteen years ago, Grant felt anger brewing. He was jealous of missing Lacey's younger years, knowing her when she was so carefree. And he was jealous of the way she looked at Brett. He couldn't remember the last time she had looked at *him* like that. Before he could ponder any further, he saw Brett pull away from Lacey and jump off the stage and hit a guy in the audience. The video went black.

Grant sat in the dark, mulling over what he'd just seen – realizing he was not competing with just a man but with all the memories that came with a first love, as well as all the "firsts" that come with it. Especially one *particular* first he had just learned about. The "first" that he and Lacey had deemed sacred. The "first" they had chosen to "wait" for. The "first" that was stolen from him. The "first" that was now stealing his daughter, his family and maybe his future.

Despite the jealous anger brewing in him, Grant knew now he wanted to keep his family in tact AND he now knew what he was up against. He was going to need all the angels of heaven fighting with him on this one.

"God help me," he prayed, as he put the video away.

THIRTY

As soon as Lacey learned Grant had talked to Pastor Holt, she knew Melissa would be calling. Even though Pastor Dan hadn't been raised in Tennessee, Melissa had grown up with Lacey and knew about both Brett and Grant. Through recent years, she and Melissa had become the best of friends, and Lacey had regretted they hadn't been closer in high school. Lacey enjoyed being with Melissa. Her deep faith showed through every word she spoke, and her sweet spirit made opening up easy – an excellent trait that aided in her counseling, no doubt.

Lacey was grateful Melissa was able to see her so soon. It'd been a week since she had told Grant. He had moved out to the pool house while she was at Vandy to have space to think. Grant always took alone time to think on serious matters. Once, toward the end of Law school, Lacey didn't see him for two entire weeks! And Grant also took his statements seriously: he said what he meant and meant what he said. He was not one to say anything in haste he'd later regret. Lacey respected that.

Melissa's Jack Russell terrier greeted Lacey as she came through the door. Lacey always loved their home. Despite having two children, their home was cozy, tidy and welcoming, and smelled of vanilla candles and coffee.

"Thanks for letting me come over so soon, Melissa," Lacey said as she patted Jack.

"Of course, Lacey! I'm sorry I was out of town and couldn't be here for you sooner," Melissa apologized as she handed Lacey a cup of coffee - in a fine china cup and saucer, no less. Melissa seemed to so easily do the homemaker things Lacey had dreamed of and fallen short.

"I bet you've got lavender springs on top of your towels!" Lacey once joked with her in good natured fun.

"And I bet the towels are even FOLDED!" Mya had chimed in – revealing how that week she had merely put the hamper of unfolded, clean towels in front of the bathroom closet.

"Life's too short to fold towels!" Mya had defended herself. The women burst into a cackle of laughs and tears ran down their cheeks, thoroughly enjoying their differences.

"So, did Dan fill you in?" Lacey asked, taking off her shoes and curling up on Melissa's couch.

Melissa nodded. "Yes, he did. How are you and Grant doing?"

Lacey shrugged. "I'm not sure about Grant. He moved out to the pool house." Melissa looked up, gravely concerned. Lacey spoke quickly to relieve her fears. "No, it's not *that* bad – he goes out there all the time when he needs to think on heavy issues. He regularly stays out there when working on cases." Melissa nodded, understandingly, relieved.

"And you?! How are you, Lacey??" Melissa asked. The care and concern gracing her words caused Lacey to break down, crying. She couldn't remember the last time someone had asked her how she was doing.

"Awful. Just awful. I've destroyed my marriage with my own hands & didn't even know!" Lacey was sniffling now. "Did Dan tell you I didn't even KNOW?! What kind of mother doesn't know the father of her *own child* 'til THIRTEEN YEARS LATER?!" Lacey was overcome. Melissa could tell Lacey had not had time to process the news herself.

"And it was ONE TIME, Melissa! The *one time* I let my guard down and took off my halo THIS is the fallout!" Years of sorrow, hidden guilt and regret poured out in tears.

"My sin has finally found me out and Grant is going to divorce me," Lacey stated factually.

Melissa was surprised at her friend's reaction. "Lacey, don't jump to conclusions…"

Lacey cut in, "No, Melissa…I *know* Grant. *YOU* know Grant - how morally excellent he is…how he thought *I* was, too… He never even told another girl he loved her until me and now *this*?!"

Lacey's eyes widened, frantic with a new realization. "And the *firm*! Oh my word! He was just put up for *partner* and was thinking of entering the Senate race! Guess I've killed that for him. He's *never* gonna forgive me. Never!" Lacey put her head in her hands, defeated, her country twang and fears creeping into her voice.

Melissa tried to console her, "I *do* know how moral he is, Lacey...and I also know he is a *good man*...We have that to cling to. Like all men, though, he needs time to process all this. My concern right now is you. Have *you* taken time to process it all?" she asked, concerned.

"No. I've been on emotional autopilot ever since we got Kit's diagnosis. And now this...I don't want to tell her all this yet, since she's got so much to handle herself already...Melissa, I honestly *didn't know*! I had finally made peace with my past and put Brett to rest. But now everything's getting dredged up all over again! What am I gonna do?"

Melissa sighed, "Lacey, I was there when you and Brett were dating and I can *imagine* how hard this is on you!" Melissa's voice softened and her eyes were sympathetic. "Everyone in Dawsonville loved Lacey and Brett back then. From the very beginning it was as if you were meant to be, entertaining everyone with your feigned, nonchalant banter and digs, but everyone knew that behind every dig and under every zinger lay a hidden "I love you." You two were head over heels in love! The perfect blend of Johnny and June, and Kenny and Dolly: true loves and best friends. Everyone was disappointed when they heard things hadn't panned out for the two of you. Disappointed, but not surprised. The people of Houston County know, more than most, the stressors deployment brings. War has a way of changing even the surest of things."

"First loves are always the hardest and, like parental love, they are *unconditional*. First love might even be MORE powerful because, unlike a parent's love, THEY have a *CHOICE*! They love us merely because there is something in their souls that connects with ours. There's no worries of, "Is he a good provider? Will he make a good father? Is he ambitious, dependable and emotionally well suited for me?" No. It is merely "I *see* you and I love *you*." You. Your real, authentic self. Not the "you" you become. Not the "you" that emerges with masks and coping behaviors after real life has gotten ahold of you. First love is love's truest, purest form – giving all and seeking nothing in return. It's hard not to respond to that, especially when you and Brett had it for so long, and assumed you would get married."

"It's deeper than that," Lacey whispered, wondering if she should reveal what was tormenting her the worst. She decided the chance at relief was worth the risk. "I had a "sense" we'd be together."

Melissa slumped back on her chair. She had the same spiritual gift as Lacey, and knew the full meaning of her words. Over the years she had seen how the devil tried to use the best of God's gifts to His advantage, and it seemed Lacey might be in that very situation now.

"Oh, honey. I *know* the weight of that, but perhaps this is part of your testing. Despite what you felt or sensed, are you going to trust your *gift* from God – or are you going to trust **God**?"

Though she and Melissa had never discussed it, Lacey had sensed they shared the same gift. It was comforting to know she was speaking to someone who truly understood.

"Could it be you got a message that the two of you would be in each other's lives forever and your young heart interpreted it as *marriage?* Possibly. But you *didn't* marry, so it's not even an issue."

"But you see, then, how that's been weighing mightily on me..." Lacey whispered. "Especially when it could happen *later...*"

Melissa could feel her friend's inner struggle. The devil was, indeed, using everything he could against her – including her spiritual gift!

"Yes, but even if it comes to pass, it will be *later*, in *God's* time and in *God's* way! His will, His way, His time! *Your* job is to obey where you are **now**...and right now you are Grant's wife." Melissa paused to let the full impact of her words seep down into Lacey's heart.

"Trust me. I *know*," Melissa whispered as she squeezed Lacey's hand.

Lacey looked up, surprised. Melissa was hinting that in the past she, too, had received a weighty message and had to "wait and see" what the Lord had in mind. Lacey had forgotten that Melissa's "best laid plans" had also been thwarted. Her first love, Scott, had returned from the Gulf a different man – a soldier boy who didn't know how to unpack all he had seen. Melissa loyally stuck by him, until a black eye and a broken rib taught her no matter how hard we try or pray, things do not always work out. She, of all people, truly understood the struggle Lacey was facing. Even in her turmoil, Lacey felt thankful for her friend. There is a special bond between people who share the same tragedies and struggles – and Gifts.

"It's gonna be the hardest thing you've ever done, but it appears the devil is using your Gift to deceive you. You're gonna have to ignore it for a while until your family gets through this crisis."

Lacey looked up, unbelieving. Asking someone with intuition to ignore it was like asking most people to start living life with their eyes closed – except harder. It was their sixth – but strongest – sense that led them through life. It was what they relied upon to navigate, like a pilot's instruments. Now she was being told to "ignore the controls" and strictly follow the manual and what it, God and godly friends were telling her to do. She honestly wasn't sure she could.

Melissa tried to encourage her, "It won't last *forever,* and I'll stay right with you and be your "discernment wingman,*"* but you've got no choice right now. Your gauges are off and you need recalibrating. But, really, there isn't anything you *can* do right now – except pray. And that's also the *best* thing we can do," Melissa said.

"But Grant is *so angry*! And rightfully so..." Lacey mumbled sadly.

"Only God can change a heart, Lacey. This is also a battle between Grant and the Lord. We need to cover him – and all of you – in prayer...even Brett," Melissa said. "We've got to remember God wants us *all* to come home to Him, and something like this could hinder Brett's spiritual walk. I know it's a lot on you right now, but don't do anything to encourage Brett to stumble. The Bible tells us there will always be temptations to sin, but great sorrow awaits the person doing the tempting! It says it would be better for him to have a big rock tied around his neck and be thrown into the ocean than to cause a new or weak believer to fall into sin. That "weak believer" would be Brett. It doesn't seem fair, but part of our Christian responsibility is to look after each other."

Lacey sighed, "Melissa, I thought when I eloped with Grant, I could pretend Brett and I had never happened, that the two of us had never existed…

Melissa sighed. "The things we run away from catch up to us eventually."

Lacey winced.

"How's Brett doing?" Melissa asked, knowing she'd probably talked with him already.

"Doing as Brett does…" Lacey shrugged.

"That's what I was afraid of," Melissa mumbled, rolling her eyes. That was all it took for Lacey to divulge the final secrets hidden in her heart.

"Oh, Melissa, I am just so confused! You *know* how in love we were! I was prepared to seal that part of my heart up forever. What I was *not* prepared for was to find out he's the *father* of my *daughter* thirteen years later and have to deal with all those buried feelings! Not to mention being tied now to him forever!"

"So, *all* those feelings are coming back?" Melissa asked, knowingly. Lacey knew better than to try to deny it.

She sighed dejectedly, and confirmed Melissa's fears, "Like a flood. The attraction I once felt for him is as intense as it once was: I get butterflies every time he's around and he's still…BRETT," Lacey looked off sadly.

"Melissa, you KNOW us! It's just so *easy* with Brett! It always has been…"

Melissa squeezed her hand sympathetically.

"Yes, I remember," Melissa admitted. "But I also remember a lot of turmoil. It might have been easier but was it **better**? I knew you and Brett, and I know you and Grant – and, from the outside looking in, your relationship with Grant is more stable, more solid, surer. Those traits don't seem very romantic, but it's hard to have a marriage last without them."

"You love Grant. You are going to have to remember those feelings that sneak up with Brett have *nothing to do with your love for Grant*, and you're gonna have to keep them in check. And if Brett hasn't changed, you'd *better* keep your guard up! The Bible even talks about not falling for smooth talking evil. The devil's gonna take advantage of the attraction you've always had with Brett and remind you of all his good traits, just like he made Eve notice the good traits of the forbidden fruit. He's gonna try to convince you of how good that fruit would *taste*…but don't fall for it! The devil can disguise himself as a smooth talking, hot military man," Melissa said.

Lacey looked up, surprised. "Oh, it's worse!" Lacey added. "He's added *tattoos* and a *motorcycle* to the mix!"

"Lord, have mercy…" Melissa whispered, fanning herself with the church bulletin. "We are gonna have to borrow some anointing oil from Mya and douse you every time you have to see him!" Melissa teased.

"No! The sparks would catch me on fire!" Lacey laughed, holding her cheeks. They were laughing so hard her cheeks were starting to ache.

"Well just remember, 'Beauty is fleeting and charm is deceptive, but the one who loves the Lord is to be praised.' I'll admit *both* men are handsome, but only *one* seems truly dedicated to walking with God right now – and, luckily, he happens to be your husband."

Melissa's words comforted Lacey. It was nice to have someone see that, yes, the bond she and Brett shared *was* strong and attractive and **real**…and a danger. The advice Melissa was giving was not the advice Lacey's flesh wanted to hear, but she knew it was what she needed to hear.

Lacey nodded, "I totally agree."

"Try not to fret - let God work on Grant's heart. He is not a foolish man, and he loves you and the kids very much. You just need to keep the faith while he's absorbing everything."

"I'll do my best," Lacey promised, still wondering if this was too tall a task even for the Lord to want to tackle.

THIRTY-ONE

Kit's follow up Vanderbilt appointment couldn't have come at a better time. Their trip would give Grant more time to think alone. Pastor Dan had suggested Lacey might further explain things in a letter, so Grant could read the details of the past when he was ready.

Lacey's parents lived in Nashville now, which had been super helpful with Kit's medical condition and doctor visits. They were both retired, and though Lacey's dad had been diagnosed with early Alzheimer's, they did pretty well, but it was sad to watch such a decline. Sometimes, her dad would mistake Lacey for her mother, and he would ask her to make him a sandwich. It was easier to do instead of trying to convince him who she really was.

Returning home had been difficult, but things got easier once her Dad's "issues" got a diagnosis: PTSD. Lacey felt guilty: all those years assuming her dad was being "mean" when he was just trying to work through things from the war.

"Always be kind," Grandpa Charlie used to say. "The older I get, the more I learn there's usually a hidden explanation for things that upset us. I have often regretted how I treated someone, but I have never regretted being kind."

Growing up, Lacey was nice to her dad on the *outside*, but she'd harbored a lot of anger in her heart. She decided the best way to make up for it was to be as understanding as she could for his remaining years.

Lacey headed to the back study to find some stationery. Even though they had moved to a different house, her Dad had kept everything just as it had been in their Houston County home. This not only made Lacey feel like she was still "at home," but also made things easy to find. "The silver lining of OCD," Lacey thought with a chuckle.

As she rummaged through the desk drawers, a large, manila envelope spilled, its contents spread all over the floor. Lacey recognized the block style writing and knew instantly who the envelopes addressed to her were from:

Brett.

Lacey opened the top letter, dated 1993 – the same month she'd had the wreck. She opened the next one with trembling hands and slid down the wall, opening and reading, savoring each word. There were long letters and short notes, funny ones and sad ones, but they all contained love and spoke of the future he wanted with her once he got home – rough house plans and baby names and honeymoon ideas. *Brett had been telling the truth*! Heartbreak and cold fear washed over her as she realized how different her life would have been if she had received these letters.

She hastily grabbed the scattered letters and ran to her Dad.

"Dad! Dad!" she yelled. Exasperated, she reverted to his first name. "Jim!" They had been taught Alzheimer's patients might respond better to their personal names than family terms, like Dad. Sure enough, he said, "Over here." She found him tinkering with a gadget in the garage.

Lacey went to him, breathless. "Jim. *Look* what I found…All these letters…"

Jim's eyes were foggy, but as soon as he saw the name on the return address, he became agitated, flailing his arms about.

"Kim! *Kim*! Hide those letters! Put those back where you found them, ya hear me?! Burn 'em! Lacey's gone and found her a real good boy and we don't need to ruin it now…"

Lacey's heart sank as she realized her Dad had intercepted and hid the letters. Then, her heart swelled, realizing Brett had written her every day, just like he said. He must've spent half his first month's salary on stamps!

"And I didn't believe him!" her heart screamed. She had been dating Grant a few months when she got her memories back of Brett, but a large factor in her deciding to marry Grant had been because Brett seemed to have disappeared without a trace – or a second thought for her. It was the most painful thing she had done: deciding to let him go and move on with Grant.

She grabbed the letters and ran out the door to see the one person who would truly understand the fullness of the situation: Jenn.

****

The two hour drive from Nashville to Jenn's house had given her a chance to cool off, pray and think things through. Lacey had been so conditioned over the years to look past her Dad's nonsensical actions so many times that the thought of being angry with him didn't even enter her mind. And, strangely, she could see how her Dad's logic DID make sense.

Lacey hadn't seen Jenn for about six months – not from lack of want, but due to their busy lives. But no matter how much time had passed between their visits, they always picked up right where they'd left off like no time had even passed.

She and Will had married right after graduation and moved wherever the Army sent them. Eight moves and four babies later they found themselves back in Dawsonville, happy to be home.

Lacey didn't know what she would do without Jenn – she alone had been by Lacey's side through her beginning with Brett, their turbulent middle, their demise and then her meeting and marrying Grant. And now, she'd be here again, as she and Brett reunited.

Lacey had called and told Jenn the news about Kit's paternity. Jenn's response had first been dead silence, followed by an immediate response of, "Figures." Jenn's crazy life had programmed her to deal with surprises and accept things quickly – but, truth be told, only Brett and Lacey could make such an unbelievable situation so believable.

Jenn was already waiting on the porch with a glass of wine. "I know you claim not to drink whiskey anymore, but you didn't say nothin' 'bout wine," Jenn said with a wink and sympathetic smile. "I thought this was called for," she whispered, as she put her arm around her bestie and walked her into the house.

Lacey breathed a sigh of relief; proof Jenn was the one who would truly "get it."

For the next two hours, they read through every letter, with Lacey's heart repeatedly soaring then breaking. The scattered and torn envelopes served as a visual for Lacey's heart.

"So, Brett was telling the truth the whole time, huh?" Jenn asked, rocking her youngest as he nursed. "I'd like to say nothing surprises me when it come to the two of you, but I gotta admit this is pretty crazy, even for y'all."

"A-par-ent-ly," Lacey drawled sarcastically.

"Wow. Just…wow." Jenn said, taking it all in, knowing full well what was playing out in Lacey's mind and heart. "And your dad just hid the letters all this time?"

"A-par-ent-ly," Lacey swooned again. Lacey understood. Even in her pain, she got it: she had started dating Grant after the wreck - a solid, good, godly man. What loving father *wouldn't* do what hers had done? He was trying to protect her happiness – and possible future - with a wonderful man. How was he to know that his daughter's full memory would return and break her heart, anyway?

She understood but hated it.

She felt lied to, cheated, and robbed…with no way to fix it.

It was a no-win situation. And it was sucking the life out of her. But what could she do?

"It is what it is," Brett used to say.

Well, this time the "it is what it is" *wasn't* what she *thought* it was! Lacey put her head down on her arms, exhausted and spent. Jenn rubbed her back sympathetically. She knew her friend was dying inside. What her friend and Brett had in the past really *was* like a fairy tale: a real life, twisted, romance novel. They belonged together, like salt and pepper. Everyone just *knew* they were going to ride off into the sunset together and live happily ever after. And now, to find out they *would have*, if not for parental involvement, was heartbreaking and overwhelming.

"Jenn, I just can't handle it! Everything was *manipulated*!" Lacey was crying now. "And all those buried emotions that I thought were done and over? Not so! Time hasn't changed anything! I'm fighting the same feelings I had fifteen years ago, only now it's worse because I *know* Brett tried! I can't run away, and I can't hide. I am having to just SIT IN THIS! I know it's awful, Jenn, but I still love him just like I did back then…" she whispered.

"I think I'm seriously starting to slip. I KNOW what the Bible teaches on divorce, but I even looked in the Bible today to confirm people can't divorce for a "Father's Intervention..."

Jenn looked up, surprised.

"And you can't. I checked," Lacey said with a sigh and a sip. "...not that I WANT a divorce! I mean, I *love* Grant, it's just...things aren't looking good between us right now. He is *really hurt*, Jenn..."

"I am so sorry, Lace. Does Brett know about these letters?" Jenn asked, pointing to the letters.

Lacey shook her head "no." Jenn remained silent, letting the question sink in. It would be Lacey's decision, of course, to tell Brett or not. There would really be no reason to – it would only make him harbor anger as well, but it might help him understand her struggle.

"Grant still giving you the silent treatment?" Jenn inquired.

"Yeah...we haven't spoken since I told him. Brother Holt suggested I write him a letter, explaining everything about me and Brett to avoid saying it all face to face..."

"Sweetie, you can't convey everything about you two in a *letter*," Jenn pointed out, stating the obvious.

Jenn was right. How in the world could she explain all the history and chemistry she and Brett had on *paper*? And would she even WANT to? To her *husband*, that is? The thought made her shiver. If she could make him see what they really WERE, it might diffuse his anger a bit. But if she DID make him see what they really were, it might push him away further: She honestly didn't know which would be worse.

"How's *Brett* acting?" Jenn gave her friend a sideways stare.

"At first he was all business," Lacey said. "But then he started dropping hints, saying how we have a "right" to be together, how we've always been "soul mates," that kinda thing...and then he kissed me," Lacey admitted.

Jenn whistled, amazed but not surprised. She was relieved to see a slight frown instead of a grin on Lacey's face. "Wow – I figured he might try something...he always was an opportunistic son of a –

"Mooom!!" Jenn's two middle kids came running in, tattling on each other, leaving Lacey to her thoughts. It was good to hear Jenn call Brett out on his actions, and see things from another perspective. Because she was starting to see the validity of some of *his* points.

"Well, I'll give him one thing: ain't nobody around's got the kind of chemistry you two had, that's for sure. And you might be soul mates, but..." Jenn paused, trying to phrase her words so that they would have an impact but not harden her friend's heart.

"Go on," Lacey encouraged.

"...but remember the cause of your breakup? That was you getting a glimpse into his heart, sweetie. He *cheated* on you, remember? And him making moves on you, as a married woman, now? He's shown you his character card, honey." The words stung, but Lacey knew her friend had her best interest at heart – and made an excellent point. "Yes, he was heartbroken and lonely back then, but he didn't have to sleep with someone! *He* made that choice. And Lacey, you were very young and idealistic. Do you really think you could've married him after you found out another girl was having his baby?! You couldn't have handled that back then!" Jenn's words were bringing a realistic perspective back to Lacey's mind.

Her friend continued, "And you never had time to really *process* all of that, just moved from Brett back to Grant after that weekend...Maybe this is your time to process things, a time of *reckoning*, so to speak,"

Lacey's head shot up. Jenn carried on feeding the baby, not realizing the impact that word had made on Lacey. It was as if Grandma Kate herself were there in the room, gently advising and directing her, just like she used to.

"I know you're Brett's girl, but you're gonna have to be extra careful, considering y'all's past chemistry and all," Jenn said.

In the South, there is an unofficial relationship so rare it doesn't even have a name. It's never spoken of and is almost always comprised of first loves - or couples that shared a deep, deep love. It is extraordinary, unpredictable and an organic bond that springs up naturally, all on its own. This special love remains with a girl forever. Not just in the cherished memories of her mind, but tangibly. It is not sexual or tawdry, but a loyal, pure love. The couples that do experience it know how truly remarkable it is. Like trying to describe a new color that has never been seen before, it is almost impossible to describe. It cannot be explained, but it cannot be denied. It usually reveals itself later in life after the two have long parted ways. It does not follow the typical path of most past romantic relationships that fizzle and fade, so those that have never experienced or witnessed such a relationship do not fully understand just what it is.

Strangers will try to force this relationship into a romantic box, not knowing it is a completely different category all its own. To imply a romantic slant is actually insulting, as such description would tarnish this kind of love. Perhaps that is why no one speaks of this relationship...others just can't grasp it. Like the perpetual Big Foot rumors: they want it to be true, and wish it to be true...but just can't wrap their minds around it. So, the love is rarely spoken of – it remains private. There is no rhyme or reason as to which couples will be blessed with this amazing souvenir from the meaningful love they once shared. It is a special, random, sacred gift known only to a few.

The South is a place of pride and integrity. Boys are taught to do the "right thing" no matter what. Many a girl has fallen for a guy who could see her true potential. But if he felt in his heart he didn't have what it took to give her the future or the home or the stability he felt she deserved, in an act of true, selfless love, he would break things off, ignoring his emotions in exchange for the honor of knowing he stepped aside to give her a better life. Like an unwed, expectant mom giving her child up for adoption, he would sacrifice his desires for the good of the one he loves the most. Many times, his girl would go off to college, or pursue big dreams elsewhere. They both will have move on and marry another, and remain happily so. But that special love remains. He is her forever shadow, the invisible hand on her back, the unseen shoulder to cry on. He is the one who stands waiting to provide for or defend her, should the need ever arise. He is her wingman, her hero-in-waiting, the unseen Best Man at her wedding. Romantic love, now buried, becomes the foundation on which their new relationship is built. An outsider might catch occasional hints of past romance, but they are subtle and fleeting, like a nickname or a friendly tease. They are innocent, but cherished, reminders of the love they once had that still remains, though kept at arms' length.

There is no name for this unseen kind of relationship – the girl is merely referred to as "his girl." She has the comfort of knowing she is looked after, and he knows that he is admired. And they both, no matter what comes or what they become, always have someone who still sees them for who they truly are, not through their masks, occupations or their mistakes. They see straight to the heart and remind each other who they really are. It is a relationship that seems to violate all good marital advice and bunks protocol, but it is a symbiotic relationship that works, somehow. It is a strong love because it is unconditional, sure and steady: nothing can shake it or change it.

In Houston County, that meant the guy would check on "his girl" if her husband was overseas – but never in an inappropriate way. Special care is given not to reignite the ever present, eternal flame between them. Never together alone, the two have little communication. There will rarely be an indication of just who is helping in times of need...no return address accompanying the letter that contains money during hard times. But his girl knows.

When Mya's husband was recovering from surgery, her "guy" paid to have her family's yard mowed and put extra money in their bank account until her husband was back on his feet.

There is no reason to worry about the ex. The ex's concern and care come from a place of wanting the absolute BEST for "his girl," arguably one of the purest forms of love there is.

Jenn knew Brett and Lacey's deep connection and chemistry posed a high risk, despite her dedication to the Lord. The low simmer between them could quickly escalate into a full-on combustible explosion without warning. And in Lacey's case, there was too much at stake.

"You might be Brett's *girl*, but you're Grant's *wife*," Jenn said.

"Don't get it twisted."

THIRTY-TWO

It had been three weeks since Lacey had told Grant the news, and one week since she had sent him the letter explaining the relationship between her and Brett. Melissa had helped her edit out what she needed to say and, more importantly, what she didn't, but Lacey hadn't heard from him. She'd tried to relay how deep her relationship with Brett had been, how they were close friends as well as a couple, bonded from similar griefs – but her words lay flat on the paper. Some things had to be experienced to be understood. She knew Grant felt betrayed on many levels. Not only was he learning of Kit's paternity, but he was also having to digest the idea that his wife had been deeply involved – a breath away from marrying – another man.

Grant had requested they do their talking in a counseling setting so they wouldn't say anything either one of them might later regret. They would meet weekly with Pastor Dan, in addition to individual talks – he, with Pastor Dan and she with Melissa. They were great counselors, both strong believers. Dan was ten years older than them and had a counseling degree, and Melissa had grown up with Lacey, knowing both Brett *and* Grant. Their first couple's appointment was scheduled for today, after church.

Not wanting to arouse suspicion from the neighbors, Grant drove the whole family to church, but kept his conversation between him and the kids. Any talking he and Lacey had was centered around schedules and logistics. It seemed "cold," but she feared once they opened up emotionally it would snowball into something they couldn't control.

They both put on friendly faces to greet their church, but there was an underlying tension present Lacey could not ignore.

Just as greeting time was about to close, they heard a commotion. Lacey knew without looking Brett had entered. She heard men calling their greetings and a sideways glance at Mya's wide eyes confirmed it.

"What is he *doing* here?!" Mya mouthed.

Lacey rolled her eyes and gave her a quick "I don't know" shrug and an "I-CANNOT-BELIEVE-THE-GALL" angry face before turning her head to the front of the church. Brett might be in her presence, but she did not have to acknowledge him.

Grant, too, had heard the commotion and had to admit he was shocked. He could tell from Lacey's letter that Brett was a lot different than him, but he wasn't quite prepared for what he saw. Standing at 6"1 and muscular, he looked every bit like a real life GI Joe.

Pastor Dan had wondered if Brett might show up for services, so he used the opportunity to nail home some important truths. He talked about the danger of gossiping and making assumptions, followed by the holy sanctity of marriage, and how the marital bonds should be guarded. He then reminded everyone how marriage represented the relationship between Christ and the church – always loving and forgiving, no matter how difficult. The lesson was not lost on Grant, who was squirming in his seat, unable to make eye contact with his Pastor. Pastor Dan closed his sermon with the advice, "When you don't know *what* to do, ask 'What is the *loving* thing to do?'" Grant tugged at his tie. Pastor Dan never shied away from hard topics. He always told the congregation what they needed to hear in a loving way.

As the service was dismissed, Lacey busied herself collecting the things, then hurried out of the sanctuary. She headed into the bathroom to bide time and catch her breath. She had just cooled her face with a wet napkin when in walked Hayley.

"Lacey! Oh my word! Did you *see* who's here?!" Hayley asked.

"Yes, I did," Lacey answered. The problem with Hayley was that she was so genuine Lacey never knew how to take her. Lacey always made a point to be polite but kept a tight rein on her tongue when she was around, never knowing when Hayley might want to share her business as a "prayer request" to the delight of her not-as-innocent cronies. Her two friends beside her were pleased Hayley lacked the social tact to *not* ask the sensitive questions they all wanted answers to. Lacey decided playing it cool would raise a red flag since they all knew her history with Brett.

"I'm glad to see he's looking well," Lacey said as she toweled off her hands.

"He certainly is! Did you know he was coming today?" Hayley continued.

"No, I was as surprised as you!" Lacey said truthfully.

"Well I wonder what's brought him to Dickson?" Hayley wondered aloud.

"Probably just passing through to Fort Campbell. I would imagine his being in Special Ops, he is always coming from or going to a mission." If one wanted to get technical, he *was* on a mission: to see if he was a match for Kit. Operation Kidney. The thought made Lacey smile.

"Why don't you ask him," Lacey dried her hands and headed out the door. She prayed she came off as cool as a cucumber and her years of performing had finally come in handy. Inside she was shaking like a leaf.

THIRTY-THREE

The afternoon sun came streaming though the red and blue stained glass of Pastor Dan's office, creating a pattern with the lead strips that made a shattered picture on the carpeted aisle beside Grant.

"Like our lives," Grant thought. Lacey had given him a letter last week, explaining just who this "Brett" was, and his presence that morning at worship only confirmed the kind of man Grant had pictured in his mind. The mind thinks strange things during stressful situations and he couldn't help but compare himself to him. They were certainly as different as two men could be: military and collegiate, sporty and nerdy, extroverted and introverted. However, they both were very intelligent, and had at least one thing in common: their love for Lacey and Kit. Grant was hoping that would be motivation enough for Brett to be willing to donate a kidney, should he be a match. Grant *was* relieved to know Kit hadn't been conceived by a random stranger, but that's about where his thankful heart left off. However, he was willing to act amicably if it meant a longer life for his child. "Brett's child, actually," he corrected himself. The thought still stung.

"So, that's Brett..." Grant said, breaking the silence.

Lacey couldn't help but hear the slight jealousy behind Grant's dig. She'd never had Grant talk like this to her, and wasn't sure how to respond really, so she just let it lie.

"How long do you think it's going to take for people to figure things out?" Grant asked, more matter of factly than emotionally.

"Hopefully quickly, because that'll mean he's a match for Kit," Lacey returned, still pointing out silver linings out of habit. Grant could only nod.

They then sat in silence as they waited for Pastor Dan to arrive. Their "talks" over the past couple of weeks had been about *anything* unemotional.

As they heard Pastor Dan climbing the stairs, they stood up and Lacey automatically plucked stray lint off Grant's blazer.

"Love is weird that way, its habits remain even after the loved one is gone," Grandpa Charlie had once said, when asked why he still set two plates at the table after Grandma Kate had died. Grandpa Charlie had taught her a lot about love. "Love is more than a feeling. It's a choice," he'd always said. "Real love comes in when the "want to" has faded." Lacey prayed he was right.

Pastor Dan started their session as he always did, with a prayer, asking God to guide them into all truth so healing could begin. He then instructed them to talk in "I feel" phrases, to limit the feeling of personal attack.

"I know Grant, you have had time to think about things. This *is* an unexpected, maybe *unprecedented* event, so how are you feeling?" Pastor Dan asked.

"Well, the numb has started wearing off," Grant admitted. "I guess right now I'm trying to come to terms with what is truth and what has been deception, and working through those emotions. I know this all happened fourteen years ago, but I'm having to deal with it afresh."

Pastor Dan nodded. "Lacey, Grant and I have been trying to sort through his emotions, and I have relayed the information I felt he needed to work through before the two of you met again. Did the letter help, Grant? I know you had a lot of questions initially about Kit's paternity."

Grant nodded, "It did. I didn't know how Lacey couldn't have known about... the paternity," Grant still couldn't bring himself to say Kit "wasn't his,"

"...but the letter helped me see she wasn't being *purposefully* deceptive."

"Is there anything you would like to say, or add to the letter?" Pastor Dan asked Lacey.

"No," Lacey cleared her throat. "I just want to reiterate that I did not know until a few weeks ago either, and how very, very sorry I am." Lacey glanced at Grant while baring her heart, but he wouldn't make eye contact. "If I could take it all back, I would."

Sensing Grant's distance, Pastor Dan decided to ask, "Grant, how do you feel now?"

It was a full minute before Grant spoke, "I feel betrayed."

There it was.

The truth.

Simple, short, exact.

And not easily fixable.

Pastor Dan was relieved to see tears welling behind Grant's austere expression. In all his years of counseling, that was a good sign someone still cared.

"Lacey, can you mirror talk what Grant said?"

"I hear you saying you feel betrayed and hurt," Lacey said. Grant nodded.

"What else, Grant?" Pastor Dan coaxed, knowing this wouldn't be an easy task for someone brought up to deny their emotions as Grant had been.

"I am struggling with what I feel, versus what I know, versus what God would have me to do," with that, he hung his head and his shoulders slumped. Lacey reached to take his hand, but he flinched away. He wasn't sure which angered him more: his feelings about the situation or the fact he was not in control of his feelings, but at the mercy of them.

Grant's physical response was not lost on Pastor Dan. He was hesitant to dig deeper, since dealing with strong emotions was a new thing for Grant. Before he could redirect the conversation, Lacey spoke up.

"Grant, I know how you feel and…"

"You know how I feel? *You know how I feel*?!" Grant was coming out of his emotional corner now, swinging, his voice exasperated, his face, red and angry, "You have *NO IDEA*, Lacey, what it feels like to find out the love of your life had a child with someone else!"

Now it was Lacey's turn to slump. "Actually, I know *exactly* how that feels," she said, mournfully, her voice reflecting Grant's emotion perfectly, remembering and reliving that day in Nashville when the same news crumbled her world. She remembered she felt engulfed in lies and betrayal and heartbreak.

She didn't know anything could ever be worse, but now she knew knowing *you* had caused the love of your life to feel such a way was worse. Much worse.

Grant looked up at her, quizzically. Her voice was seeped in genuine empathy. Pastor Dan decided to bring the session to an end for the day. Emotions were running too high to reveal any new further information. He didn't want to cause permanent damage.

"Grant, I think that idea you had is a good place to start from: what is *God's* will in this situation? Let's take a week to pray and digest this and then we'll meet back up in a few days."

They ended on a prayer, Lacey dreading her outburst was going to result in her having to divulge more information from her past. Her concerns had progressed from "worried" to "scared." Grant had never kept her at arm's length or been so cold. He had barely looked at her. "At least the meeting didn't end in a divorce," Lacey thought as they said Amen.

THIRTY-FOUR

Lacey had gotten everyone off to school, and was finishing her morning prayers. She'd made a point to pray for Grant's heart to be forgiving and heal, and for God to direct them with clarity. She sighed when she remembered how easy and simple everything used to be when they faced the difficult things together. She was determined to make her marriage work, but slowly realized so many things were not in her control. She cringed as she remembered when she used to judge others' marriage failures. She'd never really understood when people said, "They tried their hardest, but it just didn't work out." She was sad to say she now understood what they meant. It was exactly as they said: "complicated" and "not so cut and dry." She wasn't sure how her situation was going to resolve itself, but she knew one thing for certain: she would definitely have more sympathy for others going through a separation or divorce. She'd never known how truly heartbreaking it could be.

She had just finished tidying up the kitchen when she heard a knock at the door. She was not expecting anyone, so peeped through the keyhole, only to find Brett peering back at her.

"Was your door unlocked? That's not safe, Lace...I thought I taught ya better'n that," Brett jiggled the door handle as he walked through the door.

How was it that the same person could *infuriate* her as much as he *thrilled* her? Both emotions made her feel alive.

"I know how to keep myself safe, Mr. Wright. Have you already forgotten who my Daddy is? And, I'll have you know, I checked from the side window to see *who* was ringing my bell at the most *inopportune* time, so I knew it was you anyway..."

Sensing he knew he'd gotten a rise out of her, Lacey decided to push back a bit.

"*What in the world were you thinking*, showing up at church like that?!"

"Yeah, I wanted to apologize. I had *no intention* of making a scene, Lacey. My intent was to catch a glimpse of Kit, and get outta there! How was I supposed to know half of Houston County was gonna be at your church?"

Brett posed a valid question. He had no way of knowing half of the church from Houston County had diverted to Dickson from a church split after he had shipped out.

"What'd you say brought you here?" she asked, as she laced her running shoes. She was starting to get nervous about the neighbors seeing his motorcycle in her driveway. In a subdivision, appearances were very important, even if you didn't care about them.

"Well, I wanted to apologize mainly, but I also wanted to show you something. What time do you have to pick up the kids?" Brett asked.

"Not 'til three thirty, but I've got to work out and have errands to do…"

"You won't need to work out after *our* errand," Brett waved her plans away like they were excuses. "This won't take long. And you need to get some air…you were looking real stressed Sunday!" Brett winked.

"No thanks to you!" She yelled, swatting him in the arm with the kitchen towel that had hung on her shoulder.

Brett took her beating, then held out a helmet to her and nodded toward the door. He knew Lacey liked to ride, whether it was a Harley or a four wheeler on the muddy back roads.

"Only a few minutes?" Lacey asked, biting her lip.

"Thirty minutes, tops," Brett nodded.

Lacey threw the kitchen towel on the couch and adjusted the strap under her chin, vowing to not let the outing go longer than he promised. Her curiosity was getting the better of her.

They drove out of town, curving around steep hills and valleys, the suburbs morphing into the countryside. The early light glinted off the arcs of hay bales warming up to the morning sun. The sights and smells of the asphalt city gave way to fresh smelling farms. Lacey couldn't help but relax as she breathed it all in contentedly. It'd been too long since she'd gone to the country to relax. She vowed to make time for it at least once a week. As they pulled in to the park's parking lot, Lacey noticed the allotted thirty minutes was up.

Brett took her helmet and grabbed her hand like it was something he did every day and led her toward the woods.

"Just *where* are we going?" Lacey asked, thankful she had on her workout clothes.

"You'll see," Brett said, steadily looking ahead.

His spontaneity was one of the things she loved – and hated - most about him. "You gonna murder me in the woods and chop me up into little pieces?" Lacey joked.

"Only if you keep talking," Brett whispered with a grin as they walked. "Now hush, Missy," he motioned for her to crouch low. They had made their way almost to the top. The people of Dickson knew it as Almost Mountain, because it lacked being a mountain by a few feet. In the winter when all the leaves were gone, the eye could see for miles atop the cliffs.

Brett had made his way to a tall pine tree and motioned for Lacey to follow. He clasped his hands and bent over, waiting to hoist her onto the first branch. Lacey looked at him like he was crazy. Respecting his request to be quiet, she stayed silent, but gave him an "Are-you-crazy-I'm-not-sixteen-anymore-and-am-not-gonna-climb-a-tree" stare. To which he replied with a silent eye roll and "What?! Like-it's-hard? Don't-be-ridiculous-you-have-yoga-pants-on" face and yanked her yoga pants at the thigh for effect.

Lacey remained unmovable - feet solid on the ground. Brett intuitively made military hand gestures, signaling how she should proceed up the first rung of branches. Lacey, flabbergasted, responded in sign language, "What?"

Brett looked at her, genuinely confused and leaned in to whisper in her ear, "I can't tell what you are saying."

"EXACTLY!" Lacey whispered back, with an "I-don't-know-Ranger-signals-you-idiot" stare.

Brett sighed, and climbed up the first branch, and then reached his arm down to help her up. Lacey could tell he was not going to give up. With a sigh, she quietly took his hand, and was shocked to see her name peeping out from under his t-shirt cuff. She had forgotten that was there and was surprised to find she felt a bit honored.

She walked her feet up the trunk while holding onto his arm, wrapped her legs around the branch and Brett then hoisted her the rest of the way onto the branch. They continued this until they were almost at the top of the tree. At one point, midway, Lacey had almost frozen on the branch from fear. Sensing it, Brett put his index finger under her chin, pulled her face up to meet his, pointed to the sky and mouthed, "Look up!" It was enough to break her fear. When they'd almost reached the tip-top, Brett straddled the last branch, his back against the trunk.

"He makes that look easy," Lacey jealously thought, as she accepted his hand one last time. This time he motioned for her to swing her leg over and straddle the branch too, facing outward this time, her back against his.

Lacey paused, keenly aware this was not an appropriate position for a married woman to be in, especially alone in the woods with an ex...THE ex, no less.

Brett saw her pause and knew what she was thinking. Rolling his eyes, he patted the branch in front of him and gave her an "Oh-my-word-Lacey-will-you-please-get-your-head-out-of-the-gutter-and-get-your-tail-up-here" look.

Not wanting to have climbed the tree for nothing, and secretly dying to know what he was going to show her, she grabbed his hand and took her seat in front of him. It took her a minute to get adjusted and calm herself. She had never been able to tolerate heights well.

"Breathe," Brett slowly whispered in her ear, knowing heights weren't her thing, holding her securely around the waist. She tried to slow her breathing and her heart rate and ignore the memories his whispering stirred. Memories like the first day they'd talked when he'd "taught" her how to cast a line and how, from that first moment, she'd felt like she'd found home...She pushed the thoughts out of her mind. "Not an option!" she reminded herself.

As she opened her eyes, Brett's thumb slid from her eye to her chin and pulled forward, stopping in mid-air, his arm fully extended, his thumb acting as a "site," leading her eyes straight ahead. And that's when she saw it.

They overlooked the tops of the woodland trees as far as the eye could see. Pink and white dogwoods danced alongside a winding creek, the sun glinting off the trickling waters looked like a silver necklace winding through the greenery. And in the middle, deep golden daffodils were sprouting. Lacey took a deep breath, and took it all in. It was beautiful! She turned back, giving Brett a big smile. He nodded, then pulled her in close and leaned back, grabbing the leafy limb from above as he moved, pulling it over them, making a makeshift camouflaged hideout. Lacey looked at him quizzically and he again dragged his thumb across her cheek and pointed to a nearby tree at two o'clock. He then tapped the side of her eyes, indicating she should watch there.

It only took a minute for Lacey to see what she was watching for. Brett placed his sunglasses on her nose. With the push of a button, the lenses acted as binoculars. Lacey marveled at the cool "toys" he got to use in his job, and secretly wondered just how deep in Special Ops he really was. Items far away became five times closer and bigger, and Lacey saw a large nest in the crevice of a stone wall. A shadow appeared, and Lacey heard the squeaking of newborn birds moving among the leaves as the shadow loomed larger. Seconds later, a massive bald eagle swooped and soared high above, occasionally hovering above the nest as if "checking" on the little eaglets.

Brett placed the sunglasses back on himself, and tapped the side a few times, then motioned to Lacey with a "snapshot" signal. He put the glasses back on her nose and let her take a few photos before motioning for her to descend.

Silently and slowly, they climbed back down until Lacey could contain herself no longer. "Oh my WORD, Brett! Did you SEE that?! Holy Cow! We had to be five feet from them! I bet I could 'a reached out and PET them!" Lacey was ecstatic.

Brett was adjusted his equipment and smiled ear to ear, relieved to see a look of happiness on her face. He was hoping this might bring her joy. Lord knows she needed some in her life right now, and he'd do anything to make her happy.

"How in the world did you KNOW about this?!" Lacey asked, amazed.

"I saw the coordinates in that newspaper clipping y'all had on your eagle board project in your kitchen," Brett explained.

Lacey stopped, amused. "The *coordinates,* huh?" Lacey teased.

"Don't joke," Brett said, misinterpreting her comment.

"No! I'm impressed, Brett! Truly!" Lacey went into a deep, imitating voice:

"Hey, Brett, what you doing tomorrow?"

"Oh, there's some new eaglets in the Park…"

"Oh really?"

"Oh, yeah, I'm just gonna follow the coordinates, scout out the area, do surveillance, and FIND them, climb a bloody TREE and WATCH them! And then I'm gonna take my trusty spy glasses and take the first pictures of them!"

Lacey was smiling big and chuckling now, genuinely amazed. Brett laughed, too.

"It's kinda what I do," Brett shrugged. It was moments like these when he was reminded how very different his line of work must appear to civilians.

"It's *amazing!*" Lacey oozed. Brett wasn't sure if she was referring to the eagle, to his work, or both.

"I was hoping you'd like that," Brett said, nodding. It was so good to see a smile on her face again, as wild and untamed as the picture in her hallway she had of herself performing on stage in high school. Before drunken mistakes and kidney diseases and paternity tests had come into the picture. The smile of being carefree and blissful.

"Mission accomplished," he thought.

"So, you forgive me for that Sunday debacle?" He asked, leaning against the pine beside him.

Lacey couldn't help but say the line she knew he was waiting to hear, "Just this one time, I guess," she said with a knowing smile. "Here. Get a picture of me in front of this awesome tree with the daffodils behind me," Lacey said.

She stood on the large roots of a big oak tree, leaning against its massive trunk. Its roots were intertwined and exposed. Trees had always held special meaning to Lacey.

Our family, like branches on a tree,
We all grow in different directions,
But our roots remain as one.

Brett chuckled, "You and trees!" he mumbled with a grin. He snapped a couple of pictures at different angles, just to be safe.

"You gonna put this by your *other* daffodil photo in your hallway?" he asked, unashamedly. They shared a knowing look. He could always see straight through her.

"I see you still notice everything," Lacey said.

"Only the important things," Brett replied.

She looked down to deflect his gaze and started to walk across the roots to retrieve her phone from Brett. But before she could move, she heard a creak. Brett yelled her name as she looked up to see a widow maker branch land wobbly on a branch right above her. A childhood classmate had been killed by such a branch, so she knew firsthand the falling limbs rightfully deserved the name they'd been given. She moved to get out of the way, but her foot caught in a root. She was stuck.

Brett assessed the situation and his training kicked in. He leapt, tackling her, and wrapped one arm tight around her waist and the other protectively around her head. He tried to wrap her legs tight as he crossed his ankles around hers and protect her as much as he could as they rolled like a hewn log down the embankment. Luckily, the bank became grassy and wasn't as steep as Brett had thought, leveling off into a clearing. Brett had been through worse, but when they stopped Lacey's eyes were closed.

"Lacey! Lace!" Brett yelled, blowing on her face.

She slowly blinked her eyes. "Disoriented, but not dilated," Brett observed, relieved.

"You ok, baby?!" Brett asked. She lay in the same position as the night she'd found out he was joining up, and they both let their guards down and their hearts show. Her hair billowed out her – flushed faced and wide-eyed...so beautiful.

It took a minute for Lacey to get her bearings, but she, too, remembered a tumble they had once taken, falling head over heels in love fifteen years ago. And now, his arms around her and his body atop her, she once again felt herself falling hard.

"This reminds me of another time we took a tumble," she whispered with a slight grin, rubbing the scar on her forehead.

Relief washed over Brett. "Man, you scared me! You ok?" he asked, getting even closer and inspecting her scarred forehead. Lacey could smell his fear, feel his heartbeat on her own chest.

"Yeah...it's a sensitive old wound..." she whispered, her voice cracking as she glanced away.

Realizing she was fine, Brett was instantly aware of just how close they were and how they'd landed.

"Some old wounds never heal," Brett said as he looked down at her, her body under his, barely breathing. He couldn't hide the way his voice cracked. He was overcome with all he'd lost, and how he hadn't been able to be there for her when she needed him most. He kissed the scar on her forehead, then rested his forehead on hers, his eyes closed, straddling the fence of right and wrong, not knowing which one to pray for. Brett loved Lacey, but making moves on another man's wife wasn't ok by any standards, even *if* the wife was Lacey.

Despite knowing she shouldn't, Lacey looked up at Brett, her love for him clear and apparent. That was all it took.

He kissed her.

Intently, intensely and deeply.

This kiss was different than their last one – it was real and genuine, filled with all the raw emotion of past hopes, passion and love and present regret and repentance and, yes, love. He still loved her - he always had. He tried to kiss away the hurt, the mistakes, and all the misunderstandings, as if the intensity of his love could make everything right again. He tried to convey the depths of his sorrow and regret, all the things he wanted to say but couldn't. His kiss apologized for being so young and stupid. It spoke of his good intentions and deep regret. Even more, it begged for another chance.

Lacey was conflicted. Weary of struggling with her heart, deciphering what was right or wrong, and playing referee between her flesh and her spirit. She melted into Brett's kiss and for the first time in fourteen years, all felt *right* again. If only for a moment.

Brett finally stopped, but didn't pull away. He held her, cheek to cheek, too scared to move, each one of them wanting to stay locked in that moment. Fearful of what was waiting on the other side of the kiss, he waited.

That's when he felt her head rest heavily on the curve of his arm. Her spot with her name on it. He bravely opened his eyes.

Unexpected relief washed over him as his Southern angel smiled. He tightened his grip, and rested his chin on her head.

"What in the world are we gonna do?" Lacey asked, desperation, sorrow and sincere wonder filling her question.

Brett sighed, knowing there was no easy answer. Even if Lacey's conscience allowed it, getting back together would mean ripping apart a family – something even Brett wasn't ok with. But remaining apart also separated a family – THEIR family...the one that *should* have been.

Lacey was struggling, like Brett, but her struggle was with choosing to walk in the Spirit rather than give into flesh and blood. She knew it was not right to entertain the thoughts dancing through her mind, but it also wasn't right for her Dad to have hidden her letters, altering her fate. She didn't *want* to leave Grant...she loved him, truly and deeply. Nothing had changed in that area, except perhaps *Grant's* love for *her*. Her struggle violated all she'd ever believed: that one had to hate someone to contemplate cheating on them. She never would have believed it was possible for someone to have feelings for another and it have absolutely nothing at all to do with their spouse, yet here she was, stuck between two different men and two different paths – once again. However, this time *Brett* was present and *Grant* was aloof.

She'd always prided herself on being faithful, and doing the right thing, the proper thing...yet here she was, laying in an isolated field with another man.

"What is a *married wife and mother* doing LAYING IN A FIELD kissing *another man*?!" Lacey knew she was on thin ice, and started to turn away.

"Don't go," Brett begged. "Stay right here," he whispered, begging for more time.

Lacey paused, not knowing if this moment would ever come again.

"Lace..." he softly said. "You're the best thing to ever happened to me! When I didn't get a response to my letters, I thought you were done and I just couldn't handle it. I hung on for twelve weeks, baby, but then the weekend we had our first break from BASIC I just lost it. Got drunk as a skunk and woke up with someone. I don't remember hardly anything…" His words sounded generic, but they were genuine. Lacey waited, knowing he needed to have his say.

"I'm so sorry, and I'll forever regret it, and…" he paused then continued,

"… I love you."

There it was.

He'd finally said it.

There could be no more denying, no more wondering. It was not merely a sentiment.

It was a question,

a hope, a confession,

and a *proposal*

And it was a standing offer if she should ever accept it.

It was an honor,

a temptation

…and a lot of pressure!

She realized, with precise clarity, that from this moment on, whatever happened would be at *her* call… and on *her* shoulders.

She looked at him, longingly and sadly, before speaking.

"My heart was broken into a million pieces, thinking you'd just abandoned me after all that we'd shared and planned…" Lacey's voice faded out as she decided what she was or was not going to say next.

"Until a few weeks ago," Lacey finished.

"What happened?" Brett asked, hoping she was going to say she'd decided to get back together with him.

Lacey sighed; still not certain it was the right thing to do.

"I found the letters."

"Where?" Brett asked, calmly. He wasn't shocked like she'd because he knew he had written them.

"In Dad's desk drawer. All of them. A hundred of them, just like you said. Apparently, everyone thought it was better to make my future decisions for me," Lacey frowned now, mourning what should have been *her* choice.

Brett sighed and hung his head, flopping beside her on his back, mourning the same thing.

"You don't say," he mumbled. They lay in silence, but each thinking thoughts of what could've been. What should've been. What wasn't.

"Well, that would've changed a lot of things," he finally said, flatly.

Lacey began to laugh. Brett had a knack of stating the obvious. She laughed at that, and at the absurdity of the situation she now found herself in. Brett joined in, feeling it, too.

"Jenn said we are like a soap opera," Lacey said between hard laughs. They were both in a full on tizzy now, their laughs echoing off the cliffs.

"Can I ask you a question?" Brett asked after their laughter had died down.

"Shoot," Lacey said.

"How...how did you *not* know Kit was mine?" he asked gently, so as not to insult her.

Lacey took a deep breath. "When I saw the text with the picture that day, I couldn't handle it. I went to the lake house for a week to mourn and cry and then ran straight back to college and eloped with Grant the next week. He'd been wanting to get married for a while, but I kept pushing things off hoping to win his mom's favor. But after everything that happened that past week, I just wanted to be married and settled. And...I loved him...*love* him," Lacey corrected herself.

Hearing her say that cut Brett, but she continued, "I had no clue, Brett. We eloped in a frenzy a week later, so...I never thought of the possibility of you being her father," Lacey frowned. "I'm truly sorry."

Brett nodded and then sighed as Lacey's alarm sounded, reminding her of her carpool duties.

He helped her to her feet and brushed the grass out of her hair. Before she could grab her phone, he grabbed her elbow and said, "Just one more minute?"

Lacey paused, but relented, glad for the chance to let him hold her one last time before returning to reality. As he made a mental memory, they looked out over the sea of daffodils blowing in the breeze.

"We belong together, Lace...you *gotta* know that..." Brett whispered, his tone pleading. "And we have a *right* to be together!

If your dad hadn't of interfered, you would have made different choices. I *know* you would have…"

Lacey knew he was right. They *did* belong together. And things *would* be different, starting with her last name.

The alarm sounded again, pulling them back into the present.

They descended Almost Mountain, put on their helmets and mounted the bike, his last statement staying heavy in the air – and on her heart. They didn't speak. There was really nothing *to* say.

As they drove the windy back roads back toward Dickson and their problems, Lacey held on tight, vowing to hold on as tightly to her convictions, and tried to convince herself she did not desire what was forbidden.

The devil had done his homework, laying all her deepest desires at her feet - desires she didn't even know she had, ready for the taking. He had all but crammed the juicy apple down her parched throat, promising to restore everything she missed, reminding her of the things she had convinced herself she didn't want anymore…but did.

This was going to be much harder than she had thought.

As Brett pulled into the driveway, they passed Mya on her daily run. Lacey grimaced. She did not want to be asked questions she did not have answers to – or answer *truthfully* some of the ones she *did* – but the questions would come since her best friend had seen her holding onto her ex on the back of a Harley. Lacey blushed at the thought of what assumptions she and the neighbors might make, and the gossip that would follow.

Mya rounded the corner as Brett roared away. There would be no dodging her – or her questions. Instead, she opened her mailbox and pretended to rummage through the junk mail, and waited for the scolding.

She was shocked, however, when Mya did not stop. She said not a word, but kept jogging. She breathed a sigh of relief, knowing she needed to explain, but not wanting to just yet.

Her relief turned to conviction, however, when she heard Mya yell over her shoulder.

"You're not running fast enough"

To the uninformed observer, it was merely a friend ribbing her bestie for not running, but Lacey knew what Mya was referring to, remembering the first time Mya had seen Brett and she advised her to "run like Joseph". It was sharp and cutting - and exactly what she knew she needed to hear. She vowed to go see Mya later, after she'd been able to digest everything herself.

Lacey knew *exactly* the danger she was in, and what was at stake. She'd even taught the "Affair Proofing Your Marriage" classes at church, for Pete's sake! She knew of the six steps to an affair she was at five and a half, standing in the middle of the rolling blaze. None of that knowledge seemed to affect her emotions, however.

Her mind still whirled as she waited in carpool. She'd been praying fervently for God to speak to her ever since she'd gotten home from her trek in the woods. With a sigh, she grabbed her Message bible out of the console and flopped it open.

"Desperate times call for desperate measures," Lacey thought as she did a blind flip through the Scriptures. The Lord met her mustard seed of faith with a whisper in her ear, as she opened her eyes to Proverbs 6:

Dear friend, if you've gone into hock with your neighbor or locked
yourself into a deal with a stranger,
If you've impulsively promised the shirt off your back and
now find yourself shivering out in the cold,
Friend, don't waste a minute, get yourself out of that mess!
You're in that man's clutches!
Go, put on a long face; act desperate.
Don't procrastinate! There's no time to lose!
Run like a deer from the hunter!
Fly like a bird from the trapper!

Amazed, she continued to read until her doubt was replaced with assurance of an undeniable answer to prayer:

Adultery is a brainless act,
soul-destroying, self-destructive!
Expect a bloody nose, a black eye,
and a reputation ruined for good.
For jealousy detonates rage in a cheated husband;

wild for revenge, he won't make allowances.
Nothing you say or pay will make it all right;
neither bribes nor reason will satisfy him.

"I hear you, Lord," Lacey whispered as the kids climbed into the car.

THIRTY-FIVE

By the time Will and Jenn arrived at the hospital, the surgeons at Vanderbilt had already finished Kit's exploratory surgery and she was sleeping off the anesthesia. It was a necessary and standard procedure, but lengthy. Surgical procedures had, sadly, become routine for Kit. Will and Jenn made a habit of heading to Vanderbilt to keep Grant and Lacey company during surgery to help pass the time, and today was no different.

Jenn ran to Lacey for a hug, and Will made his way to Grant.

"So, how're things going?" Will asked.

"Okay…" Will gave Grant a quizzical look.

"Not so good, honestly…Still trying to find my bearings," Grant admitted, fumbling with his coffee cup.

"Things ok with Lacey?" Will asked more directly.

Grant took a big breath in. He wasn't used to divulging personal information – especially the sort of an emotional nature. But even *he* had to admit it felt good to be able to talk about the situation with someone who knew what was going on. He and Will had become close friends through Lacey and Jenn's relationship. Grant knew fifteen years ago he was a good guy when he saw him hauling Lacey, wheelchair and all, up the stairs to her parents' house – and did so everyday the entire time she was bound to it. He had proven himself to be a valuable asset to her family. Grant now saw him as an invaluable well of knowledge about Lacey – Will knew her both before and after Brett had entered the picture.

"Not really. I've seen and learned things about Lacey I never knew and…it's like she was a whole different person! My reserved wife used to be an extroverted singer performer?! Oh, and

I saw Mr. Wright at church…" The two men shared knowing nods. "It's a lot to take in…not to mention the other…" Grant's voice - and gaze - faded off into the distance.

Will knew he needed some encouragement – and insight. "I can't even imagine, man. And Brett? Yeah, he'd make *anyone* feel insecure!" Will shook his head as he raised his Coke to his lips. "Once we were all shooting skeet - he had never shot before – so we all thought we would take advantage of his inflated ego to make a little money. We told him we'd all give him a dollar for every skeet he shot, but he'd have to give a dollar to the ammo fund for every one he missed," Will grinned just thinking about it, and then turned to face Grant, stone faced. "Do you know that turkey walked away with a hundred and thirty-two dollars?! He hit TWENTY-TWO outta TWENTY-FOUR, I kid you not! And had never shot skeet a day in his life!" Will shook his head. "I think that was the day I told him he needed to join the Rangers, what with his hand-eye coordination, and all…"

Will sympathized with Grant. He could only imagine how hard it would be to discover your daughter of thirteen years was not really yours, compiled by having to deal with the thought of your wife being with another man. He felt an obligation to help Grant. After all, he would want someone to do the same for him, if he were in the same situation.

"As far as Lacey's concerned…she *did* have a personality shift right after the wreck, that's for sure. She used to be the life of the party – always full of energy, always positive with a spring in her step, not reserved like she is now. And, boy, could she sing!" Will shook his head, smiling, just thinking about those bonfire jams. "Maybe her hit to the head subdued her a bit? I don't know. But what I *do* know is that if you are worried about her turning into the woman she used to be, don't. You'd be pleased as punch if she reverted back to her old self. She was spunky and lively and fun, but she was always also a good girl, dedicated to the Lord and her family. She's not gonna lose that." Will shook his head, assuredly.

"*Good* girl, huh?" Grant mumbled, genuinely asking.

Will paused, knowing the real question he was asking. "*Yes*, good girl. Did you *see* Brett?" Will shot back.

Grant nodded affirmatively and cringed. "Oh, I *saw* him, alright!"

"Well, Lacey dated him for nigh on *four years* and nothing happened…'til the night she thought they were gonna elope. If you ask me, she's got the strength of Job, what with his charm and their chemistry and all…"

Grant nodded understandingly and seemed a bit relieved. He knew Will would cut straight with him.

"Yeah," Grant mumbled, letting his veneer crack a bit.

"Y'all talkin' to anybody?" Will asked.

"Pastor Holt," Grant said, knowing he was referring to a counselor. "But overnight I found out my wife and my life's been a lie. I honestly don't know *what* to believe!"

Will could feel Grant's frustration. "Listen, I don't know what Brother Dan's been telling you, Grant, but I've always heard, "The truth shall set you free."

Grant laughed, "Well, that's ironic, because that's actually what he's been saying."

"Did he also tell you the truth hurts sometimes?" Will asked. Grant's smile faded.

"I know that full well, already," Grant said, looking over at Kit.

"Well, I know you might not want to hear this, but you're not ever gonna break the bond they got. Don't even try."

Grant looked up, surprised. Will continued.

"They go way back. He was the first person who wasn't intimidated by her pain, and understood her brokenness. They got a bond stronger than steel, and you can't compete with that…But you don't need to."

Grant gave Will a quizzical look, before Will went on, "They came into each other's lives with deep wounds, at a time when they had no one else. And no one could remotely understand all they'd been through. They found a *comfort* in each other, *grew up* together, *relied* on each other, *competed* and *pushed* each other to become the best they could be."

Grant was getting perturbed. "Is there a point to this, Will?"

"Point is, there's something in each of them the other one *still* needs. It's not romantic, but it runs deep." Grant looked at him, unbelieving.

Will sighed. "Yes, it *was* once wrapped in romance, but not anymore. You're gonna have to respect that bond, though, or you might be left with nothing more than a shell of her. I know you're worried about them, and yes, Lacey's got a lot of kinks to work out – but I think Brett is pivotal in her healing. It's gonna work out, Grant. You just gotta hold steady."

"How do I do that?" Grant asked.

"Let go," Will said. "Think about it, Grant - with *all* they had in common, despite *all* that, she Still. Chose. You." Will poked Grant in the chest for emphasis. "You gotta trust that, man."

"But how am I gonna move forward? It's bad enough I gotta share Kit, but now it feels like I'm also sharing *Lacey* with another man…"

Will shook his head, "It feels like that right *now*, sure. But you know the only thing worse than "sharing" her?" Will asked. Grant looked at him silently.

"Losing her."

Grant glanced at Lacey across the room and nodded in agreement.

Will went on, "You're gonna have to be patient. You both need time to let your hearts catch up with all your minds just learned. I know you feel betrayed, but don't *stay* in that place. You don't have the luxury or the right to be vengeful. That's God's job. *Your* job is to be *loving* and *obey*. You got bigger things at stake than your ego right now, anyway. Kit needs ya'll."

"But what am I gonna do?" Grant asked. "I saw a video of Brett and Lacey singing from high school…how can I compete with *that*?!"

"Well, you're gonna have to bring your best game. You need to woo her like you're about to lose her, cause if you *don't*, you *will*. He's got chemistry, but you two have substance. Remember back to what bonded you two together and do that stuff. And pray. The devil is doing double duty on you two, and you can't let him win this one. You might get bloody, bruised and broken but you've got to come out *together*."

Grant nodded in agreement

"You go back further with Brett than you do with me, Will…why are you helping *me* so much?" Grant asked, genuinely wondering.

"Cause I can't get legal advice any cheaper than you…" he said with a grin.

"Hey, why *did* they officially break up?" Grant asked.

"Well, *I* heard she met a better man," Will said with a wink, as he bent over to tie his toddler's shoe.

"That, and him getting another girl pregnant on his first night's leave sure didn't help," Will mumbled.

The words rang in Grant's head. He knew by the way Will answered so nonchalantly that Will thought he knew already, so he played it off cool. But inside he was a mess. Empathy and anger and thankfulness all flooded his heart at once. Anger that he felt second fiddle: thankfulness that Brett *did* slip, and newfound empathy for Lacey started to bubble up.

"So *that's* what she meant when she said she knew what it felt like to have the love of your life have a baby with someone else!" Grant mused.

The thought was a comfort to him. As he looked across the waiting room at his wife, his heart ached for her, wondering what other hidden wounds she bore. Suddenly he was given a window into her soul and he saw how much more difficult this was on her than him. She *also* knew the pain of betrayal, having the "worst case scenario" dumped your lap. And it would be her, not him, neighbors would judge. Something that might be a fleeting embarrassment for a man could *ruin* a woman in a small town. Despite his own pain, his heart ached for his wife. Thank God she was tough! She constantly showed him just how strong she was, with all she'd had to carry through the years. He longed to wrap his arms around her, but that seemed awkward at this point, so he settled on getting her a coffee. As he went to fill up their cups, Will joined him at the cart.

"I'll tell you one thing, though," Will said in a whisper. "If Brett Wright was coming back into *my* wife's life?" he paused, clucked his tongue, and shook his head, "I *sure* wouldn't be sleeping in no pool house!"

Grant handed Lacey a coffee and took the chair beside her. She was surprised, but pleased.

"This reminds me of when you had Kit," Grant said. "I sat in this waiting room while they prepared you for the C-section."

"Really?" Lacey asked, happy he was talking to her.

"Yeah…And just like then, I was scared to death I might lose everything that meant anything to me…"

Lacey was shocked speechless. Before she could respond, they were interrupted by Kit's surgeon. Dr. Schwartz updated them on Kit's progress. The tests weren't currently showing the numbers they wanted, so they could not proceed with a kidney transplant even if they *had* a donor.

"Lacey, why don't you get out of here and get a shower and sleep in your own bed. I'll watch over Kit tonight." Grant encouraged.

Lacey was adamant. "No, I need to stay…"

"Honey, she's gonna be doped up all night anyway. Go get some sleep and come back tomorrow when she's awake."

Lacey relented, "I guess you're right…"

Out of habit Grant hugged her and kissed her head. Surprisingly, it didn't feel awkward. Grant asked Jenn and Will to escort to her car before she could change her mind.

THIRTY-SIX

It had been a very long day at the hospital, but Lacey couldn't bring herself to go home just yet. She had too much on her mind to spend all night in a quiet house.

"A quiet house does not respect the boundaries of a troubled mind," Lacey thought. She pulled into a parking spot on the town square to call Mya, succumbing to hot tears.

"Yeah, it's not the news we wanted to hear, but not a deal breaker...and Grant is acting weird. First, cold- then, hot...and I can't be around Brett cause I don't want to add a big red "A" to my sweater collection...I'm just gonna grab a bite to eat and head home to sleep the day off," She heard Mya send her love before hanging up.

The Boardwalk's neon lights bounced off her hood, boasting of the truly awesome sandwiches they served, reminding Lacey she hadn't eaten since breakfast.

****

By the time Brett showed up, news had spread through town Lacey had hit the stage, and the Boardwalk was busting at the seams! Brett had started getting sporadic texts from Lacey that got progressively more frequent, until his phone was buzzing hotter than an M-60d during a surprise enemy attack.

The music hit him hard as he stepped through the door. He made his way to the bar, where he was greeted by Bulldog.

"Brett Wright! Well, slap my momma! How in the world you doin?!" Bulldog yelled over the roar.

"Good, man!" Brett said, accepting the big bear hug and beer Bulldog gave him. He learned that Bulldog had taken over the

Boardwalk after his Mom had passed, and was the creator of their famous sandwiches.

Lacey was back in her element. It was amazing how well she could sing, when obviously tipsy. Her voice was still strong and powerful. The karaoke machine had been replaced by home-grown musicians, and every toe in the audience was tapping. She still had it.

Brett leaned over to Bulldog, "She been here long?"

Bulldog nodded as he dried the clean glasses with a towel, "Since about nine thirty...drinkin' since ten. Said she "didn't get the news she was hoping for," he shrugged, not knowing what specific news that might be.

Brett knew.

"What's she drinkin'?" Brett asked.

"Jack," Bulldog answered. Brett's head shot up.

"*STRAIGHT*," Bulldog added, sharing a "knowing look" with Brett.

"Yep. She's hurtin," Brett mumbled as he took a swig of his beer and turned toward the stage. He hoped her drinking didn't mean she'd heard he wasn't a match for Kit. He'd only known her to drink Jack straight once, and that was the night they'd gotten word her classmate had died in the Gulf.

"The stronger the drink, the deeper the sorrow," he thought with dismay.

He wasn't planning on staying, but he was committed. She was his girl, and her well-being was in his hands.

Lacey was singing one of her favorite sad songs, *Release Me*, when she spotted Brett. Her voice was a soft, melodic ribbon and wrapped around Brett like a lasso, binding him tight and pulling him toward her. Her eyes were speaking volumes as her voice slid over the words:

Is there any other way we can do this without you leaving?
Is there any other way I can still stay?
I love you, but it's a draining battle,
My salvation and destruction, loving you this way.
Release me... *

The audience turned to see who she was looking at so intensely. The ones who knew their history nodded and turned back around. They knew Lacey was Brett's girl, and they figured he would show up, stopping all their fun. Brett wouldn't shirk his duty; he would protect his girl…even if she was in her thirties and married. Brett watched in wide-eyed wonder. Even sloppy drunk, she sang like an angel.

After the song ended, she managed to walk down the stage steps and sauntered over to Brett's stool. She fell heavily onto him and instinctively Brett grabbed her around the waist to hold her steady, more protective than romantic.

"Well, speak of the devil! You's just the man I's hopin' to see!" she swooned, wrapping her arms around him and entwining her fingers behind his neck, taking advantage of his protective move.

"I kinda figured that by the thirty-eight text messages you sent me," he said, pulling away from her as he eased her onto the bar stool facing him.

The crowd turned to see what the commotion was, but quickly turned their attention back to their own tables once they realized Lacey wasn't going to sing anymore. Being a small town, they all knew about Kit's situation, and most were surprised they hadn't seen her in the Boardwalk sooner. They knew stress can get to a body. Brett didn't have to worry about any of them spreading word of Lacey's condition. They had their own share of problems. Sorrow forms tight bonds between people, creating an atmosphere of shared camaraderie. Pain and empathy run so deep all judgments are pushed aside - sad but comforting quality that made bars more welcoming than church, at times. These people understood needing to escape from things you cannot change and provided space to heal, with anonymity.

Lacey gave him a tipsy smile before turning to order another drink.

"Kami!" She shouted her kamikaze order to Bulldog, but Brett was behind her shaking his head "no" and gave Bulldog a "slit throat" signal indicating he should cut her off. He had just enough time to bring his hand up to his mouth and do a "chewing" motion silently to order her some "sober food" before Lacey whirled back around and leaned into him. As she gave him another hug, he took the opportunity to shove away her partially filled drink glasses, lest she find more alcohol some other way. He detangled her arms from around his neck before interrogating her.

"So, Lace, d'you hear anything from Vandy yet?" he asked as he handed her a water.

"As a matter of fact, I did! Just tonight!" she yelled, over emphasizing the last word, her cheery tone not matching the emotions that lay underneath. He was hoping those sad feelings would hurry the sobering process…if not physically, at least mentally. It worked. He'd used that tactic more than a few times on his Army buddies.

"Good news?" he asked, keeping a steady hand on her hip, to keep her from slipping off the stool.

Lacey shrugged. "Not so good. Not "rejection," but the numbers aren't what they want yet. Even if you come back as a match, they won't do surgery until her numbers go up."

"But that's not what I's gonna talk to you about… I've been doin a lot – and I mean a LOT – of thinking and I've decided something," her voice got steadily slower and lower. She absent-mindedly picked a stray thread off his shoulder before rubbing the back of his head with her fingers, like she used to, before continuing, "You are right, Mister Wright! You are 100% absolutely, t-totally right! We do deserve to be together! I mean, we can't stop destiny, right?! I'm tired of fightin' it, Brett…"

Just then, Bulldog placed the hamburger and fries in front of her.

Lacey looked at them warily. "You tryin' to sober me up, Private?" she asked. Brett couldn't help but chuckle.

"Well that's a first!" she laughed as she shrugged and started eating, but even a burger and fries couldn't stop her rampant words. Lacey continued proclaiming her undying love, but it didn't give Brett joy. Yes, she was saying what he had been praying to hear, but it wasn't the way he'd imagined it. Still, "a drunk mind speaks the truth," he thought. Maybe there was hope, yet.

"Oh! And did I tell you I found the letters?! Over a *hundred* of them Brett, and so lovely!" she swooned, as she caressed his cheek and laid her hand – heavily – on his shoulder.

"Anyway, my point, Private, is this," she interrupted. "I want to be with you."

Her words were sober, solid and sure, her gaze steady. It caught Brett off guard. The conditions weren't perfect, but could she be having a change of heart?

Before he could respond, Lacey grabbed his hand and jumped off her stool. "Oh my word, Brett! This is my song!" Brett cringed. At the rate of her sobering, he might be dancing for a very long time.

"C'mon, Cowboy! You still owe me a dance!" She cajoled as *Cowboys** started playing.

He knew better than to argue, but he led her onto the patio, hoping the cool air would speed the sobering process. Luckily, the next song was a slow one.

"Thank God for small favors," Brett thought, as she placed her hand in his and she rested her heavy head on his shoulder. He felt himself relax, lowering his head and inhibitions as they swayed to the music.

Well ,you say this is hard on you
But, baby, do you know what it puts me through?
Seeing him holding you, and touching you
Doing all the little things I had planned to do,
Playing Daddy to our kids, swapping out my name for his.
I know it's hard, but it's harder watching him
*Livin' my should've been...**

He could feel himself getting lost. The scent of her hair and perfume, the sway of her body on his...he had decided to keep things on the "up and up" - but that was before he held the woman of his dreams in his arms. Brett was conflicted about acting on his desires. He let his mind, and his hands, wander down to the small of her back and around her waist – holding both her and their memories tightly. He was thankful she let him.

Before he could get too nostalgic, the next song started – an upbeat, country dance song and Lacey twirled away, skipping into the bar saying, "Yesss! This is my fave-or-ite!"

"Oh no, little lady! You are DONE for the night!" He said, grabbing her wrist and flipping her over his shoulder like a sack of taters.

He motioned to Bulldog that he'd pay up later while Lacey threw an old fashioned, child-like fit – failing her arms and kicking. Half the people in the bar turned to stare and laughed as Brett swatted her fanny.

"A'ight, now! Enough with that! Don't make me have to spank you when you get home!" he threatened.

That subdued her, at least until he'd safely buckled her in his truck.

By the time Brett ran around to the other side, however, Lacey had unlocked his door and slid to the middle seat.

"Lord, help me," he muttered under his breath before climbing in to the cab. Brett was a Ranger. He spent most of his time in combat on missions so secret he wasn't sure even the President knew all the details. He knew five different ways to kill a man with a dull spoon, and had performed two of them. He'd once spent a night under a pile of dead bodies waiting for his relief helicopter to pick him up. Nothing scared him.

Nothing but her.

Like Lacey, the past week he'd also been thinking and vowed he wasn't going to pursue her. She had a life – a good life – with Grant and the kids. He didn't want to be the man to break up a family – it violated the Code. But now, with Lacey putting the schmooze on so hard? He was going to have to stay extra focused to keep that vow tonight.

As he drove Lacey home, she wasn't making things easy. The alcohol had made her extra touchy-feely, and if he wasn't shifting gears, he was pushing her hands away. First, she rubbed his biceps, then the back of his hair. At the red light, she started to go in for a kiss but spotted some women in the car beside them she knew, and started waving frantically at them.

"Roll the window down, Brett! I know them from church and I need to tell Sheryl that I'll return her casserole dish this Sunday!" Lacey begged, still waving and grinning like a goon.

Brett glanced down, and the juxtaposition made him laugh out loud. The women surely knew Lacey! Their mouths were agape in stunned amazement. He grabbed Lacey's hands, but he couldn't stop her from then coming at him with a kiss on his cheek. Not sure what to do, he nodded to the ladies and smiled politely before speeding on under the green light.

"Oh, I'm pretty sure you're gonna hear from her before Sunday, babe. Probably first thing tomorrow morning!" he laughed out loud, imagining the stories they'd concoct and spread.

Brett had finally relented and let her rest her head on his shoulder, hoping for a reprieve. He had hoped she'd sobered up a bit, but she stopped at every flower along the drive, telling it how much she loved it. At this rate it was going to take an hour to get her into the house. He again tossed her over his shoulder and wrangled with the key at the front door.

"I hear you grunting," she teased him. "You're not as fit as you used to be!" she sang out.

"You either, Missy. Thus, the grunting," Brett retorted.

His words must've cut. It caused her to hush, so at least there was a silver lining.

"Shoulda insulted her first thing," he thought with a laugh, knowing she wouldn't remember it in the morning anyway.

She had told him yesterday Jake would be spending the night at Mya's and he knew Grant was with Kit, so he didn't worry when he made a racket getting in the house.

"Shhhhhh! You're gonna wake up the kids!" Lacey whispered in a non-whisper.

"They're at Mya's," Brett reminded her as he toted her back through her hallway of memories toward her room. The imagery wasn't lost on him. It seemed symbolic - him walking back into her life - still supporting her in her weak times.

"And what she didn't know, because she couldn't see," he thought, reciting a song lyric, "is how I needed her as much as she needed me."

He still needed her. She brought out the best in him. She was his cheerleader and coach – believing in him and challenging him to do better things and things better. He didn't know what direction their lives were going to take now, but he knew one thing: he'd accept whatever she'd give him, even if only friendship, to keep her in his life.

The full moonlight streamed through the open plantation blinds, allowing Brett to walk her safely to the bed. He couldn't help but remember the last time he was carried her to bed.

"Focus," Brett reprimanded himself.

As he reached for a blanket, she grabbed him around the neck and kissed him – from the whiskey or desire, Brett wasn't sure. Her quick move had surprised him, threw him off balance and he landed on top of her, just as she'd hoped. He was able to pull away, but her mouth formed the word,

"Stay."

He paused. The moonlight created a glow around her, making her look seventeen again. He took a mental snapshot, their memories both comforted and haunted him. They tortured him daily. He was tempted, but shook his head instead.

"No?" Lacey asked, sincerely.

Brett shook his head again. "Not like this, babygirl," Brett whispered, kissing her forehead as he got up to get the blanket. Lacey was not so easily deterred. She pulled him in, kissing him like she used to: boldly, unapologetically and unashamedly. It was intoxicating. Brett had been desired many times by many women, but rarely loved. And never loved *and* desired.

At the risk of hurting her feelings, he pulled away quickly without saying a word, knowing if he stayed, he'd soon cross the point of no return. He grabbed a blanket from the hope chest at the foot of her bed, noticing Grandpa Charlie's initials carved in the far corner. The same chest, ironically, that Grandpa Charlie had made thinking a marriage – to Brett - would be eminent. No telling how many hopes and dreams and assumptions lay invisibly hidden within that chest. As he wrapped the blanket tightly around her, Lacey broke the silence.

"Brett, it's you. It's always been you! I was so wrong to run away! I was young and confused and just…prideful! I am so, so sorry…I know I'm too sloppy for you to even consider being with me right now, but…will you ever forgive me?"

Brett didn't hesitate. "Always. Now get some sleep," he whispered as he slowly closed the door. What he heard next was barely a whisper, but distinct and clear,

"I love you, Brett."

And there it was.

Brett walked down the hall of memories with a huge smile. He didn't know the future. He didn't know if they would ride off into the sunset or only become "co-parents." He didn't even know where Uncle Sam was gonna send him tomorrow. Nothing in his life was sure, but this one thing was: *whatever* happened tomorrow or any other day, nothing on earth could ever steal that moment or knowledge from him. The knowledge that Lacey Wilson loved him. Truly.

THIRTY-SEVEN

It wasn't an alarm clock, but the smell of bacon that woke Lacey up the next day. Like a college frat boy after a three day weekend binge, she stumbled into the bathroom to be greeted by a frizzy haired, raccoon eyed, crumbled-shirted reflection, screaming a silent testimony of her raucous behavior the night before.

She faced herself in the mirror, and tried to remember. She remembered having a few drinks and singing and texting, before Brett showed up.

"Oh, yes! Then Brett bought me some food…" the scenes slowly came to mind, though fuzzy and in flashes.

"Brett! Oh my word! BRETT!" Lacey's mind raced and become frantic, not being able to remember much after that. Somehow, she had gotten back to the house…

She ran to the master window and looked out front. Her heart sank as she saw her van was, indeed, missing – and in it's place an F150.

"Oh my word! He stayed the night!" A mortifying chill ran up the back of her neck.

As she walked back to the bedroom, she saw an envelope on the pillow next to hers.

"*Take two of these. -B*" was written on the front.

She opened the envelope to find two Alka-Seltzers and writing on the inside flap:

PS. Nothing happened. Unfortunately.

She fell to the floor in relief. Typical Brett, always a step ahead. And always using humor to lighten an awkward situation. Surprisingly, the thought annoyed her. It was nice to be cared for and so well known by someone, but…

"Always thinking of me, except *once*," she reminded herself with a frown. "The one time that had changed everything."

She quickly swiped the mascara rings under her eyes, pulled her hair back in a messy bun and threw on a pair of sunglasses and a clean t-shirt before trudging down the hall toward the scent.

Brett stood in front of the stove, lit from the morning sun dancing off the pool. Before turning around, and before Lacey had had a chance to say anything, Brett spoke.

"Well, hello, sleepy head…'bout time you rolled out of bed," he said as he flipped an omelet.

"What're you doing?" Lacey, still groggy headed, was "with it" enough to know it wasn't proper for an ex to be cooking in a married woman's kitchen.

"Don't u mean thank you?" Brett asked in a serious tone.

"For what?" Lacey asked, half scared to hear the answer.

"For holding your hair about four times last night, that's what," Brett said, smirking. He knew he was treading on thin ice, but he couldn't resist.

"You know, for a lady, you sure do drink a lot," he continued, ribbing her "..and about hold it like one of 'em, too…" he teased.

"And I bet you're the only woman in Hickman county who's gotten tipsy at the Boardwalk in a twin sweater set and pearls!" He chuckled.

She let him get his punches in as she silently sipped the coffee he put before her. She knew she deserved it.

"So, fill in the blanks for me," she mumbled.

"Well, by the time I got there, you were singing which, even three sheets to the wind sounded FABULOUS, and then you proceeded to make me dance every song with you… and then you hopped up on the bar and began to take your clothes off but only wiggled out of your bra, thankfully…"

At that point Lacey stopped sipping.

"Just kiddin'!" Brett said "about undressing on top of the bar, anyway." Lacey went back to sipping, unamused.

"And after convincing you not to tarnish my virtue, I managed to wrangle you into the truck and get you home. Oh, and on the way, we saw some of your church friends and you gave a SUPER DOOPER wave to them before trying to kiss me…"

Lacey continued to drink her coffee. Sometimes Brett didn't know when to let the kidding go…

"…A "Sheryl" I think it was…"

Lacey instantly sobered up.

"Sheryl?!" Lacey managed to sputter, her voice barely louder than a whisper.

"Yeah, she asked me just how long you were planning on keeping her casserole dish," Brett continued eating his toast, completely unaware of the bomb he'd just dropped and the impending havoc it was sure to bring.

"No! No! No! No!" Lacey's mind yelled. Of all the people in town to see her that time of night…SHERYL! Allegedly the biggest gossip of the church!

"You talked to her?" Lacey asked, still shell shocked.

"Yeah, I told her I'd bring it over to her house…tomorrow…after we woke up," Brett said with a wink. He was prepared for her to throw something, but was met with a speechless, pale face.

"Man, Lacey, you are *still* so gullible!" He said, laughing under his breath.

Color slowly returned to Lacey's cheeks. "BRETT!" Lacey screamed, finally finding her voice. "That is NOT FUNNY!! I'm serious!"

Brett shook his head, still cooking, laughing, "Women."

"I would'a DIED if Sheryl had seen us," Lacey muttered, relieved he was joking about it all. "Wait. How'd you know about the casserole dish if you didn't talk to her? Did you see her name on her dish in the dry rack?" Lacey asked, curious (and half impressed) as to just HOW he knew to use the name "Sheryl".

"Oh, she saw us alright! She DEFINITELY saw us…but we didn't get the chance to talk, per say – what with you hanging all over me and all…"

Lacey's knees felt weak again. "So what part were you joking about?" she asked, confused.

Brett rolled his eyes. "I was joking about telling her I'd return her dish in the morning, silly! I'm not that cruel."

Lacey's mind raced, trying to make sense of it all.

"So we did see her?"

"Yes."

"And she saw us?"

"Yes," Brett answered between bites, his nonchalant attitude quickly becoming a big irritation.

"But you didn't tell her anything about returning the dish?"

"No." Relief started to wash over Lacey.

"And she didn't see me hanging all over you?"

Brett shook his head negative while swallowing and relief started to wash over Lacey until –

"No, she SAW you, all right…"

"Oh, Lord, help me…" Lacey crumbled onto the island stool.

Brett shrugged. "You care too much about what other people think, Lace. They're not gonna bring you taters if you're ever hungry…"

Lacey cut him a mean look, knowing he was quoting one of Grandpa Charlie's favorite sayings.

"Well, she most certainly WOULD bring me taters! And DID! Which is WHYYYY I have one of her CASSEROLE DISHES TO RETURN!" Lacey was screaming now, flailing her arms in the air. She picked up the casserole dish and pumped it in the air as if trying to prove a point.

"Oh, chill Lacey! You don't think people aren't gonna be talking anyway, do you, once they hear about Kit?" he asked.

Lacey sighed. "I guess, but there's just a difference between past and present sins, Brett," Lacey tried to explain.

Brett shrugged and tried to distract her. "Here. It's apple," he said, holding up a fork of streusel for her to try. Brett was trying to comfort her, but Lacey thought of Melissa's words, "You're in so deep, the devil's practically forcing that apple down your throat…" It was all just too much. She threw up her hands, sending the fork flying.

"What in the world, Lace?" Brett asked, bewildered.

Grant and the kids were due back this morning, by now the whole town was talking about her and Brett, and Brett was in her kitchen, cooking for her! But she didn't have time to explain all of the absurdities to Brett.

"You gotta leave, Brett – now!" Lacey's legs were shaky, but she managed to maneuver him to the side door by his elbow.

"Okay, okay! I'm going! But lemme tell you this: Drunken lips speak truth, Lacey, and let's just say last night you were very drunk when you told me you love me..."

Lacey knew better than to deny her feelings, but she felt she needed to explain where her mind was. "You're not the *only* one I love, though. I know you don't understand this, Brett, but I don't just live by what I *feel*. Whatever the past held, at the end of the day, vows were exchanged and a *family* was made..." Lacey's voice reflected the struggle and desperation she felt in her soul.

Brett nodded, sympathetically. "I get that, I do. And I'm the last person to want to break up a family...But where is *HE*, Lace? 'Cause I can tell you this, if you were ever *my* wife, there's no way I'd be staying in a pool house."

"This is a lot for him to digest, Brett," Lacey interjected. "He didn't know about Kit, much less you. And...it's complicated."

Brett shook his head, unempathetic, "Man has a great wife, learns she slipped up, forgives her, moves on...Doesn't seem that complicated to me.."

"It's... not just that...." Lacey hesitated, stuck between protecting a secret or making her husband look bad. She chose her husband.

"Kit is our only biological child. Jake is adopted," She hoped this news would dispel the need to explain further. It didn't.

"So?" Brett said, not comprehending the implication she was trying to send.

Lacey sighed, "So, after Kit was born, we couldn't conceive. We tried everything, but nothing worked. We finally adopted Jake five years later, after all the failed attempts." Brett still looked at her blankly.

Lacey continued, "So getting *this* news...Grant has to deal with feeling like you've not only taken his *daughter* away, but his *manhood*, too."

"Oh, wow," Brett whistled, genuinely sympathetic for him.

"Yeah." Lacey nodded, sadly, fiddling with the doorknob. "Speaking of which, they are all set to come home soon so you need to skedaddle," she instructed, opening the door.

Brett walked through the door, but turned before heading down the steps. "Oh! I almost forgot to tell you," Brett said, facing her from the porch.

"What?" Lacey asked.

"You're awful cute when you're tipsy." Brett gave her a sly grin as she slammed the door in his face.

"You know you love me!" she heard him yell as he hopped down the porch steps and jogged to his truck.

Lacey rolled her eyes.

"That's the problem," she said under her breath.

****

Grant and the kids were scheduled to be home around noon, which gave Lacey just enough time to tidy herself up. But before she could get started, the doorbell – and her phone – lit up.

"Open the door. It's us," the text read. Mya and Melissa.

"It's worse than I thought," Mya said to Melissa, when Lacey opened the door, looking Lacey up and down like the disaster she was.

"I guess the rumors *are* true," Melissa agreed, shaking her head in disappointment as they walked across the threshold.

"What're y'all talking' 'bout?" Lacey squeaked out as she took the bread from Melissa's hand, her voice raw from singing and screaming the night before. The ladies silently dared the other one to tell Lacey the news.

"Go for it," Mya's glance told Melissa. "You're the preacher's wife."

Melissa responded with a silent, "But YOU are the best friend" stare. To which Mya just shook her head in defiance, only to have Melissa nod toward the bread, indicating she'd already done *something*. As always, friendship trumped status, so Mya took a deep breath before beginning.

"Sheryl's been calling everyone around town, saying you were drunk –"

"as a skunk," Melissa interrupted.

"…last night," Mya finished.

"With *Brett*," Melissa added, raising her eyebrow questioningly.

"Oh no…" Lacey said, furrowing her brow.

"And now everyone's rumoring that you're cheating on Grant," Mya continued.

"With *Brett,*" Melissa interrupted again, wide-eyed, before clasping her hands over her mouth, as if pushing the words back in could make it all magically not true.

"And getting back together with Brett," Melissa continued.

Lacey suddenly remembered waving to Sheryl the night before, just before wrapping her arms around Brett and kissing him on the cheek as they peeled away.

"Oh no!" Lacey gasped, horrified, clasping her hands over her eyes as Mya clasped her own hands over her ears at the news. The ladies stood in the foyer, looking like the famous "three monkeys", ironically symbolizing "see no evil, say no evil, hear no evil" – two of which were hoping to hear Lacey deny the claims.

Lacey's hands finally slid down her face. "Well, nothing happened," Lacey assured them. "At least THAT," she said, popping a piece of bread in her mouth. "Truth don't matter much in a small town, though," Lacey muttered between bites. The ladies remained unconvinced.

"Then why did we just see his truck go roarin' up the street five minutes ago?" Mya asked, not fully convinced.

"He stayed to make sure I didn't die in my own… "misery," Lacey said, trying to phrase it nicely for Melissa. They continued to look at her, unbelieving.

"Look! Here's proof!" she said, tossing Brett's handwritten envelope confession toward them. They both breathed a sigh of relief when they read "Nothing happened" before Lacey spoke.

"Trust me, last night was anything BUT romantic…"

"Well what *did* happen?" Mya asked.

Lacey paused to think. "I think I finally cracked. I got the news that Kit's numbers aren't "ideal" and just lost it. I *did* get sloshed," she gave an apologetic look to Melissa, "but I did *not* sleep with Brett…not that I didn't *want* to…" her voice trailed off reluctantly as she looked away.

"Well, that's the other reason we're here," Melissa said. Lacey looked at them quizzically.

"This is an intervention," Mya explained sternly. Lacey looked at them in shock before erupting into a gale of laughter.

"Oh man! Y'all are TOO MUCH!" Lacey wiped at happy tears in the corner of her eyes.

"We're serious," Mya said.

"Y'all, I do not have a problem with alcohol! Yes, I got tipsy last night, but…"

"It's not that kind of an intervention," Melissa interruption.

"This is a *Brett* intervention!" Mya clarified.

Now it was Lacey who was stone-faced. Despite the façade she put on, she emotionally clung to Brett. His memory – even though scarred - had always been a source of comfort for her. This talk of "intervention" sent a cold chill up her spine. If there were any alcohol effects left in her system, she was completely sober now.

"What do you mean?" Lacey asked apprehensively.

Melissa sighed, took Lacey's hand and said, "You've got to let him go."

The words cut her to the core. Melissa and Mya – both very loving people – looked at Lacey sternly.

"Lacey, we know how hard this has been for you. We know you've been trying to put closure on the past in addition to shouldering all of Kit's medical issues, but sometimes, closure never happens. We know your will *wants* to do what God wants – but your emotions are getting in the way. We can see objectively just how hard this struggle is for you, and last night proves it. Your emotions can't make sense of it all, because they aren't logical. If you don't walk away from this, from *him*, you are going to lose everything precious to you." Melissa's words were sincere and true.

Mya interjected, "Lacey, you could lose your husband, your kids…it's just not worth it."

Lacey nodded in agreement. She knew they were right, and she honestly felt relief that someone finally saw how hard the struggle was and were giving her some boundaries – but she didn't know what that meant, really.

"So, what are you saying?" Lacey asked.

"We're gonna do our own rehab," Mya said boldly, "We've set you up an appointment with Dr. Laney, gonna have a "goodbye past" ceremony, and then you're going to detox: we're gonna cut off all direct contact with Mr. Dimples," Mya said, barely suppressing a grin. "So, I'm gonna need your phone to BLOCK HIM," she said, putting her hand out.

"Oh, you mean *now*!" Lacey said, surprised.

"Yes, Ma'am," Mya said.

Lacey had no choice but to hand over her phone – and her crutch.

THIRTY-EIGHT

"Well, I guess the whole town knows my halo fell off," Lacey said as she walked through Melissa's side door. They hadn't seen each other since their "Brett intervention" and Lacey was feeling the full weight of Sheryl's tongue.

Melissa sighed and put her arm around her, "When your husband is in the ministry, you find out real quick how riddled EVERYONE is with issues and problems. And don't let 'em fool you, some of the ones with the best reputations have the worst skeletons! I'm just worried about YOU...how are you doing?"

Lacey sighed, "OK...I mean, beside the public drunkenness and Kit's daily fight for survival and my marriage hanging in the balance...other than that, I'm peachy keen!" Lacey said sarcastically.

Melissa gave her a sympathetic nod, "Any new news on Kit?"

Lacey nodded, "Her numbers have gone up a bit, but still no news on a match yet."

"Well, that is good news! Praise the Lord!" Melissa cheered. "How's everything else, then? The last time we talked we were going to pray double time for Grant's heart."

Lacey looked down, embarrassed. "Well, now it's my heart you probably need to pray for. I know Sheryl's been letting everyone think I slept with Brett, but you know I didn't. But I wanted to. And, if not for his being a gentleman, I probably would have. Grant is still distant, and said at our last counseling session he wasn't sure if he could get past all this and I am just so lonely right now! All alone in the worst time of my life!" Lacey wailed.

"Lacey I'm not gonna lie, you're in the fight of your life and being sifted. The devil is throwing everything he's got at you – temptation, trials, *and* tribulation! Not to mention all the past wounds to be dealt with, and judgment from others...you're in your Job phase!" Melissa agreed.

"Melissa, I'm trying *so hard* to do the right thing! But it's difficult when your husband virtually abandons you and Prince Charming whispers all the things you want to hear, how we "deserve to be together" and have a "right" to...and, honestly, I'm beginning to see his point...I mean, don't we have a *right* to be together? If my Dad hadn't interfered, we would've been, right?" Lacey looked off, sadly.

Melissa sighed. It was clear the strain of life was starting to affect her thinking. "Sweetie, we gotta be real careful any time we start thinking we have a "right" to do something. Usually when you say you have a "right" to do something, it is a telltale sign you DON'T. You have free will like everyone else, but you gave up all your "rights" when you laid them down at the foot of the cross. That is what dying to yourself is. There's a reason it's called *dying.* It's like the Pearl of Great Price parable, where the man sold all his little treasures for the master Pearl. Brett might be the "treasure" you are going to have to give up for the Great Pearl (your marriage), but it is worth it. I promise. *"*

Lacey remembered the pearl engagement ring still waiting for her, should she accept it. Lacey knew Melissa was speaking truth, but she felt irritated, "But I'm honestly conflicted! One minute I feel one way and the next, another. I just don't know *how* I feel, Melissa!"

"Well, that's part of the problem," Melissa replied. "When did you start making decisions based on how you FEEL? Are you gonna bow to the god of Feelings or trust and obey God? The Bible says the heart is deceptive so if you start making decisions just on how you feel it can lead you down the wrong path." Melissa paused to let her words sink in. "And I know you got it in you. You don't feel like exercising but you *do* it. You don't feel *like* abstaining from desserts, but I've seen you do that, too."

Melissa continued, "Grant has done nothing *to* you, Lacey. You don't have a right *or* a reason to divorce him - Biblically, legally *or* morally! Just like GRANT doesn't have a "right" to divorce *you*! This new information doesn't change the *facts*! The fact that you and Grant promised God you would stay together for LIFE. You don't have a *marriage* problem, Lacey – you have an *obedience* problem."

Melissa was coming in tough on her, but Lacey knew she was right.

"But this is so *hard*!" Lacey cried.

"I know! Like Abraham, you feel like you are being asked to give up the one thing you've always wanted, deep down. Brett is your Isaac and you feel he's being ripped away from you. That kind of obedience is *supposed* to be hard! You are trying to keep your feelings in check with your FIRST LOVE, for Pete's sake!"

"It feels like I'm sinning *against* love!" Lacey admitted.

"I'm sure that's how Abraham felt, too, when he was asked to sacrifice his son," Melissa continued. "First love is extremely powerful, but it's not the only form of love. The deepest form of love is when it does what is best for others, regardless of the level of attraction because then it is a choice.

That's why Jesus says to love our enemies. Love is not a feeling, but a choice. It should not be, "I *feel* love for you." That's not love, it's *attraction*! We should rather say, "I DO love FOR you!" THAT is LOVE! *Anyone* can act lovingly when they *feel* it Agape love is the highest order of love, and it says, "I'm not feeling it, but I'm going to be loving because I want to give another person joy. That's the "meaty" love. People always write novels and make movies and write songs about romantic love, but they really are speaking of "attraction." Real love isn't so glorious. It's feeding your spouse who's had a stroke, or getting up to feed a newborn four times a night for months. It is selfless and rarely gets acclaim or honor. But that's the *real* stuff. God's inviting you to go deeper, Lacey, by truly *loving*.

"It's just so hard!" Lacey cried.

Melissa gaffed, "Of course it is! Obedience is *always* hard! Tony Evans said obedience without struggle isn't *obedience*, it's *agreement*. You've been thinking you were obeying the Lord all these years, when you were just walking in agreement with him. Now your feet are in the fire, and you've got to walk on hot coals!"

Lacey nodded in agreement.

"You are falling for every one of the devil's lies, Lacey. The first lie is that you alone are in total control of your life. That "right" was washed away the day you put on Christ. God is hemming you in. While you have been making plans for your life, the LORD wants to direct your steps. But that is *such* a *blessing*, Lacey! Can you imagine how things would've worked out if He *wasn't* at the helm?"

Lacey cringed at the thought. "But don't I have a right to be happy? Doesn't God want me happy?"

Melissa leaned in. "The Lord wants us HOLY, Lacey. Lots of times we get "happy" along with it – but "happy" was never promised to us. And sometimes we're in a position where we have to choose: Happy versus Holy."

"But, Melissa, you *know* us…it's just so much *easier* with Brett! It always has been! We're like soul mates! He was my first love…and he still feels like home! It's always taken more effort with Grant…I just don't know what to do."

"Well, no matter how badly we sometimes want to, you can't go home again…" Lacey knew Melissa was remembering from experience. "There are some things in life we have to accept and people we have to let go, even though we don't want to. Sometimes the hardest and bravest and most necessary thing in life we will ever do is walk away…

And Brett Wright might just *be* your soul mate, Lacey…but he's not your *husband*." Lacey looked up, surprised at Melissa's firm tone.

"Have you been talking to Jenn?" Lacey asked sullenly, remembering she had heard those almost exact words before.

Melissa continued, "And Brett was *not* your first love, Lacey! **GOD** was!" Melissa was not backing down – realizing Who she was actually fighting. Lacey had swallowed the devil's lies hook, line and sinker and Melissa knew she had to speak truth to them.

Lacey sighed. "I *never* thought I would be in this position, Melissa! Never in a million years! I mean, I love Grant to death…but he's shut down and shut me out! And Brett says he still loves me, and always has…"

"Lacey, honey, God and the devil are *both* battling for you! Luckily, you are God's child, but there are *rights and responsibilities* that come with that relationship! Sometimes we get so confused we need to step back and simplify. Sometimes the question comes down to this: are you going to trust and obey or not?"

Lacey was wringing her hands, now, her face reflecting the inner turmoil she felt. Melissa wasn't letting up, though. She loved her too much to not tell her what she needed to hear.

"But know this: God *always* blesses obedience, Lacey! Always." Melissa nodded affirmatively. "You *have* got to stay STRONG! Think of the two people who also struggled with the idea of adultery. David gave in, and we KNOW how badly that ended up. But Joseph took a different route…

"I know…he ran…" Lacey interjected.

"But do you remember the last thing he said before he ran?" Melissa asked. Lacey met her question with an empty stare.

"He said, how can I do this to the *LORD*?" Melissa quoted. "Sweetie, this is more than just about you and Brett, Grant and your family. It's about you denying what you've always wanted and choosing and trusting the Lord. Go home and pray on that. I can't *imagine* how hard this is for you, but you have to remember Lacey, the vows you and Grant made to love, honor, and stay together are still in effect – despite everything."

"Don't indulge your flesh at the expense of your soul…for you are 'a chosen race, a royal priesthood, a holy nation, a people for God's own possession, For you once were not (such) a people, but now you are a people of God.'" Melissa let the Word of God speak for her.

Lacey sighed heavily, "You're right, I know. You and Dan will keep praying for us?"

"Of course. And keep your guard up. Remember what we said a few weeks ago: The devil doesn't come around in horns and a long tail – he's usually disguised as a smooth talking, hot military man," she said, "or a delicious cupcake!"

Lacey laughed as she bit into her cupcake. As soon as the dessert hit her taste buds, she spit it out!

"What in the WORLD?!" Lacey sputtered, and grabbed the nearest water. It was the nastiest cake she'd ever tasted!

"And that, my dear, is sin. Looks and smells tasty. Might even be delicious at first," Melissa said, licking the icing off her fork. "But it's only a lure. It leaves an awful aftertaste and makes you wish you'd never taken the first bite," Melissa said, pointing to the salt on the table in front of them.

"You sure know how to make a point!" Lacey said.

She left Melissa's with spiritual ammunition – and a couple cupcakes to remind her that sin, though tempting, isn't worth it in the long run.

THIRTY-NINE

Will had heard about Lacey's night at the Boardwalk and decided it was time to step into his older brother role and moseyed in beside Lacey in the potluck line.

"Heard you was having a high old time with Brett the other night," he said, as he filled his plate.

Lacey turned, ready to give the speaker a piece of her mind. She swallowed her words when she saw it was Will. "Nothing happened, Will," she said soberly.

Will was quick to respond. The last thing he needed was for the old Lacey to get her dander up. "No, no...I don't doubt that," he said, quickly reassuring her of his confidence in her. "I'm just worried how you're holding up under temptation, little sister?"

Lacey looked at him, thankful he was concerned about her. "I'm makin' it," Lacey admitted. "I want our marriage to work out, but I still have all these feelings for Brett. You know how we are...*were*...It's hard. I keep praying, and nothin's changin'."

"With all due respect, Lacey, I just gotta ask, which god are you prayin to?"

Lacey whirled and looked at him, insulted. Will stayed silent and steady, unwilling to let her hurt feelings stand in the way of her hearing the truth.

"Seems to me you're cow tailin to the false god of Feelings, and gettin fairy tales and God's will confused. You show me somewhere in the Bible about you being directed to break up your family to be with your "soulmate" and I'll support you, but it ain't there, Lace. The devil's making you think you got options you don't."

Will knew he was coming in hard and strong, but he didn't feel he had a choice. Will knew the direction of Brett and Lacey's relationship rested squarely on Lacey's shoulders. And, based on what he heard about the Boardwalk, she was growing weary.

"God's not gonna contradict himself. The devil's coming after you strong…when the enemy whispers in your ear all the things about Brett you miss, you know what you need to tell him?" Will paused. "You need to tell him, 'So?"

He summoned his best devilish voice, "Brett is your soul mate…"

"So?" he said in his best, high-pitched feminine voice.

"But you two belong together…" he growled.

"So?" he squealed.

"But you deserve to be together…" he said in a tempting tone.

"So?" he said again, laughing this time.

Lacey grinned. For some people a gentle word gets through to their psyche, but for Lacey it had always been the strong, no-nonsense pep talks that worked best. Will was making a lot of sense and telling her all the things she needed to hear. She knew how much he cared by how firm he was speaking to her. Even though it irritated her, it was also a comfort.

"But he loves me…" Lacey whispered, a tear sliding down her nose.

It broke Will's heart to see Lacey hurting so. Even though she was younger, he'd always looked up to her spiritually. Her life had given him a tangible example of what a strong love for God looked like in real life. And now, she needed guidance and encouragement. It was an honor to help her out. He was determined to do all he could to help her get through this crisis – even if it meant making her uncomfortable and angry.

"He *does* love you, Lacey, but he don't love you with *Christian* love."

Lacey looked up as she wiped away another tear. "He's a good guy Lace, and would probably love you somethin fierce the rest of y'alls lives…but He don't have the Holy Spirit guiding him."

The words stung, but were dead on. It was a relief to have someone ADMIT they saw the love between her and Brett and not deny it – and also have the main issue that would cause the most problems pointed out to her.

"I guess sometimes it comes down to guilt or regret," Lacey said. "Do what you *want* and live with the *guilt*, or do the *right* thing and have *regret*. Choose your poison," she said with a frown. "Either way, it hurts the same…"

Will shook his head, "But if you do what you *want* you get both guilt and regret."

He let the full weight of his words seep into her mind before continuing, "Anytime you're fraught, you gotta ask yourself: Is there a lie in what I'm thinking? The devil deals in lies: white lies, half lies, full-on lies… Well, there's a lie in your thinkin' Lace. First one being that doing the right thing holds regret. Doing the right thing might bring temporary sadness, but you know as well as I do it's not regrettable. Doing the right thing is always right." Will muttered between bites.

"Second lie is "this world is supposed to feel like home." The truth is, little sister, this *ISN'T* home! It's a journey on the way *TO* home! You gotta stop trying to wiggle your reality into a shoe that don't fit," Will nodded at her, before he started singing with a grin, "This world is not my home, I'm just a passin' through…"

Lacey smiled. There was truth in his words. "I just don't know what to do…I don't know what I want…" she said.

"There you go again, 'What do *I* want?' Why don't you take a step back and look at the big picture? Life ain't just about you! And your actions will sure enough affect others besides you, so broaden your focus and ask what would be best for *them*?"

"Maybe that's a question you need to pose to Grant," Lacey mumbled, blinking back tears.

Will sighed. He knew the situation wasn't as cut and dry emotionally as he was making it out to be.

"Oh, I've been giving him an earful! No doubt! Brett, too!" He assured her.

"And just what have you been telling him?" Lacey asked, surprised.

"Same thing's I been telling you…reminding him to stay in his lane and that closure is a lie."

Lacey looked at him, surprised he knew exactly what she'd been hoping for and shocked he'd say it didn't exist.

Will continued, "You two go too deep and have been through too much to ever be at total peace with things ending. Don't chase after "closure," but pursue "acceptance" instead. As soon as you *accept* that there's always going to be a part of your heart that belongs to Brett, you'll be halfway to healed. But you're gonna have to mourn that loss. And, I ain't gonna lie, it's gonna hurt like crazy, but I've learned over time that many times the healing is in the aching…"

He softened his voice before continuing, "Lace…anyone with eyes can see how charming Brett is, so I'm not frontin' you for feeling torn – ESPECIALLY with the added childhood bond y'all got. But you've always been a strong girl and I don't want to see you taken down by a pack of devil lies!" Will's concern was shown in his furrowed brow. "Y'all got too much to lose!"

Lacey was touched. "I know you love us, Will, and I'm grateful you're lookin' after me the way you are. I'm just so weary! You struggle with a sin long enough, you feel like you've committed it," Lacey hung her head. "All I know to say is just please keep praying for me and Grant. I'm just not sure how to break through that wall I helped build between us…"

"Don't give up, Lace…He'll do the right thing. But he *does* come from proud stock and you can't trollop around the honky tonks with GI Joe making it hard for Grant to come home."

"I know," Lacey hung her head. "It wasn't planned. I'd just gotten news about Kit and had had enough, I guess."

"Well, nobody rightly blames you for fallin' apart with all you got on you – but don't stay in that ditch," Will said.

"I won't," Lacey said. "Anyway, the girls have already instituted a "Brett intervention" and I have no contact with him." Lacey smiled.

Will laughed, "No way!"

Lacey nodded, "Melissa blocked his number on my phone and Mya diverted his number to her phone anytime he calls!"

"Man!" Will chuckled respectfully. "Those girls don't play!" he said between laughs.

"They most certainly do not!" Lacey agreed. Despite the "big brother" talk and the fact she felt emotionally beat up on, Lacey felt loved more. She knew it was a rare blessing to have friends that loved her enough to tell her what she needed, but didn't want, to hear. She quickly thanked God for them as she prayed over her food.

After Lacey put the kids to bed later that night, she prayed again – but this time she took her time. It'd been a while since she'd prayed deeply. Seemed when troubles hit, she actually prayed less than other times…perhaps because she didn't want to face the depth of her problems? She wasn't sure. But what she was sure of was she was long over-due.

"Dear God, I haven't talked to you face to face in a while, and I'm sorry for that. Between Kit's issues and now my past returning to be dealt with, I feel like a hamster on a wheel, like I'm drowning! If I were to tell someone all we've been through in the past year no one would believe it. Kit's health issues, finding out Brett was her father, the shame I've brought on Grant…and now to be estranged from him at a time like this? And, on top of everything else, facing the temptation of my *life* with Brett?! *How much longer, Lord*??

I've prayed in the past for Kit's healing. Insulted you by trying to make deals with you for her returned health…I've wondered if I brought this upon her by my sin with Brett…but I know you, Lord. I've walked with you so long, I can't even be mad at you, which makes this all the harder. It's easier when there is someone to blame, when you can focus all your pain on someone else – and even if it's wrong, on You. But now, this time, I just have to sit in this! There's no *reason*, there's no one to *blame*, it's all a hot mess!" Lacey was past bawling and now blubbering.

"I can't do it anymore, God! I just *can't*!"

Overwhelmed, she lay her head in her arm and cried, letting the Holy Spirit interpret HER moans and groans. She cried for the life she'd lost with Brett, and her unknown future with Grant. She cried for the lies she'd been fed and the lies she'd served, the life she'd lost and the life that had been decided for her. She cried for the moments she and Kit had lost because of her illness and the moments she had lost because of her own Dad's illness. She cried for a past she couldn't change and a future still unknown. She cried until she was empty.

"God, I've never worn masks with you and I'm not going to start now, but I want to be with Brett. I love him the same as I did fifteen years ago. Please change that or at least help my heart to want to work things out with Grant. I know that sounds awful, God, but it's all I've got right now. You promised to meet us where we are, well that's where I am. I am glad you are the God of miracles 'cause I sure need a few right now! Thank You for your gracious blessings through all of this, Lord, but we need you more than ever right now. Help soften both our hearts so we can do what *You* want us to do, despite what *we* want to do. I love you, God. I'm so sorry I've brought all this on the family..."

In desperation, she opened her Bible, doubtfully hoping she would find something to speak to her problem and pain. She knew people made fun of folks that flopped open the Bible expecting an answer from the Lord, but God had "talked" to her once before in this way. Effective or not, pride is of no value when you are out of options.

Gingerly, she opened her eyes and read the words her eyes had landed on:

*"And don't be wishing you were someplace else or **with** someone else. Where you are right now is God's place for you. Live and obey and love and believe right there. **God**, not your marital status, defines your life.... As the Lord has assigned to each one, as the Lord has called each, in this manner let him walk...Circumcision or uncircumcision are nothing but what matters is the keeping of the commandments of God." (1 Cor. 7:17-20)*

Lacey sat, stunned at the way the verses precisely spoke to every issue she had just prayed about. To Lacey the message was clear: whether she had married Brett or Grant, it didn't matter. What was important was obeying the Lord NOW in the place she found herself NOW, and living for the Lord in a way to give Him glory.

It said GOD had assigned a path for each person. It was almost as if God had written on her bedroom wall with his hand "You're *Grant's* wife. Be true to THAT." And "You are not the controller of your destiny...I AM."

She reread verse 17:

"Don't go wishing you were somewhere else or with someone else. Where you are right now is God's place for you. Live and obey and love and believe right there...remain in the condition in which you are..."

In three short verses God not only told her to stop wishing she was elsewhere, but let her know she was exactly where God wanted her, calming her worries that she or her Dad had "messed everything up." In addition, He reminded her that the most important thing was keeping the commandments of God.

She was amazed, but asked the one question that plagued her heart: how did God feel about how she was handling things? She knew she hadn't behaved perfectly, but did her attempts to stay straight count for anything?

She opened the Bible again, a hopeful prayer rising from her heart that she would not land on some abstract verse like "Obed begat Jethro, begat Samuel…" because she wanted desperately to believe He had heard her heart and had answered her a few moments before.

She opened her eyes to the words:

*"And while there has never been a question about your honesty in these matters – **I couldn't be prouder of you!** – I want you to be **smart**, making sure every "good" thing is the "**real deal**." Don't be gullible in regards to smooth talking evil. Stay alert like this and before you know it the God of Peace will come down on Satan with both feet, stomping Him into the dirt. Enjoy the best of Jesus!" (Romans 16:19-20)*

Lacey bowed her head in humble appreciation, overwhelmingly grateful for the fact that, despite her doubts, God had showed up - in brilliant display with undeniable clarity.

Just like He always does.

Every. Single. Time.

FORTY

It'd been three weeks since Lacey's infamous Boardwalk debacle, twenty-one days since she'd seen or talked to Brett. "Twenty days and fourteen hours, to be exact," Lacey thought with a sigh. When the girls had asked for her phone and said they were conducting an intervention she had laughed, thinking they were being a bit ridiculous...but she wasn't laughing now. As much as she wanted to deny it, she missed Brett. Terribly. She was shocked that after only being back in touch for a few months he had gotten so deep into her system.

In the short time she'd been out of contact with Brett, she was able to focus more on the kids and redirect her thoughts in the direction they needed to go. She and Melissa had been walking every night, and Melissa listened and prayed with her. In addition to comparing Joseph and David's reactions and consequences to sexual temptation, the other story that encouraged her most were the thoughts Melissa had shared on Rahab.

Rahab was a brothel owner living in the Isrealite enemy city of Jericho. Even so, she had heard of the God of Isreal and His mighty works and believed in Him. But her faith didn't stop there. When the Isrealite spies entered the city, she hid them and asked them to spare her and her family when they invaded the city. They were true to their promise, and she found herself a member of God's family. This is awesome, but there was more to the story.

Melissa pointed out how hard this transition was for Rahab, a prostitute living in a foreign land. In Jericho, she did as she pleased. There were no laws, or restrictive commandments. Her new life was different. The food, the language, the clothes, and the customs were different. Some things *were* the same, however, like whispering gossip and darting eyes. Rahab had exchanged her old, dead life for a new one filled with life.

But it wasn't easy.

It didn't *look* like home, or *taste* like home.

But it was *God's* home.

"Sometimes where we are called to be isn't where we feel most comfortable, or gifted or even where we feel we *want* to be. But it's where we *need* to be. Because that is where God is." Melissa's words were echoing in her mind. "I know sometimes the life you're living doesn't feel like the "home" you imagined, but you've gotta trust God in this. Don't even give yourself permission to ask what you *want*…ask what *God* wants and do *that*."

"That's a lot harder than it sounds," Lacey said dejectedly.

"But do you know what happened to Rahab?" Melissa asked.

Lacey shook her head "no."

Melissa smiled, "Well, because of her faithfulness she became the great-great-great-great-whatever-grandmother of Jesus." Melissa paused a minute to let the full meaning of those words sink in. "God always rewards obedience, Lacey. Sometimes in ways we get to *see*, and sometimes in ways we *don't*, but *Always*! *Every* time!"

Those thoughts comforted Lacey when she was torn between her flesh and what the Lord wanted. She clung to that story, hoping she and Grant could be a family again soon. It was a comfort to know someone else – even a woman centuries ago - understood her struggle of following God's or returning back to the comforts of home.

In her own studies, she read the story of Abraham and Isaac. God had told Abraham to take Isaac, the one he loved the most, up the mountain to sacrifice. The story did not give any details about how Abraham felt or how many tears he shed…it only said "he went the next morning" and set out to obey. Lacey longed to know what must have been going on in his heart during that time! She was pretty sure he was confused, saddened, and probably angry. Did he pray all night for God to change his request? Did he set out a fleece to verify what he'd heard? Did he feel abandoned, betrayed and unloved by his Lord? It doesn't say. What the Bible DID say was that Abraham WENT. And obeyed.

THE PEARL OF GREAT PRICE

Even though he didn't want to. Even though it didn't make sense. Even though God had promised him a nation, and his obedience would seemingly prevent that. Even though it meant giving up his heart's desire…second only, and barely, to his love for the Lord. Even through the confusion and the anger and the loss and the tears, he obeyed. Even when Isaac "caught on" after he asked where the sacrifice was, and he saw his son's feelings of betrayal and fear toward *him* flash in his eyes – he obeyed. Even when he had to use one hand to steady his trembling, knife bearing hand and close his eyes so he wouldn't see the death of his dream, he obeyed.

And at the very last moment, with heart already broken and his finest and best on the altar, and angel of the Lord stopped him and said, "Because you *obeyed* me, NOW I know that you (truly) love me."

Obedience = love

Lacey reminded herself this wasn't just about avoiding adultery or a divorce, but also a way to show God how much she loved Him. This gave her motivation and strength because, honestly, it wasn't getting easier, but harder to remain strong, especially when the benefits of sin seemed to outweigh the rewards of being faithful – to God *and* Grant.

She wrote out and posted the scriptures around her house and even made bracelets that displayed the verses "Genesis 39:9" and "Phil. 1:24" to remind her daily – sometimes hourly – of what was at stake.

Mya, Melissa and Lacey planned to meet at Curlz for a Beauty day. Between running back and forth to Nashville for Kit's Vanderbilt appointments, Lacey looked forward to the pampering. Curlz was famous for two things: their gossip and their famous broccoli muffins and fruit tea they served their customers as they were doing their pedis. It was often said that more ladies booked pedicures for the muffins than the actual pedicures.

While enjoying the delicious muffins, Mya broached the subject.

"So how many days clean are you?" she asked, jokingly.

Lacey grinned at both the reference and the similarity. "Twenty and holding," Lacey answered to their applause.

"We are so proud of you!" Melissa praised her. "We know how hard this must be for you!"

"The deeper the love, the deeper the sorrow," Grandpa Charlie had said a few years after Grandma Kate's death. Lacey was finding out how true those words were, and how much pain was involved.

"Things going better with Grant?" Melissa's voice broke into her thoughts.

"A little, I guess," Lacey sighed. "We've been talking more in counseling...I wanted to quit, honestly, but the counselor said it gets worse before it gets better so I'm praying the "better" will come...I guess I deserve it to be hard, though, especially after the ruckus I caused at The Boardwalk a few weeks back."

"If it helps, I haven't heard any new whispers," Mya said.

"And at least Grant's trying to work on things," Melissa encouraged. Lacey shook her foil laden head in agreement.

"Any news from Vandy yet?"

"They called last week and said Kit's numbers were finally high enough to attempt a transplant," Lacey said.

"Oh my heart!" Melissa exclaimed. "Lacey! That is *wonderful!*" she was almost squealing.

Lacey nodded, unable to stop her bright smile. "Yes! Just waiting for Vandy to finish Brett's test..."

Almost as if on cue, Lacey's phone rang. Her fingernails still wet, Lacey had Melissa accept the call for her and placed the phone to her ear. As soon as Melissa saw "Vandy" on Lacey's phone, she shushed the talking women nearby. They gave her some perturbed looks until she mouthed, "It's the doctor" before they turned around quietly. Out of respect, or so they could hear better, Melissa wasn't sure. Everyone in Dickson knew about Kit's situation, what with Grant being on the City Council and all. Kit was on every prayer list, from the First Baptist on Main to the Church of Christ in the boonies and every Methodist, Church of God and Community church in-between. Not to mention the Amish community on the outskirts. If any child was covered in prayer, it was Kit.

"Yes?" Lacey asked, the salon dead quiet. "Uh-huh..." It was as if the seconds were years. Every eye and ear were on Lacey, waiting and praying.

"I see," Lacey said. Mya's shoulders slumped. She'd been friends with Lacey long enough to know "I see" was not a sign of good news.

"Ok," Lacey continued, now grabbing a pencil and ripping out the postcard insert from her People magazine to write down some info. "Yes. Yes. Will do. Thank you," she said, grinning and scribbling away.

Mya was confused. At this point she had no clue if the call was the news they'd wanted.

"They're putting me through to Dr. Schwartz," Lacey mouthed, her foam-spaced toes tapping nervously. She grabbed Mya's hand anxiously.

"Hi, Doctor," Lacey said, "Uh-huh…. uh-huh…yes…"

The tension in the beauty shop was thick.

"Uh-uh…uh-huh…" Lacey's voice grew louder. "Yes, sir, yes." Lacey was now hitting the table excitedly, looking at the girls wide-eyed and hopeful.

"I understand *completely*," Lacey said, this time taking the phone, wet-nailed and all, and jumping up out of her seat. "I can do that! I will do that *right now*!!" Lacey yelled, as she hobbled on her bare feet toward her purse. In between hobbles she had just enough time to lower the phone and say the words they had all been dying to hear:

"It's a match!!"

The salon erupted in glorious cheers and the right rear corner broke out into a literal hallelujah chorus, hands raised high and unashamed. Mya jumped as high as a kangaroo multiple times and Melissa crumbled into a ball of tears. Lacey yelled, "Call Brett!" over her shoulder as she continued to talk to Dr. Schwartz as she slung her purse on her shoulder and hobbled out the door. Curlz was in the center of town, five stores down from the Court House, Grant's second home. She looked like a hot mess, with her hair frizzed and foiled, her salon cape flying out around her like a superhero reject, hobbling with the pedi tissue stuck between her piggies – but she didn't care. She had to tell Grant ASAP!

She climbed the Court House steps three at a time, thanking Ray, the Courthouse security guard, as he opened the door, still talking to Dr. Schwartz. She paused only to turn the doorknob before running into the packed Courtroom.

She was halfway down the aisle before remembering the Perry murder case was in session. Instead of the normal fifteen people usually in attendance, she was greeted by the stares of a packed house and three television crews. Her brisk entrance jostled the judge to attention and caused the whole room to turn and stare. Lacey was surprised but not embarrassed. Grant turned just in time to see his lovely bride, as he used to always call her, stop mid-aisle, to stand before him in all her foiled glory. He stopped, mid-sentence, thinking she'd finally lost her mind.

Lacey didn't know it, but the ladies, suspecting where she was headed, had all left the salon and followed her up the street, not wanting to miss the scene of the decade. As she stopped, the other women silently streamed in behind her.

Forgetting for a moment the seriousness of the setting and the space that distanced the two of them, she acted on pure impulse and adrenaline as she threw the phone up in the air and once again yelled,

"IT'S A MATCH!!"

Like the salon, every person in attendance knew Kit's situation and erupted into deafening applause and cheers. Grant hopped the small gate that separated the attorneys from the spectators, and ran to Lacey. Relieved and ecstatic, he twirled her around, burying his head in her shoulder. Try as he might, the Judge could not regain order. Being a man up in years, he knew when he was in a hopeless situation and promptly and happily dismissed court.

By the time Grant stopped twirling Lacey, they were locked in a long overdue kiss. Lacey pulled away to see his smiling face, covered in happy tears.

"You sure know how to clear a room!" Grant laughed, pulling at her silver foil. "Look at you!" They both collapsed into each other, laughing. "You're definitely gonna make the evening news, honey!" Grant said, wiping the tears from the corner of his eyes, and pointing to her bare feet.

"Trish should give me a free manicure for all the free advertising I'll be giving her salon tonight!" Lacey joked before heading to the waving newscasters, hand in hand with Grant.

FORTY-ONE

It had been two months since Grant had played with his church's baseball team. It wasn't that he didn't want to, but prepping for the Perry murder case had him too swamped to do much else. It felt good to be back in the game. He was always able to forget work and worries on the field. He usually pitched, but this season he'd sat out due to the trial. Today he arrived early and decided to set up. As he was looking through the bag for the helmets, other teammates arrived. They were playing their nemesis, Fellowship Church, so the stands were going to be full. In most towns, church ball doesn't get a lot of attention, but in Dickson it takes on a whole other dimension! Most games happen on a Tuesday or Thursday and get full radio coverage since church ball is the only real sport going on in Dickson during the summer. The gate tickets fully support Operation Christmas Child and the winning team gets free BBQ ribs on Saturday nights at Squealers. The local cheerleaders get some extra practice in, cheering once a week for the teams. Church ball in Dickson is a very big deal.

Grant was rummaging through the bag, still trying to find the last batter glove, when some teammates walked into the dugout.

"Don't tell me that's Brett Wright!" he heard one say, pointing to Fellowship's side. The name perked Grant's attention.

"Yeah it is… Josh injured his heel on a descent so Wright's subbing," the other player said, tying his cleat.

"I hear he's subbing for *Grant*, too," the first player said under his breath.

"I sure hope not," his friend said, shaking his head, concerned.

"Word is he's wiggled back into Lacey's life," player #12 said, sadly. "And Grant's living in the pool house. And Sheryl told Grace Lacey was all over Brett, drunk as a skunk few weeks back."

Player #6 spit through the fence before replying. If this were true, it would be the fourth couple in their church in a year that'd fallen on hard times. Deacon Williams didn't wanna see the same fate come their way, too. "Anybody checked on 'em yet?"

"No, they haven't," Grant said, standing up and turning around. Player #12 looked down, embarrassed, but Deacon Williams leaned in.

"So, y'all need anything?" he asked, his sincere concern felt.

"Prayers," Grant said. "We're doing better, just got a lot to digest." Grant didn't want to talk further with all the guys about to pile in but made a note to call Deacon Williams soon. News of what was really going on was bound to break soon, and he felt he deserved to give the leaders a heads up beforehand.

"You got it," Deacon Williams said, patting him on the shoulder.

The game went smoothly the first few innings, with each team taking turns in the lead. By the eighth inning it was five to six, Fellowship – thanks in part to Brett's homerun in the bottom of the sixth. It was now the ninth inning and Brett was up to bat.

Lacey and the kids had arrived late, taking their usual spot between Mya and Melissa's clans. Jenn had come, too, since Will was announcing, and had spread their whole troop out to save Lacey some seats.

"What'd I miss?" Lacey asked, winded. Her hair had been ruined by keeping the foils on too long in the Courtroom, so Trish had to take her back to her natural color of red. She was lucky she didn't lose her hair from the root, as long as the foil was on! She was met with "wows" and compliments from the ladies.

"Five to six, Fellowship. Brett is up to bat," Melissa said over her shoulder.

"Brett?!" Lacey asked, confused.

"He's filling in for Josh," Mya said. Lacey slumped in her seat. Had she known Brett was going to be playing she definitely would not have come. She and Grant had enjoyed a nice night by the fire with the kids the night before last and the last thing she needed was Brett casting a shadow over them. She was hoping he'd stick to playing ball and not cause any trouble.

"Well, my, my, Lacey!" Sheryl's shrill voice carried to her from two rows back. She practically felt her hot breath on the back of her neck. "It's like the Dessert Auction fifteen years ago! I'm sure you don't know *which* team to root for..." she said, fanning and smirking. Lacey was mortified. She was sure Jake had heard her, and didn't know how to respond. But Jenn did.

"You either, huh, Sheryl?" Jenn asked, referring to Player #22 on the other team, Brandon, Sheryl's ex-boyfriend from high school and her current boyfriend on shortstop. Sheryl looked at Jenn, caught off guard. "By the way, how's your sister doing?" Jenn asked. Sheryl quickly turned away, yelling at her child for something he *didn't* do, giving her an excuse to leave the scene.

"Oh, my!" Melissa whispered, laughing, knowing that Jenn was referring to the rumor that Sheryl and her boyfriend had broken up after she'd caught him with her own sister the morning after Prom. "You don't pull any punches, do you?" she whispered to Jenn.   "Thank you," Lacey silently mouthed to Jenn as she squeezed her hand.

Deacon Williams gave his best curve ball and got a strike from Brett. Lacey looked for Grant. Glad he was in the dugout so he wouldn't be pitching or having any contact with Brett at any of the bases. She sighed with relief. Maybe it wouldn't be so bad after all.

"Strike TWO!" the umpire's voice rang out across the field. All the people in the stand got excited. It wasn't everyday a minor league player played church ball, and even rarer he would strike "out." The fans were on the edge of their seats, but not Lacey. She knew Brett. He was too gentlemanly to make a small game pitcher look bad, but too stubborn to take an "out." He also liked drama. She knew what he was planning, and it was no surprise when, on the third pitch, she heard a crack of the bat. Out of habit, Brett pointed to the flying ball with one hand and threw Lacey a kiss with the other, just like old times. Lacey prayed Grant hadn't noticed.

Will's voice echoed across the fence and through the airwaves. "And that's a hoooomeruuuunnnnnn by number fourteen, Brett Wright, subbing for me, Josh Evans. He's no Josh

Evans, but looks like he'll do in a pinch, ladies and gentlemen." Will couldn't help joking. "A bat to the left and a kiss to the stands and he is OFF!"

Grant had, indeed, seen the kiss and knew exactly to whom it was directed. He'd held it together all night – through the first homerun and the cocky strut – but this? This was too much. He felt his fists clench and before he knew what he was doing, he was running across the field at full speed! Instantly, the associate minister took off after him, only to be stopped by Pastor Holt.

"Aren't we gonna stop 'em?!" Brother Mullins asked Pastor Holt.

"Now, son, the Bible says there is a time for everything. A time to plant and a time to reap, a time for peace…and a time to fight. We should pray about this," he said, as they watched Grant run past the pitching mound heading straight for Brett between second and third base. "Three o'clock, Grant!" he yelled, seeing Brett turn his way.

Brett heard the cheers and thought they were for him, never realizing he was about to be bulldozed by Grant. Will's voice continued to ring out over the field. He heard Will yell "Holy Smokes!" before seeing someone coming at his waist from behind. He swung to his right to sucker punch the guy with his left arm. Only then did he see the last name on his attacker's jersey, Andrews, before they both tumbled into a heap in the red clay.

Will was torn between the action on the field and his duties in the booth. "Holy smokes, people! In the history of church ball I don't think we've ever had an actual fist fight but that's what we've got tonight! Grant Andrews has charged out of Cornerstone's dugout, heading straight for Brett Wright who's rounding Second. You should see it folks! He's like a bull in a bullfight!" Will could contain himself no longer. "GET HIM, GRANT! I mean, uh, hold on folks – I've been called up." He took off his headphones, hopped out of the booth, donned a helmet and ran onto the field, looking at both men, not knowing who to help. Finally he jumped in between, trying to separate them, thankful he'd grabbed a helmet first.

Lacey stood in shock. "Oh my!" Sheryl yelled in her best snooty voice. It was all too much for Lacey. "I'm taking Jake home," she told the girls, and headed out of the park as the field filled with deacons and elders trying to separate the men that had jumped in on the action. Eventually, everyone got separated and they dispersed, heading home.

****

Lacey saw Grant's headlights pull into the backyard a couple hours later. Curious, she made sure the kids were asleep before grabbing a pack of frozen peas and a piece of pie and headed out to the pool house.

Just when it seemed she and Grant were making headway; the guys had to get into a fight. She quietly knocked on the door and held up her peace offering.

"I thought you might need these," she said, holding up the peas and pie with a grin. She was relieved to see he had only one swollen eye. He smiled and opened the door for her to come in.

"What happened out there tonight?" She asked, wringing out the washcloth she'd just wet.

"I guess I just couldn't take anymore," Grant said, shrugging. He winced as Lacey cleaned his eye. She was sitting on the arm of the couch, and he'd forgotten how much he'd missed her. He wrapped his hand around her waist as she tended to his eye.

"Well, I wish I'd known 'cause I could've warned you about his left hook," Lacey said, laughing. "He always leads with his left," she said quietly.

Grant laughed, too. "Yeah, that would've been good information to have," he said.

"Well, either way, you looked mighty fine out there today..." Lacey said, her bodice at his eye level.

"Yeah?" Grant asked, his other hand finding its way to her other hip, and letting his guard down long enough to look her in the eyes.

"Um-huh," Lacey said as she leaned in for a kiss.

Grant did wind up staying in the pool house that night.

And so did Lacey.

FORTY-TWO

For the first time in months, Lacey did not wake up with a sense of dread. Even though they had a lot of things to work out, last night was their start to a new beginning and held promise of something she had lost a long time ago:

Hope.

It's a word that most cling to for comfort or to inspire themselves or others. But there was a time when hope was not Lacey's friend. Life had gotten so stressful and upside-down that she would get angry when well-meaning people would say, "Don't lose hope." The saying felt like just another thing on her "to do" list, and another thing she would fail at. For her, hope had led to nothing but disappointment and heartbreak, and still required *something* on her part. She'd been so overwhelmed, even *hope* was too much pressure. So, she asked herself, what could she do?

Trust.

She *could* trust.

It required nothing of her, and put all the pressure on God.

So, after searching in vain for a "trust" charm, she had one made and wore it every day. Every time they did not get the test results they wanted, she saw the charm and, ironically, it *gave* her what temporarily eluded her: *hope*. However, this time her hope was not in the situation, but in the Lord.

Lacey knew Grant had one last trip to make to Memphis to prepare for his trial - but was surprised to find a gift waiting for her when she woke up. As she walked toward the kitchen, between her living and sitting room she saw a four-foot long tree branch suspended in mid-air, hanging by clear fishing line! Green leaves and all!

Perplexed, Lacey made her way around to get a better view. That's when she saw it. There, on the branch, were the carved initials: GA + LA, inside a deep heart. Lacey instantly teared up, overwhelmed with Grant's show of love for her.

Lacey immediately called Grant.

"Did you like your gift?" Grant asked mischievously.

"Yes!" Lacey couldn't keep the squeal out of her voice.

Grant chuckled happily, "Yeah, Mom's gonna freak when she sees it…"

"Oh, my word, Grant?! That's not from the Burning Bush is it?!" Lacey yelled, taken aback.

"Sure is," Grant said. "I figured it was about time we were on it…"

Lacey collapsed in a fit of laughter and tears. She was slightly horrified, but she had never felt so loved!

"Don't worry…we can use the bare spot to put our initials ON the tree next Thanksgiving," Grant said, already a step ahead – smoothing things over.

"I love you, honey," he said, his voice low and serious. "We have a lot to work through, but we're gonna be okay."

Lacey hung up the phone, truly feeling at home in her own home…

Wanted.

Cherished.

Loved.

THE PEARL OF GREAT PRICE

FORTY-THREE

Lacey put the last of the pre-made meals in the freezer before heading upstairs. She knew the ladies of church were going to keep her family well fed during the transplant surgery and recovery, but she wanted to make sure she had some meals in stock just in case they were needed. She also needed to keep herself busy. She did her best thinking when she was cleaning and cooking.

Even though she missed Brett like crazy and was dying to talk to him, she'd stayed true to her promise at the "intervention" and stayed away. It was crazy how deep he'd become imbedded in her schedule, mind and heart in the short few months since they had gotten back in touch. And the news about Kit had welded them tighter. She knew she needed to reach out to him, but wanted to make sure her heart was solid before doing so. Jenn's warning wasn't unmerited, nor did it fall on deaf ears.

"It's a fierce battle between the flesh and the soul," Pastor Holt had once said. "And as Christians, lots of times our feelings and minds are in line with God's will, but sometimes they're not – which is why it is so important to be in the Word every day, those Words of Life are going to guide and direct you during your trying times. Sometimes the enemy will deceive us and when we check what we are thinking or feeling with Scripture there is a disconnect. Either the Word is right or you are. In those situations, you have to do like pilots do: when they find themselves in the storm, TRUST YOUR INSTRUMENTS. Even if you think you are going East, if the instruments say you are going West TRUST THE INSTRUMENTS. And when you find yourself in that kind of situation, TRUST YOUR MANUAL, THE BIBLE. Act from your

THE PEARL OF GREAT PRICE

WILL, not your feelings. You don't have to be led around willy-nilly by your ever changing, faulty feelings! You are a HUMAN, not an animal: Show your feelings who is in charge!"

Lacey was trying to do what she'd been taught: ignore her selfish flesh, go on "auto pilot" and trust the manual. *Knowing* she'd been so close to being deceived, she relied heavily on her Christian sisters to keep her on the right track and hold her accountable. It was embarrassing, honestly, for her - a girl who'd grown up "teething on the pews" and such a strong woman of faith - to be in this situation, but her girlfriends were so supportive.

"That is the devil talkin'!" Mya would say, mimicking Melissa, every time Lacey would bemoan being a "burden" or "weak". "For some reason, right now you and your family are being sifted, tempted, tested, tried AND pruned! These are the times you're *supposed* to lean on us! One of the devil's best tools is pride, and don't let that work on you! Lean on us, and that's *just fine* 'cause there's gonna come a day when we are gonna need the same from you...maybe not in the same form, but the day will come." Mya always had a way of putting things in perspective, and her friends had been true to their word: taking texts late at night to reassure her, sending her scriptures and quotes through Pinterest that spoke to her situation, running pass interference between her and Brett, and even being brave and loving enough to tell her what she needed to hear – when it was the last thing she wanted. All of these were a tremendous help, but she felt there was one last thing she needed to do before moving on.

In two days, Kit needed to be at Vandy to prep for the transplant, and tomorrow night Grant would return from his work trip, so that meant she only had tonight to do what she'd planned. And thank God the forecast was clear.

She waited 'til the kids were settled in bed, left Kit a note, and quietly pulled out of the drive. It was nine o'clock on a Friday night, and she was hoping Brett would be home. She texted Jenn she had arrived before cutting the engine in front of his apartment. She'd run her idea by Jenn to make sure her idea was "sister approved." Lacey, if she was totally honest, had asked the most "relaxed" of all her Christian sisters to approve her plan, but Jenn went all the way back to their beginning. She understood "them" like none of her other friends would. Jenn had, indeed, approved her outing – but only if she took Will as a chaperone.

Right before she got out of the car, she had a terrorizing thought.

"Oh my word! What if he's on a date?" Lacey texted.

"If he's *there*, then he's not on a date!" Jenn texted back.

"No! What if he's on a date…at *HOME*?!" Lacey returned. The thought terrified her, especially considering everyone knew everyone in Dickson. What if she came face to face with someone she KNEW?! Worse, what if she came face to face with a FRIEND?! Worse still, what if…

"What if he's with *SHERYL*?!?!" Lacey's mind was running wild now.

"HE IS NOT WITH SHERYL. GO TO THE DOOR! And remind Will to pick up some milk," Jenn wrote. Luckily, Will had agreed and was waiting at their forthcoming destination.

"Just pretend it's a performance," she said to herself through deep breaths.

Her plan was to boldly go up to the door, ring the bell and if a female answered the door, say in a nice, professional way she needed to talk to Brett for a second about their daughter. If he did indeed have a date, she would act like she had a question about the surgery and scrap Plan A.

Lacey didn't make a habit of praying selfish prayers, but tonight she caved.

"Please, Lord, don't let him have a girl in there," she whispered. "And if he does, please – if there's any way possible – don't let her be younger or prettier than me," she thought. "And if there's any chance there's a girl and it happens to be Sheryl, could you please kill me dead on the spot?" Lacey asked, not half joking. In a situation like this, she thought it best to cover all her bases.

Brett's apartment was a corner one, on the ground level. Lacey could see what looked like the light of the TV.

She crept quietly toward his back patio. The rear streetlight provided some light for her to see, but her knee still managed to find his boat hitch.

"Mrrrrowww!" she meowed, hoping Brett would think a stray cat was trekking through his yard. She waited a second before peeking through the mini blinds, but all she could see was the glow of the TV reflecting off the coffee table.

She headed toward the back door, but before she could knock the door FLEW open and a bright light was flashed into her eyes. She screamed before ducking down on the ground.

"Dawg, Lacey! You trying to get shot?!" Brett yelled, fear quickly turning into relief as he switched off his torch light, tucked his handgun into his waist band, then reached out to help her up.

"I didn't know if you had a girl with you…" Lacey tried to explain, too scared to think of a white lie.

Brett laughed. "No, I don't have a girl with me, silly…" he felt honored that she cared enough to be sensitive to the idea, anyway. Back in the day she would'a busted through the door with both guns blazing. The thought of the juxtapose realities made him a bit sad.

"You know there's these things called cell phones now…" Brett started to tease her.

"Are you kidding?! The girls have got me tied in tighter than my *Dad*! I'm lucky Melissa didn't put an ankle monitor on me and Mya isn't sleeping with me!" Lacey stumbled as Brett led her into the apartment.

"So am I going to be permanently blind?" she asked, rubbing her eyes and blinking.

Brett laughed, "No, you'll be good in a couple minutes." He uncapped a bottle of water and placed it in her hands.

"How did you know I was out there? Did my "meow" give it away?" Lacey asked through closed eyes. Brett didn't know which was funnier – the fact that she'd tried to imitate a cat, or that she'd thought it would actually work.

"Well, no, I didn't hear a "meow" over the gunfire on the tv. Could you do it for me and I'll tell you if it would'a worked," Brett kept his voice steady as he pushed the record button on his phone. He was definitely gonna save this as his ringtone!

Lacey wasn't falling for it. "I might be blind, Brett, but I see what you're doing. So how *did* you know I was here?" She asked, schluffing off his request.

"Well, next time you decide to spy on someone, you might wanna make sure there's no backlight to cast a shadow on the window you pick to look through," Brett said. "I'm surprised you didn't think of that, with your photography background," Brett said.

"I guess I was too focused on my mission," Lacey laughed. She was now almost able to make out his silhouette.

"So what brings you out here so late? If you're here for a booty call, you could 'a dressed a little more appropriately," Brett teased, eyeing her old jeans and climbing boots.

"Ha, ha," Lacey mumbled. "Speaking of clothes, could you go put some on? I don't wanna *stay* blind," she teased, trying to avert her eyes and attention from his bare, chiseled chest. Seeing her name on his arm made her uncomfortable this time. "Maybe that's a sign I'm making progress," she wondered.

"Hey. *You* invaded *my* space," Brett said. "And eyes up here," he teased, returning the words she'd always thrown his way in days past when *she'd* caught *his* eyes wandering.

"I'll have you know..." Lacey began, but stopped mid-sentence.

"BRETT!" she gasped. "Your face!" Brett had a purple-blue eye, and a matching bruise on his left chin.

Brett chuckled. "Your husband's tougher than he looks..."

"*Grant* did that?!" Lacey asked, surprised. She then lowered her voice to a whisper as if others might hear. "D'you let him get a couple in?"

"Shoot, naw!" Brett yelled. "*HE's* the one shoulda joined the Army...I'm gonna request him as my battle buddy if they ever institute the draft!" he said.

"Well, you kinda had it coming after blowing that kiss my way..." Lacey said, frowning.

"Yeah, it was pure muscle memory...I wasn't really thinkin'. I deserved everything he gave me, and if not for that, for everything else, I'm sure," he admitted as he pulled on a t-shirt.

"You know you're gonna have to go forward at church for that..." Lacey said, not half-joking.

Brett chuckled, "Of all the things I'd have to go forward for..." Brett and Lacey laughed. "Maybe we should announce Kit's situation at the same time cause I'm not going forward twice in one month!" Brett shook his head.

"I think we're *all* gonna be sitting front and center come Sunday morning," Lacey said, "...all broken and bruised..."

"It'll be a sight for sure! How's Grant look?" Brett asked.

"Not as bad as you!" Lacey retorted.

Brett grimaced. "Can't you lie to me just *once*, babe?"

Lacey shrugged, "I never thought *you'd* have a problem with your ego…"

"You'd be surprised…" Brett murmured.

"Well, grab your boots and flashlight. I wanna show you something," Lacey commanded.

"Are you kidnapping me, babygirl?" Brett asked cheerfully.

"I wouldn't get enough ransom to make it worth it," She shot back. "Now grab your gear." Brett did as he was told, wondering just what she had planned.

They drove for about thirty minutes, winding through the back roads from Dickson to Cheatham County. The flat, wide highway narrowed into tight curves, winding them back in time. They drove past small homes and occasional two-room churches until the only thing that surrounded them was the trees and the night. Lacey rolled her windows down, letting the crickets and cicadas fill her car with their songs as they traveled down the road. If it weren't for Brett not holding her hand, she would have sworn it was fifteen years ago.

When they arrived at their destination, Brett was surprised to see Will's truck there.

"You giving me a surprise party or a tail whoopin?" Brett asked, a little scared and unsure of the answer.

"I told you I'm on lock down! We gotta have a chaperone until I'm no longer a temptation for you,"

"Pa-shaw!" Brett grunted. "I'm pretty sure it goes the other way around, sweetie!"

Lacey let Brett and Will talk a minute while she got her Thirty-One blanket and flashlight out of the trunk. Will was kind enough to keep his distance as they walked toward the nature trail. Distant, but present – like the current state of Brett and Lacey's relationship.

"This is Kit's favorite nature spot," Lacey told Brett. They walked in silence on level, wooded trails. Eventually they arrived at a flat, open clearing.

Lacey stopped and unwrapped the blanket, laying it fleece-side up near the creek.

"You know, I never took you for the adventurous sort, but we could 'a done this at my house. In a comfortable bed. With no mosquitoes or witnesses," Brett said, teasingly as he took off his jacket.

Lacey gave him an exasperated look, "There's gonna be mating alright, but it won't be us."

"Darn," Brett said. Lacey had to laugh. His quick wit was one of his best traits. He always managed to say exactly what one would expect him to be feeling, and it was that genuine transparency that endeared him to so many. She was grateful for his humor, especially at this transitional time in their relationship. She could feel their dynamic changing, and his jokes made the moments not so awkward.

She sat on the blanket and checked her watch. It was almost ten o'clock. Perfect timing! She patted the blanket beside her to indicate Brett should take a seat.

"This is the creek we used to bring Kit to wade in when she was young," Lacey whispered. "She would go wading all day if we'd have let her, bringing me all kinds of "treasures" every so often. Sometimes a leaf, or a snail, or a pretty stone..." Lacey's voice trailed off remembering. "One time she brought me a snake!"

"A snake?!" Brett was genuinely surprised. "How old was she?"

"Around seven. Old enough to know she should be scared, but too stubborn to let fear stop her."

"Just like her momma," Brett nodded, impressed. "Fearless."

"Oh, I have my share of fear," Lacey said.

"Courageous, then," Brett said with a nudge and a smile. "Why are we whisperin'?" Brett asked, still whispering.

Just as Brett was asking, Lacey saw the first sign she'd been watching for and put her index finger up in a shushing motion. As much as Brett wanted to pull her hand down and plant a kiss on her pursed lips, he didn't. He felt the shift between them, but what was there was still nice. Different, but nice.

"Y'all being appropriate down there? Y'all are mighty quiet," Will's voice came booming from up the hill behind them.

"Of course, goober! Don't you trust me?!" Lacey yelled back.

"Oh, I trust YOU just FINE!" Will responded, letting his insinuation sink in.

"Thanks, Man. I appreciate that vote of confidence," Brett said between Will's chuckles.

"Just doin my job!" Will retorted.

"Y'all hush it up, or my surprise is never gonna happen!" Lacey yelled and turned back and watched, completely still. Finally, Brett leaned in and whispered in her ear, "This reminds me of a time we were near another willow tree," Brett said, smiling softly. Lacey returned his smile and squeezed his hand.

"I'm surprised you still remember that," Lacey whispered.

"You never forget your first kiss, Lace," Brett said. Lacey never thought their kiss was his first, too.

"You were pretty much all my firsts," he whispered, nostalgia creeping in. "Now, just what are we waiting on?" he asked again, clearing his throat. She finger shushed him again and he hung his head in exasperation. She leaned in to whisper, "Pretend you're on a stakeout."

Just then, she saw a bright yellow blink, down at the beginning of the creek bend. Lacey pointed, knowing the show was about to begin. Thirty or more lightning bugs began to blink their mating calls in synchronized fashion. As the "glow show" progressed and hundreds of lightning bugs joined the starters, Brett resisted the urge to put his arm around her. They watched the lights in silence as the bugs slowly made their way toward them, and Lacey nodded for him to look up. As the male lightning bugs began to flash at the base of their tree, the females returned their signals high above them, steadily spiraling up the height of the tree. The long branches of the willow made a canopy enclosing the bursts of light, making it truly magical. They continued to watch, amazed, in silent wonder.

"Kit calls this God's Christmas lights," Lacey said. "It never gets old."

"Definitely worth the wait," Brett admitted.

"If there's noise or movement in the beginning, they will not come out. But once they start their mating dance, it doesn't seem to bother them," Lacey said. "It happens this time every year.

We learned about it when we lived in Knoxville. The Smoky Mountains have a special show every year at a park there, but we have our own show right here," Lacey explained.

"I can't wait to get to know Kit," Brett said.

"Me, too," Lacey said. "That's one of the reasons I wanted to talk to you in person. She knows."

"You don't say. How'd you tell her?"

"I didn't. *She* told *me,*" Lacey shook her head in amazement. "Just like she did when she was five years old and told me about Santa Clause."

"*Five*?!" Brett whistled. "She truly *IS* a blend of you and me!" Brett said.

"Pretty as an angel but fierce as the devil...that's what her Papaw said about her," Lacey said. "I'd say that pretty much sums her up." Lacey nodded, agreeing.

"After the ball game she asked me straight up if you were her Dad," Lacey said. "I had to tell her. She's like you in that way, always seeing though me..." Lacey cleared her throat. "I asked her how she figured it out and she said, "Well, for one, he's a *MATCH*..." like, "Duh, Mom."

Brett laughed. "How else did she know?" he asked.

Lacey waited before answering. "She said it was the way you looked at me when I wasn't looking..."

They were both quiet for a minute.

"You seem more at peace since the last time I saw you..." Brett said, turning to face her with his good eye.

"I've done a lot of thinking and praying. And talking to the girls," Lacey admitted.

"Uh-oh," Brett moaned.

Lacey ignored him. "They said some things that have helped me a lot and will help us, I hope."

"Hit me," Brett said.

"Well, Mya kept saying to be honest and Melissa kept quoting the scripture about the truth setting me free, so I got honest with myself and realized I'd been *fighting* truth. So, I asked myself, "What *is* the truth?""

Brett held his breath, not knowing what she was going to say, and not knowing at this point what to even hope for. He had her ring in his pants pocket, just in case things took a big turn in his favor, but he wasn't going to jump the gun on this one.

"The truth is… I love you. I've loved you since I was fifteen, and I'm *always* gonna love you, Brett. Ever since you came back in my life, it's like my world is right again. And I've missed you so much these past couple of weeks…"

"Me, too, babe," Brett said, edging a bit closer. He knew she didn't know the extent of his loneliness, and having her back in his life and then torn away without a warning about near killed him.

"And it's no doubt…I still need you," Lacey said with pleading eyes.

"Ditto," Brett said, slowly inching his left hand into his pocket for her ring.

"And, I've finally accepted I'm always *gonna* love you…I'm never gonna *not* love you…"

He looked at her inquisitively, hopefully.

Lacey turned to him. "…it's just gotta be in a different way from now on."

Brett loosened his grip, feeling the ring – along with his hopes and dreams - fall out of his grasp once again.

"Cause the *other* truth is… I'm married," Lacey continued, soberly.

He exhaled, disheartened, but was surprised at the slight relief he felt. He lay back on the blanket, and smiled – although if someone had asked him, he couldn't honestly say why. Perhaps because all his romantic relationships always fizzled, and if he and Lacey gave it a try, they might end in flames as well. And that's something he just couldn't take. In an ideal world, he'd selfishly choose Lacey in a heartbeat – but, being a gambler, he knew he'd be better off to get out of the game with *something* rather than walk away empty handed. He'd rather be her friend than nothing at all.

"So, friends?" Brett asked. "I like that idea…" he said finally.

"Really?" Lacey asked, overwhelmed with relief at his response.

"Well, my first pick, of course, would be steamy lovers," Brett dodged the elbow nudge he knew was coming. "But "best of friends" would be my next choice. Sounds better than the "baby momma" title I was gonna give you, I guess," Brett smiled.

"I'll take ya any way I can get ya, Lace..." Brett said, seriously and truthfully, as he pulled her in for a hug. Out of habit, he kissed the top of her head.

Lacey smiled, knowing the depth of his sincerity on that statement, for she felt the same way.

"I don't know how that's gonna work, though..." Brett said.

Lacey looked up, concerned.

"Bein' as how you've never been able to keep your hands off of me," he said, laughing.

Lacey slapped his leg as she rested her head on his arm. They sat in the silence for a while, happy to have a defined relationship now, and feeling contentment in their discontent.

Lacey was the first to break the silence. "Who would 'a thought a year ago we'd have a *baby*?" Lacey asked, amused.

"I know, right?!" Brett said as he flicked a stray firefly that had landed on Lacey's arm. "When we spill the beans to the church, I just might pass out pink cigars as Pastor Holt's shaking them out after services."

Lacey laughed heartily. "He would actually love that," she nodded.

They sat like they used to; her head nestled comfortably on his shoulder. It was bittersweet how they still fit together. They were a beautiful tragedy.

Brett was well aware this would be his last private moment with Lacey. Once they returned home, they would be Mrs. Lacey Andrews and Brett Wright once again. At the risk of breaking all rules of protocol, he couldn't let this moment pass him by.

"You know, I always thought we'd end up together in a DIFFERENT way..." he said, still looking at the sky.

"Me, too," Lacey said. Lacey knew he was speaking from his heart. He always avoided eye contact when he was revealing things that meant the most to him. Lacey also knew this was the time to "speak now or forever hold her peace," but there was so much to say...and so much she didn't feel she should say, as a married woman. She longed to tell him how much he meant to her, how losing him about killed her, how it took everything within her not to run off with him again, and how she loved him almost too much, which is why she had to back away. She longed to have him "see" just why she couldn't merely do what she wanted to do – how there was more at stake than just her family and marriage, and how following Christ is about sacrifice and self-denial, and even though at times like these it was painful, it was best. She knew he didn't fully understand it, but he did respect it. Some emotions run so deep they can't be put into words. Nevertheless, she tried.

"Melissa always reminds me that God's ways are not our ways...and even though we might want something different than the place he calls us, He knows what He is doing, and His ways are best," Lacey said. "...even if we would choose *differently* if we could..."

She hoped the meaning behind her words would somehow travel from her heart to his.

It did.

And even though there were going to be many things, sadly, left unsaid and undone between them, they were somehow *known*, felt and *understood* that night near the aptly named Weeping Willow. Not a kiss was exchanged that night, but hidden truths were revealed without a word or a touch. They sat in the grass - not skin on skin but soul to soul - the heavy silence holding the things they did NOT say as they made a mental memory of the moment, wrapping their minds around this new relationship – this "friendship kinship" – they were creating.

"I really do miss what we almost had," Lacey whispered.

Brett sighed contentedly. "You comfort my soul, babe," he said, giving her shoulder a friendly squeeze.

"You ignite mine!" Lacey said with a grin. "For good or ill..."

"It's always been like that, hasn't it?" Brett chuckled. "You keep me in line, and I keep you on your toes," he said, smiling.

"You did give me a great gift, though," Lacey confessed.

"Oh? What was that?" Brett asked.

"You reminded me of who I am," Lacey said. "I'd forgotten."

Brett nodded in agreement, knowing exactly what she meant. "Yeah, and you helped get me back on track. You *are* the only one I would keep the rules for..." his voice trailed off. "Case in point," he said with a chuckle, pointing to them lying in the grass doing nothing.

"And you're the only one I'd bend 'em for!" Lacey said, laughing, pointing to the same. They basked in the laughter that bubbled up between them before falling back into content silence.

"I love you, Kiddo," Brett whispered.

"Love you, too," Lacey whispered back, firmly this time, and unashamedly. They felt themselves saying good-bye to the romantic connection they cherished and walking toward something new, building upon the childhood friendship that had always gotten them through the hardest times.

She didn't know what lay before them or even what that new relationship could be categorized as, but she knew it would be something very, very special.

FORTY-FOUR

By the time Sunday morning rolled around, it seemed everyone from Waverly to Nashville had heard about the fight on the field and decided to pay Cornerstone Church a visit. Pastor Holt had spoken with Pastor Galloway and they decided to combine their services to facilitate an environment of forgiveness and solidarity. All the players had agreed to sit on the front rows to serve as an example of what brotherly love looked like, complete with their matching black eyes and bruises. Most of the men in the area still served in the military in some form or another, but the extra people from Pastor Galloway's church didn't account for such a massive turn out! Cars filled the lot and lined the streets a good two miles in both directions! Pastor Holt even thought he spied a Channel 4 news crew van!

Pastor Holt decided to use the current events to shape his sermon for the week, choosing to speak on how all Christians are imperfect and strive like everyone else to do the right thing when their flesh wars against the Spirit. Forgiveness is both a balm and a glue to heal our hurts and bind us together. He began his sermon from the wings, unseen, so the congregation could focus solely on the Word and message.

As he concluded the Scriptures on forgiving your brother up to "seventy times seven" he emerged from stage left to walk toward the podium...revealing a black eye, matching the players!

The congregation erupted into spontaneous laughter!

"Like I said, we're all human! Thank God for forgiveness!" Pastor Holt went on to apologize for the players and then extend the invitation. Lacey and Grant had already decided to fill the congregation in on the transplant that would be happening in two days, and Lacey decided it would also be the opportune time to address the rumors that had been flying for a couple of months. Showing a united front, Grant walked up with Lacey, and, as chance would have it, took a seat on the pew opposite the isle of Brett.

"Grant Andrews is asking for forgiveness for starting the fight at the field this Tuesday…along with the bruised up players here from each team…The adrenaline just got to us, I guess," Pastor Holt said. "In addition, Grant and Lacey wanted to let everyone know that, if you have not heard or seen the clip on channel 2 from the courthouse this week, a match has been found for Sister Kit!" Pastor Holt waited as the applause and cheers subsided. "She and Lacey will be traveling to Vanderbilt today to prep for surgery on Tuesday, and in the theme of mistakes and forgiveness, Lacey comes forward today to talk to you…" He assisted Lacey up the stairs to the podium before taking his seat beside Brother Mullins.

Despite feeling at home on stage and performing half her life, Lacey was filled with fear as she climbed the wine colored, carpeted steps. She was about to speak before more than four hundred people without a prepared script or song. It was just her and her sins. She'd never felt so naked or vulnerable and prayed for strength as she looked over the audience. With a supportive wink from Brett and smile from Grant, she began.

"I'm sure you've all noticed that Brett Wright has been back in town for a while, and that we have been spending time together," Lacey cleared her throat and took a deep breath. "I've heard there's been some rumors that he and I are having a fling, and I don't blame you for the whispers because of how I've been acting lately…but we're not," she could hear the church exhale a collective, relieved sigh.

"Brett is back because, thankfully, he's a transplant match for Kit." Grant led the sporadic applause that trickled across the audience, knowing people would be concerned about his feelings in the situation. He hoped to show them he was choosing to focus on the joy of the situation, especially since he and Lacey were now moving in a forward direction. The rest of the crowd joined in when they saw him clap.

"Grant and I are so thankful Brett was a match and is stepping up to save our daughter…" she looked at Brett, choking up, with tears in her eyes. Grant led the congregation in applause again.

"Their surgery is this Tuesday, so we ask for prayers for both of them…" Before continuing, Lacey paused, trying to collect her thoughts.

"Since most of us go far back, I'm assuming you can derive what this match means," Lacey waited for the explanatory whispers she knew would come to die down before continuing. "This is not the time for details, but I wanted to let everyone know that neither Grant *nor I* knew Brett could even remotely be of help to Kit until a few months ago…" Lacey paused to let the reality of her message sink in. "Needless to say, this has been an emotional roller coaster for us all. We have a lot more healing ahead of us, but Grant and I are committed to our family no matter what, so we ask for prayer for that as well." This time it was Brett that led the applause.

"As for me, the rumors of adultery are **not** true…but for the recent public drunkenness, cussing, and that one act of fornication fourteen years ago…I **do** repent and apologize!" Lacey said, with a little sass in her voice.

This time the Pastor led the congregation in a rousing round of applause as he nudged the associate minister and excitedly said, "She's back!!" happy to see the spark that had flickered out thirteen years ago returning. He hugged her as she approached the podium.

"Isn't it wonderful to see how God can take the craziest circumstances and bring new life from them?" Pastor Holt began. "I have been with these three throughout this strange ordeal, and I am here to tell you the devil was fighting as hard as the Lord was on this one. But, praise God, what the devil had meant for evil to tear apart a family, low and behold, the Lord is using for good – to heal past wounds and give life to our sweet Kit! Gather around with me, would you? And let's all pray for these…"

Lacey was relieved to see the congregation filing down the aisles like water from a cistern, with nothing on the members' faces except love and relief and praise. As the crowd closed in, she held the hand of her daughter on one side and the hand of her husband in the other. No longer fearful, but joyful and full of hope for the future that belonged to the One who makes all things work for the Good…even in the Bad.

FORTY-FIVE

Lacey and Kit left for the hospital right after church, so Grant had the day to think alone, in the quiet. He had moved back into the house a week ago, and things were better. Still a little awkward at times, but better. The counselor had told them it would take time for their minds and emotions to process everything, but moving back in was a step in the right direction. It showed unity, and didn't allow the devil as much wiggle room for a stronger foothold.

Grant had just finished edging the lawn and was turning on the tv for Sunday night football. Grant had been feeling the Holy Spirit whispering to him lately about approaching Brett, but he was having a hard time figuring out just how to go about doing that. He'd seen him at church today, but it wasn't really the time or place to have such a private conversation. It wasn't like they ever ran into each other, but Grant knew he was using that as an excuse. He was a lawyer for Pete's sake! He knew how to find and summon anyone! And did. Regularly! Grant's final prayer was that God show him when and how to have that conversation.

Not that he was sure he could. Grant knew logically there was nothing for him to forgive: Brett had not sinned against *him*, had not tried to purposefully harm *him*. But the ramifications of his actions were sure wreaking havoc on him and his family, now!

"But he holds the key to your family's healing," Grant heard God whisper to his heart. "Particularly Kit."

Grant sometimes resisted when God whispered to him. Sometimes the message was uncomfortable or hurt. This time, it was excruciating.

Through it all, Grant was forced to see some truths in himself he didn't like. He'd discovered a lot of pride issues that he had never known he had. He had also seen how hard forgiving was for him. Even in his pain, Grant could see God using the situation to buff off some of the "bad fruits" he'd accumulated. It was painful, but the only silver lining he could think of.

"Help me to fight past my feelings and do the right thing," Grant prayed.

Just as he was putting away his mowing shoes, he heard a knock at the door. He glanced out the living room window on his way to answer it and stopped in his tracks. There, in the middle of the driveway sat Brett's pickup.

"Seriously, Lord?" Grant asked, looking up shaking his head. A story came to mind about a general wouldn't *go* into battle, so God brought the battle *to* the general. "God don't play," Grant groaned. "Okay, okay," Grant mumbled, apologetically. He had no clue what was waiting for him on the other side of the door. Grant had been relieved that Brett had not filed any charges against him, but now he wondered if he was just biding his time for some vigilante justice.

"I bet he can break a neck with his bare hands," Grant thought, correctly.

"I come in peace!" Grant heard Brett yell toward the door. Relieved, Grant prayed for strength as he fumbled with the bolt.

Brett held a six pack of Bud Light in his right hand, and a six pack of root beer in his left.

"Pick your poison," Brett said with a smile, holding up the options.

"Either way, we're gonna have to drink it out back so we don't have to go forward again next Sunday," Grant said with a chuckle, as he led Brett through the house to the back patio.

"Wasn't that something today?" Brett said. "Pastor Holt told me if he'd known a fight was gonna bring that many visitors to church he would 'a staged one years ago!" The both chuckled at the idea as they sat down by the pool.

"Your eye looks like it's healing well," Grant said as he popped the top. "I've been meaning to apologize for that in person…"

"Naw…I had it coming," Brett said with a shy grin. "You know, I'm not as bad as they say I am," Brett continued, looking off.

Grant nodded and laughed along.

"I'm not gonna lie, though. My first intentions when I got here were to win Lacey back, and make the home we'd always planned on," Brett said before taking a swig.

"And?" Grant asked.

Brett looked at Grant, then said, "She's already got a home…and a fine one at that," Brett shook his head affirmatively. "You've done real good by her, Grant," he continued. "And I just want to let you know, man to man, my intentions are 100% honorable, now. You got nothing to worry about from me."

"Thank you," Grant said. "I greatly appreciate that. And I can't tell you how much it means to us that you're stepping up the way you have…"

"Glad to do it…Can you *believe* all this?" Brett said, changing the subject.

"Crazy," Grant agreed, laughing. "Will said it's like a real life soap opera!"

They continued talking, as men do, about nothing and everything into the evening, swapping war and courtroom stories and bonding over football, developing a deep respect for each other. Grant could see that, while they walked different paths in life, they shared lots of the same traits: determination, intellect, diligence, perseverance and, of course, the same taste in women. One woman, in particular. The same woman who had divided them would now unite them, forever, through Kit, another young woman they both shared an unconditional love for.

"Say, what time are you getting to the hospital tomorrow?" Grant asked as they walked toward the door.

"Probably eight. You ain't gonna slip somethin in my IV, are you?" Brett asked over his shoulder.

Grant gave a chuckle, "No. I was going to ask Pastor Holt to come join us to pray over you."

Brett was used to being attacked and fought with. In life he'd been starved, spat upon, abused, left for dead…and that was his biological family, not to mention all his tours had thrown at him. He was not used to surprise kindness, especially from someone who had every right to hate him. It caught him off guard, and, even in the dim light, Grant could see his eyes had grown misty.

"Would that be alright?" Grant asked, sincerely.

Brett nodded affirmatively before clearing his throat, "That'd be just fine," he said, before turning to go.

Brett knew the reason why Grant was so quick to bury the hatchet and extend an olive branch wasn't because his daughter needed a kidney. It was the same reason Lacey was so loving and Jenn was so giving and Will was so supportive. They all had the same Father. And, once again, Brett felt Him whisper to his soul, gently inviting him to come back home.

FORTY-SIX

Lacey had gotten Kit situated, and she was napping before the surgery. She took the opportunity to slip out and check on Brett. He would've already been prepped and she hated to think of him being alone at a time like this. He never did well with hospitals – or waiting.

"Double whammy today," Lacey thought.

She peeped in through his curtain to see him fiddling with the remote, IVs already in his arm. "You ready for this, soldier?" she asked, sliding his curtain back. Brett chuckled, surprised and relieved to see a familiar face.

"You better get outta here, little lady! I promised your husband I was gonna leave you alone," he teased.

Lacey laughed. "Grant told me the two of you had a nice talk yesterday…"

"Yeah, we decided we're gonna dual it out for your hand at high noon after I get outta here," he said in the most serious tone he could muster, but Lacey saw him clench his jaw.

"Oh hush!" Lacey said, throwing a towel at him as she sat down beside him.

"He really is a really good man, Lace," Brett said, his gaze and voice steady and sincere.

"Well, I've been blessed to have been loved by *two* good men," Lacey said with a wink and friendly smile.

"How's Kit?" Brett asked, quickly changing the subject, while popping his knuckles.

"A little anxious," Lacey said. "She pops her knuckles when she's nervous, too," Lacey said as she covered his crackling hands with hers. "You're gonna be *fine*," she whispered, reassuring him.

Just as she had taken his hands, Grant rounded the corner at the end of the hall. He instantly felt the chill of fear wash over him. Luckily, Will was there and saw what he was seeing.

"It's ok, man," he said. "Remember: they're just finding their footing."

Grant nodded and took a deep breath before heading over to hand Lacey her coffee.

"I told you about flirtin' with my wife, and look at you, holding her hand..." Grant said through a good natured smile. Brett smiled back, thankful they were now communicating in a language he understood well: humor and camaraderie.

"It's her, not me! She won't keep her grabby hands off of me!" Brett joked, "Control your woman, man!" He schluffed off Lacey's hand. "You're gonna get me beat up again, Lacey!"

Lacey was happy to hear their laughter fill the air. Just then, Pastor Holt made his way into the room.

"Now that's what I like to hear!" he said, relieved. "The nurse said it's time to wheel you back, so let's all pray, and then we will head over to pray with Kit," he said, motioning them into a huddle around Brett.

They circled together, hand in hand and heart to heart. Past and current loves coming together for the good of a child - *their* child.

The Good Book says "A little child shall lead them," and in this case, it was true. It was a child that had led the wayward and lonely back home. It was a child that helped bring reconciliation to two past lovers and heal their long, over-due wounds. It was a child that showed the prideful his need for others, and melted a mother's heart of stone. It was a child that caused a community to come together for a greater good. And it was a child who showed them that, with a little faith, God can move mountains.

Just like Jesus did.

I'd like to say they all lived happily ever after, but that's only in fairy tales. Real life is unpredictable and messy and complicated. Brett and Kit both came through the surgery, and Kit became healthy and strong. But, like everything else in life, it wasn't a constant ball of happy: there were counseling sessions and explanations, and long night talks in the night, some shouting matches, and, finally, reluctant acceptance. Eventually they all found their footing and became a "family plus one." Brett became known as "Uncle Brett" and visited between missions. Grant and Lacey moved forward, accepting what they could not change and clinging to every silver lining they found.

And Lacey and Brett?

It took a while, but they, too, plowed their own way. Even though it was awkward in the beginning, they keep things appropriate - their relationship a mixture of competitive, encouraging, teasing friends who shared a unique love. And it continues to change and grow, because, as we all know, love never dies.

And the devil?
He's still a sneaky, cunning scoundrel.

But let me tell you about the Lord.

He is patient.
And loving.
And good.
And kind.
Ever present, and always on time.
*His timing is **perfect** and His ways are **right.***
He is the Master Restorer – taking the absolute worst parts of our lives - sands, prunes and polishes them - until they shine and emerge better than new and even stronger than before.
Yes, the devil is bad.
But God?
He is stronger.
He is greater.
He is tougher
And He is able.

He is a magnificent magician who brings beauty from ashes, and turns our mourning into dancing.

He's a front liner – staying by his soldiers in the thick of battle.

He is a good Father, directing and guiding the paths before us when the unexpected comes our way.

He is our ultimate hero, who moves into hopeless situations and what the devil had meant for evil, uses it for good.

He is forgiving,
A keeper of promises
And he is everlasting.

And, he is oh, so very, very Good!

****

To listen to or purchase the songs from the book, go to "Reverbnation" or "CD Baby" and search "April Estes" or go to:
https://www.reverbnation.com/artist/songwriteraprilestes
https://store.cdbaby.com/cd/dixielace

Study guide also available for Bible Study or Book Clubs.
For ordering or speaking engagements: april.estes@gmail.com

Subscribe to April's blog at: https://sweetmimosa.blog
or join *Sweet Mimosa* (Facebook)

Download or listen online at "Reverbnation" or "CD Baby" (search: April Estes)

* Songs from book:

This One's For You, God (page 53)

Real Good Girl (page 58)

Southern Chic (page 82)

Boomerang (page 83)

50 Years Ago/All Those Years Ago (page 84)

First Love Rights (page 118)

Before We Let Love Go (page 119)

Release Me (page 210)

Cowboys (page 213)

Livin' My Should've Been (page 213)

Other applicable songs:

Warrior Mother (Lacey)

Up and Down (Lacey & Grant)

Made in the USA
Lexington, KY
29 October 2019

56257752R10177